THE
MYSTIC WRITINGS
of
ALGERNON BLACKWOOD

---

14 SHORT STORIES FROM
THE PEN OF ENGLAND'S MOST
PROLIFIC WRITER OF GHOST STORIES

Fantasy and Horror Classics

Read & Co.

Copyright © 2023 Fantasy and Horror Classics

This edition is published by Fantasy and Horror Classics,
an imprint of Read & Co.

British Library Cataloguing-in-Publication Data
A catalogue record for this book is available
from the British Library.

Read & Co. is part of Read Books Ltd.
For more information visit
www.readandcobooks.co.uk

CONTENTS

Algernon Blackwood..5

A HAUNTED ISLAND 9

A CASE OF EAVESDROPPING.......................27

THE OLD MAN OF VISIONS 45

ANCIENT SORCERIES...............................55

SECRET WORSHIP 109

THE ATTIC 147

THE TRANSFER..155

THE EMPTY SLEEVE 167

THE TERROR OF THE TWINS 185

THE WOLVES OF GOD 193

THE TARN OF SACRIFICE 217

"VENGEANCE IS MINE"............................243

KING'S EVIDENCE....................................285

THE MAGIC MIRROR 293

Algernon Blackwood

Algernon Henry Blackwood was born in Shooter's Hill, South East England, in 1869. In his youth he trained as a doctor at Wellington College in Berkshire, and went on to pursue a number of careers, in areas as varied as milk farming, modelling, journalism and violin teaching. In his thirties, Blackwood returned to England from New York, where he had spent a number of years, and began to write stories of the supernatural.

Blackwood was extremely prolific, producing over the course of his life some ten original collections of short stories, fourteen novels, several children's books, and a number of plays. Most of his work was concerned with the ghostly, mythical or occult—themes which Blackwood was attracted to his whole life—and he is regarded as one of the earlier practitioners of 'weird fiction'. Amongst his best known short stories are 'The Wendigo', and 'The Willows'—a work which H. P. Lovecraft called "the finest weird story I have ever read." In 1914, he produced his short story collection *Incredible Adventures*, which leading literary critic S. T. Joshi has said "may be the premier weird collection of this or any other century." Blackwood worked as an undercover agent for Britain during the First World War, and during the 1920s became famous for reading his ghost stories live on BBC radio and television.

After a number of strokes, Blackwood died in old age in Kent, England.

THE
MYSTIC WRITINGS
of
ALGERNON BLACKWOOD

A HAUNTED ISLAND

The following events occurred on a small island of isolated position in a large Canadian lake, to whose cool waters the inhabitants of Montreal and Toronto flee for rest and recreation in the hot months. It is only to be regretted that events of such peculiar interest to the genuine student of the psychical should be entirely uncorroborated. Such unfortunately, however, is the case.

Our own party of nearly twenty had returned to Montreal that very day, and I was left in solitary possession for a week or two longer, in order to accomplish some important "reading" for the law which I had foolishly neglected during the summer.

It was late in September, and the big trout and maskinonge were stirring themselves in the depths of the lake, and beginning slowly to move up to the surface waters as the north winds and early frosts lowered their temperature. Already the maples were crimson and gold, and the wild laughter of the loons echoed in sheltered bays that never knew their strange cry in the summer.

With a whole island to oneself, a two-storey cottage, a canoe, and only the chipmunks, and the farmers weekly visit with eggs and bread, to disturb one, the opportunities for hard reading might be very great. It all depends!

The rest of the party had gone off with many warnings to beware of Indians, and not to stay late enough to be the victim of a frost that thinks nothing of forty below zero. After they had gone, the loneliness of the situation made itself unpleasantly felt. There were no other islands within six or seven miles, and though the mainland forests lay a couple of miles behind me, they stretched for a very great distance unbroken by any signs of human habitation. But, though the island was completely deserted and silent, the rocks and trees that had echoed human laughter and voices almost every hour of the day for two months could not fail to retain some memories of it all; and I was not surprised to fancy I heard a shout or a cry as I passed from rock to rock, and more than once to imagine that I heard my own name called aloud.

In the cottage there were six tiny little bed-rooms divided from one another by plain unvarnished partitions of pine. A wooden bedstead, a mattress, and a chair, stood in each room, but I only found two mirrors, and one of these was broken.

The boards creaked a good deal as I moved about, and the signs of occupation were so recent that I could hardly believe I was alone. I half expected to find someone left behind, still trying to crowd into a box more than it would hold. The door of one room was stiff, and refused for a moment to open, and it required very little persuasion to imagine someone was holding the handle on the inside, and that when it opened I should meet a pair of human eyes.

A thorough search of the floor led me to select as my own sleeping quarters a little room with a diminutive balcony over the verandah roof. The room was very small, but the bed was large, and had the best mattress of them all. It was situated directly over the sitting-room where I should live and do my "reading," and the miniature window looked out to the rising sun. With the exception of a narrow path which led from the front door and verandah through the trees to the boat-landing, the island was densely covered with maples, hemlocks, and cedars. The trees gathered in round the cottage so closely that the slightest wind made the branches scrape the roof and tap the wooden walls. A few moments after sunset the darkness became impenetrable, and ten yards beyond the glare of the lamps that shone through the sitting-room windows—of which there were four—you could not see an inch before your nose, nor move a step without running up against a tree.

The rest of that day I spent moving my belongings from my

tent to the sitting-room, taking stock of the contents of the larder, and chopping enough wood for the stove to last me for a week. After that, just before sunset, I went round the island a couple of times in my canoe for precaution's sake. I had never dreamed of doing this before, but when a man is alone he does things that never occur to him when he is one of a large party.

How lonely the island seemed when I landed again! The sun was down, and twilight is unknown in these northern regions. The darkness comes up at once. The canoe safely pulled up and turned over on her face, I groped my way up the little narrow pathway to the verandah. The six lamps were soon burning merrily in the front room; but in the kitchen, where I "dined," the shadows were so gloomy, and the lamplight was so inadequate, that the stars could be seen peeping through the cracks between the rafters.

I turned in early that night. Though it was calm and there was no wind, the creaking of my bedstead and the musical gurgle of the water over the rocks below were not the only sounds that reached my ears. As I lay awake, the appalling emptiness of the house grew upon me. The corridors and vacant rooms seemed to echo innumerable footsteps, shufflings, the rustle of skirts, and a constant undertone of whispering. When sleep at length overtook me, the breathings and noises, however, passed gently to mingle with the voices of my dreams.

A week passed by, and the "reading" progressed favourably. On the tenth day of my solitude, a strange thing happened. I awoke after a good night's sleep to find myself possessed with a marked repugnance for my room. The air seemed to stifle me. The more I tried to define the cause of this dislike, the more unreasonable it appeared. There was something about the room that made me afraid. Absurd as it seems, this feeling clung to me obstinately while dressing, and more than once I caught myself shivering, and conscious of an inclination to get out of the room as quickly as possible. The more I tried to laugh it away, the more real it became; and when at last I was dressed, and went out into the passage, and down-stairs into the kitchen, it was with feelings of relief, such as I might imagine would accompany one's escape from the presence of a dangerous contagious disease.

While cooking my breakfast, I carefully recalled every night spent in the room, in the hope that I might in some way connect the dislike I now felt with some disagreeable incident that had occurred in it. But the only thing I could recall was one stormy night when I suddenly awoke and heard the boards creaking so loudly in the corridor that I was convinced there were people in the house. So certain was I of this, that I had descended the stairs, gun in hand, only to find the doors and windows securely fastened, and the mice and black-beetles in sole possession of the floor. This was certainly not sufficient to account for the strength of my feelings.

The morning hours I spent in steady reading; and when I broke off in the middle of the day for a swim and luncheon, I was very much surprised, if not a little alarmed, to find that my dislike for the room had, if anything, grown stronger. Going upstairs to get a book, I experienced the most marked aversion to entering the room, and while within I was conscious all the time of an uncomfortable feeling that was half uneasiness and half apprehension. The result of it was that, instead of reading, I spent the afternoon on the water paddling and fishing, and when I got home about sundown, brought with me half a dozen delicious black bass for the supper-table and the larder.

As sleep was an important matter to me at this time, I had decided that if my aversion to the room was so strongly marked on my return as it had been before, I would move my bed down into the sitting-room, and sleep there. This was, I argued, in no sense a concession to an absurd and fanciful fear, but simply a precaution to ensure a good night's sleep. A bad night involved the loss of the next day's reading,—a loss I was not prepared to incur.

I accordingly moved my bed downstairs into a corner of the

sitting-room facing the door, and was moreover uncommonly glad when the operation was completed, and the door of the bedroom closed finally upon the shadows, the silence, and the strange *fear* that shared the room with them.

The croaking stroke of the kitchen clock sounded the hour of eight as I finished washing up my few dishes, and closing the kitchen door behind me, passed into the front room. All the lamps were lit, and their reflectors, which I had polished up during the day, threw a blaze of light into the room.

Outside the night was still and warm. Not a breath of air was stirring; the waves were silent, the trees motionless, and heavy clouds hung like an oppressive curtain over the heavens. The darkness seemed to have rolled up with unusual swiftness, and not the faintest glow of colour remained to show where the sun had set. There was present in the atmosphere that ominous and overwhelming silence which so often precedes the most violent storms.

I sat down to my books with my brain unusually clear, and in my heart the pleasant satisfaction of knowing that five black bass were lying in the ice-house, and that to-morrow morning the old farmer would arrive with fresh bread and eggs. I was soon absorbed in my books.

As the night wore on the silence deepened. Even the chipmunks were still; and the boards of the floors and walls ceased creaking. I read on steadily till, from the gloomy shadows of the kitchen, came the hoarse sound of the clock striking nine. How loud the strokes sounded! They were like blows of a big hammer. I closed one book and opened another, feeling that I was just warming up to my work.

This, however, did not last long. I presently found that I was reading the same paragraphs over twice, simple paragraphs that did not require such effort. Then I noticed that my mind began to wander to other things, and the effort to recall my thoughts became harder with each digression. Concentration was growing momentarily more difficult. Presently I discovered that

I had turned over two pages instead of one, and had not noticed my mistake until I was well down the page. This was becoming serious. What was the disturbing influence? It could not be physical fatigue. On the contrary, my mind was unusually alert, and in a more receptive condition than usual. I made a new and determined effort to read, and for a short time succeeded in giving my whole attention to my subject. But in a very few moments again I found myself leaning back in my chair, staring vacantly into space.

Something was evidently at work in my subconsciousness. There was something I had neglected to do. Perhaps the kitchen door and windows were not fastened. I accordingly went to see, and found that they were! The fire perhaps needed attention. I went in to see, and found that it was all right! I looked at the lamps, went upstairs into every bedroom in turn, and then went round the house, and even into the ice-house. Nothing was wrong; everything was in its place. Yet something *was* wrong! The conviction grew stronger and stronger within me.

When I at length settled down to my books again and tried to read, I became aware, for the first time, that the room seemed growing cold. Yet the day had been oppressively warm, and evening had brought no relief. The six big lamps, moreover, gave out heat enough to warm the room pleasantly. But a chilliness, that perhaps crept up from the lake, made itself felt in the room, and caused me to get up to close the glass door opening on to the verandah.

For a brief moment I stood looking out at the shaft of light that fell from the windows and shone some little distance down the pathway, and out for a few feet into the lake.

As I looked, I saw a canoe glide into the pathway of light, and immediately crossing it, pass out of sight again into the darkness. It was perhaps a hundred feet from the shore, and it moved swiftly.

I was surprised that a canoe should pass the island at that time of night, for all the summer visitors from the other side of the lake had gone home weeks before, and the island was a long way out of any line of water traffic.

My reading from this moment did not make very good progress, for somehow the picture of that canoe, gliding so dimly and swiftly across the narrow track of light on the black waters, silhouetted itself against the background of my mind with singular vividness. It kept coming between my eyes and the printed page. The more I thought about it the more surprised I became. It was of larger build than any I had seen during the past summer months, and was more like the old Indian war canoes with the high curving bows and stern and wide beam. The more I tried to read, the less success attended my efforts; and finally I closed my books and went out on the verandah to walk up and down a bit, and shake the chilliness out of my bones.

The night was perfectly still, and as dark as imaginable. I stumbled down the path to the little landing wharf, where the water made the very faintest of gurgling under the timbers. The sound of a big tree falling in the mainland forest, far across the lake, stirred echoes in the heavy air, like the first guns of a distant night attack. No other sound disturbed the stillness that reigned supreme.

As I stood upon the wharf in the broad splash of light that followed me from the sitting-room windows, I saw another canoe cross the pathway of uncertain light upon the water, and disappear at once into the impenetrable gloom that lay beyond. This time I saw more distinctly than before. It was like the former canoe, a big birch-bark, with high-crested bows and stern and broad beam. It was paddled by two Indians, of whom the one in the stern—the steerer—appeared to be a very large man. I could see this very plainly; and though the second canoe was much nearer the island than the first, I judged that they were both on their way home to the Government Reservation, which was situated some fifteen miles away upon the mainland.

I was wondering in my mind what could possibly bring any Indians down to this part of the lake at such an hour of the night, when a third canoe, of precisely similar build, and also occupied by two Indians, passed silently round the end of the wharf. This time the canoe was very much nearer shore, and it suddenly flashed into my mind that the three canoes were in reality one and the same, and that only one canoe was circling the island!

This was by no means a pleasant reflection, because, if it were the correct solution of the unusual appearance of the three canoes in this lonely part of the lake at so late an hour, the purpose of the two men could only reasonably be considered to be in some way connected with myself. I had never known of the Indians attempting any violence upon the settlers who shared the wild, inhospitable country with them; at the same time, it was not beyond the region of possibility to suppose . . . But then I did not care even to think of such hideous possibilities, and my imagination immediately sought relief in all manner of other solutions to the problem, which indeed came readily enough to my mind, but did not succeed in recommending themselves to my reason.

Meanwhile, by a sort of instinct, I stepped back out of the bright light in which I had hitherto been standing, and waited in the deep shadow of a rock to see if the canoe would again make its appearance. Here I could see, without being seen, and the precaution seemed a wise one.

After less than five minutes the canoe, as I had anticipated, made its fourth appearance. This time it was not twenty yards from the wharf, and I saw that the Indians meant to land. I recognised the two men as those who had passed before, and the steerer was certainly an immense fellow. It was unquestionably the same canoe. There could be no longer any doubt that for some purpose of their own the men had been going round and round the island for some time, waiting for an opportunity to land. I strained my eyes to follow them in the darkness, but the night had completely swallowed them up, and not even the faintest swish of the paddles reached my ears as the Indians plied their long and powerful strokes. The canoe would be round again in a few moments, and this time it was possible that the men might land. It was well to be prepared. I knew nothing of their intentions, and two to one (when the two are big Indians!) late at night on a lonely island was not exactly my idea of pleasant intercourse.

In a corner of the sitting-room, leaning up against the back wall, stood my Marlin rifle, with ten cartridges in the magazine and one lying snugly in the greased breech. There was just time to get up to the house and take up a position of defence in that corner. Without an instant's hesitation I ran up to the verandah, carefully picking my way among the trees, so as to avoid being seen in the light. Entering the room, I shut the door leading to the verandah, and as quickly as possible turned out every one of the six lamps. To be in a room so brilliantly lighted, where my every movement could be observed from outside, while I could see nothing but impenetrable darkness at every window, was by all laws of warfare an unnecessary concession to the enemy. And this enemy, if enemy it was to be, was far too wily and dangerous to be granted any such advantages.

I stood in the corner of the room with my back against the wall, and my hand on the cold rifle-barrel. The table, covered with my books, lay between me and the door, but for the first few minutes after the lights were out the darkness was so intense that nothing could be discerned at all. Then, very gradually, the outline of the room became visible, and the framework of the windows began to shape itself dimly before my eyes.

After a few minutes the door (its upper half of glass), and the two windows that looked out upon the front verandah, became specially distinct; and I was glad that this was so, because if the Indians came up to the house I should be able to see their approach, and gather something of their plans. Nor was I mistaken, for there presently came to my ears the peculiar hollow sound of a canoe landing and being carefully dragged up over the rocks. The paddles I distinctly heard being placed underneath, and the silence that ensued thereupon I rightly interpreted to mean that the Indians were stealthily approaching the house. . . .

While it would be absurd to claim that I was not alarmed—even frightened—at the gravity of the situation and its possible outcome, I speak the whole truth when I say that I was not overwhelmingly afraid for myself. I was conscious that even at this stage of the night I was passing into a psychical condition in which my sensations seemed no longer normal. Physical fear at no time entered into the nature of my feelings; and though I kept my hand upon my rifle the greater part of the night, I was all the time conscious that its assistance could be of little avail against the terrors that I had to face. More than once I seemed to feel most curiously that I was in no real sense a part of the proceedings, nor actually involved in them, but that I was playing the part of a spectator—a spectator, moreover, on a psychic rather than on a material plane. Many of my sensations that night were too vague for definite description and analysis, but the main feeling that will stay with me to the end of my days is the awful horror of it all, and the miserable sensation that if the strain had lasted a little longer than was actually the case my mind must inevitably have given way.

Meanwhile I stood still in my corner, and waited patiently for what was to come. The house was as still as the grave, but the inarticulate voices of the night sang in my ears, and I seemed to hear the blood running in my veins and dancing in my pulses.

If the Indians came to the back of the house, they would find the kitchen door and window securely fastened. They could not get in there without making considerable noise, which I was bound to hear. The only mode of getting in was by means of the door that faced me, and I kept my eyes glued on that door without taking them off for the smallest fraction of a second.

My sight adapted itself every minute better to the darkness. I saw the table that nearly filled the room, and left only a narrow passage on each side. I could also make out the straight backs of the wooden chairs pressed up against it, and could even distinguish my papers and inkstand lying on the white oilcloth covering. I thought of the gay faces that had gathered round that table during the summer, and I longed for the sunlight as I had never longed for it before.

Less than three feet to my left the passage-way led to the kitchen, and the stairs leading to the bedrooms above commenced in this passage-way, but almost in the sitting-room itself. Through the windows I could see the dim motionless outlines of the trees: not a leaf stirred, not a branch moved.

A few moments of this awful silence, and then I was aware of a soft tread on the boards of the verandah, so stealthy that it seemed an impression directly on my brain rather than upon the nerves of hearing. Immediately afterwards a black figure darkened the glass door, and I perceived that a face was pressed against the upper panes. A shiver ran down my back, and my hair was conscious of a tendency to rise and stand at right angles to my head.

It was the figure of an Indian, broad-shouldered and immense; indeed, the largest figure of a man I have ever seen outside of a circus hall. By some power of light that seemed to generate itself in the brain, I saw the strong dark face with the aquiline nose and high cheek-bones flattened against the glass. The direction of the gaze I could not determine; but faint gleams of light as the big eyes rolled round and showed their whites, told me plainly that no corner of the room escaped their searching.

For what seemed fully five minutes the dark figure stood there, with the huge shoulders bent forward so as to bring the head down to the level of the glass; while behind him, though not nearly so large, the shadowy form of the other Indian swayed to and fro like a bent tree. While I waited in an agony of suspense and agitation for their next movement little currents of icy sensation ran up and down my spine and my heart seemed alternately to stop beating, and then start off again with terrifying rapidity. They must have heard its thumping and the singing of the blood in my head! Moreover, I was conscious, as

I felt a cold stream of perspiration trickle down my face, of a desire to scream, to shout, to bang the walls like a child, to make a noise, or do anything that would relieve the suspense and bring things to a speedy climax.

It was probably this inclination that led me to another discovery, for when I tried to bring my rifle from behind my back to raise it and have it pointed at the door ready to fire, I found that I was powerless to move. The muscles, paralysed by this strange fear, refused to obey the will. Here indeed was a terrifying complication!

* * * * *

There was a faint sound of rattling at the brass knob, and the door was pushed open a couple of inches. A pause of a few seconds, and it was pushed open still further. Without a sound of footsteps that was appreciable to my ears, the two figures glided into the room, and the man behind gently closed the door after him.

They were alone with me between the four walls. Could they see me standing there, so still and straight in my corner? Had they, perhaps, already seen me? My blood surged and sang like the roll of drums in an orchestra; and though I did my best to suppress my breathing, it sounded like the rushing of wind through a pneumatic tube.

My suspense as to the next move was soon at an end— only, however, to give place to a new and keener alarm. The men had hitherto exchanged no words and no signs, but there were general indications of a movement across the room, and whichever way they went they would have to pass round the table. If they came my way they would have to pass within six inches of my person. While I was considering this very disagreeable possibility, I perceived that the smaller Indian (smaller by comparison) suddenly raised his arm and pointed to the ceiling. The other fellow raised his head and followed the direction of his companion's arm. I began to understand at last. They were going upstairs, and the room directly overhead to which they pointed had been until this night my bedroom. It was the room in which I had experienced that very morning so strange a sensation of fear, and but for which I should then have been lying asleep in the narrow bed against the window.

The Indians then began to move silently around the room; they were going upstairs, and they were coming round my side of the table. So stealthy were their movements that, but for the abnormally sensitive state of the nerves, I should never have heard them. As it was, their cat-like tread was distinctly audible. Like two monstrous black cats they came round the table toward me, and for the first time I perceived that the smaller of the two dragged something along the floor behind him. As it trailed along over the floor with a soft, sweeping sound, I somehow got the impression that it was a large dead thing with outstretched wings, or a large, spreading cedar branch. Whatever it was, I was unable to see it even in outline, and I was too terrified, even had I possessed the power over my muscles, to move my neck forward in the effort to determine its nature.

Nearer and nearer they came. The leader rested a giant hand upon the table as he moved. My lips were glued together, and the air seemed to burn in my nostrils. I tried to close my eyes, so that I might not see as they passed me; but my eyelids had stiffened, and refused to obey. Would they never get by me? Sensation seemed also to have left my legs, and it was as if I were standing on mere supports of wood or stone. Worse still, I was conscious that I was losing the power of balance, the power to stand upright, or even to lean backwards against the wall. Some force was drawing me forward, and a dizzy terror seized me that I should lose my balance, and topple forward against the Indians just as they were in the act of passing me.

Even moments drawn out into hours must come to an end some time, and almost before I knew it the figures had passed me and had their feet upon the lower step of the stairs leading to the upper bedrooms. There could not have been six inches between us, and yet I was conscious only of a current of cold air that followed them. They had not touched me, and I was convinced that they had not seen me. Even the trailing thing on the floor behind them had not touched my feet, as I had dreaded it would, and on such an occasion as this I was grateful even for the smallest mercies.

The absence of the Indians from my immediate neighbourhood brought little sense of relief. I stood shivering and shuddering in my corner, and, beyond being able to breathe more freely, I felt no whit less uncomfortable. Also, I was aware that a certain light, which, without apparent source or rays, had enabled me to follow their every gesture and movement, had gone out of the room with their departure. An unnatural darkness now filled the room, and pervaded its every corner so that I could barely make out the positions of the windows and the glass doors.

As I said before, my condition was evidently an abnormal one. The capacity for feeling surprise seemed, as in dreams, to be wholly absent. My senses recorded with unusual accuracy every smallest occurrence, but I was able to draw only the simplest deductions.

The Indians soon reached the top of the stairs, and there they halted for a moment. I had not the faintest clue as to their next movement. They appeared to hesitate. They were listening attentively. Then I heard one of them, who by the weight of his soft tread must have been the giant, cross the narrow corridor and enter the room directly overhead—my own little bedroom. But for the insistence of that unaccountable dread I had experienced there in the morning, I should at that very moment have been lying in the bed with the big Indian in the room standing beside me.

For the space of a hundred seconds there was silence, such as might have existed before the birth of sound. It was followed by a long quivering shriek of terror, which rang out into the night, and ended in a short gulp before it had run its full course. At the same moment the other Indian left his place at the head of the stairs, and joined his companion in the bedroom. I heard the "thing" trailing behind him along the floor. A thud followed, as of something heavy falling, and then all became as still and silent as before.

It was at this point that the atmosphere, surcharged all day with the electricity of a fierce storm, found relief in a dancing flash of brilliant lightning simultaneously with a crash of loudest thunder. For five seconds every article in the room was visible to me with amazing distinctness, and through the windows I saw the tree trunks standing in solemn rows. The thunder pealed and echoed across the lake and among the distant islands, and the flood-gates of heaven then opened and let out their rain in streaming torrents.

The drops fell with a swift rushing sound upon the still waters of the lake, which leaped up to meet them, and pattered with the rattle of shot on the leaves of the maples and the roof of the cottage. A moment later, and another flash, even more brilliant and of longer duration than the first, it up the sky from zenith to horizon, and bathed the room momentarily in dazzling whiteness. I could see the rain glistening on the leaves and branches outside. The wind rose suddenly, and in less than a minute the storm that had been gathering all day burst forth in its full fury.

Above all the noisy voices of the elements, the slightest sounds in the room overhead made themselves heard, and in the few seconds of deep silence that followed the shriek of terror and pain I was aware that the movements had commenced again. The men were leaving the room and approaching the top of the stairs. A short pause, and they began to descend. Behind them, tumbling from step to step, I could hear that trailing "thing" being dragged along. It had become ponderous!

I awaited their approach with a degree of calmness, almost of apathy, which was only explicable on the ground that after a certain point Nature applies her own anæsthetic, and a merciful condition of numbness supervenes. On they came, step by step, nearer and nearer, with the shuffling sound of the burden behind growing louder as they approached.

They were already half-way down the stairs when I was galvanised afresh into a condition of terror by the consideration of a new and horrible possibility. It was the reflection that if another vivid flash of lightning were to come when the shadowy procession was in the room, perhaps when it was actually passing in front of me, I should see everything in detail, and worse, be seen myself! I could only hold my breath and wait—wait while the minutes lengthened into hours, and the procession made its slow progress round the room.

The Indians had reached the foot of the staircase. The form of the huge leader loomed in the doorway of the passage, and the burden with an ominous thud had dropped from the last step to the floor. There was a moment's pause while I saw the Indian turn and stoop to assist his companion. Then the procession moved forward again, entered the room close on my left, and began to move slowly round my side of the table. The leader was already beyond me, and his companion, dragging on the floor behind him the burden, whose confused outline I could dimly make out, was exactly in front of me, when the cavalcade came to a dead halt. At the same moment, with the strange suddenness of thunderstorms, the splash of the rain ceased altogether, and the wind died away into utter silence.

For the space of five seconds my heart seemed to stop beating, and then the worst came. A double flash of lightning lit up the room and its contents with merciless vividness.

The huge Indian leader stood a few feet past me on my right. One leg was stretched forward in the act of taking a step. His immense shoulders were turned toward his companion, and in all their magnificent fierceness I saw the outline of his features. His gaze was directed upon the burden his companion was dragging along the floor; but his profile, with the big aquiline nose, high cheekbone, straight black hair and bold chin, burnt itself in that brief instant into my brain, never again to fade.

Dwarfish, compared with this gigantic figure, appeared the proportions of the other Indian, who, within twelve inches of my face, was stooping over the thing he was dragging in a position that lent to his person the additional horror of deformity. And the burden, lying upon a sweeping cedar branch which he held and dragged by a long stem, was the body of a white man. The scalp had been neatly lifted, and blood lay in a broad smear upon the cheeks and forehead.

Then, for the first time that night, the terror that had paralysed my muscles and my will lifted its unholy spell from my soul. With a loud cry I stretched out my arms to seize the big Indian by the throat, and, grasping only air, tumbled forward unconscious upon the ground.

I had recognised the body, and *the face was my own!* . . .

It was bright daylight when a man's voice recalled me to consciousness. I was lying where I had fallen, and the farmer was standing in the room with the loaves of bread in his hands. The horror of the night was still in my heart, and as the bluff settler helped me to my feet and picked up the rifle which had fallen with me, with many questions and expressions of condolence, I imagine my brief replies were neither self-explanatory nor even intelligible.

That day, after a thorough and fruitless search of the house, I left the island, and went over to spend my last ten days with the farmer; and when the time came for me to leave, the necessary reading had been accomplished, and my nerves had completely recovered their balance.

On the day of my departure the farmer started early in his big boat with my belongings to row to the point, twelve miles distant, where a little steamer ran twice a week for the accommodation of hunters. Late in the afternoon I went off in another direction in my canoe, wishing to see the island once again, where I had been the victim of so strange an experience.

In due course I arrived there, and made a tour of the island. I also made a search of the little house, and it was not without a curious sensation in my heart that I entered the little upstairs bedroom. There seemed nothing unusual.

Just after I re-embarked, I saw a canoe gliding ahead of me around the curve of the island. A canoe was an unusual sight at this time of the year, and this one seemed to have sprung from nowhere. Altering my course a little, I watched it disappear around the next projecting point of rock. It had high curving bows, and there were two Indians in it. I lingered with some excitement, to see if it would appear again round the other side of the island; and in less than five minutes it came into view. There were less than two hundred yards between us, and the Indians, sitting on their haunches, were paddling swiftly in my direction.

I never paddled faster in my life than I did in those next few minutes. When I turned to look again, the Indians had altered their course, and were again circling the island.

The sun was sinking behind the forests on the mainland, and the crimson-coloured clouds of sunset were reflected in the waters of the lake, when I looked round for the last time, and saw the big bark canoe and its two dusky occupants still going round the island. Then the shadows deepened rapidly; the lake grew black, and the night wind blew its first breath in my face as I turned a corner, and a projecting bluff of rock hid from my view both island and canoe.

The Empty House, 1906

A CASE OF
EAVESDROPPING

Jim Shorthouse was the sort of fellow who always made a mess of things. Everything with which his hands or mind came into contact issued from such contact in an unqualified and irremediable state of mess. His college days were a mess: he was twice rusticated. His schooldays were a mess: he went to half a dozen, each passing him on to the next with a worse character and in a more developed state of mess. His early boyhood was the sort of mess that copy-books and dictionaries spell with a big "M," and his babyhood—ugh! was the embodiment of howling, yowling, screaming mess.

At the age of forty, however, there came a change in his troubled life, when he met a girl with half a million in her own right, who consented to marry him, and who very soon succeeded in reducing his most messy existence into a state of comparative order and system.

Certain incidents, important and otherwise, of Jim's life would never have come to be told here but for the fact that in getting into his "messes" and out of them again he succeeded in drawing himself into the atmosphere of peculiar circumstances and strange happenings. He attracted to his path the curious adventures of life as unfailingly as meat attracts flies, and jam wasps. It is to the meat and jam of his life, so to speak, that he owes his experiences; his after-life was all pudding, which attracts nothing but greedy children. With marriage the interest of his life ceased for all but one person, and his path became regular as the sun's instead of erratic as a comet's.

The first experience in order of time that he related to me

shows that somewhere latent behind his disarranged nervous system there lay psychic perceptions of an uncommon order. About the age of twenty-two—I think after his second rustication—his father's purse and patience had equally given out, and Jim found himself stranded high and dry in a large American city. High and dry! And the only clothes that had no holes in them safely in the keeping of his uncle's wardrobe.

Careful reflection on a bench in one of the city parks led him to the conclusion that the only thing to do was to persuade the city editor of one of the daily journals that he possessed an observant mind and a ready pen, and that he could "do good work for your paper, sir, as a reporter." This, then, he did, standing at a most unnatural angle between the editor and the window to conceal the whereabouts of the holes.

"Guess we'll have to give you a week's trial," said the editor, who, ever on the lookout for good chance material, took on shoals of men in that way and retained on the average one man per shoal. Anyhow it gave Jim Shorthouse the wherewithal to sew up the holes and relieve his uncle's wardrobe of its burden.

Then he went to find living quarters; and in this proceeding his unique characteristics already referred to—what theosophists would call his Karma—began unmistakably to assert themselves, for it was in the house he eventually selected that this sad tale took place.

There are no "diggings" in American cities. The alternatives for small incomes are grim enough—rooms in a boarding-house where meals are served, or in a room -house where no meals are served—not even breakfast. Rich people live in palaces, of course, but Jim had nothing to do with "sich-like." His horizon was bounded by boarding-houses and room-houses; and, owing to the necessary irregularity of his meals and hours, he took the latter.

It was a large, gaunt-looking place in a side street, with dirty windows and a creaking iron gate, but the rooms were large, and the one he selected and paid for in advance was on the top floor.

The landlady looked gaunt and dusty as the house, and quite as old. Her eyes were green and faded, and her features large.

"Waal," she twanged, with her electrifying Western drawl, "that's the room, if you like it, and that's the price I said. Now, if you want it, why, just say so; and if you don't, why, it don't hurt me any."

Jim wanted to shake her, but he feared the clouds of long-accumulated dust in her clothes, and as the price and size of the room suited him, he decided to take it.

"Anyone else on this floor?" he asked.

She looked at him queerly out of her faded eyes before she answered.

"None of my guests ever put such questions to me before," she said; "but I guess you're different. Why, there's no one at all but an old gent that's stayed here every bit of five years. He's over thar," pointing to the end of the passage.

"Ah! I see," said Shorthouse feebly. "So I'm alone up here?"

"Reckon you are, pretty near," she twanged out, ending the conversation abruptly by turning her back on her new "guest," and going slowly and deliberately downstairs.

The newspaper work kept Shorthouse out most of the night. Three times a week he got home at 1 a.m., and three times at 3 a.m. The room proved comfortable enough, and he paid for a second week. His unusual hours had so far prevented his meeting any inmates of the house, and not a sound had been heard from the "old gent" who shared the floor with him. It seemed a very quiet house.

One night, about the middle of the second week, he came home tired after a long day's work. The lamp that usually stood all night in the hall had burned itself out, and he had to stumble upstairs in the dark. He made considerable noise in doing so, but nobody seemed to be disturbed. The whole house was utterly quiet, and probably everybody was asleep. There were no lights under any of the doors. All was in darkness. It was after two o'clock. After reading some English letters that had come during the day, and dipping for a few minutes into a book, he became drowsy and got ready for bed. Just as he was about to get in between the sheets, he stopped for a moment and listened. There rose in the night, as he did so, the sound of steps somewhere in the house below. Listening attentively, he heard that it was somebody coming upstairs—a heavy tread, and the owner taking no pains to step quietly. On it came up the stairs, tramp, tramp, tramp—evidently the tread of a big man, and one in something of a hurry.

At once thoughts connected somehow with fire and police flashed through Jim's brain, but there were no sounds of voices with the steps, and he reflected in the same moment that it could only be the old gentleman keeping late hours and tumbling upstairs in the darkness. He was in the act of turning out the gas and stepping into bed, when the house resumed its former stillness by the footsteps suddenly coming to a dead stop immediately outside his own room.

With his hand on the gas, Shorthouse paused a moment before turning it out to see if the steps would go on again, when he was startled by a loud knocking on his door. Instantly, in obedience to a curious and unexplained instinct, he turned out the light, leaving himself and the room in total darkness.

He had scarcely taken a step across the room to open the door, when a voice from the other side of the wall, so close it almost sounded in his ear, exclaimed in German, "Is that you, father? Come in."

The speaker was a man in the next room, and the knocking, after all, had not been on his own door, but on that of the adjoining chamber, which he had supposed to be vacant.

Almost before the man in the passage had time to answer in German, "Let me in at once," Jim heard someone cross the floor and unlock the door. Then it was slammed to with a bang, and there was audible the sound of footsteps about the room, and of chairs being drawn up to a table and knocking against furniture on the way. The men seemed wholly regardless of their neighbour's comfort, for they made noise enough to waken the dead.

"Serves me right for taking a room in such a cheap hole," reflected Jim in the darkness. "I wonder whom she's let the room to!"

The two rooms, the landlady had told him, were originally one. She had put up a thin partition—just a row of boards—to increase her income. The doors were adjacent, and only separated by the massive upright beam between them. When one was opened or shut the other rattled.

With utter indifference to the comfort of the other sleepers in the house, the two Germans had meanwhile commenced to talk both at once and at the top of their voices. They talked emphatically, even angrily. The words "Father" and "Otto" were freely used. Shorthouse understood German, but as he stood listening for the first minute or two, an eavesdropper in spite of himself, it was difficult to make head or tail of the talk, for neither would give way to the other, and the jumble of guttural sounds and unfinished sentences was wholly unintelligible. Then, very suddenly, both voices dropped together; and, after a moment's pause, the deep tones of one of them, who seemed to be the "father," said, with the utmost distinctness—

"You mean, Otto, that you refuse to get it?"

There was a sound of someone shuffling in the chair before the answer came. "I mean that I don't know how to get it. It is so much, father. It is *too* much. A part of it——"

"A part of it!" cried the other, with an angry oath, "a part of it, when ruin and disgrace are already in the house, is worse than useless. If you can get half you can get all, you wretched fool. Half-measures only damn all concerned."

"You told me last time——" began the other firmly, but was not allowed to finish. A succession of horrible oaths drowned his sentence, and the father went on, in a voice vibrating with anger—

"You know she will give you anything. You have only been

married a few months. If you ask and give a plausible reason you can get all we want and more. You can ask it temporarily. All will be paid back. It will re-establish the firm, and she will never know what was done with it. With that amount, Otto, you know I can recoup all these terrible losses, and in less than a year all will be repaid. But without it. . . . You must get it, Otto. Hear me, you must. Am I to be arrested for the misuse of trust moneys? Is our honoured name to be cursed and spat on?" The old man choked and stammered in his anger and desperation.

Shorthouse stood shivering in the darkness and listening in spite of himself. The conversation had carried him along with it, and he had been for some reason afraid to let his neighbourhood be known. But at this point he realised that he had listened too long and that he must inform the two men that they could be overheard to every single syllable. So he coughed loudly, and at the same time rattled the handle of his door. It seemed to have no effect, for the voices continued just as loudly as before, the son protesting and the father growing more and more angry. He coughed again persistently, and also contrived purposely in the darkness to tumble against the partition, feeling the thin boards yield easily under his weight, and making a considerable noise in so doing. But the voices went on unconcernedly, and louder than ever. Could it be possible they had not heard?

By this time Jim was more concerned about his own sleep than the morality of overhearing the private scandals of his neighbours, and he went out into the passage and knocked smartly at their door. Instantly, as if by magic, the sounds ceased. Everything dropped into utter silence. There was no light under the door and not a whisper could be heard within. He knocked again, but received no answer.

"Gentlemen," he began at length, with his lips close to the keyhole and in German, "please do not talk so loud. I can overhear all you say in the next room. Besides, it is very late, and I wish to sleep."

He paused and listened, but no answer was forthcoming.

He turned the handle and found the door was locked. Not a sound broke the stillness of the night except the faint swish of the wind over the skylight and the creaking of a board here and there in the house below. The cold air of a very early morning crept down the passage, and made him shiver. The silence of the house began to impress him disagreeably. He looked behind him and about him, hoping, and yet fearing, that something would break the stillness. The voices still seemed to ring on in his ears; but that sudden silence, when he knocked at the door, affected him far more unpleasantly than the voices, and put strange thoughts in his brain—thoughts he did not like or approve.

Moving stealthily from the door, he peered over the banisters into the space below. It was like a deep vault that might conceal in its shadows anything that was not good. It was not difficult to fancy he saw an indistinct moving to-and-fro below him. Was that a figure sitting on the stairs peering up obliquely at him out of hideous eyes? Was that a sound of whispering and shuffling down there in the dark halls and forsaken landings? Was it something more than the inarticulate murmur of the night?

The wind made an effort overhead, singing over the skylight, and the door behind him rattled and made him start. He turned to go back to his room, and the draught closed the door slowly in his face as if there were someone pressing against it from the other side. When he pushed it open and went in, a hundred shadowy forms seemed to dart swiftly and silently back to their corners and hiding-places. But in the adjoining room the sounds had entirely ceased, and Shorthouse soon crept into bed, and left the house with its inmates, waking or sleeping, to take care of themselves, while he entered the region of dreams and silence.

Next day, strong in the common sense that the sunlight brings, he determined to lodge a complaint against the noisy occupants of the next room and make the landlady request them to modify their voices at such late hours of the night and morning. But it so happened that she was not to be seen that day, and when he returned from the office at midnight it was, of course, too late.

Looking under the door as he came up to bed he noticed that there was no light, and concluded that the Germans were not in. So much the better. He went to sleep about one o'clock, fully decided that if they came up later and woke him with their horrible noises he would not rest till he had roused the landlady and made her reprove them with that authoritative twang, in which every word was like the lash of a metallic whip.

However, there proved to be no need for such drastic measures, for Shorthouse slumbered peacefully all night, and his dreams—chiefly of the fields of grain and flocks of sheep on the far-away farms of his father's estate—were permitted to run their fanciful course unbroken.

Two nights later, however, when he came home tired out, after a difficult day, and wet and blown about by one of the wickedest storms he had ever seen, his dreams—always of the fields and sheep—were not destined to be so undisturbed.

He had already dozed off in that delicious glow that follows the removal of wet clothes and the immediate snuggling under warm blankets, when his consciousness, hovering on the borderland between sleep and waking, was vaguely troubled by a sound that rose indistinctly from the depths of the house, and, between the gusts of wind and rain, reached his ears with an accompanying sense of uneasiness and discomfort. It rose on the night air with some pretence of regularity, dying away again in the roar of the wind to reassert itself distantly in the deep, brief hushes of the storm.

For a few minutes Jim's dreams were coloured only—tinged, as it were, by this impression of fear approaching from somewhere insensibly upon him. His consciousness, at first, refused to be drawn back from that enchanted region where it had wandered, and he did not immediately awaken. But the nature of his dreams changed unpleasantly. He saw the sheep suddenly run huddled together, as though frightened by the neighbourhood of an enemy, while the fields of waving corn became agitated as though some monster were moving uncouthly among the crowded stalks. The sky grew dark, and in his dream an awful sound came somewhere from the clouds. It was in reality the sound downstairs growing more distinct.

Shorthouse shifted uneasily across the bed with something like a groan of distress. The next minute he awoke, and found himself sitting straight up in bed—listening. Was it a nightmare? Had he been dreaming evil dreams, that his flesh crawled and the hair stirred on his head?

The room was dark and silent, but outside the wind howled dismally and drove the rain with repeated assaults against the rattling windows. How nice it would be—the thought flashed through his mind—if all winds, like the west wind, went down with the sun! They made such fiendish noises at night, like the crying of angry voices. In the daytime they had such a different sound. If only——

Hark! It was no dream after all, for the sound was momentarily growing louder, and its cause was coming up the stairs. He found himself speculating feebly what this cause might be, but the sound was still too indistinct to enable him to arrive at any definite conclusion.

The voice of a church clock striking two made itself heard above the wind. It was just about the hour when the Germans had commenced their performance three nights before. Shorthouse made up his mind that if they began it again he would not put up with it for very long. Yet he was already horribly conscious of the difficulty he would have of getting out of bed. The clothes were so warm and comforting against his back. The sound, still steadily coming nearer, had by this time become differentiated from the confused clamour of the elements, and had resolved itself into the footsteps of one or more persons.

"The Germans, hang 'em!" thought Jim. "But what on earth is

the matter with me? I never felt so queer in all my life."

He was trembling all over, and felt as cold as though he were in a freezing atmosphere. His nerves were steady enough, and he felt no diminution of physical courage, but he was conscious of a curious sense of malaise and trepidation, such as even the most vigorous men have been known to experience when in the first grip of some horrible and deadly disease. As the footsteps approached this feeling of weakness increased. He felt a strange lassitude creeping over him, a sort of exhaustion, accompanied by a growing numbness in the extremities, and a sensation of dreaminess in the head, as if perhaps the consciousness were leaving its accustomed seat in the brain and preparing to act on another plane. Yet, strange to say, as the vitality was slowly withdrawn from his body, his senses seemed to grow more acute.

Meanwhile the steps were already on the landing at the top of the stairs, and Shorthouse, still sitting upright in bed, heard a heavy body brush past his door and along the wall outside, almost immediately afterwards the loud knocking of someone's knuckles on the door of the adjoining room.

Instantly, though so far not a sound had proceeded from within, he heard, through the thin partition, a chair pushed back and a man quickly cross the floor and open the door.

"Ah! it's you," he heard in the son's voice. Had the fellow, then, been sitting silently in there all this time, waiting for his father's arrival? To Shorthouse it came not as a pleasant reflection by any means.

There was no answer to this dubious greeting, but the door was closed quickly, and then there was a sound as if a bag or parcel had been thrown on a wooden table and had slid some distance across it before stopping.

"What's that?" asked the son, with anxiety in his tone.

"You may know before I go," returned the other gruffly. Indeed his voice was more than gruff: it betrayed ill-suppressed passion.

Shorthouse was conscious of a strong desire to stop the

conversation before it proceeded any further, but somehow or other his will was not equal to the task, and he could not get out of bed. The conversation went on, every tone and inflexion distinctly audible above the noise of the storm. In a low voice the father continued. Jim missed some of the words at the beginning of the sentence. It ended with: ". . . but now they've all left, and I've managed to get up to you. You know what I've come for." There was distinct menace in his tone.

"Yes," returned the other; "I have been waiting."

"And the money?" asked the father impatiently.

No answer.

"You've had three days to get it in, and I've contrived to stave off the worst so far—but to-morrow is the end."

No answer.

"Speak, Otto! What have you got for me? Speak, my son; for God's sake, tell me."

There was a moment's silence, during which the old man's vibrating accents seemed to echo through the rooms. Then came in a low voice the answer—

"I have nothing."

"Otto!" cried the other with passion, "nothing!"

"I can get nothing," came almost in a whisper.

"You lie!" cried the other, in a half-stifled voice. "I swear you lie. Give me the money."

A chair was heard scraping along the floor. Evidently the men had been sitting over the table, and one of them had risen. Shorthouse heard the bag or parcel drawn across the table, and then a step as if one of the men was crossing to the door.

"Father, what's in that? I must know," said Otto, with the first signs of determination in his voice. There must have been an effort on the son's part to gain possession of the parcel in question, and on the father's to retain it, for between them it fell to the ground. A curious rattle followed its contact with the floor. Instantly there were sounds of a scuffle. The men were struggling for the possession of the box. The elder man with oaths, and blasphemous imprecations, the other with short gasps that betokened the strength of his efforts. It was of short duration, and the younger man had evidently won, for a minute later was heard his angry exclamation.

"I knew it. Her jewels! You scoundrel, you shall never have them. It is a crime."

The elder man uttered a short, guttural laugh, which froze Jim's blood and made his skin creep. No word was spoken, and for the space of ten seconds there was a living silence. Then the air trembled with the sound of a thud, followed immediately by a groan and the crash of a heavy body falling over on to the table. A second later there was a lurching from the table on to the floor and against the partition that separated the rooms. The bed quivered an instant at the shock, but the unholy spell was lifted from his soul and Jim Shorthouse sprang out of bed and across the floor in a single bound. He knew that ghastly murder had been done—the murder by a father of his son.

With shaking fingers but a determined heart he lit the gas, and the first thing in which his eyes corroborated the evidence of his ears was the horrifying detail that the lower portion of the partition bulged unnaturally into his own room. The glaring paper with which it was covered had cracked under the tension and the boards beneath it bent inwards towards him. What hideous load was behind them, he shuddered to think.

All this he saw in less than a second. Since the final lurch against the wall not a sound had proceeded from the room, not even a groan or a footstep. All was still but the howl of the wind, which to his ears had in it a note of triumphant horror.

Shorthouse was in the act of leaving the room to rouse the house and send for the police—in fact his hand was already on the door-knob—when something in the room arrested his attention. Out of the corner of his eyes he thought he caught sight of something moving. He was sure of it, and turning his eyes in the direction, he found he was not mistaken.

Something was creeping slowly towards him along the floor.

It was something dark and serpentine in shape, and it came from the place where the partition bulged. He stooped down to examine it with feelings of intense horror and repugnance, and he discovered that it was moving toward him from the *other side* of the wall. His eyes were fascinated, and for the moment he was unable to move. Silently, slowly, from side to side like a thick worm, it crawled forward into the room beneath his frightened eyes, until at length he could stand it no longer and stretched out his arm to touch it. But at the instant of contact he withdrew his hand with a suppressed scream. It was sluggish— and it was warm! and he saw that his fingers were stained with living crimson.

A second more, and Shorthouse was out in the passage with his hand on the door of the next room. It was locked. He plunged forward with all his weight against it, and, the lock giving way, he fell headlong into a room that was pitch dark and very cold. In a moment he was on his feet again and trying to penetrate the blackness. Not a sound, not a movement. Not even the sense of a presence. It was empty, miserably empty!

Across the room he could trace the outline of a window with rain streaming down the outside, and the blurred lights of the city beyond. But the room was empty, appallingly empty; and so still. He stood there, cold as ice, staring, shivering listening. Suddenly there was a step behind him and a light flashed into the room, and when he turned quickly with his arm up as if to ward off a terrific blow he found himself face to face with the landlady. Instantly the reaction began to set in.

It was nearly three o'clock in the morning, and he was standing there with bare feet and striped pyjamas in a small room, which in the merciful light he perceived to be absolutely empty, carpetless, and without a stick of furniture, or even a window-blind. There he stood staring at the disagreeable landlady. And there she stood too, staring and silent, in a black wrapper, her head almost bald, her face white as chalk, shading a sputtering candle with one bony hand and peering over it at him with her blinking green eyes. She looked positively hideous.

"Waal?" she drawled at length, "I heard yer right enough. Guess you couldn't sleep! Or just prowlin' round a bit— is that it?"

The empty room, the absence of all traces of the recent tragedy, the silence, the hour, his striped pyjamas and bare feet— everything together combined to deprive him momentarily of speech. He stared at her blankly without a word.

"Waal?" clanked the awful voice.

"My dear woman," he burst out finally, "there's been something awful——" So far his desperation took him, but no farther. He positively stuck at the substantive.

"Oh! there hasn't been nothin'" she said slowly still peering at him. "I reckon you've only seen and heard what the others did. I never can keep folks on this floor long. Most of 'em catch on sooner or later—that is, the ones that's kind of quick and sensitive. Only you being an Englishman I thought you wouldn't mind. Nothin' really happens; it's only thinkin' like."

Shorthouse was beside himself. He felt ready to pick her up and drop her over the banisters, candle and all.

"Look there," he said, pointing at her within an inch of her blinking eyes with the fingers that had touched the oozing blood; "look there, my good woman. Is that only thinking?"

She stared a minute, as if not knowing what he meant.

"I guess so," she said at length.

He followed her eyes, and to his amazement saw that his fingers were as white as usual, and quite free from the awful stain that had been there ten minutes before. There was no sign of blood. No amount of staring could bring it back. Had he gone out of his mind? Had his eyes and ears played such tricks with him? Had his senses become false and perverted? He dashed past the landlady, out into the passage, and gained his own room in a couple of strides. Whew! . . . the partition no longer bulged. The paper was not torn. There was no creeping, crawling thing on the faded old carpet.

"It's all over now," drawled the metallic voice behind him. "I'm going to bed again."

He turned and saw the landlady slowly going downstairs again, still shading the candle with her hand and peering up at him from time to time as she moved. A black, ugly, unwholesome object, he thought, as she disappeared into the darkness below, and the last flicker of her candle threw a queer-shaped shadow along the wall and over the ceiling.

Without hesitating a moment, Shorthouse threw himself into his clothes and went out of the house. He preferred the storm to the horrors of that top floor, and he walked the streets till daylight. In the evening he told the landlady he would leave next day, in spite of her assurances that nothing more would happen.

"It never comes back," she said—"that is, not after he's killed."

Shorthouse gasped.

"You gave me a lot for my money," he growled.

"Waal, it aren't my show," she drawled. "I'm no spirit medium. You take chances. Some'll sleep right along and never hear nothin'. Others, like yourself, are different and get the whole thing."

"Who's the old gentleman?—does he hear it?" asked Jim.

"There's no old gentleman at all," she answered coolly. "I just told you that to make you feel easy like in case you did hear anythin'. You were all alone on the floor."

"Say now," she went on, after a pause in which Shorthouse could think of nothing to say but unpunishable things, "say now, do tell, did you feel sort of cold when the show was on, sort of tired and weak, I mean, as if you might be going to die?"

"How can I say?" he answered savagely; "what I felt God only knows."

"Waal, but He won't tell," she drawled out. "Only I was wonderin' how you really did feel, because the man who had that room last was found one morning in bed——"

"In bed?"

"He was dead. He was the one before you. Oh! You don't need to get rattled so. You're all right. And it all really happened, they do say. This house used to be a private residence some twenty-five years ago, and a German family of the name of Steinhardt lived here. They had a big business in Wall Street, and stood 'way up in things."

"Ah!" said her listener.

"Oh yes, they did, right at the top, till one fine day it all bust and the old man skipped with the boodle——"

"Skipped with the boodle?"

"That's so," she said; "got clear away with all the money, and the son was found dead in his house, committed soocide it was thought. Though there was some as said he couldn't have stabbed himself and fallen in that position. They said he was murdered. The father died in prison. They tried to fasten the murder on him, but there was no motive, or no evidence, or no somethin'. I forget now."

"Very pretty," said Shorthouse.

"I'll show you somethin' mighty queer anyways," she drawled, "if you'll come upstairs a minute. I've heard the steps and voices lots of times; they don't pheaze me any. I'd just as lief hear so many dogs barkin'. You'll find the whole story in the newspapers if you look it up—not what goes on here, but the story of the Germans. My house would be ruined if they told all, and I'd sue for damages."

They reached the bedroom, and the woman went in and pulled up the edge of the carpet where Shorthouse had seen the blood soaking in the previous night.

"Look thar, if you feel like it," said the old hag. Stooping down, he saw a dark, dull stain in the boards that corresponded exactly to the shape and position of the blood as he had seen it.

That night he slept in a hotel, and the following day sought new quarters. In the newspapers on file in his office after a long search he found twenty years back the detailed story, substantially as the woman had said, of Steinhardt & Co.'s failure, the absconding and subsequent arrest of the senior partner, and the suicide, or murder, of his son Otto. The landlady's room-house had formerly been their private residence.

The Empty House, 1906

THE OLD
MAN OF VISIONS

I

The image of Teufelsdröckh, sitting in his watchtower, "alone with the stars," leapt into my mind the moment I saw him; and the curious expression of his eyes proclaimed at once that here was a being who allowed he world of small effects to pass him by, while he himself dwelt among the eternal verities. It was only necessary to catch a glimpse of the bent grey figure, so slight yet so tremendous, to realise that he carried staff and wallet, and was travelling along in a spiritual region, uncharted, and full of wonder, difficulty, and fearful joy.

The inner eye perceived this quite as clearly as the outer was aware of his Hebraic ancestry; but along what winding rivers, through what haunted woods, by the shored of what singing seas he pressed forward towards the mountains of his goal, no one could guess from a mere inspection of that wonderful old face.

To have stumbled upon such a figure in the casual way I did seemed incredible to me even at the time, yet I at once caught something of the uplifting airs that followed this inhabitant of a finer world, and I spent days—and considered them well spent— trying to get into conversation with him, so that I might know something more than the thin disguise of his holding a reader's ticket for the Museum Library.

To reach the stage of intimacy where actual speech is a hindrance to close understanding, one need not in some cases have spoken at all, thus by merely setting my mind, and above all my imagination, into tune with his, and by steeping myself so much in his atmosphere that I absorbed and then gave back to him with my own stamp the forces he exhaled, it was at length possible to persuade those vast-seeing eyes to turn in my direction; and our glances having once met, I simply rose when he rose, and followed him out of the smokey restaurant so closely up the street that our clothes brushed, and I thought I could even catch the sound of his breathing.

Whether, having already weighed me, he accepted the office, or whether he was grateful for the arm to lean upon, with his many years' burden, I do not know; but the sympathy between us was such that, without a single word, we walked up that foggy London street to the door of his lodging in Bloomsbury, where I noticed that at the touch of his arm the noise of the town seemed to turn into deep singing, and even the hurrying passers-by seemed bent upon noble purposes; and though he barely reached to my shoulder, his grey beard almost touched my glove as I bent my arm to hold his own, there was something immense about his figure that sent him with towering stature above me and filled my thoughts with enchanting dreams of grandeur and high beauty.

But it was only when the door had closed on him with a little rush of wind, and I was walking home alone, that I fully realized the shock of my return to earth; and on reaching my own rooms I shook with laughter to think I had walked a mile and a half with a complete stranger without uttering a single syllable. Then the laughter suddenly hushed as I caught my face in the glass with the expression of the soul still lingering about the eyes and forehead, and for a brief moment my heart leapt to a sort of noble fever in the blood, leaving me with the smart of the soul's wings stirring beneath the body's crushing weight. And when it passed I found myself dwelling upon the only words he had spoken when I left him at the door:

"I am the Old Man of Visions, and I am *at your service*."

I think he never had a name—at least, it never passed his lips, and perhaps lay buried with so much else of the past that he clearly deemed unimportant. To me, at any rate, he became simply the Old Man of Visions, and the the little waiting-maid and the landlady he was known simply as "Mister"—Mister, neither more nor less. The impenetrable veil that hung over his past never lifted for any vital revelations of his personal history, though he evidently knew all the countries of the world, and had absorbed into his heart and brain the experience of all possible types of human nature; and there was an air about him not so much of "Ask me no questions," as "Do not ask me, for I cannot answer you *in words*."

He could satisfy, but not in mere language; he would reveal, but by the wonderful words of silence only; for he was the Old Man of Visions, and visions need no words, being swift and of the spirit.

Moreover, the landlady—poor, dusty, faded woman—the landlady stood in awe, and disliked being probed for information in a passage-way down which he might any moment tread, for she could only tell me, "He just came in one night, years ago, and he's been here ever since!" And more than that I never knew. "Just came in—one night—years ago." This adequately explained him, for where he came *from*, or was journeying *to* was something quite beyond the scope of ordinary limited language.

I pictured him suddenly turning aside from the stream of unimportant events, quietly stepping out of the world of straining, fighting, and shouting, and moving to take his rightful place among the forces of the still, spiritual region where belonged by virtue of long pain and difficult attainment. For he was unconnected from any conceivable network of relations, friends, or family, and his terrible aloofness could not be disturbed by any one unless with his permission and by his express wish. Nor could he be imagined has "belonging" to any definitely set of souls. He was apart from the world— and above it.

But it was only when I began to creep a little nearer to him, and our strange, silent intimacy passed from mental to spiritual, that I began really to understand more of this wonderful Old Man of Visions.

Steeped in the tragedy, and convulsed with laughter at the comedy, of life, he yet lived there in his high attic wrapped in silence as in a golden cloud; and so seldom did he actually speak to me that each time the sound of his voice, that had something elemental in it—something of winds and waters—thrilled me with the power of the first time. He lived, like Teufelsdröckh, "alone with the stars," and it seemed impossible, more and more, to link him on anywhere into practical dealings with ordinary men and women. Life somehow seemed to pass *below* him. Yet the small, selfish spirit of the recluse was far from him, and he was tenderly and deeply responsive to pain and suffering, and more particularly to genuine yearnings for the far things of beauty. The unsatisfied longings of other could move him at once to tears.

"Me relations with men are perfect," he said one night as we neared his dwelling. "I give them all sympathy out of my stores of knowledge and experience, and they give me what kindness I need. My outer shell lies within impenetrable solitude, for only so can my inner life move freely along the paths and terraces that are thronged with the beings to whom I belong." And when I asked him how he maintained such deep sympathy with humanity, and yet absolved himself apparently from action as from speech, he stopped against an area railing and turned his eyes to my face, as though their fire could communicate his thought without the husk of words:

"I have peered too profoundly into life and beyond it," he murmured, "and wish to express in language what I *know*. Action is not for all, always; and I am in touch with the cistern of thought that lie behind action. I ponder the mysteries. What may solve is not lost for lack of either speech or action for the true mystic is ever the true man of action, and my thought will reach others as soon as they are ready for it in the same way that it reaches you. All who strongly yearn, must, sooner or later, find me and be comforted."

His eyes shifted from my face towards the stars, softly shining above the dark Museum roof, and a moment later he had disappeared into the hall-way of his house.

"An old poet who has strayed afield and lost his way," I mused; but through the door where he had just vanished the words came back to me as from a great distance: "A priest, rather who has begun to find his way."

For a space I stood, pondering on his face and words:—that mercilessly intelligent look of the Hebrew woven in with the expression of the sadness of a whole race, yet touched with the glory of the spirit; and his utterance—that he had passed through all the traditions and no longer needed a formal, limited creed to hold to. I forget how I reached my own door several miles away, but it seemed to me that I flew.

In this way, and by unregistered degrees, we came to know each other better, and he accepted me and took me into his life. Always wrapped in the great calm of his delightful silence, he taught me more, and told me more, than could ever lie within the confines of mere words; and in moments of need, no matter when or where, I always knew exactly how to find him, reaching him in a few seconds by some swift way that disdained the means of ordinary locomotion.

Then at last one day he gave me the key of his house. And the first time I found my way into his eyry, and realised that it was a haven I could always fly to when the yearnings of the heart and soul struggled vainly for recompense, the full meaning and importance of the Old Man of Visions became finally clear to me.

II

The room, high up creaky, darkened stairs in the ancient house, was bare and fireless, looking through a single patched window across a tumbled sea of roofs and chimneys; yet there was that in it which instantly proclaimed it a little holy place out of the world, a temple in which some one with spiritual vitality had worshipped, prayed, wept, and sung.

It was dusty and unswept, yet it was utterly *unsoiled*; and the Old Man of Visions who lived there, for all his shabby and stained garments, his uncombed beard and broken shoes, stood within it door revealed in his real self, moving in a sort of divine whiteness, iridescent, shining, And here, in this attic (lampless and unswept), high up under the old roofs of Bloomsbury, the window scarred with rain and the corners dropping cobwebs, I heard his silver whisper issue from the shadows:

"Here may you satisfy you soul's desire and may commune with the Invisibles; only, to find the Invisibles, you must first be able to lose yourself."

Ah! through that stained window-pane, the sign leaping at a single bound from black roofs up to the stars, what pictures, dreams, and vision of the Old Man has summoned to my eyes! Distances, measureless and impossible hitherto, became easy, and from the oppression of dead bricks and the market-place he transported me in a moment to the slopes of the Mountains of Dream; leading me to little places near the summits where the pines grew thinly and the stars were visible through their branches, fading into the rose of dawn; where the winds tasted of the desert, and the voices of the wilderness fled upwards with a sound of wings and falling streams. At his word houses melted away, and the green waves of all the seas flowed into their places; forests waves themselves into the coastline of dull streets; and the power of the old earth, with all her smells and the flowers and wild life, thrilled down among the dead roofs and caught me away into freedom among the sunshine of meadows and the music of sweet pipings. And with the divine deliverance came the crying of sea-gulls, the glimmer of reedy tarns, the whispering of wind among grasses, and the healing scorch of a real sun upon the skin.

And poetry such was never known of heard before clothed all he uttered, yet even when took no form in actual words, for it was of the substance of aspiration and yearning, voicing adequately all the busy, high-born dreams that haunt the soul yet never live in the uttered line. He breathed it about him in the air so that it filled my being. It was part of him—beyond words; and it sang my own longings, and sang them perfectly so that I was satisfied; for my own mood never failed to touch him instantly and to waken the right response. In its essence it was spiritual—the mystic poetry of heaven; still, the love of humanity informed it, for star-fire and heart's blood were about equally mingled there, while the mystery of unattainable beauty moved through it like a white flame.

With other dreams and longings, too, it was the same; and all the most beautiful ideas that ever haunted a soul endowed with expression here floated with satisfied eyes and smiling lips before one—floated in silence, unencumbered, unlimited, unrestrained by words.

In this dim room, never made ugly by artificial light, but always shadowy in a kind of gentle dusk, the Old Man of Visions had only to lead me to the window to bring peace. Music, that rendered the soul fluid, as it poured across the old roofs into the room, was summoned by him at need; and when one's wings beat sometimes against the prison walls and the yearning for escape oppressed the heart, I have heard the little room rush and fill with the sound of trees, wind among grasses, whispering branches and lapping waters. The very odours of space and mountain-side came too, and the looming of noble seemed visible overhead against the stars, as though the ceiling had suddenly become transparent.

For the Old Man of Visions had the power of instantly

satisfying an ideal when once that ideal created a yearning that could tear and burn its way out with sufficient force to set the will a-moving.

III

But, as the time passed and I came to depend more and more upon the intimacy with my strange old friend, new light fell upon the nature and possibilities of our connection. I discovered, for instance, that though I held the key to his dwelling, and was familiar with the way, he was nevertheless not always available. Two things, in different fashion, rendered him in accessible, or mute; and, for the first, I gradually learned that when life was prosperous, and the body singing aloud, I could not find my way to his house. No amount of wondering , calculation, or persevering effort enabled me even to find the street again. With any burst of worldly success, however fleeting, the Old Man of Visions somehow slipped away into remote shadows and became unreal and misty. A merely passing desire to be with him, to seek his inspiration by a glimpse though the magic window-pane, resulted only in vain and tiresome pacing to and fro along ugly streets that produced weariness and depression; and after these periods it became, I noticed, less and less easy to discover the house, to fit the key in the door, or, having gained access to the temple, to realise visions I *thought* I craved for.

Often, in this way, have I searched in vain for days, but only succeeded in losing myself in the murky purlieus of of quite strange Bloomsbury; stopping outside numberless counterfeit doors, and struggling vainly with locks that knew nothing of my little shining key.

But, on the other hand, pain, loneliness, sorrow—the merest whisper of spiritual affliction—and, lo, in a single moment the difficult geography became plain, and without hesitation, when I was unhappy or distressed, I found the way to his house as by a bird's instinctive flight, and the key slipped into the lock as though it loved it and was returning home.

The other cause to render him inaccessible, though not so determined—since it never concealed the way the house—was even more distressing, for it depended wholly on myself; and I cam to know how by the least ugly action, involving a depreciation of ideals, so confused to the mind that, when I got into the house, with difficulty, and found him in the little room after much searching, he was able to do or say scarcely at all for me. The mirror facing the door then gave back, I saw, no proper reflection of his his person, but only a faded and wavering shadow with dim eye and stooping, indistinct outline, and I even fancied I could see the pattern of the wall and shape of the furniture *through* his body, as though he had grown semi-transparent.

"You must not expect yearnings to weight," came his whisper, like wind far overhead "unless you lend to them *your own* substance; and your own substance you cannot both keep and lend. If you would know the Invisibles, forget yourself."

And later, as the years slipped away one after another into the mists, and the frontier between the real and unreal began to shift amazingly with his teachings, it became more and more clear to me that he belonged to a permanent region that, with all the changes in the world's history, has itself never altered in any essential particular. This immemorial Old Man of Visions, as I grew to thin of him, had existed always; he was old as the sea and coeval with the stars; and he dwelt beyond time and space, reaching out a hand to all those who, weary of the shadows and illusions of practical life, really call to him with their heart of hears. To me, indeed, the touch of sorrow was always near enough to prevent his becoming often inaccessible, and after a while even his voice became so *living* that I sometimes heard it calling to me in the street and in the fields.

Oh, wonderful Old Man of Visions! Happy the days of disaster, since they taught me how to know you, the Unraveller of Problems, the Destroyer of Doubts, who bore me ever away with soft flight down the long, long vistas of the heart and soul!

And his loneliness in that temple attic under the stars, his loneliness, too, had a meaning I did not fail to understand later, and why he was always available for me and seemed to belong to no other.

"To every one who finds me," he said, with the strange smile that wrapped his whole being and not his face alone, "to every one I am the same, and yet different. I am not really ever alone. The whole world, nay"—his voice rose to a singing cry—"the whole universe lies in this room, or just beyond that window-pane; for here past and future meet and all real dreams find completeness. But remember," he added—and there was a sound as of soft wind and rain in the room with his voice—"no true dream can ever be shared, and should you seek to explain me to another you must lose me beyond recall. You have never asked my name, nor must you ever tell it. Each must find me in his own way."

Yet one day, for all my knowledge and his warnings, I felt so sure of my intimacy with this immemorial being, that I spoke of him to a friend who was, I had thought, so much a part of myself that it seemed no betrayal. And my friend, who went to search and found nothing, returned with the fool's laughter on his face, and swore that no street or number existed, for he had looked in vain, and had repeatedly *asked the way.*

And, from that day to this, the Old Man of Visions has neither called to me nor let his place be found; the streets are strange and empty, and I have even lost the little shining key.

The Listener and Other Stories, 1907

ANCIENT SORCERIES

I

There are, it would appear, certain wholly unremarkable persons, with none of the characteristics that invite adventure, who yet once or twice in the course of their smooth lives undergo an experience so strange that the world catches its breath—and looks the other way! And it was cases of this kind, perhaps, more than any other, that fell into the wide-spread net of John Silence, the psychic doctor, and, appealing to his deep humanity, to his patience, and to his great qualities of spiritual sympathy, led often to the revelation of problems of the strangest complexity, and of the profoundest possible human interest.

Matters that seemed almost too curious and fantastic for belief he loved to trace to their hidden sources. To unravel a tangle in the very soul of things—and to release a suffering human soul in the process—was with him a veritable passion. And the knots he untied were, indeed, after passing strange.

The world, of course, asks for some plausible basis to which it can attach credence—something it can, at least, pretend to explain. The adventurous type it can understand: such people carry about with them an adequate explanation of their exciting lives, and their characters obviously drive them into the circumstances which produce the adventures. It expects nothing else from them, and is satisfied. But dull, ordinary folk have no right to out-of-the-way experiences, and the world having been led to expect otherwise, is disappointed with them, not to say shocked. Its complacent judgment has been rudely disturbed.

"Such a thing happened to *that* man!" it cries—"a

55

commonplace person like that! It is too absurd! There must be something wrong!"

Yet there could be no question that something did actually happen to little Arthur Vezin, something of the curious nature he described to Dr. Silence. Outwardly or inwardly, it happened beyond a doubt, and in spite of the jeers of his few friends who heard the tale, and observed wisely that "such a thing might perhaps have come to Iszard, that crack-brained Iszard, or to that odd fish Minski, but it could never have happened to commonplace little Vezin, who was fore-ordained to live and die according to scale."

But, whatever his method of death was, Vezin certainly did not "live according to scale" so far as this particular event in his otherwise uneventful life was concerned; and to hear him recount it, and watch his pale delicate features change, and hear his voice grow softer and more hushed as he proceeded, was to know the conviction that his halting words perhaps failed sometimes to convey. He lived the thing over again each time he told it. His whole personality became muffled in the recital. It subdued him more than ever, so that the tale became a lengthy apology for an experience that he deprecated. He appeared to excuse himself and ask your pardon for having dared to take part in so fantastic an episode. For little Vezin was a timid, gentle, sensitive soul, rarely able to assert himself, tender to man and beast, and almost constitutionally unable to say No, or to claim many things that should rightly have been his. His whole scheme of life seemed utterly remote from anything more exciting than missing a train or losing an umbrella on an omnibus. And when this curious event came upon him he was already more years beyond forty than his friends suspected or he cared to admit.

John Silence, who heard him speak of his experience more than once, said that he sometimes left out certain details and put in others; yet they were all obviously true. The whole scene was unforgettably cinematographed on to his mind. None of the details were imagined or invented. And when he told the story with them all complete, the effect was undeniable. His appealing brown eyes shone, and much of the charming personality, usually so carefully repressed, came forward and revealed itself. His modesty was always there, of course, but in the telling he forgot the present and allowed himself to appear almost vividly as he lived again in the past of his adventure.

He was on the way home when it happened, crossing northern France from some mountain trip or other where he buried himself solitary-wise every summer. He had nothing but an unregistered bag in the rack, and the train was jammed to suffocation, most of the passengers being unredeemed holiday English. He disliked them, not because they were his fellow-countrymen, but because they were noisy and obtrusive, obliterating with their big limbs and tweed clothing all the quieter tints of the day that brought him satisfaction and enabled him to melt into insignificance and forget that he was anybody. These English clashed about him like a brass band, making him feel vaguely that he ought to be more self-assertive and obstreperous, and that he did not claim insistently enough all kinds of things that he didn't want and that were really valueless, such as corner seats, windows up or down, and so forth.

So that he felt uncomfortable in the train, and wished the journey were over and he was back again living with his unmarried sister in Surbiton.

And when the train stopped for ten panting minutes at the little station in northern France, and he got out to stretch his legs on the platform, and saw to his dismay a further batch of the British Isles debouching from another train, it suddenly seemed impossible to him to continue the journey. Even *his* flabby soul revolted, and the idea of staying a night in the little town and going on next day by a slower, emptier train, flashed into his mind. The guard was already shouting "*en voiture*" and the corridor of his compartment was already packed when the thought came to him. And, for once, he acted with decision and rushed to snatch his bag.

Finding the corridor and steps impassable, he tapped at the window (for he had a corner seat) and begged the Frenchman who sat opposite to hand his luggage out to him, explaining in his wretched French that he intended to break the journey there. And this elderly Frenchman, he declared, gave him a look, half of warning, half of reproach, that to his dying day he could never forget; handed the bag through the window of the moving train; and at the same time poured into his ears a long sentence, spoken rapidly and low, of which he was able to comprehend only the last few words: "*à cause du sommeil et à cause des chats.*"

In reply to Dr. Silence, whose singular psychic acuteness at once seized upon this Frenchman as a vital point in the adventure, Vezin admitted that the man had impressed him favourably from the beginning, though without being able to explain why. They had sat facing one another during the four hours of the journey, and though no conversation had passed between them—Vezin was timid about his stuttering French—he confessed that his eyes were being continually drawn to his face, almost, he felt, to rudeness, and that each, by a dozen nameless little politenesses and attentions, had evinced the desire to be kind. The men liked each other and their personalities did not clash, or would not have clashed had they chanced to come to terms of acquaintance. The Frenchman, indeed, seemed to have exercised a silent protective influence over the insignificant little Englishman, and without words or gestures betrayed that he wished him well and would gladly have been of service to him.

"And this sentence that he hurled at you after the bag?" asked John Silence, smiling that peculiarly sympathetic smile that always melted the prejudices of his patient, "were you unable to follow it exactly?"

"It was so quick and low and vehement," explained Vezin, in his small voice, "that I missed practically the whole of it. I only caught the few words at the very end, because he spoke them so clearly, and his face was bent down out of the carriage window so near to mine."

"'*À cause du sommeil et à cause des chats*'?" repeated Dr. Silence, as though half speaking to himself.

"That's it exactly," said Vezin; "which, I take it, means something like 'because of sleep and because of the cats,' doesn't it?"

"Certainly, that's how I should translate it," the doctor observed shortly, evidently not wishing to interrupt more than necessary.

"And the rest of the sentence—all the first part I couldn't understand, I mean—was a warning not to do something—not to stop in the town, or at some particular place in the town, perhaps. That was the impression it made on me."

Then, of course, the train rushed off, and left Vezin standing on the platform alone and rather forlorn.

The little town climbed in straggling fashion up a sharp hill rising out of the plain at the back of the station, and was crowned by the twin towers of the ruined cathedral peeping over the summit. From the station itself it looked uninteresting and modern, but the fact was that the mediaeval position lay out of sight just beyond the crest. And once he reached the top and entered the old streets, he stepped clean out of modern life into a bygone century. The noise and bustle of the crowded train seemed days away. The spirit of this silent hill-town, remote from tourists and motor-cars, dreaming its own quiet life under the autumn sun, rose up and cast its spell upon him. Long before he recognised this spell he acted under it. He walked softly, almost on tiptoe, down the winding narrow streets where the gables all but met over his head, and he entered the doorway of the solitary inn with a deprecating and modest demeanour that was in itself an apology for intruding upon the place and disturbing its dream.

At first, however, Vezin said, he noticed very little of all this. The attempt at analysis came much later. What struck him then was only the delightful contrast of the silence and peace after the dust and noisy rattle of the train. He felt soothed and stroked like a cat.

"Like a cat, you said?" interrupted John Silence, quickly catching him up.

"Yes. At the very start I felt that." He laughed apologetically. "I felt as though the warmth and the stillness and the comfort made me purr. It seemed to be the general mood of the whole place—then."

The inn, a rambling ancient house, the atmosphere of the old coaching days still about it, apparently did not welcome him too warmly. He felt he was only tolerated, he said. But it was cheap and comfortable, and the delicious cup of afternoon tea he ordered at once made him feel really very pleased with himself for leaving the train in this bold, original way. For to him it had seemed bold and original. He felt something of a dog. His room, too, soothed him with its dark panelling and low irregular ceiling, and the long sloping passage that led to it seemed the natural pathway to a real Chamber of Sleep—a little dim cubby hole out of the world where noise could not enter. It looked upon the courtyard at the back. It was all very charming, and made him think of himself as dressed in very soft velvet somehow, and the floors seemed padded, the walls provided with cushions. The sounds of the streets could not penetrate there. It was an atmosphere of absolute rest that surrounded him.

On engaging the two-franc room he had interviewed the only person who seemed to be about that sleepy afternoon, an elderly waiter with Dundreary whiskers and a drowsy courtesy, who had ambled lazily towards him across the stone yard; but on coming downstairs again for a little promenade in the town before dinner he encountered the proprietress herself. She was a large woman whose hands, feet, and features seemed to swim towards him out of a sea of person. They emerged, so to speak. But she had great dark, vivacious eyes that counteracted the bulk of her body, and betrayed the fact that in reality she was both vigorous and alert. When he first caught sight of her she was knitting in a low chair against the sunlight of the wall, and something at once made him see her as a great tabby cat, dozing, yet awake, heavily sleepy, and yet at the same time prepared for instantaneous action. A great mouser on the watch occurred to him.

She took him in with a single comprehensive glance that was polite without being cordial. Her neck, he noticed, was extraordinarily supple in spite of its proportions, for it turned so easily to follow him, and the head it carried bowed so very flexibly.

"But when she looked at me, you know," said Vezin, with that little apologetic smile in his brown eyes, and that faintly deprecating gesture of the shoulders that was characteristic of him, "the odd notion came to me that really she had intended to make quite a different movement, and that with a single bound she could have leaped at me across the width of that stone yard and pounced upon me like some huge cat upon a mouse."

He laughed a little soft laugh, and Dr. Silence made a note in his book without interrupting, while Vezin proceeded in a tone as though he feared he had already told too much and more than we could believe.

"Very soft, yet very active she was, for all her size and mass, and I felt she knew what I was doing even after I had passed and was behind her back. She spoke to me, and her voice was smooth and running. She asked if I had my luggage, and was comfortable in my room, and then added that dinner was at seven o'clock, and that they were very early people in this little country town. Clearly, she intended to convey that late hours were not encouraged."

Evidently, she contrived by voice and manner to give him the impression that here he would be "managed," that everything would be arranged and planned for him, and that he had nothing to do but fall into the groove and obey. No decided action or sharp personal effort would be looked for from him. It was the very reverse of the train. He walked quietly out into the street feeling soothed and peaceful. He realised that he was in a *milieu* that suited him and stroked him the right way. It was so much easier to be obedient. He began to purr again, and to feel that all the town purred with him.

About the streets of that little town he meandered gently, falling deeper and deeper into the spirit of repose that characterised it. With no special aim he wandered up and down, and to and fro. The September sunshine fell slantingly over the roofs. Down winding alleyways, fringed with tumbling gables and open casements, he caught fairylike glimpses of the great plain below, and of the meadows and yellow copses lying like a dream-map in the haze. The spell of the past held very potently here, he felt.

The streets were full of picturesquely garbed men and women, all busy enough, going their respective ways; but no one took any notice of him or turned to stare at his obviously English appearance. He was even able to forget that with his tourist appearance he was a false note in a charming picture, and he melted more and more into the scene, feeling delightfully insignificant and unimportant and unselfconscious. It was like becoming part of a softly coloured dream which he did not even realise to be a dream.

On the eastern side the hill fell away more sharply, and the plain below ran off rather suddenly into a sea of gathering shadows in which the little patches of woodland looked like islands and the stubble fields like deep water. Here he strolled along the old ramparts of ancient fortifications that once had been formidable, but now were only vision-like with their charming mingling of broken grey walls and wayward vine and ivy. From the broad coping on which he sat for a moment, level with the rounded tops of clipped plane trees, he saw the esplanade far below lying in shadow. Here and there a yellow sunbeam crept in and lay upon the fallen yellow leaves, and from the height he looked down and saw that the townsfolk were walking to and fro in the cool of the evening. He could just hear the sound of their slow footfalls, and the murmur of their voices floated up to him through the gaps between the trees. The figures looked like shadows as he caught glimpses of their quiet movements far below.

He sat there for some time pondering, bathed in the waves of murmurs and half-lost echoes that rose to his ears, muffled by the leaves of the plane trees. The whole town, and the little hill out of which it grew as naturally as an ancient wood, seemed to him like a being lying there half asleep on the plain and crooning to itself as it dozed.

And, presently, as he sat lazily melting into its dream, a sound of horns and strings and wood instruments rose to his ears, and the town band began to play at the far end of the crowded terrace below to the accompaniment of a very soft, deep-throated drum. Vezin was very sensitive to music, knew about it intelligently, and had even ventured, unknown to his friends, upon the composition of quiet melodies with low-running chords which he played to himself with the soft pedal when no one was about. And this music floating up through the trees from an invisible and doubtless very picturesque band of the townspeople wholly charmed him. He recognised nothing that they played, and it sounded as though they were simply improvising without a conductor. No definitely marked time ran through the pieces, which ended and began oddly after the fashion of wind through an Aeolian harp. It was part of the place and scene, just as the dying sunlight and faintly breathing wind were part of the scene and hour, and the mellow notes of old-fashioned plaintive horns, pierced here and there by the sharper strings, all half smothered by the continuous booming of the deep drum, touched his soul with a curiously potent spell that was almost too engrossing to be quite pleasant.

There was a certain queer sense of bewitchment in it all. The music seemed to him oddly unartificial. It made him think of trees swept by the wind, of night breezes singing among wires and chimney-stacks, or in the rigging of invisible ships; or—and the simile leaped up in his thoughts with a sudden sharpness of suggestion—a chorus of animals, of wild creatures, somewhere in desolate places of the world, crying and singing as animals will, to the moon. He could fancy he heard the wailing, half-human cries of cats upon the tiles at night, rising and falling with weird intervals of sound, and this music, muffled by distance and the trees, made him think of a queer company of these creatures on some roof far away in the sky, uttering their solemn music to one another and the moon in chorus.

It was, he felt at the time, a singular image to occur to him, yet it expressed his sensation pictorially better than anything else. The instruments played such impossibly odd intervals, and the crescendos and diminuendos were so very suggestive of cat-land on the tiles at night, rising swiftly, dropping without warning to deep notes again, and all in such strange confusion of discords and accords. But, at the same time a plaintive sweetness resulted on the whole, and the discords of these half-broken instruments were so singular that they did not distress his musical soul like fiddles out of tune.

He listened a long time, wholly surrendering himself as his character was, and then strolled homewards in the dusk as the air grew chilly.

"There was nothing to alarm?" put in Dr. Silence briefly.

"Absolutely nothing," said Vezin; "but you know it was all so fantastical and charming that my imagination was profoundly impressed. Perhaps, too," he continued, gently explanatory, "it was this stirring of my imagination that caused other impressions; for, as I walked back, the spell of the place began to steal over me in a dozen ways, though all intelligible ways. But there were other things I could not account for in the least, even then."

"Incidents, you mean?"

"Hardly incidents, I think. A lot of vivid sensations crowded themselves upon my mind and I could trace them to no causes.

It was just after sunset and the tumbled old buildings traced magical outlines against an opalescent sky of gold and red. The dusk was running down the twisted streets. All round the hill the plain pressed in like a dim sea, its level rising with the darkness. The spell of this kind of scene, you know, can be very moving, and it was so that night. Yet I felt that what came to me had nothing directly to do with the mystery and wonder of the scene."

"Not merely the subtle transformations of the spirit that come with beauty," put in the doctor, noticing his hesitation.

"Exactly," Vezin went on, duly encouraged and no longer so fearful of our smiles at his expense. "The impressions came from somewhere else. For instance, down the busy main street where men and women were bustling home from work, shopping at stalls and barrows, idly gossiping in groups, and all the rest of it, I saw that I aroused no interest and that no one turned to stare at me as a foreigner and stranger. I was utterly ignored, and my presence among them excited no special interest or attention.

"And then, quite suddenly, it dawned upon me with conviction that all the time this indifference and inattention were merely feigned. Everybody as a matter of fact was watching me closely. Every movement I made was known and observed. Ignoring me was all a pretence—an elaborate pretence."

He paused a moment and looked at us to see if we were smiling, and then continued, reassured—

"It is useless to ask me how I noticed this, because I simply cannot explain it. But the discovery gave me something of a shock. Before I got back to the inn, however, another curious thing rose up strongly in my mind and forced my recognition of it as true. And this, too, I may as well say at once, was equally inexplicable to me. I mean I can only give you the fact, as fact it was to me."

The little man left his chair and stood on the mat before the fire. His diffidence lessened from now onwards, as he lost himself again in the magic of the old adventure. His eyes shone a little already as he talked.

"Well," he went on, his soft voice rising somewhat with his excitement, "I was in a shop when it came to me first—though the idea must have been at work for a long time subconsciously to appear in so complete a form all at once. I was buying socks, I think," he laughed, "and struggling with my dreadful French, when it struck me that the woman in the shop did not care two pins whether I bought anything or not. She was indifferent whether she made a sale or did not make a sale. She was only pretending to sell.

"This sounds a very small and fanciful incident to build upon what follows. But really it was not small. I mean it was the spark that lit the line of powder and ran along to the big blaze in my mind.

"For the whole town, I suddenly realised, was something other than I so far saw it. The real activities and interests of the people were elsewhere and otherwise than appeared. Their true lives lay somewhere out of sight behind the scenes. Their busy-ness was but the outward semblance that masked their actual purposes. They bought and sold, and ate and drank, and walked about the streets, yet all the while the main stream of their existence lay somewhere beyond my ken, underground, in secret places. In the shops and at the stalls they did not care whether I purchased their articles or not; at the inn, they were indifferent to my staying or going; their life lay remote from my own, springing from hidden, mysterious sources, coursing out of sight, unknown. It was all a great elaborate pretence, assumed possibly for my benefit, or possibly for purposes of their own. But the main current of their energies ran elsewhere. I almost felt as an unwelcome foreign substance might be expected to feel when it has found its way into the human system and the whole body organises itself to eject it or to absorb it. The town was doing this very thing to me.

"This bizarre notion presented itself forcibly to my mind as I walked home to the inn, and I began busily to wonder wherein the true life of this town could lie and what were the actual interests and activities of its hidden life.

"And, now that my eyes were partly opened, I noticed other things too that puzzled me, first of which, I think, was the extraordinary silence of the whole place. Positively, the town was muffled. Although the streets were paved with cobbles the people moved about silently, softly, with padded feet, like cats. Nothing made noise. All was hushed, subdued, muted. The very voices were quiet, low-pitched like purring. Nothing clamorous, vehement or emphatic seemed able to live in the drowsy atmosphere of soft dreaming that soothed this little hill-town into its sleep. It was like the woman at the inn—an outward repose screening intense inner activity and purpose.

"Yet there was no sign of lethargy or sluggishness anywhere about it. The people were active and alert. Only a magical and uncanny softness lay over them all like a spell."

Vezin passed his hand across his eyes for a moment as though the memory had become very vivid. His voice had run off into a whisper so that we heard the last part with difficulty. He was telling a true thing obviously, yet something that he both liked and hated telling.

"I went back to the inn," he continued presently in a louder voice, "and dined. I felt a new strange world about me. My old world of reality receded. Here, whether I liked it or no, was something new and incomprehensible. I regretted having left the train so impulsively. An adventure was upon me, and I loathed adventures as foreign to my nature. Moreover, this was the beginning apparently of an adventure somewhere deep within me, in a region I could not check or measure, and a feeling of alarm mingled itself with my wonder—alarm for the stability of what I had for forty years recognised as my 'personality.'

"I went upstairs to bed, my mind teeming with thoughts that were unusual to me, and of rather a haunting description. By way of relief I kept thinking of that nice, prosaic noisy train and all those wholesome, blustering passengers. I almost wished

I were with them again. But my dreams took me elsewhere. I dreamed of cats, and soft-moving creatures, and the silence of life in a dim muffled world beyond the senses."

II

Vezin stayed on from day to day, indefinitely, much longer than he had intended. He felt in a kind of dazed, somnolent condition. He did nothing in particular, but the place fascinated him and he could not decide to leave. Decisions were always very difficult for him and he sometimes wondered how he had ever brought himself to the point of leaving the train. It seemed as though some one else must have arranged it for him, and once or twice his thoughts ran to the swarthy Frenchman who had sat opposite. If only he could have understood that long sentence ending so strangely with "*à cause du sommeil et à cause des chats.*" He wondered what it all meant.

Meanwhile the hushed softness of the town held him prisoner and he sought in his muddling, gentle way to find out where the mystery lay, and what it was all about. But his limited French and his constitutional hatred of active investigation made it hard for him to buttonhole anybody and ask questions. He was content to observe, and watch, and remain negative.

The weather held on calm and hazy, and this just suited him. He wandered about the town till he knew every street and alley. The people suffered him to come and go without let or hindrance, though it became clearer to him every day that he was never free himself from observation. The town watched him as a cat watches a mouse. And he got no nearer to finding out what they were all so busy with or where the main stream of their activities lay. This remained hidden. The people were as soft and mysterious as cats.

But that he was continually under observation became more evident from day to day.

For instance, when he strolled to the end of the town and entered a little green public garden beneath the ramparts and seated himself upon one of the empty benches in the sun, he was quite alone—at first. Not another seat was occupied; the little park was empty, the paths deserted. Yet, within ten minutes of his coming, there must have been fully twenty persons scattered about him, some strolling aimlessly along the gravel walks, staring at the flowers, and others seated on the wooden benches enjoying the sun like himself. None of them appeared to take any notice of him; yet he understood quite well they had all come there to watch. They kept him under close observation. In the street they had seemed busy enough, hurrying upon various errands; yet these were suddenly all forgotten and they had nothing to do but loll and laze in the sun, their duties unremembered. Five minutes after he left, the garden was again deserted, the seats vacant. But in the crowded street it was the same thing again; he was never alone. He was ever in their thoughts.

By degrees, too, he began to see how it was he was so cleverly watched, yet without the appearance of it. The people did nothing *directly*. They behaved *obliquely*. He laughed in his mind as the thought thus clothed itself in words, but the phrase exactly described it. They looked at him from angles which naturally should have led their sight in another direction altogether. Their movements were oblique, too, so far as these concerned himself. The straight, direct thing was not their way evidently. They did nothing obviously. If he entered a shop to buy, the woman walked instantly away and busied herself with something at the farther end of the counter, though answering at once when he spoke, showing that she knew he was there and that this was only her way of attending to him. It was the fashion of the cat she followed. Even in the dining-room of the inn, the be-whiskered and courteous waiter, lithe and silent in all his movements, never seemed able to come straight to his table for an order or a dish. He came by zigzags, indirectly, vaguely, so that he appeared to be going to another table altogether, and only turned suddenly at the last moment, and was there beside him.

Vezin smiled curiously to himself as he described how he began to realize these things. Other tourists there were none in the hostel, but he recalled the figures of one or two old men, inhabitants, who took their *déjeuner* and dinner there, and remembered how fantastically they entered the room in similar fashion. First, they paused in the doorway, peering about the room, and then, after a temporary inspection, they came in, as it were, sideways, keeping close to the walls so that he wondered which table they were making for, and at the last minute making almost a little quick run to their particular seats. And again he thought of the ways and methods of cats.

Other small incidents, too, impressed him as all part of this queer, soft town with its muffled, indirect life, for the way some of the people appeared and disappeared with extraordinary swiftness puzzled him exceedingly. It may have been all perfectly natural, he knew, yet he could not make it out how the alleys swallowed them up and shot them forth in a second of time when there were no visible doorways or openings near enough to explain the phenomenon. Once he followed two elderly women who, he felt, had been particularly examining him from across the street—quite near the inn this was—and saw them turn the corner a few feet only in front of him. Yet when he sharply followed on their heels he saw nothing but an utterly deserted alley stretching in front of him with no sign of a living thing. And the only opening through which they could have escaped was a porch some fifty yards away, which not the swiftest human runner could have reached in time.

And in just such sudden fashion people appeared, when he never expected them. Once when he heard a great noise of fighting going on behind a low wall, and hurried up to see what was going on, what should he see but a group of girls and women engaged in vociferous conversation which instantly hushed itself to the normal whispering note of the town when his head appeared over the wall. And even then none of them turned to look at him directly, but slunk off with the most unaccountable rapidity into doors and sheds across the yard. And their voices, he thought, had sounded so like, so strangely like, the angry snarling of fighting animals, almost of cats.

The whole spirit of the town, however, continued to evade him as something elusive, protean, screened from the outer world, and at the same time intensely, genuinely vital; and, since he now formed part of its life, this concealment puzzled and irritated him; more—it began rather to frighten him.

Out of the mists that slowly gathered about his ordinary surface thoughts, there rose again the idea that the inhabitants were waiting for him to declare himself, to take an attitude, to do this, or to do that; and that when he had done so they in their turn would at length make some direct response, accepting or rejecting him. Yet the vital matter concerning which his decision was awaited came no nearer to him.

Once or twice he purposely followed little processions or groups of the citizens in order to find out, if possible, on what purpose they were bent; but they always discovered him in time and dwindled away, each individual going his or her own way. It was always the same: he never could learn what their main interest was. The cathedral was ever empty, the old church of St. Martin, at the other end of the town, deserted. They shopped because they had to, and not because they wished to. The booths stood neglected, the stalls unvisited, the little *cafés* desolate. Yet the streets were always full, the townsfolk ever on the bustle.

"Can it be," he thought to himself, yet with a deprecating laugh that he should have dared to think anything so odd, "can it be that these people are people of the twilight, that they live only at night their real life, and come out honestly only with the dusk? That during the day they make a sham though brave pretence, and after the sun is down their true life begins? Have they the souls of night-things, and is the whole blessed town in the hands of the cats?"

The fancy somehow electrified him with little shocks of shrinking and dismay. Yet, though he affected to laugh, he knew that he was beginning to feel more than uneasy, and that strange forces were tugging with a thousand invisible cords at the very centre of his being. Something utterly remote from his ordinary life, something that had not waked for years, began faintly to stir in his soul, sending feelers abroad into his brain and heart, shaping queer thoughts and penetrating even into certain of his minor actions. Something exceedingly vital to himself, to his soul, hung in the balance.

And, always when he returned to the inn about the hour of sunset, he saw the figures of the townsfolk stealing through the dusk from their shop doors, moving sentry-wise to and fro at the corners of the streets, yet always vanishing silently like shadows at his near approach. And as the inn invariably closed its doors at ten o'clock he had never yet found the opportunity he rather half-heartedly sought to see for himself what account the town could give of itself at night.

"—*à cause du sommeil et à cause des chats*"—the words now rang in his ears more and more often, though still as yet without any definite meaning.

Moreover, something made him sleep like the dead.

III

It was, I think, on the fifth day—though in this detail his story sometimes varied—that he made a definite discovery which increased his alarm and brought him up to a rather sharp climax. Before that he had already noticed that a change was going forward and certain subtle transformations being brought about in his character which modified several of his minor habits. And he had affected to ignore them. Here, however, was something he could no longer ignore; and it startled him.

At the best of times he was never very positive, always

negative rather, compliant and acquiescent; yet, when necessity arose he was capable of reasonably vigorous action and could take a strongish decision. The discovery he now made that brought him up with such a sharp turn was that this power had positively dwindled to nothing. He found it impossible to make up his mind. For, on this fifth day, he realised that he had stayed long enough in the town and that for reasons he could only vaguely define to himself it was wiser *and safer* that he should leave.

And he found that he could not leave!

This is difficult to describe in words, and it was more by gesture and the expression of his face that he conveyed to Dr. Silence the state of impotence he had reached. All this spying and watching, he said, had as it were spun a net about his feet so that he was trapped and powerless to escape; he felt like a fly that had blundered into the intricacies of a great web; he was caught, imprisoned, and could not get away. It was a distressing sensation. A numbness had crept over his will till it had become almost incapable of decision. The mere thought of vigorous action—action towards escape—began to terrify him. All the currents of his life had turned inwards upon himself, striving to bring to the surface something that lay buried almost beyond reach, determined to force his recognition of something he had long forgotten—forgotten years upon years, centuries almost ago. It seemed as though a window deep within his being would presently open and reveal an entirely new world, yet somehow a world that was not unfamiliar. Beyond that, again, he fancied a great curtain hung; and when that too rolled up he would see still farther into this region and at last understand something of the secret life of these extraordinary people.

"Is this why they wait and watch?" he asked himself with rather a shaking heart, "for the time when I shall join them—or refuse to join them? Does the decision rest with me after all, and not with them?"

And it was at this point that the sinister character of the

adventure first really declared itself, and he became genuinely alarmed. The stability of his rather fluid little personality was at stake, he felt, and something in his heart turned coward.

Why otherwise should he have suddenly taken to walking stealthily, silently, making as little sound as possible, for ever looking behind him? Why else should he have moved almost on tiptoe about the passages of the practically deserted inn, and when he was abroad have found himself deliberately taking advantage of what cover presented itself? And why, if he was not afraid, should the wisdom of staying indoors after sundown have suddenly occurred to him as eminently desirable? Why, indeed?

And, when John Silence gently pressed him for an explanation of these things, he admitted apologetically that he had none to give.

"It was simply that I feared something might happen to me unless I kept a sharp look-out. I felt afraid. It was instinctive," was all he could say. "I got the impression that the whole town was after me—wanted me for something; and that if it got me I should lose myself, or at least the Self I knew, in some unfamiliar state of consciousness. But I am not a psychologist, you know," he added meekly, "and I cannot define it better than that."

It was while lounging in the courtyard half an hour before the evening meal that Vezin made this discovery, and he at once went upstairs to his quiet room at the end of the winding passage to think it over alone. In the yard it was empty enough, true, but there was always the possibility that the big woman whom he dreaded would come out of some door, with her pretence of knitting, to sit and watch him. This had happened several times, and he could not endure the sight of her. He still remembered his original fancy, bizarre though it was, that she would spring upon him the moment his back was turned and land with one single crushing leap upon his neck. Of course it was nonsense, but then it haunted him, and once an idea begins to do that it ceases to be nonsense. It has clothed itself in reality.

He went upstairs accordingly. It was dusk, and the oil lamps had not yet been lit in the passages. He stumbled over the uneven surface of the ancient flooring, passing the dim outlines of doors along the corridor—doors that he had never once seen opened—rooms that seemed never occupied. He moved, as his habit now was, stealthily and on tiptoe.

Half-way down the last passage to his own chamber there was a sharp turn, and it was just here, while groping round the walls with outstretched hands, that his fingers touched something that was not wall—something that moved. It was soft and warm in texture, indescribably fragrant, and about the height of his shoulder; and he immediately thought of a furry, sweet-smelling kitten. The next minute he knew it was something quite different.

Instead of investigating, however,—his nerves must have been too overwrought for that, he said,—he shrank back as closely as possible against the wall on the other side. The thing, whatever it was, slipped past him with a sound of rustling and, retreating with light footsteps down the passage behind him, was gone. A breath of warm, scented air was wafted to his nostrils.

Vezin caught his breath for an instant and paused, stockstill, half leaning against the wall—and then almost ran down the remaining distance and entered his room with a rush, locking the door hurriedly behind him. Yet it was not fear that made him run: it was excitement, pleasurable excitement. His nerves were tingling, and a delicious glow made itself felt all over his body. In a flash it came to him that this was just what he had felt twenty-five years ago as a boy when he was in love for the first time. Warm currents of life ran all over him and mounted to his brain in a whirl of soft delight. His mood was suddenly become tender, melting, loving.

The room was quite dark, and he collapsed upon the sofa by the window, wondering what had happened to him and what it all meant. But the only thing he understood clearly in that instant was that something in him had swiftly, magically changed: he no longer wished to leave, or to argue with himself about leaving. The encounter in the passage-way had changed all that. The strange perfume of it still hung about him, bemusing his heart and mind. For he knew that it was a girl who had passed him, a girl's face that his fingers had brushed in the darkness, and he felt in some extraordinary way as though he had been actually kissed by her, kissed full upon the lips.

Trembling, he sat upon the sofa by the window and struggled to collect his thoughts. He was utterly unable to understand how the mere passing of a girl in the darkness of a narrow passage-way could communicate so electric a thrill to his whole being that he still shook with the sweetness of it. Yet, there it was! And he found it as useless to deny as to attempt analysis. Some ancient fire had entered his veins, and now ran coursing through his blood; and that he was forty-five instead of twenty did not matter one little jot. Out of all the inner turmoil and confusion emerged the one salient fact that the mere atmosphere, the merest casual touch, of this girl, unseen, unknown in the darkness, had been sufficient to stir dormant fires in the centre of his heart, and rouse his whole being from a state of feeble sluggishness to one of tearing and tumultuous excitement.

After a time, however, the number of Vezin's years began to assert their cumulative power; he grew calmer, and when a knock came at length upon his door and he heard the waiter's voice suggesting that dinner was nearly over, he pulled himself together and slowly made his way downstairs into the dining-room.

Every one looked up as he entered, for he was very late, but he took his customary seat in the far corner and began to eat. The trepidation was still in his nerves, but the fact that he had passed through the courtyard and hall without catching sight of a petticoat served to calm him a little. He ate so fast that he had almost caught up with the current stage of the table d'hôte, when a slight commotion in the room drew his attention.

His chair was so placed that the door and the greater portion of the long *salle à manger* were behind him, yet it was not necessary to turn round to know that the same person he had passed in the dark passage had now come into the room. He felt the presence long before he heard or saw any one. Then he became aware that the old men, the only other guests, were rising one by one in their places, and exchanging greetings with some one who passed among them from table to table. And when at length he turned with his heart beating furiously to ascertain for himself, he saw the form of a young girl, lithe and slim, moving down the centre of the room and making straight for his own table in the corner. She moved wonderfully, with sinuous grace, like a young panther, and her approach filled him with such delicious bewilderment that he was utterly unable to tell at first what her face was like, or discover what it was about the whole presentment of the creature that filled him anew with trepidation and delight.

"Ah, Ma'mselle est de retour!" he heard the old waiter murmur at his side, and he was just able to take in that she was the daughter of the proprietress, when she was upon him, and he heard her voice. She was addressing him. Something of red lips he saw and laughing white teeth, and stray wisps of fine dark hair about the temples; but all the rest was a dream in which his own emotion rose like a thick cloud before his eyes and prevented his seeing accurately, or knowing exactly what he did. He was aware that she greeted him with a charming little bow; that her beautiful large eyes looked searchingly into his own; that the perfume he had noticed in the dark passage again assailed his nostrils, and that she was bending a little towards him and leaning with one hand on the table at this side. She was quite close to him—that was the chief thing he knew—explaining that she had been asking after the comfort of her mother's guests, and now was introducing herself to the latest arrival—himself.

"M'sieur has already been here a few days," he heard the waiter say; and then her own voice, sweet as singing, replied—

"Ah, but M'sieur is not going to leave us just yet, I hope. My mother is too old to look after the comfort of our guests properly, but now I am here I will remedy all that." She laughed deliciously. "M'sieur shall be well looked after."

Vezin, struggling with his emotion and desire to be polite, half rose to acknowledge the pretty speech, and to stammer some sort of reply, but as he did so his hand by chance touched her own that was resting upon the table, and a shock that was for all the world like a shock of electricity, passed from her skin into his body. His soul wavered and shook deep within him. He caught her eyes fixed upon his own with a look of most curious intentness, and the next moment he knew that he had sat down wordless again on his chair, that the girl was already half-way across the room, and that he was trying to eat his salad with a dessert-spoon and a knife.

Longing for her return, and yet dreading it, he gulped down the remainder of his dinner, and then went at once to his bedroom to be alone with his thoughts. This time the passages were lighted, and he suffered no exciting contretemps; yet the winding corridor was dim with shadows, and the last portion, from the bend of the walls onwards, seemed longer than he had ever known it. It ran downhill like the pathway on a mountain side, and as he tiptoed softly down it he felt that by rights it ought to have led him clean out of the house into the heart of a great forest. The world was singing with him. Strange fancies filled his brain, and once in the room, with the door securely locked, he did not light the candles, but sat by the open window thinking long, long thoughts that came unbidden in troops to his mind.

<h1 style="text-align:center">IV</h1>

This part of the story he told to Dr. Silence, without special coaxing, it is true, yet with much stammering embarrassment. He could not in the least understand, he said, how the girl had managed to affect him so profoundly, and even before he had set eyes upon her. For her mere proximity in the darkness had been sufficient to set him on fire. He knew nothing of enchantments, and for years had been a stranger to anything approaching tender relations with any member of the opposite sex, for he was encased in shyness, and realised his overwhelming defects only too well. Yet this bewitching young creature came to him deliberately. Her manner was unmistakable, and she sought him out on every possible occasion. Chaste and sweet she was undoubtedly, yet frankly inviting; and she won him utterly with the first glance of her shining eyes, even if she had not already done so in the dark merely by the magic of her invisible presence.

"You felt she was altogether wholesome and good!" queried the doctor. "You had no reaction of any sort—for instance, of alarm?"

Vezin looked up sharply with one of his inimitable little apologetic smiles. It was some time before he replied. The mere memory of the adventure had suffused his shy face with blushes, and his brown eyes sought the floor again before he answered.

"I don't think I can quite say that," he explained presently. "I acknowledged certain qualms, sitting up in my room afterwards. A conviction grew upon me that there was something about her—how shall I express it?—well, something unholy. It is not impurity in any sense, physical or mental, that I mean, but something quite indefinable that gave me a vague sensation of the creeps. She drew me, and at the same time repelled me, more than—than—"

He hesitated, blushing furiously, and unable to finish the sentence.

"Nothing like it has ever come to me before or since," he concluded, with lame confusion. "I suppose it was, as you suggested just now, something of an enchantment. At any rate, it was strong enough to make me feel that I would stay in that awful little haunted town for years if only I could see her every day, hear her voice, watch her wonderful movements, and sometimes, perhaps, touch her hand."

"Can you explain to me what you felt was the source of her power?" John Silence asked, looking purposely anywhere but at the narrator.

"I am surprised that *you* should ask me such a question," answered Vezin, with the nearest approach to dignity he could manage. "I think no man can describe to another convincingly wherein lies the magic of the woman who ensnares him. I certainly cannot. I can only say this slip of a girl bewitched me, and the mere knowledge that she was living and sleeping in the same house filled me with an extraordinary sense of delight.

"But there's one thing I can tell you," he went on earnestly, his eyes aglow, "namely, that she seemed to sum up and synthesise in herself all the strange hidden forces that operated so mysteriously in the town and its inhabitants. She had the silken movements of the panther, going smoothly, silently to and fro, and the same indirect, oblique methods as the townsfolk, screening, like them, secret purposes of her own—purposes that I was sure had *me* for their objective. She kept me, to my terror and delight, ceaselessly under observation, yet so carelessly, so consummately, that another man less sensitive, if I may say so"—he made a deprecating gesture—"or less prepared by what had gone before, would never have noticed it at all. She was always still, always reposeful, yet she seemed to be everywhere at once, so that I never could escape from her. I was continually meeting the stare and laughter of her great eyes, in the corners of the rooms, in the passages, calmly looking at me through the windows, or in the busiest parts of the public streets."

Their intimacy, it seems, grew very rapidly after this first encounter which had so violently disturbed the little man's equilibrium. He was naturally very prim, and prim folk live mostly in so small a world that anything violently unusual may shake them clean out of it, and they therefore instinctively distrust originality. But Vezin began to forget his primness after awhile. The girl was always modestly behaved, and as her mother's representative she naturally had to do with the guests in the hotel. It was not out of the way that a spirit of camaraderie should spring up. Besides, she was young, she was charmingly pretty, she was French, and—she obviously liked him.

At the same time, there was something indescribable—a certain indefinable atmosphere of other places, other times— that made him try hard to remain on his guard, and sometimes made him catch his breath with a sudden start. It was all rather like a delirious dream, half delight, half dread, he confided in a whisper to Dr. Silence; and more than once he hardly knew quite what he was doing or saying, as though he were driven forward by impulses he scarcely recognised as his own.

And though the thought of leaving presented itself again and again to his mind, it was each time with less insistence, so that he stayed on from day to day, becoming more and more a part of the sleepy life of this dreamy mediaeval town, losing more and more of his recognisable personality. Soon, he felt, the Curtain within would roll up with an awful rush, and he would find himself suddenly admitted into the secret purposes of the hidden life that lay behind it all. Only, by that time, he would have become transformed into an entirely different being.

And, meanwhile, he noticed various little signs of the intention to make his stay attractive to him: flowers in his bedroom, a more comfortable arm-chair in the corner, and even special little extra dishes on his private table in the dining-room. Conversations, too, with "Mademoiselle Ilsé" became more and more frequent and pleasant, and although they seldom travelled beyond the weather, or the details of the town, the girl, he noticed, was never in a hurry to bring them to an end, and often contrived to interject little odd sentences that he never properly understood, yet felt to be significant.

And it was these stray remarks, full of a meaning that evaded him, that pointed to some hidden purpose of her own and made him feel uneasy. They all had to do, he felt sure, with reasons for his staying on in the town indefinitely.

"And has M'sieur not even yet come to a decision?" she said softly in his ear, sitting beside him in the sunny yard before *déjeuner*, the acquaintance having progressed with significant rapidity. "Because, if it's so difficult, we must all try together to help him!"

The question startled him, following upon his own thoughts. It was spoken with a pretty laugh, and a stray bit of hair across one eye, as she turned and peered at him half roguishly. Possibly he did not quite understand the French of it, for her near presence always confused his small knowledge of the language distressingly. Yet the words, and her manner, and something else that lay behind it all in her mind, frightened him. It gave such point to his feeling that the town was waiting for him to make his mind up on some important matter.

At the same time, her voice, and the fact that she was there so close beside him in her soft dark dress, thrilled him inexpressibly.

"It is true I find it difficult to leave," he stammered, losing his way deliciously in the depths of her eyes, "and especially now that Mademoiselle Ilsé has come."

He was surprised at the success of his sentence, and quite delighted with the little gallantry of it. But at the same time he could have bitten his tongue off for having said it.

"Then after all you like our little town, or you would not be pleased to stay on," she said, ignoring the compliment.

"I am enchanted with it, and enchanted with you," he cried, feeling that his tongue was somehow slipping beyond the control of his brain. And he was on the verge of saying all manner of other things of the wildest description, when the girl sprang lightly up from her chair beside him, and made to go.

"It is *soupe à l'onion* to-day!" she cried, laughing back at him through the sunlight, "and I must go and see about it. Otherwise, you know, M'sieur will not enjoy his dinner, and then, perhaps, he will leave us!"

He watched her cross the courtyard, moving with all the

grace and lightness of the feline race, and her simple black dress clothed her, he thought, exactly like the fur of the same supple species. She turned once to laugh at him from the porch with the glass door, and then stopped a moment to speak to her mother, who sat knitting as usual in her corner seat just inside the hall-way.

But how was it, then, that the moment his eye fell upon this ungainly woman, the pair of them appeared suddenly as other than they were? Whence came that transforming dignity and sense of power that enveloped them both as by magic? What was it about that massive woman that made her appear instantly regal, and set her on a throne in some dark and dreadful scenery, wielding a sceptre over the red glare of some tempestuous orgy? And why did this slender stripling of a girl, graceful as a willow, lithe as a young leopard, assume suddenly an air of sinister majesty, and move with flame and smoke about her head, and the darkness of night beneath her feet?

Vezin caught his breath and sat there transfixed. Then, almost simultaneously with its appearance, the queer notion vanished again, and the sunlight of day caught them both, and he heard her laughing to her mother about the *soupe à l'onion*, and saw her glancing back at him over her dear little shoulder with a smile that made him think of a dew-kissed rose bending lightly before summer airs.

And, indeed, the onion soup was particularly excellent that day, because he saw another cover laid at his small table, and, with fluttering heart, heard the waiter murmur by way of explanation that "Ma'mselle Ilsé would honour M'sieur to-day at *déjeuner*, as her custom sometimes is with her mother's guests."

So actually she sat by him all through that delirious meal, talking quietly to him in easy French, seeing that he was well looked after, mixing the salad-dressing, and even helping him with her own hand. And, later in the afternoon, while he was smoking in the courtyard, longing for a sight of her as soon as her duties were done, she came again to his side, and when he rose to meet her, she stood facing him a moment, full of a perplexing sweet shyness before she spoke—

"My mother thinks you ought to know more of the beauties of our little town, and *I* think so too! Would M'sieur like me to be his guide, perhaps? I can show him everything, for our family has lived here for many generations."

She had him by the hand, indeed, before he could find a single word to express his pleasure, and led him, all unresisting, out into the street, yet in such a way that it seemed perfectly natural she should do so, and without the faintest suggestion of boldness or immodesty. Her face glowed with the pleasure and interest of it, and with her short dress and tumbled hair she looked every bit the charming child of seventeen that she was, innocent and playful, proud of her native town, and alive beyond her years to the sense of its ancient beauty.

So they went over the town together, and she showed him what she considered its chief interest: the tumble-down old house where her forebears had lived; the sombre, aristocratic-looking mansion where her mother's family dwelt for centuries, and the ancient market-place where several hundred years before the witches had been burnt by the score. She kept up a lively running stream of talk about it all, of which he understood not a fiftieth part as he trudged along by her side, cursing his forty-five years and feeling all the yearnings of his early manhood revive and jeer at him. And, as she talked, England and Surbiton seemed very far away indeed, almost in another age of the world's history. Her voice touched something immeasurably old in him, something that slept deep. It lulled the surface parts of his consciousness to sleep, allowing what was far more ancient to awaken. Like the town, with its elaborate pretence of modern active life, the upper layers of his being became dulled, soothed, muffled, and what lay underneath began to stir in its sleep. That big Curtain swayed a little to and fro. Presently it might lift altogether . . .

He began to understand a little better at last. The mood of

the town was reproducing itself in him. In proportion as his ordinary external self became muffled, that inner secret life, that was far more real and vital, asserted itself. And this girl was surely the high-priestess of it all, the chief instrument of its accomplishment. New thoughts, with new interpretations, flooded his mind as she walked beside him through the winding streets, while the picturesque old gabled town, softly coloured in the sunset, had never appeared to him so wholly wonderful and seductive.

And only one curious incident came to disturb and puzzle him, slight in itself, but utterly inexplicable, bringing white terror into the child's face and a scream to her laughing lips. He had merely pointed to a column of blue smoke that rose from the burning autumn leaves and made a picture against the red roofs, and had then run to the wall and called her to his side to watch the flames shooting here and there through the heap of rubbish. Yet, at the sight of it, as though taken by surprise, her face had altered dreadfully, and she had turned and run like the wind, calling out wild sentences to him as she ran, of which he had not understood a single word, except that the fire apparently frightened her, and she wanted to get quickly away from it, and to get him away too.

Yet five minutes later she was as calm and happy again as though nothing had happened to alarm or waken troubled thoughts in her, and they had both forgotten the incident.

They were leaning over the ruined ramparts together listening to the weird music of the band as he had heard it the first day of his arrival. It moved him again profoundly as it had done before, and somehow he managed to find his tongue and his best French. The girl leaned across the stones close beside him. No one was about. Driven by some remorseless engine within he began to stammer something—he hardly knew what—of his strange admiration for her. Almost at the first word she sprang lightly off the wall and came up smiling in front of him, just touching his knees as he sat there. She was hatless as usual, and the sun caught her hair and one side of her cheek and throat.

"Oh, I'm *so* glad!" she cried, clapping her little hands softly in his face, "so very glad, because that means that if you like me you must also like what I do, and what I belong to."

Already he regretted bitterly having lost control of himself. Something in the phrasing of her sentence chilled him. He knew the fear of embarking upon an unknown and dangerous sea.

"You will take part in our real life, I mean," she added softly, with an indescribable coaxing of manner, as though she noticed his shrinking. "You will come back to us."

Already this slip of a child seemed to dominate him; he felt her power coming over him more and more; something emanated from her that stole over his senses and made him aware that her personality, for all its simple grace, held forces that were stately, imposing, august. He saw her again moving through smoke and flame amid broken and tempestuous scenery, alarmingly strong, her terrible mother by her side. Dimly this shone through her smile and appearance of charming innocence.

"You will, I know," she repeated, holding him with her eyes.

They were quite alone up there on the ramparts, and the sensation that she was overmastering him stirred a wild sensuousness in his blood. The mingled abandon and reserve in her attracted him furiously, and all of him that was man rose up and resisted the creeping influence, at the same time acclaiming it with the full delight of his forgotten youth. An irresistible desire came to him to question her, to summon what still remained to him of his own little personality in an effort to retain the right to his normal self.

The girl had grown quiet again, and was now leaning on the broad wall close beside him, gazing out across the darkening plain, her elbows on the coping, motionless as a figure carved in stone. He took his courage in both hands.

"Tell me, Ilsé," he said, unconsciously imitating her own purring softness of voice, yet aware that he was utterly in earnest, "what is the meaning of this town, and what is this real life you speak of? And why is it that the people watch me from morning to night? Tell me what it all means? And, tell me," he added more quickly with passion in his voice, "what you really are—yourself?"

She turned her head and looked at him through half-closed eyelids, her growing inner excitement betraying itself by the faint colour that ran like a shadow across her face.

"It seems to me,"—he faltered oddly under her gaze—"that I have some right to know—"

Suddenly she opened her eyes to the full. "You love me, then?" she asked softly.

"I swear," he cried impetuously, moved as by the force of a rising tide, "I never felt before—I have never known any other girl who—"

"Then you *have* the right to know," she calmly interrupted his confused confession, "for love shares all secrets."

She paused, and a thrill like fire ran swiftly through him. Her words lifted him off the earth, and he felt a radiant happiness, followed almost the same instant in horrible contrast by the thought of death. He became aware that she had turned her eyes upon his own and was speaking again.

"The real life I speak of," she whispered, "is the old, old life within, the life of long ago, the life to which you, too, once belonged, and to which you still belong."

A faint wave of memory troubled the deeps of his soul as her low voice sank into him. What she was saying he knew instinctively to be true, even though he could not as yet understand its full purport. His present life seemed slipping from him as he listened, merging his personality in one that was far older and greater. It was this loss of his present self that brought to him the thought of death.

"You came here," she went on, "with the purpose of seeking it, and the people felt your presence and are waiting to know what you decide, whether you will leave them without having found it, or whether—"

Her eyes remained fixed upon his own, but her face began to change, growing larger and darker with an expression of age.

"It is their thoughts constantly playing about your soul that makes you feel they watch you. They do not watch you with their eyes. The purposes of their inner life are calling to you, seeking to claim you. You were all part of the same life long, long ago, and now they want you back again among them."

Vezin's timid heart sank with dread as he listened; but the girl's eyes held him with a net of joy so that he had no wish to escape. She fascinated him, as it were, clean out of his normal self.

"Alone, however, the people could never have caught and held you," she resumed. "The motive force was not strong enough; it has faded through all these years. But I"—she paused a moment and looked at him with complete confidence in her splendid eyes—"I possess the spell to conquer you and hold you: the spell of old love. I can win you back again and make you live the old life with me, for the force of the ancient tie between us, if I choose to use it, is irresistible. And I do choose to use it. I still want you. And you, dear soul of my dim past"—she pressed closer to him so that her breath passed across his eyes, and her voice positively sang—"I mean to have you, for you love me and are utterly at my mercy."

Vezin heard, and yet did not hear; understood, yet did not understand. He had passed into a condition of exaltation. The world was beneath his feet, made of music and flowers, and he was flying somewhere far above it through the sunshine of pure delight. He was breathless and giddy with the wonder of her words. They intoxicated him. And, still, the terror of it all, the dreadful thought of death, pressed ever behind her sentences. For flames shot through her voice out of black smoke and licked at his soul.

And they communicated with one another, it seemed to him, by a process of swift telepathy, for his French could never have compassed all he said to her. Yet she understood perfectly, and what she said to him was like the recital of verses long since known. And the mingled pain and sweetness of it as he listened were almost more than his little soul could hold.

"Yet I came here wholly by chance—" he heard himself saying.

"No," she cried with passion, "you came here because I called to you. I have called to you for years, and you came with the whole force of the past behind you. You had to come, for I own you, and I claim you."

She rose again and moved closer, looking at him with a certain insolence in the face—the insolence of power.

The sun had set behind the towers of the old cathedral and the darkness rose up from the plain and enveloped them. The music of the band had ceased. The leaves of the plane trees hung motionless, but the chill of the autumn evening rose about them and made Vezin shiver. There was no sound but the sound of their voices and the occasional soft rustle of the girl's dress. He could hear the blood rushing in his ears. He scarcely realised where he was or what he was doing. Some terrible magic of the imagination drew him deeply down into the tombs of his own being, telling him in no unfaltering voice that her words shadowed forth the truth. And this simple little French maid, speaking beside him with so strange authority, he saw curiously alter into quite another being. As he stared into her eyes, the picture in his mind grew and lived, dressing itself vividly to his inner vision with a degree of reality he was compelled to acknowledge. As once before, he saw her tall and stately, moving through wild and broken scenery of forests and mountain caverns, the glare of flames behind her head and clouds of shifting smoke about her feet. Dark leaves encircled her hair, flying loosely in the wind, and her limbs shone through the merest rags of clothing. Others were about her, too, and ardent eyes on all sides cast delirious glances upon her, but her own eyes were always for One only, one whom she held by the hand. For she was leading the dance in some tempestuous orgy to the music of chanting voices, and the dance she led circled about a great and awful Figure on a throne, brooding over the scene through lurid vapours, while innumerable other wild faces and forms crowded furiously about her in the dance. But the one she held by the hand he knew to be himself, and the monstrous shape upon the throne he knew to be her mother.

The vision rose within him, rushing to him down the long years of buried time, crying aloud to him with the voice of memory reawakened . . . And then the scene faded away and he saw the clear circle of the girl's eyes gazing steadfastly into his own, and she became once more the pretty little daughter of the innkeeper, and he found his voice again.

"And you," he whispered tremblingly—"you child of visions and enchantment, how is it that you so bewitch me that I loved you even before I saw?"

She drew herself up beside him with an air of rare dignity.

"The call of the Past," she said; "and besides," she added proudly, "in the real life I am a princess—"

"A princess!" he cried.

"—and my mother is a queen!"

At this, little Vezin utterly lost his head. Delight tore at his heart and swept him into sheer ecstasy. To hear that sweet singing voice, and to see those adorable little lips utter such things, upset his balance beyond all hope of control. He took her in his arms and covered her unresisting face with kisses.

But even while he did so, and while the hot passion swept him, he felt that she was soft and loathsome, and that her answering kisses stained his very soul . . . And when, presently, she had freed herself and vanished into the darkness, he stood there, leaning against the wall in a state of collapse, creeping with horror from the touch of her yielding body, and inwardly raging at the weakness that he already dimly realised must prove his undoing.

And from the shadows of the old buildings into which she disappeared there rose in the stillness of the night a singular, long-drawn cry, which at first he took for laughter, but which later he was sure he recognised as the almost human wailing of a cat.

<h2 style="text-align:center">V</h2>

For a long time Vezin leant there against the wall, alone with his surging thoughts and emotions. He understood at length that he had done the one thing necessary to call down upon him the whole force of this ancient Past. For in those passionate kisses he had acknowledged the tie of olden days, and had revived it. And the memory of that soft impalpable caress in the darkness of the inn corridor came back to him with a shudder. The girl had first mastered him, and then led him to the one act that was necessary for her purpose. He had been waylaid, after the lapse of centuries—caught, and conquered.

Dimly he realised this, and sought to make plans for his escape. But, for the moment at any rate, he was powerless to manage his thoughts or will, for the sweet, fantastic madness of the whole adventure mounted to his brain like a spell, and he gloried in the feeling that he was utterly enchanted and moving in a world so much larger and wilder than the one he had ever been accustomed to.

The moon, pale and enormous, was just rising over the sea-like plain, when at last he rose to go. Her slanting rays drew all the houses into new perspective, so that their roofs, already glistening with dew, seemed to stretch much higher into the sky than usual, and their gables and quaint old towers lay far away in its purple reaches.

The cathedral appeared unreal in a silver mist. He moved softly, keeping to the shadows; but the streets were all deserted and very silent; the doors were closed, the shutters fastened. Not a soul was astir. The hush of night lay over everything; it was like a town of the dead, a churchyard with gigantic and grotesque tombstones.

Wondering where all the busy life of the day had so utterly disappeared to, he made his way to a back door that entered the inn by means of the stables, thinking thus to reach his room unobserved. He reached the courtyard safely and crossed it by keeping close to the shadow of the wall. He sidled down it, mincing along on tiptoe, just as the old men did when they entered the *salle à manger*. He was horrified to find himself doing this instinctively. A strange impulse came to him, catching him somehow in the centre of his body—an impulse to drop upon all fours and run swiftly and silently. He glanced upwards and the idea came to him to leap up upon his window-sill overhead instead of going round by the stairs. This occurred to him as the easiest, and most natural way. It was like the beginning of some horrible transformation of himself into something else. He was fearfully strung up.

The moon was higher now, and the shadows very dark along the side of the street where he moved. He kept among the deepest of them, and reached the porch with the glass doors.

But here there was light; the inmates, unfortunately, were still about. Hoping to slip across the hall unobserved and reach the stairs, he opened the door carefully and stole in. Then he saw that the hall was not empty. A large dark thing lay against the wall on his left. At first he thought it must be household articles. Then it moved, and he thought it was an immense cat, distorted in some way by the play of light and shadow. Then it rose straight up before him and he saw that it was the proprietress.

What she had been doing in this position he could only venture a dreadful guess, but the moment she stood up and faced him he was aware of some terrible dignity clothing her about that instantly recalled the girl's strange saying that she was a queen. Huge and sinister she stood there under the little oil lamp; alone with him in the empty hall. Awe stirred in his heart, and the roots of some ancient fear. He felt that he must bow to her and make some kind of obeisance. The impulse was fierce and irresistible, as of long habit. He glanced quickly about him. There was no one there. Then he deliberately inclined his head toward her. He bowed.

"Enfin! M'sieur s'est donc décidé. C'est bien alors. J'en suis contente."

Her words came to him sonorously as through a great open space.

Then the great figure came suddenly across the flagged hall at him and seized his trembling hands. Some overpowering force moved with her and caught him.

"On pourrait faire un p'tit tour ensemble, n'est-ce pas? Nous y allons cette nuit et il faut s'exercer un peu d'avance pour cela. Ilsé, Ilsé, viens donc ici. Viens vite!"

And she whirled him round in the opening steps of some dance that seemed oddly and horribly familiar. They made no sound on the stones, this strangely assorted couple. It was all soft and stealthy. And presently, when the air seemed to thicken like smoke, and a red glare as of flame shot through it, he was aware that some one else had joined them and that his hand the mother had released was now tightly held by the daughter. Ilsé had come in answer to the call, and he saw her with leaves of vervain twined in her dark hair, clothed in tattered vestiges of some curious garment, beautiful as the night, and horribly, odiously, loathsomely seductive.

"To the Sabbath! to the Sabbath!" they cried. "On to the Witches' Sabbath!"

Up and down that narrow hall they danced, the women on each side of him, to the wildest measure he had ever imagined, yet which he dimly, dreadfully remembered, till the lamp on the wall flickered and went out, and they were left in total darkness. And the devil woke in his heart with a thousand vile suggestions and made him afraid.

Suddenly they released his hands and he heard the voice of the mother cry that it was time, and they must go. Which way they went he did not pause to see. He only realised that he was free, and he blundered through the darkness till he found the stairs and then tore up them to his room as though all hell was at his heels.

He flung himself on the sofa, with his face in his hands, and groaned. Swiftly reviewing a dozen ways of immediate escape, all equally impossible, he finally decided that the only thing to do for the moment was to sit quiet and wait. He must see what was going to happen. At least in the privacy of his own bedroom he would be fairly safe. The door was locked. He crossed over and softly opened the window which gave upon the courtyard and also permitted a partial view of the hall through the glass doors.

As he did so the hum and murmur of a great activity reached his ears from the streets beyond—the sound of footsteps and voices muffled by distance. He leaned out cautiously and listened. The moonlight was clear and strong now, but his own window was in shadow, the silver disc being still behind the house. It came to him irresistibly that the inhabitants of the town, who a little while before had all been invisible behind closed doors, were now issuing forth, busy upon some secret and unholy errand. He listened intently.

At first everything about him was silent, but soon he became aware of movements going on in the house itself. Rustlings and cheepings came to him across that still, moonlit yard. A concourse of living beings sent the hum of their activity into the night. Things were on the move everywhere. A biting, pungent odour rose through the air, coming he knew not whence. Presently his eyes became glued to the windows of the opposite wall where the moonshine fell in a soft blaze. The roof overhead, and behind him, was reflected clearly in the panes of glass, and he saw the outlines of dark bodies moving with long footsteps over the tiles and along the coping. They passed swiftly and silently, shaped like immense cats, in an endless procession across the pictured glass, and then appeared to leap down to a lower level where he lost sight of them. He just caught the soft thudding of their leaps. Sometimes their shadows fell upon the white wall opposite, and then he could not make out whether they were the shadows of human beings or of cats. They seemed to change swiftly from one to the other. The transformation looked horribly real, for they leaped like human beings, yet changed swiftly in the air immediately afterwards, and dropped like animals.

The yard, too, beneath him, was now alive with the creeping movements of dark forms all stealthily drawing towards the porch with the glass doors. They kept so closely to the wall that he could not determine their actual shape, but when he saw that they passed on to the great congregation that was gathering in the hall, he understood that these were the creatures whose leaping shadows he had first seen reflected in the windowpanes opposite. They were coming from all parts of the town, reaching the appointed meeting-place across the roofs and tiles, and springing from level to level till they came to the yard.

Then a new sound caught his ear, and he saw that the windows all about him were being softly opened, and that to each window came a face. A moment later figures began dropping hurriedly down into the yard. And these figures, as they lowered themselves down from the windows, were human, he saw; but once safely in the yard they fell upon all fours and changed in the swiftest possible second into—cats—huge, silent cats. They ran in streams to join the main body in the hall beyond.

So, after all, the rooms in the house had not been empty and unoccupied.

Moreover, what he saw no longer filled him with amazement. For he remembered it all. It was familiar. It had all happened before just so, hundreds of times, and he himself had taken part in it and known the wild madness of it all. The outline of the old building changed, the yard grew larger, and he seemed to be staring down upon it from a much greater height through smoky vapours. And, as he looked, half remembering, the old pains of long ago, fierce and sweet, furiously assailed him, and the blood stirred horribly as he heard the Call of the Dance again in his heart and tasted the ancient magic of Ilsé whirling by his side.

Suddenly he started back. A great lithe cat had leaped softly up from the shadows below on to the sill close to his face, and was staring fixedly at him with the eyes of a human. "Come," it seemed to say, "come with us to the Dance! Change as of old! Transform yourself swiftly and come!" Only too well he understood the creature's soundless call.

It was gone again in a flash with scarcely a sound of its padded feet on the stones, and then others dropped by the score down the side of the house, past his very eyes, all changing as they fell and darting away rapidly, softly, towards the gathering point. And again he felt the dreadful desire to do likewise; to murmur the old incantation, and then drop upon hands and knees and run swiftly for the great flying leap into the air. Oh, how the passion of it rose within him like a flood, twisting his very entrails, sending his heart's desire flaming forth into the night for the old, old Dance of the Sorcerers at the Witches' Sabbath! The whirl of the stars was about him; once more he met the magic of the moon. The power of the wind, rushing from precipice and forest, leaping from cliff to cliff across the valleys, tore him away . . . He heard the cries of the dancers and their wild laughter, and with this savage girl in his embrace he danced furiously about the dim Throne where sat the Figure with the sceptre of majesty . . .

Then, suddenly, all became hushed and still, and the fever died down a little in his heart. The calm moonlight flooded a courtyard empty and deserted. They had started. The procession was off into the sky. And he was left behind—alone.

Vezin tiptoed softly across the room and unlocked the door. The murmur from the streets, growing momentarily as he advanced, met his ears. He made his way with the utmost caution down the corridor. At the head of the stairs he paused and listened. Below him, the hall where they had gathered was dark and still, but through opened doors and windows on the far side of the building came the sound of a great throng moving farther and farther into the distance.

He made his way down the creaking wooden stairs, dreading yet longing to meet some straggler who should point the way, but finding no one; across the dark hall, so lately thronged with living, moving things, and out through the opened front doors into the street. He could not believe that he was really left behind, really forgotten, that he had been purposely permitted to escape. It perplexed him.

Nervously he peered about him, and up and down the street; then, seeing nothing, advanced slowly down the pavement.

The whole town, as he went, showed itself empty and deserted, as though a great wind had blown everything alive out of it. The doors and windows of the houses stood open to the night; nothing stirred; moonlight and silence lay over all. The night lay about him like a cloak. The air, soft and cool, caressed his cheek like the touch of a great furry paw. He gained confidence and began to walk quickly, though still keeping to the shadowed side. Nowhere could he discover the faintest sign of the great unholy exodus he knew had just taken place. The moon sailed high over all in a sky cloudless and serene.

Hardly realising where he was going, he crossed the open market-place and so came to the ramparts, whence he knew a pathway descended to the high road and along which he could make good his escape to one of the other little towns that lay to the northward, and so to the railway.

But first he paused and gazed out over the scene at his feet where the great plain lay like a silver map of some dream country. The still beauty of it entered his heart, increasing his sense of bewilderment and unreality. No air stirred, the leaves of the plane trees stood motionless, the near details were defined with the sharpness of day against dark shadows, and in the distance the fields and woods melted away into haze and shimmering mistiness.

But the breath caught in his throat and he stood stockstill as though transfixed when his gaze passed from the horizon and fell upon the near prospect in the depth of the valley at his feet. The whole lower slopes of the hill, that lay hid from the brightness of the moon, were aglow, and through the glare he saw countless moving forms, shifting thick and fast between the openings of the trees; while overhead, like leaves driven by the wind, he discerned flying shapes that hovered darkly one moment against the sky and then settled down with cries and weird singing through the branches into the region that was aflame.

Spellbound, he stood and stared for a time that he could not measure. And then, moved by one of the terrible impulses that seemed to control the whole adventure, he climbed swiftly upon the top of the broad coping, and balanced a moment where the valley gaped at his feet. But in that very instant, as he stood hovering, a sudden movement among the shadows of the houses caught his eye, and he turned to see the outline of a large animal dart swiftly across the open space behind him, and land with a flying leap upon the top of the wall a little lower down. It ran like the wind to his feet and then rose up beside him upon the ramparts. A shiver seemed to run through the moonlight, and his sight trembled for a second. His heart pulsed fearfully. Ilsé stood beside him, peering into his face.

Some dark substance, he saw, stained the girl's face and skin, shining in the moonlight as she stretched her hands towards him; she was dressed in wretched tattered garments that yet became her mightily; rue and vervain twined about her temples; her eyes glittered with unholy light. He only just controlled the wild impulse to take her in his arms and leap with her from their giddy perch into the valley below.

"See!" she cried, pointing with an arm on which the rags fluttered in the rising wind towards the forest aglow in the distance. "See where they await us! The woods are alive! Already the Great Ones are there, and the dance will soon begin! The salve is here! Anoint yourself and come!"

Though a moment before the sky was clear and cloudless, yet even while she spoke the face of the moon grew dark and the wind began to toss in the crests of the plane trees at his feet.

Stray gusts brought the sounds of hoarse singing and crying from the lower slopes of the hill, and the pungent odour he had already noticed about the courtyard of the inn rose about him in the air.

"Transform, transform!" she cried again, her voice rising like a song. "Rub well your skin before you fly. Come! Come with me to the Sabbath, to the madness of its furious delight, to the sweet abandonment of its evil worship! See! the Great Ones are there, and the terrible Sacraments prepared. The Throne is occupied. Anoint and come! Anoint and come!"

She grew to the height of a tree beside him, leaping upon the wall with flaming eyes and hair strewn upon the night. He too began to change swiftly. Her hands touched the skin of his face and neck, streaking him with the burning salve that sent the old magic into his blood with the power before which fades all that is good.

A wild roar came up to his ears from the heart of the wood, and the girl, when she heard it, leaped upon the wall in the frenzy of her wicked joy.

"Satan is there!" she screamed, rushing upon him and striving to draw him with her to the edge of the wall. "Satan has come. The Sacraments call us! Come, with your dear apostate soul, and we will worship and dance till the moon dies and the world is forgotten!"

Just saving himself from the dreadful plunge, Vezin struggled to release himself from her grasp, while the passion tore at his reins and all but mastered him. He shrieked aloud, not knowing what he said, and then he shrieked again. It was the old impulses, the old awful habits instinctively finding voice; for though it seemed to him that he merely shrieked nonsense, the words he uttered really had meaning in them, and were intelligible. It was the ancient call. And it was heard below. It was answered.

The wind whistled at the skirts of his coat as the air round him darkened with many flying forms crowding upwards out of the valley. The crying of hoarse voices smote upon his ears, coming closer. Strokes of wind buffeted him, tearing him this way and that along the crumbling top of the stone wall; and Ilsé clung to him with her long shining arms, smooth and bare, holding him fast about the neck. But not Ilsé alone, for a dozen of them surrounded him, dropping out of the air. The pungent odour of the anointed bodies stifled him, exciting him to the old madness of the Sabbath, the dance of the witches and sorcerers doing honour to the personified Evil of the world.

"Anoint and away! Anoint and away!" they cried in wild chorus about him. "To the Dance that never dies! To the sweet and fearful fantasy of evil!"

Another moment and he would have yielded and gone, for his will turned soft and the flood of passionate memory all but overwhelmed him, when—so can a small thing after the whole course of an adventure—he caught his foot upon a loose stone in the edge of the wall, and then fell with a sudden crash on to the ground below. But he fell towards the houses, in the open space of dust and cobblestones, and fortunately not into the gaping depth of the valley on the farther side.

And they, too, came in a tumbling heap about him, like flies upon a piece of food, but as they fell he was released for a moment from the power of their touch, and in that brief instant of freedom there flashed into his mind the sudden intuition that saved him. Before he could regain his feet he saw them scrabbling awkwardly back upon the wall, as though bat-like they could only fly by dropping from a height, and had no hold upon him in the open. Then, seeing them perched there in a row like cats upon a roof, all dark and singularly shapeless, their eyes like lamps, the sudden memory came back to him of Ilsé's terror at the sight of fire.

Quick as a flash he found his matches and lit the dead leaves that lay under the wall.

Dry and withered, they caught fire at once, and the wind carried the flame in a long line down the length of the wall, licking upwards as it ran; and with shrieks and wailings, the crowded row of forms upon the top melted away into the air on the other side, and were gone with a great rush and whirring of their bodies down into the heart of the haunted valley, leaving Vezin breathless and shaken in the middle of the deserted ground.

"Ilsé!" he called feebly; "Ilsé!" for his heart ached to think that she was really gone to the great Dance without him, and that he had lost the opportunity of its fearful joy. Yet at the same time his relief was so great, and he was so dazed and troubled in mind with the whole thing, that he hardly knew what he was saying, and only cried aloud in the fierce storm of his emotion . . .

The fire under the wall ran its course, and the moonlight came out again, soft and clear, from its temporary eclipse. With one last shuddering look at the ruined ramparts, and a feeling of horrid wonder for the haunted valley beyond, where the shapes still crowded and flew, he turned his face towards the town and slowly made his way in the direction of the hotel.

And as he went, a great wailing of cries, and a sound of howling, followed him from the gleaming forest below, growing fainter and fainter with the bursts of wind as he disappeared between the houses.

VI

"It may seem rather abrupt to you, this sudden tame ending," said Arthur Vezin, glancing with flushed face and timid eyes at Dr. Silence sitting there with his notebook, "but the fact is—er—from that moment my memory seems to have failed rather. I have no distinct recollection of how I got home or what precisely I did.

"It appears I never went back to the inn at all. I only dimly recollect racing down a long white road in the moonlight, past woods and villages, still and deserted, and then the dawn came up, and I saw the towers of a biggish town and so came to a station.

"But, long before that, I remember pausing somewhere on the road and looking back to where the hill-town of my adventure stood up in the moonlight, and thinking how exactly like a great monstrous cat it lay there upon the plain, its huge front paws lying down the two main streets, and the twin and broken towers of the cathedral marking its torn ears against the sky. That picture stays in my mind with the utmost vividness to this day.

"Another thing remains in my mind from that escape—namely, the sudden sharp reminder that I had not paid my bill, and the decision I made, standing there on the dusty highroad, that the small baggage I had left behind would more than settle for my indebtedness.

"For the rest, I can only tell you that I got coffee and bread at a café on the outskirts of this town I had come to, and soon after found my way to the station and caught a train later in the day. That same evening I reached London."

"And how long altogether," asked John Silence quietly, "do you think you stayed in the town of the adventure?"

Vezin looked up sheepishly.

"I was coming to that," he resumed, with apologetic wrigglings of his body. "In London I found that I was a whole week out in my reckoning of time. I had stayed over a week in the town, and it ought to have been September 15th,—instead of which it was only September 10th!"

"So that, in reality, you had only stayed a night or two in the inn?" queried the doctor.

Vezin hesitated before replying. He shuffled upon the mat.

"I must have gained time somewhere," he said at length—"somewhere or somehow. I certainly had a week to my credit. I can't explain it. I can only give you the fact."

"And this happened to you last year, since when you have never been back to the place?"

"Last autumn, yes," murmured Vezin; "and I have never dared to go back. I think I never want to."

"And, tell me," asked Dr. Silence at length, when he saw that the little man had evidently come to the end of his words and had nothing more to say, "had you ever read up the subject of the old witchcraft practices during the Middle Ages, or been at all interested in the subject?"

"Never!" declared Vezin emphatically. "I had never given a thought to such matters so far as I know—"

"Or to the question of reincarnation, perhaps?"

"Never—before my adventure; but I have since," he replied significantly.

There was, however, something still on the man's mind that he wished to relieve himself of by confession, yet could only with difficulty bring himself to mention; and it was only after the sympathetic tactfulness of the doctor had provided numerous openings that he at length availed himself of one of them, and stammered that he would like to show him the marks he still had on his neck where, he said, the girl had touched him with her anointed hands.

He took off his collar after infinite fumbling hesitation, and lowered his shirt a little for the doctor to see. And there, on the surface of the skin, lay a faint reddish line across the shoulder and extending a little way down the back towards the spine. It certainly indicated exactly the position an arm might have taken in the act of embracing. And on the other side of the neck, slightly higher up, was a similar mark, though not quite so clearly defined.

"That was where she held me that night on the ramparts," he whispered, a strange light coming and going in his eyes.

It was some weeks later when I again found occasion to consult John Silence concerning another extraordinary case that had come under my notice, and we fell to discussing Vezin's story. Since hearing it, the doctor had made investigations on his own account, and one of his secretaries had discovered that

Vezin's ancestors had actually lived for generations in the very town where the adventure came to him. Two of them, both women, had been tried and convicted as witches, and had been burned alive at the stake. Moreover, it had not been difficult to prove that the very inn where Vezin stayed was built about 1700 upon the spot where the funeral pyres stood and the executions took place. The town was a sort of headquarters for all the sorcerers and witches of the entire region, and after conviction they were burnt there literally by scores.

"It seems strange," continued the doctor, "that Vezin should have remained ignorant of all this; but, on the other hand, it was not the kind of history that successive generations would have been anxious to keep alive, or to repeat to their children. Therefore I am inclined to think he still knows nothing about it.

"The whole adventure seems to have been a very vivid revival of the memories of an earlier life, caused by coming directly into contact with the living forces still intense enough to hang about the place, and, by a most singular chance, too, with the very souls who had taken part with him in the events of that particular life. For the mother and daughter who impressed him so strangely must have been leading actors, with himself, in the scenes and practices of witchcraft which at that period dominated the imaginations of the whole country.

"One has only to read the histories of the times to know that these witches claimed the power of transforming themselves into various animals, both for the purposes of disguise and also to convey themselves swiftly to the scenes of their imaginary orgies. Lycanthropy, or the power to change themselves into wolves, was everywhere believed in, and the ability to transform themselves into cats by rubbing their bodies with a special salve or ointment provided by Satan himself, found equal credence. The witchcraft trials abound in evidences of such universal beliefs."

Dr. Silence quoted chapter and verse from many writers on the subject, and showed how every detail of Vezin's adventure had a basis in the practices of those dark days.

"But that the entire affair took place subjectively in the man's own consciousness, I have no doubt," he went on, in reply to my questions; "for my secretary who has been to the town to investigate, discovered his signature in the visitors' book, and proved by it that he had arrived on September 8th, and left suddenly without paying his bill. He left two days later, and they still were in possession of his dirty brown bag and some tourist clothes. I paid a few francs in settlement of his debt, and have sent his luggage on to him. The daughter was absent from home, but the proprietress, a large woman very much as he described her, told my secretary that he had seemed a very strange, absent-minded kind of gentleman, and after his disappearance she had feared for a long time that he had met with a violent end in the neighbouring forest where he used to roam about alone.

"I should like to have obtained a personal interview with the daughter so as to ascertain how much was subjective and how much actually took place with her as Vezin told it. For her dread of fire and the sight of burning must, of course, have been the intuitive memory of her former painful death at the stake, and have thus explained why he fancied more than once that he saw her through smoke and flame."

"And that mark on his skin, for instance?" I inquired.

"Merely the marks produced by hysterical brooding," he replied, "like the stigmata of the *religieuses*, and the bruises which appear on the bodies of hypnotised subjects who have been told to expect them. This is very common and easily explained. Only it seems curious that these marks should have remained so long in Vezin's case. Usually they disappear quickly."

"Obviously he is still thinking about it all, brooding, and living it all over again," I ventured.

"Probably. And this makes me fear that the end of his trouble is not yet. We shall hear of him again. It is a case, alas! I can do little to alleviate."

Dr. Silence spoke gravely and with sadness in his voice.

"And what do you make of the Frenchman in the train?"
I asked further—"the man who warned him against the
place, *à cause du sommeil et à cause des chats?* Surely a very
singular incident?"

"A *very* singular incident indeed," he made answer slowly,
"and one I can only explain on the basis of a highly improbable
coincidence—"

"Namely?"

"That the man was one who had himself stayed in the town
and undergone there a similar experience. I should like to find
this man and ask him. But the crystal is useless here, for I have
no slightest clue to go upon, and I can only conclude that some
singular psychic affinity, some force still active in his being out
of the same past life, drew him thus to the personality of Vezin,
and enabled him to fear what might happen to him, and thus to
warn him as he did.

"Yes," he presently continued, half talking to himself, "I
suspect in this case that Vezin was swept into the vortex of forces
arising out of the intense activities of a past life, and that he
lived over again a scene in which he had often played a leading
part centuries before. For strong actions set up forces that are
so slow to exhaust themselves, they may be said in a sense never
to die. In this case they were not vital enough to render the
illusion complete, so that the little man found himself caught
in a very distressing confusion of the present and the past; yet
he was sufficiently sensitive to recognise that it was true, and to
fight against the degradation of returning, even in memory, to a
former and lower state of development.

"Ah yes!" he continued, crossing the floor to gaze at the
darkening sky, and seemingly quite oblivious of my presence,
"subliminal up-rushes of memory like this can be exceedingly
painful, and sometimes exceedingly dangerous. I only trust
that this gentle soul may soon escape from this obsession of a
passionate and tempestuous past. But I doubt it, I doubt it."

His voice was hushed with sadness as he spoke, and when

he turned back into the room again there was an expression of profound yearning upon his face, the yearning of a soul whose desire to help is sometimes greater than his power.

Case II, *John Silence: Physician Extraordinary*, 1908

SECRET WORSHIP

Harris, the silk merchant, was in South Germany on his way home from a business trip when the idea came to him suddenly that he would take the mountain railway from Strassbourg and run down to revisit his old school after an interval of something more than thirty years. And it was to this chance impulse of the junior partner in Harris Brothers of St. Paul's Churchyard that John Silence owed one of the most curious cases of his whole experience, for at that very moment he happened to be tramping these same mountains with a holiday knapsack, and from different points of the compass the two men were actually converging towards the same inn.

Now, deep down in the heart that for thirty years had been concerned chiefly with the profitable buying and selling of silk, this school had left the imprint of its peculiar influence, and, though perhaps unknown to Harris, had strongly coloured the whole of his subsequent existence. It belonged to the deeply religious life of a small Protestant community (which it is unnecessary to specify), and his father had sent him there at the age of fifteen, partly because he would learn the German requisite for the conduct of the silk business, and partly because the discipline was strict, and discipline was what his soul and body needed just then more than anything else.

The life, indeed, had proved exceedingly severe, and young Harris benefited accordingly; for though corporal punishment was unknown, there was a system of mental and spiritual correction which somehow made the soul stand proudly erect to receive it, while it struck at the very root of the fault and taught the boy that his character was being cleaned and strengthened, and that he was not merely being tortured in a kind of personal revenge.

That was over thirty years ago, when he was a dreamy and impressionable youth of fifteen; and now, as the train climbed slowly up the winding mountain gorges, his mind travelled back somewhat lovingly over the intervening period, and forgotten details rose vividly again before him out of the shadows. The life there had been very wonderful, it seemed to him, in that remote mountain village, protected from the tumults of the world by the love and worship of the devout Brotherhood that ministered to the needs of some hundred boys from every country in Europe. Sharply the scenes came back to him. He smelt again the long stone corridors, the hot pinewood rooms, where the sultry hours of summer study were passed with bees droning through open windows in the sunshine, and German characters struggling in the mind with dreams of English lawns—and then the sudden awful cry of the master in German—

"Harris, stand up! You sleep!"

And he recalled the dreadful standing motionless for an hour, book in hand, while the knees felt like wax and the head grew heavier than a cannon-ball.

The very smell of the cooking came back to him—the daily *Sauerkraut*, the watery chocolate on Sundays, the flavour of the stringy meat served twice a week at *Mittagessen*; and he smiled to think again of the half-rations that was the punishment for speaking English. The very odour of the milk-bowls,—the hot sweet aroma that rose from the soaking peasant-bread at the six-o'clock breakfast,—came back to him pungently, and he saw the huge *Speisesaal* with the hundred boys in their school uniform, all eating sleepily in silence, gulping down the coarse bread and scalding milk in terror of the bell that would presently cut them short—and, at the far end where the masters sat, he saw the narrow slit windows with the vistas of enticing field and forest beyond.

And this, in turn, made him think of the great barnlike room on the top floor where all slept together in wooden cots, and he heard in memory the clamour of the cruel bell that woke them on winter mornings at five o'clock and summoned them to the stone-flagged *Waschkammer*, where boys and masters alike, after scanty and icy washing, dressed in complete silence.

From this his mind passed swiftly, with vivid picture-thoughts, to other things, and with a passing shiver he remembered how the loneliness of never being alone had eaten into him, and how everything—work, meals, sleep, walks, leisure—was done with his "division" of twenty other boys and under the eyes of at least two masters. The only solitude possible was by asking for half an hour's practice in the cell-like music rooms, and Harris smiled to himself as he recalled the zeal of his violin studies.

Then, as the train puffed laboriously through the great pine forests that cover these mountains with a giant carpet of velvet, he found the pleasanter layers of memory giving up their dead, and he recalled with admiration the kindness of the masters, whom all addressed as Brother, and marvelled afresh at their devotion in burying themselves for years in such a place, only to leave it, in most cases, for the still rougher life of missionaries in the wild places of the world.

He thought once more of the still, religious atmosphere that hung over the little forest community like a veil, barring the distressful world; of the picturesque ceremonies at Easter, Christmas, and New Year; of the numerous feast-days and charming little festivals. The *Beschehr-Fest*, in particular, came back to him,—the feast of gifts at Christmas,—when the entire community paired off and gave presents, many of which had taken weeks to make or the savings of many days to purchase. And then he saw the midnight ceremony in the church at New Year, with the shining face of the *Prediger* in the pulpit,—the village preacher who, on the last night of the old year, saw in the empty gallery beyond the organ loft the faces of all who were to die in the ensuing twelve months, and who at last recognised himself among them, and, in the very middle of his sermon, passed into a state of rapt ecstasy and burst into a torrent of praise.

Thickly the memories crowded upon him. The picture of the small village dreaming its unselfish life on the mountain-tops, clean, wholesome, simple, searching vigorously for its God, and training hundreds of boys in the grand way, rose up in his mind with all the power of an obsession. He felt once more the old mystical enthusiasm, deeper than the sea and more wonderful than the stars; he heard again the winds sighing from leagues of forest over the red roofs in the moonlight; he heard the Brothers' voices talking of the things beyond this life as though they had actually experienced them in the body; and, as he sat in the jolting train, a spirit of unutterable longing passed over his seared and tired soul, stirring in the depths of him a sea of emotions that he thought had long since frozen into immobility.

And the contrast pained him,—the idealistic dreamer then, the man of business now,—so that a spirit of unworldly peace and beauty known only to the soul in meditation laid its feathered finger upon his heart, moving strangely the surface of the waters.

Harris shivered a little and looked out of the window of his empty carriage. The train had long passed Hornberg, and far below the streams tumbled in white foam down the limestone rocks. In front of him, dome upon dome of wooded mountain stood against the sky. It was October, and the air was cool and sharp, woodsmoke and damp moss exquisitely mingled in it with the subtle odours of the pines. Overhead, between the tips of the highest firs, he saw the first stars peeping, and the sky was a clean, pale amethyst that seemed exactly the colour all these memories clothed themselves with in his mind.

He leaned back in his corner and sighed. He was a heavy man, and he had not known sentiment for years; he was a big man, and it took much to move him, literally and figuratively; he was a man in whom the dreams of God that haunt the soul in youth, though overlaid by the scum that gathers in the fight for money, had not, as with the majority, utterly died the death.

He came back into this little neglected pocket of the years, where so much fine gold had collected and lain undisturbed, with all his semispiritual emotions aquiver; and, as he watched the mountain-tops come nearer, and smelt the forgotten odours of his boyhood, something melted on the surface of his soul and left him sensitive to a degree he had not known since, thirty years before, he had lived here with his dreams, his conflicts, and his youthful suffering.

A thrill ran through him as the train stopped with a jolt at a tiny station and he saw the name in large black lettering on the grey stone building, and below it, the number of metres it stood above the level of the sea.

"The highest point on the line!" he exclaimed. "How well I remember it—Sommerau—Summer Meadow. The very next station is mine!"

And, as the train ran downhill with brakes on and steam shut off, he put his head out of the window and one by one saw the old familiar landmarks in the dusk. They stared at him like dead faces in a dream. Queer, sharp feelings, half poignant, half sweet, stirred in his heart.

"There's the hot, white road we walked along so often with the two Brüder always at our heels," he thought; "and there, by Jove, is the turn through the forest to *Die Galgen*, the stone gallows where they hanged the witches in olden days!"

He smiled a little as the train slid past.

"And there's the copse where the Lilies of the Valley powdered the ground in spring; and, I swear,"—he put his head out with a sudden impulse—"if that's not the very clearing where Calame, the French boy, chased the swallow-tail with me, and Bruder Pagel gave us half-rations for leaving the road without permission, and for shouting in our mother tongues!" And he laughed again as the memories came back with a rush, flooding his mind with vivid detail.

The train stopped, and he stood on the grey gravel platform

like a man in a dream. It seemed half a century since he last waited there with corded wooden boxes, and got into the train for Strassbourg and home after the two years' exile. Time dropped from him like an old garment and he felt a boy again. Only, things looked so much smaller than his memory of them; shrunk and dwindled they looked, and the distances seemed on a curiously smaller scale.

He made his way across the road to the little Gasthaus, and, as he went, faces and figures of former schoolfellows,—German, Swiss, Italian, French, Russian,—slipped out of the shadowy woods and silently accompanied him. They flitted by his side, raising their eyes questioningly, sadly, to his. But their names he had forgotten. Some of the Brothers, too, came with them, and most of these he remembered by name—Bruder Röst, Bruder Pagel, Bruder Schliemann, and the bearded face of the old preacher who had seen himself in the haunted gallery of those about to die—Bruder Gysin. The dark forest lay all about him like a sea that any moment might rush with velvet waves upon the scene and sweep all the faces away. The air was cool and wonderfully fragrant, but with every perfumed breath came also a pallid memory . . .

Yet, in spite of the underlying sadness inseparable from such an experience, it was all very interesting, and held a pleasure peculiarly its own, so that Harris engaged his room and ordered supper feeling well pleased with himself, and intending to walk up to the old school that very evening. It stood in the centre of the community's village, some four miles distant through the forest, and he now recollected for the first time that this little Protestant settlement dwelt isolated in a section of the country that was otherwise Catholic. Crucifixes and shrines surrounded the clearing like the sentries of a beleaguering army. Once beyond the square of the village, with its few acres of field and orchard, the forest crowded up in solid phalanxes, and beyond the rim of trees began the country that was ruled by the priests of another faith. He vaguely remembered, too, that the Catholics had showed sometimes a certain hostility towards the little Protestant oasis that flourished so quietly and benignly in their midst. He had quite forgotten this. How trumpery it all seemed now with his wide experience of life and his knowledge of other countries and the great outside world. It was like stepping back, not thirty years, but three hundred.

There were only two others besides himself at supper. One of them, a bearded, middle-aged man in tweeds, sat by himself at the far end, and Harris kept out of his way because he was English. He feared he might be in business, possibly even in the silk business, and that he would perhaps talk on the subject. The other traveller, however, was a Catholic priest. He was a little man who ate his salad with a knife, yet so gently that it was almost inoffensive, and it was the sight of "the cloth" that recalled his memory of the old antagonism. Harris mentioned by way of conversation the object of his sentimental journey, and the priest looked up sharply at him with raised eyebrows and an expression of surprise and suspicion that somehow piqued him. He ascribed it to his difference of belief.

"Yes," went on the silk merchant, pleased to talk of what his mind was so full, "and it was a curious experience for an English boy to be dropped down into a school of a hundred foreigners. I well remember the loneliness and intolerable Heimweh of it at first." His German was very fluent.

The priest opposite looked up from his cold veal and potato salad and smiled. It was a nice face. He explained quietly that he did not belong here, but was making a tour of the parishes of Wurttemberg and Baden.

"It was a strict life," added Harris. "We English, I remember, used to call it *Gefängnisleben*—prison life!"

The face of the other, for some unaccountable reason, darkened. After a slight pause, and more by way of politeness than because he wished to continue the subject, he said quietly—

"It was a flourishing school in those days, of course. Afterwards, I have heard—" He shrugged his shoulders slightly, and the odd look—it almost seemed a look of alarm—came back into his eyes. The sentence remained unfinished.

Something in the tone of the man seemed to his listener uncalled for—in a sense reproachful, singular. Harris bridled in spite of himself.

"It has changed?" he asked. "I can hardly believe—"

"You have not heard, then?" observed the priest gently, making a gesture as though to cross himself, yet not actually completing it. "You have not heard what happened there before it was abandoned—?"

It was very childish, of course, and perhaps he was overtired and overwrought in some way, but the words and manner of the little priest seemed to him so offensive—so disproportionately offensive—that he hardly noticed the concluding sentence. He recalled the old bitterness and the old antagonism, and for a moment he almost lost his temper.

"Nonsense," he interrupted with a forced laugh, "*Unsinn!* You must forgive me, sir, for contradicting you. But I was a pupil there myself. I was at school there. There was no place like it. I cannot believe that anything serious could have happened to— to take away its character. The devotion of the Brothers would be difficult to equal anywhere—"

He broke off suddenly, realising that his voice had been raised unduly and that the man at the far end of the table might understand German; and at the same moment he looked up and saw that this individual's eyes were fixed upon his face intently. They were peculiarly bright. Also they were rather wonderful eyes, and the way they met his own served in some way he could not understand to convey both a reproach and a warning. The whole face of the stranger, indeed, made a vivid impression upon him, for it was a face, he now noticed for the first time, in whose presence one would not willingly have said or done anything unworthy. Harris could not explain to himself how it was he had not become conscious sooner of its presence.

But he could have bitten off his tongue for having so far

forgotten himself. The little priest lapsed into silence. Only once he said, looking up and speaking in a low voice that was not intended to be overheard, but that evidently *was* overheard, "You will find it different." Presently he rose and left the table with a polite bow that included both the others.

And, after him, from the far end rose also the figure in the tweed suit, leaving Harris by himself.

He sat on for a bit in the darkening room, sipping his coffee and smoking his fifteen-pfennig cigar, till the girl came in to light the oil lamps. He felt vexed with himself for his lapse from good manners, yet hardly able to account for it. Most likely, he reflected, he had been annoyed because the priest had unintentionally changed the pleasant character of his dream by introducing a jarring note. Later he must seek an opportunity to make amends. At present, however, he was too impatient for his walk to the school, and he took his stick and hat and passed out into the open air.

And, as he crossed before the Gasthaus, he noticed that the priest and the man in the tweed suit were engaged already in such deep conversation that they hardly noticed him as he passed and raised his hat.

He started off briskly, well remembering the way, and hoping to reach the village in time to have a word with one of the Brüder. They might even ask him in for a cup of coffee. He felt sure of his welcome, and the old memories were in full possession once more. The hour of return was a matter of no consequence whatever.

It was then just after seven o'clock, and the October evening was drawing in with chill airs from the recesses of the forest. The road plunged straight from the railway clearing into its depths, and in a very few minutes the trees engulfed him and the clack of his boots fell dead and echoless against the serried stems of a million firs. It was very black; one trunk was hardly distinguishable from another. He walked smartly, swinging his holly stick. Once or twice he passed a peasant on his way to bed, and the guttural "Gruss Got," unheard for so long, emphasised the passage of time, while yet making it seem as nothing. A fresh group of pictures crowded his mind. Again the figures of former schoolfellows flitted out of the forest and kept pace by his side, whispering of the doings of long ago. One reverie stepped hard upon the heels of another. Every turn in the road, every clearing of the forest, he knew, and each in turn brought forgotten associations to life. He enjoyed himself thoroughly.

He marched on and on. There was powdered gold in the sky till the moon rose, and then a wind of faint silver spread silently between the earth and stars. He saw the tips of the fir trees shimmer, and heard them whisper as the breeze turned their needles towards the light. The mountain air was indescribably sweet. The road shone like the foam of a river through the gloom. White moths flitted here and there like silent thoughts across his path, and a hundred smells greeted him from the forest caverns across the years.

Then, when he least expected it, the trees fell away abruptly on both sides, and he stood on the edge of the village clearing.

He walked faster. There lay the familiar outlines of the houses, sheeted with silver; there stood the trees in the little central square with the fountain and small green lawns; there loomed the shape of the church next to the Gasthof der Brüdergemeinde; and just beyond, dimly rising into the sky, he saw with a sudden thrill the mass of the huge school building, blocked castlelike with deep shadows in the moonlight, standing square and formidable to face him after the silences of more than a quarter of a century.

He passed quickly down the deserted village street and stopped close beneath its shadow, staring up at the walls that had once held him prisoner for two years—two unbroken years of discipline and homesickness. Memories and emotions surged through his mind; for the most vivid sensations of his youth had focused about this spot, and it was here he had first begun to live and learn values. Not a single footstep broke the silence, though lights glimmered here and there through cottage windows; but when he looked up at the high walls of the school, draped now in shadow, he easily imagined that well-known faces crowded to the windows to greet him—closed windows that really reflected only moonlight and the gleam of stars.

This, then, was the old school building, standing foursquare to the world, with its shuttered windows, its lofty, tiled roof, and the spiked lightning-conductors pointing like black and taloned fingers from the corners. For a long time he stood and stared. Then, presently, he came to himself again, and realised to his joy that a light still shone in the windows of the *Bruderstube*.

He turned from the road and passed through the iron railings; then climbed the twelve stone steps and stood facing the black wooden door with the heavy bars of iron, a door he had once loathed and dreaded with the hatred and passion of an imprisoned soul, but now looked upon tenderly with a sort of boyish delight.

Almost timorously he pulled the rope and listened with a tremor of excitement to the clanging of the bell deep within the building. And the long-forgotten sound brought the past before him with such a vivid sense of reality that he positively shivered. It was like the magic bell in the fairy-tale that rolls back the curtain of Time and summons the figures from the shadows of the dead. He had never felt so sentimental in his life. It was like being young again. And, at the same time, he began to bulk rather large in his own eyes with a certain spurious importance. He was a big man from the world of strife and action. In this little place of peaceful dreams would he, perhaps, not cut something of a figure?

"I'll try once more," he thought after a long pause, seizing the iron bell-rope, and was just about to pull it when a step sounded on the stone passage within, and the huge door slowly swung open.

A tall man with a rather severe cast of countenance stood facing him in silence.

"I must apologise—it is somewhat late," he began a trifle pompously, "but the fact is I am an old pupil. I have only just arrived and really could not restrain myself." His German seemed not quite so fluent as usual. "My interest is so great. I was here in '70."

The other opened the door wider and at once bowed him in with a smile of genuine welcome.

"I am Bruder Kalkmann," he said quietly in a deep voice. "I myself was a master here about that time. It is a great pleasure always to welcome a former pupil." He looked at him very keenly for a few seconds, and then added, "I think, too, it is splendid of you to come—very splendid."

"It is a very great pleasure," Harris replied, delighted with his reception.

The dimly lighted corridor with its flooring of grey stone, and the familiar sound of a German voice echoing through it,—with the peculiar intonation the Brothers always used in speaking,—all combined to lift him bodily, as it were, into the dream-atmosphere of long-forgotten days. He stepped gladly into the building and the door shut with the familiar thunder that completed the reconstruction of the past. He almost felt the old sense of imprisonment, of aching nostalgia, of having lost his liberty.

Harris sighed involuntarily and turned towards his host, who returned his smile faintly and then led the way down the corridor.

"The boys have retired," he explained, "and, as you remember, we keep early hours here. But, at least, you will join us for a little while in the *Bruderstube* and enjoy a cup of coffee." This was precisely what the silk merchant had hoped, and he accepted with an alacrity that he intended to be tempered by graciousness. "And to-morrow," continued the Bruder, "you must come and spend a whole day with us. You may even find acquaintances, for several pupils of your day have come back here as masters."

For one brief second there passed into the man's eyes a look that made the visitor start. But it vanished as quickly as it came. It was impossible to define. Harris convinced himself it was the effect of a shadow cast by the lamp they had just passed on the wall. He dismissed it from his mind.

"You are very kind, I'm sure," he said politely. "It is perhaps a greater pleasure to me than you can imagine to see the place again. Ah,"—he stopped short opposite a door with the upper half of glass and peered in—"surely there is one of the music rooms where I used to practise the violin. How it comes back to me after all these years!"

Bruder Kalkmann stopped indulgently, smiling, to allow his guest a moment's inspection.

"You still have the boys' orchestra? I remember I used to play *'zweite Geige'* in it. Bruder Schliemann conducted at the piano. Dear me, I can see him now with his long black hair and—and—" He stopped abruptly. Again the odd, dark look passed over the stern face of his companion. For an instant it seemed curiously familiar.

"We still keep up the pupils' orchestra," he said, "but Bruder Schliemann, I am sorry to say—" he hesitated an instant, and then added, "Bruder Schliemann is dead."

"Indeed, indeed," said Harris quickly. "I am sorry to hear it." He was conscious of a faint feeling of distress, but whether it arose from the news of his old music teacher's death, or—from something else—he could not quite determine. He gazed down the corridor that lost itself among shadows. In the street and village everything had seemed so much smaller than he remembered, but here, inside the school building, everything seemed so much bigger. The corridor was loftier and longer, more spacious and vast, than the mental picture he had preserved. His thoughts wandered dreamily for an instant.

He glanced up and saw the face of the Bruder watching him with a smile of patient indulgence.

"Your memories possess you," he observed gently, and the stern look passed into something almost pitying.

"You are right," returned the man of silk, "they do. This was the most wonderful period of my whole life in a sense. At the time I hated it—" He hesitated, not wishing to hurt the Brother's feelings.

"According to English ideas it seemed strict, of course," the other said persuasively, so that he went on.

"—Yes, partly that; and partly the ceaseless nostalgia, and the solitude which came from never being really alone. In English schools the boys enjoy peculiar freedom, you know."

Bruder Kalkmann, he saw, was listening intently.

"But it produced one result that I have never wholly lost," he continued self-consciously, "and am grateful for."

"Ach! Wie so, denn?"

"The constant inner pain threw me headlong into your religious life, so that the whole force of my being seemed to project itself towards the search for a deeper satisfaction—a real resting-place for the soul. During my two years here I yearned for God in my boyish way as perhaps I have never yearned for anything since. Moreover, I have never quite lost that sense of peace and inward joy which accompanied the search. I can never quite forget this school and the deep things it taught me."

He paused at the end of his long speech, and a brief silence fell between them. He feared he had said too much, or expressed himself clumsily in the foreign language, and when Bruder Kalkmann laid a hand upon his shoulder, he gave a little involuntary start.

"So that my memories perhaps do possess me rather strongly," he added apologetically; "and this long corridor, these rooms, that barred and gloomy front door, all touch chords that—that—" His German failed him and he glanced at his companion with an explanatory smile and gesture. But the Brother had removed the hand from his shoulder and was standing with his back to him, looking down the passage.

"Naturally, naturally so," he said hastily without turning round. "*Es ist doch selbstverständlich*. We shall all understand."

Then he turned suddenly, and Harris saw that his face had turned most oddly and disagreeably sinister. It may only have been the shadows again playing their tricks with the wretched oil lamps on the wall, for the dark expression passed instantly as they retraced their steps down the corridor, but the Englishman somehow got the impression that he had said something to give offence, something that was not quite to the other's taste. Opposite the door of the *Bruderstube* they stopped. Harris realised that it was late and he had possibly stayed talking too long. He made a tentative effort to leave, but his companion would not hear of it.

"You must have a cup of coffee with us," he said firmly as though he meant it, "and my colleagues will be delighted to see you. Some of them will remember you, perhaps."

The sound of voices came pleasantly through the door, men's voices talking together. Bruder Kalkmann turned the handle and they entered a room ablaze with light and full of people.

"Ah,—but your name?" he whispered, bending down to catch the reply; "you have not told me your name yet."

"Harris," said the Englishman quickly as they went in. He felt nervous as he crossed the threshold, but ascribed the momentary trepidation to the fact that he was breaking the strictest rule of the whole establishment, which forbade a boy under severest penalties to come near this holy of holies where the masters took their brief leisure.

"Ah, yes, of course—Harris," repeated the other as though he remembered it. "Come in, Herr Harris, come in, please. Your visit will be immensely appreciated. It is really very fine, very wonderful of you to have come in this way."

The door closed behind them and, in the sudden light which made his sight swim for a moment, the exaggeration of the language escaped his attention. He heard the voice of Bruder Kalkmann introducing him. He spoke very loud, indeed, unnecessarily,—absurdly loud, Harris thought.

"Brothers," he announced, "it is my pleasure and privilege to introduce to you Herr Harris from England. He has just arrived to make us a little visit, and I have already expressed to him on behalf of us all the satisfaction we feel that he is here. He was, as you remember, a pupil in the year '70."

It was a very formal, a very German introduction, but Harris rather liked it. It made him feel important and he appreciated the tact that made it almost seem as though he had been expected.

The black forms rose and bowed; Harris bowed; Kalkmann bowed. Every one was very polite and very courtly. The room swam with moving figures; the light dazzled him after the gloom of the corridor, there was thick cigar smoke in the atmosphere. He took the chair that was offered to him between two of the Brothers, and sat down, feeling vaguely that his perceptions were not quite as keen and accurate as usual. He felt a trifle dazed perhaps, and the spell of the past came strongly over him, confusing the immediate present and making everything dwindle oddly to the dimensions of long ago. He seemed to pass under the mastery of a great mood that was a composite reproduction of all the moods of his forgotten boyhood.

Then he pulled himself together with a sharp effort and entered into the conversation that had begun again to buzz round him. Moreover, he entered into it with keen pleasure, for the Brothers—there were perhaps a dozen of them in the little room—treated him with a charm of manner that speedily made him feel one of themselves. This, again, was a very subtle delight to him. He felt that he had stepped out of the greedy, vulgar, self-seeking world, the world of silk and markets and profit-making—stepped into the cleaner atmosphere where spiritual ideals were paramount and life was simple and devoted. It all charmed him inexpressibly, so that he realised—yes, in a sense— the degradation of his twenty years' absorption in business. This keen atmosphere under the stars where men thought only of their souls, and of the souls of others, was too rarefied for the world he was now associated with. He found himself making comparisons to his own disadvantage,—comparisons with the mystical little dreamer that had stepped thirty years before from the stern peace of this devout community, and the man of the world that he had since become,—and the contrast made him shiver with a keen regret and something like self-contempt.

He glanced round at the other faces floating towards him through tobacco smoke—this acrid cigar smoke he remembered so well: how keen they were, how strong, placid, touched with the nobility of great aims and unselfish purposes. At one or two he looked particularly. He hardly knew why. They rather fascinated him. There was something so very stern and uncompromising about them, and something, too, oddly, subtly, familiar, that yet just eluded him. But whenever their eyes met his own they held undeniable welcome in them; and some held more—a kind of perplexed admiration, he thought, something that was between esteem and deference. This note of respect in all the faces was very flattering to his vanity.

Coffee was served presently, made by a black-haired Brother who sat in the corner by the piano and bore a marked resemblance to Bruder Schliemann, the musical director of thirty years ago. Harris exchanged bows with him when he took the cup from his white hands, which he noticed were like the hands of a woman. He lit a cigar, offered to him by his neighbour, with whom he was chatting delightfully, and who, in the glare of the lighted match, reminded him sharply for a moment of Bruder Pagel, his former room-master.

"*Es ist wirklich merkwürdig,*" he said, "how many resemblances I see, or imagine. It is really *very* curious!"

"Yes," replied the other, peering at him over his coffee cup, "the spell of the place is wonderfully strong. I can well understand that the old faces rise before your mind's eye—almost to the exclusion of ourselves perhaps."

They both laughed presently. It was soothing to find his mood understood and appreciated. And they passed on to talk of the mountain village, its isolation, its remoteness from worldly life, its peculiar fitness for meditation and worship, and for spiritual development—of a certain kind.

"And your coming back in this way, Herr Harris, has pleased us all so much," joined in the Bruder on his left. "We esteem you for it most highly. We honour you for it."

Harris made a deprecating gesture. "I fear, for my part, it is only a very selfish pleasure," he said a trifle unctuously.

"Not all would have had the courage," added the one who resembled Bruder Pagel.

"You mean," said Harris, a little puzzled, "the disturbing memories—?"

Bruder Pagel looked at him steadily, with unmistakable admiration and respect. "I mean that most men hold so strongly to life, and can give up so little for their beliefs," he said gravely.

The Englishman felt slightly uncomfortable. These worthy men really made too much of his sentimental journey. Besides, the talk was getting a little out of his depth. He hardly followed it.

"The worldly life still has *some* charms for me," he replied smilingly, as though to indicate that sainthood was not yet quite within his grasp.

"All the more, then, must we honour you for so freely coming," said the Brother on his left; "so unconditionally!"

A pause followed, and the silk merchant felt relieved when the conversation took a more general turn, although he noted that it never travelled very far from the subject of his visit and the wonderful situation of the lonely village for men who wished to develop their spiritual powers and practise the rites of a high worship. Others joined in, complimenting him on his knowledge of the language, making him feel utterly at his ease, yet at the same time a little uncomfortable by the excess of their admiration. After all, it was such a very small thing to do, this sentimental journey.

The time passed along quickly; the coffee was excellent, the cigars soft and of the nutty flavour he loved. At length, fearing to outstay his welcome, he rose reluctantly to take his leave. But the others would not hear of it. It was not often a former pupil returned to visit them in this simple, unaffected way. The night was young. If necessary they could even find him a corner in the great *Schlafzimmer* upstairs. He was easily persuaded to stay a little longer. Somehow he had become the centre of the little party. He felt pleased, flattered, honoured.

"And perhaps Bruder Schliemann will play something for us—now."

It was Kalkmann speaking, and Harris started visibly as he heard the name, and saw the black-haired man by the piano turn with a smile. For Schliemann was the name of his old music director, who was dead. Could this be his son? They were so exactly alike.

"If Bruder Meyer has not put his Amati to bed, I will accompany him," said the musician suggestively, looking across at a man whom Harris had not yet noticed, and who, he now saw, was the very image of a former master of that name.

Meyer rose and excused himself with a little bow, and the Englishman quickly observed that he had a peculiar gesture as though his neck had a false join on to the body just below the collar and feared it might break. Meyer of old had this trick of movement. He remembered how the boys used to copy it.

He glanced sharply from face to face, feeling as though some silent, unseen process were changing everything about him. All the faces seemed oddly familiar. Pagel, the Brother he had been talking with, was of course the image of Pagel, his former room-master, and Kalkmann, he now realised for the first time, was the very twin of another master whose name he had quite forgotten, but whom he used to dislike intensely in the old days. And, through the smoke, peering at him from the corners of the room, he saw that all the Brothers about him had the faces he had known and lived with long ago—Röst, Fluheim, Meinert, Rigel, Gysin.

He stared hard, suddenly grown more alert, and everywhere saw, or fancied he saw, strange likenesses, ghostly resemblances,—more, the identical faces of years ago. There was something queer about it all, something not quite right, something that made him feel uneasy. He shook himself, mentally and actually, blowing the smoke from before his eyes with a long breath, and as he did so he noticed to his dismay that every one was fixedly staring. They were watching him.

This brought him to his senses. As an Englishman, and a foreigner, he did not wish to be rude, or to do anything to make himself foolishly conspicuous and spoil the harmony of the evening. He was a guest, and a privileged guest at that. Besides, the music had already begun. Bruder Schliemann's long white fingers were caressing the keys to some purpose.

He subsided into his chair and smoked with half-closed eyes that yet saw everything.

But the shudder had established itself in his being, and, whether he would or not, it kept repeating itself. As a town, far up some inland river, feels the pressure of the distant sea, so he became aware that mighty forces from somewhere beyond his ken were urging themselves up against his soul in this smoky little room. He began to feel exceedingly ill at ease.

And as the music filled the air his mind began to clear. Like a lifted veil there rose up something that had hitherto obscured his vision. The words of the priest at the railway inn flashed across his brain unbidden: "You will find it different." And also, though why he could not tell, he saw mentally the strong, rather wonderful eyes of that other guest at the supper-table, the man who had overheard his conversation, and had later got into earnest talk with the priest. He took out his watch and stole a glance at it. Two hours had slipped by. It was already eleven o'clock.

Schliemann, meanwhile, utterly absorbed in his music, was playing a solemn measure. The piano sang marvellously. The power of a great conviction, the simplicity of great art, the vital spiritual message of a soul that had found itself—all this, and more, were in the chords, and yet somehow the music was what can only be described as impure—atrociously and diabolically impure. And the piece itself, although Harris did not recognise it as anything familiar, was surely the music of a Mass—huge, majestic, sombre? It stalked through the smoky room with slow power, like the passage of something that was mighty, yet profoundly intimate, and as it went there stirred into each and every face about him the signature of the enormous forces of which it was the audible symbol. The countenances round him turned sinister, but not idly, negatively sinister: they grew dark with purpose. He suddenly recalled the face of Bruder Kalkmann in the corridor earlier in the evening. The motives of their secret souls rose to the eyes, and mouths, and foreheads, and hung there for all to see like the black banners of an assembly of ill-starred and fallen creatures. Demons—was the horrible word that flashed through his brain like a sheet of fire.

When this sudden discovery leaped out upon him, for a moment he lost his self-control. Without waiting to think and weigh his extraordinary impression, he did a very foolish but a very natural thing. Feeling himself irresistibly driven by the sudden stress to some kind of action, he sprang to his feet— and screamed! To his own utter amazement he stood up and shrieked aloud!

But no one stirred. No one, apparently, took the slightest notice of his absurdly wild behaviour. It was almost as if no one but himself had heard the scream at all—as though the music had drowned it and swallowed it up—as though after all perhaps he had not really screamed as loudly as he imagined, or had not screamed at all.

Then, as he glanced at the motionless, dark faces before him, something of utter cold passed into his being, touching his very soul . . . All emotion cooled suddenly, leaving him like a receding tide. He sat down again, ashamed, mortified, angry with himself for behaving like a fool and a boy. And the music, meanwhile, continued to issue from the white and snakelike fingers of Bruder Schliemann, as poisoned wine might issue from the weirdly fashioned necks of antique phials.

And, with the rest of them, Harris drank it in.

Forcing himself to believe that he had been the victim of some kind of illusory perception, he vigorously restrained his feelings. Then the music presently ceased, and every one applauded and began to talk at once, laughing, changing seats, complimenting the player, and behaving naturally and easily as though nothing out of the way had happened. The faces appeared normal once more. The Brothers crowded round their visitor, and he joined in their talk and even heard himself thanking the gifted musician.

But, at the same time, he found himself edging towards the door, nearer and nearer, changing his chair when possible, and joining the groups that stood closest to the way of escape.

"I must thank you all *tausendmal* for my little reception and the great pleasure—the very great honour you have done me," he began in decided tones at length, "but I fear I have trespassed far too long already on your hospitality. Moreover, I have some distance to walk to my inn."

A chorus of voices greeted his words. They would not hear of his going,—at least not without first partaking of refreshment. They produced pumpernickel from one cupboard, and rye-bread and sausage from another, and all began to talk again and eat. More coffee was made, fresh cigars lighted, and Bruder Meyer took out his violin and began to tune it softly.

"There is always a bed upstairs if Herr Harris will accept it," said one.

"And it is difficult to find the way out now, for all the doors are locked," laughed another loudly.

"Let us take our simple pleasures as they come," cried a third. "Bruder Harris will understand how we appreciate the honour of this last visit of his."

They made a dozen excuses. They all laughed, as though the politeness of their words was but formal, and veiled thinly—more and more thinly—a very different meaning.

"And the hour of midnight draws near," added Bruder

Kalkmann with a charming smile, but in a voice that sounded to the Englishman like the grating of iron hinges.

Their German seemed to him more and more difficult to understand. He noted that they called him "Bruder" too, classing him as one of themselves.

And then suddenly he had a flash of keener perception, and realised with a creeping of his flesh that he had all along misinterpreted—grossly misinterpreted all they had been saying. They had talked about the beauty of the place, its isolation and remoteness from the world, its peculiar fitness for certain kinds of spiritual development and worship—yet hardly, he now grasped, in the sense in which he had taken the words. They had meant something different. Their spiritual powers, their desire for loneliness, their passion for worship, were not the powers, the solitude, or the worship that *he* meant and understood. He was playing a part in some horrible masquerade; he was among men who cloaked their lives with religion in order to follow their real purposes unseen of men.

What did it all mean? How had he blundered into so equivocal a situation? Had he blundered into it at all? Had he not rather been led into it, deliberately led? His thoughts grew dreadfully confused, and his confidence in himself began to fade. And why, he suddenly thought again, were they so impressed by the mere fact of his coming to revisit his old school? What was it they so admired and wondered at in his simple act? Why did they set such store upon his having the courage to come, to "give himself so freely," "unconditionally" as one of them had expressed it with such a mockery of exaggeration?

Fear stirred in his heart most horribly, and he found no answer to any of his questionings. Only one thing he now understood quite clearly: it was their purpose to keep him here. They did not intend that he should go. And from this moment he realised that they were sinister, formidable and, in some way he had yet to discover, inimical to himself, inimical to his life. And the phrase one of them had used a moment ago—"this *last* visit of his"—rose before his eyes in letters of flame.

Harris was not a man of action, and had never known in all the course of his career what it meant to be in a situation of real danger. He was not necessarily a coward, though, perhaps, a man of untried nerve. He realised at last plainly that he was in a very awkward predicament indeed, and that he had to deal with men who were utterly in earnest. What their intentions were he only vaguely guessed. His mind, indeed, was too confused for definite ratiocination, and he was only able to follow blindly the strongest instincts that moved in him. It never occurred to him that the Brothers might all be mad, or that he himself might have temporarily lost his senses and be suffering under some terrible delusion. In fact, nothing occurred to him—he realised nothing—except that he meant to escape—and the quicker the better. A tremendous revulsion of feeling set in and overpowered him.

Accordingly, without further protest for the moment, he ate his pumpernickel and drank his coffee, talking meanwhile as naturally and pleasantly as he could, and when a suitable interval had passed, he rose to his feet and announced once more that he must now take his leave. He spoke very quietly, but very decidedly. No one hearing him could doubt that he meant what he said. He had got very close to the door by this time.

"I regret," he said, using his best German, and speaking to a hushed room, "that our pleasant evening must come to an end, but it is now time for me to wish you all good-night." And then, as no one said anything, he added, though with a trifle less assurance, "And I thank you all most sincerely for your hospitality."

"On the contrary," replied Kalkmann instantly, rising from his chair and ignoring the hand the Englishman had stretched out to him, "it is we who have to thank you; and we do so most gratefully and sincerely."

And at the same moment at least half a dozen of the Brothers took up their position between himself and the door.

"You are very good to say so," Harris replied as firmly as he could manage, noticing this movement out of the corner of his eye, "but really I had no conception that—my little chance visit could have afforded you so much pleasure." He moved another step nearer the door, but Bruder Schliemann came across the room quickly and stood in front of him. His attitude was uncompromising. A dark and terrible expression had come into his face.

"But it was *not* by chance that you came, Bruder Harris," he said so that all the room could hear; "surely we have not misunderstood your presence here?" He raised his black eyebrows.

"No, no," the Englishman hastened to reply, "I was—I am delighted to be here. I told you what pleasure it gave me to find myself among you. Do not misunderstand me, I beg." His voice faltered a little, and he had difficulty in finding the words. More and more, too, he had difficulty in understanding *their* words.

"Of course," interposed Bruder Kalkmann in his iron bass, "*we* have not misunderstood. You have come back in the spirit of true and unselfish devotion. You offer yourself freely, and we all appreciate it. It is your willingness and nobility that have so completely won our veneration and respect." A faint murmur of applause ran round the room. "What we all delight in—what our great Master will especially delight in—is the value of your spontaneous and voluntary—"

He used a word Harris did not understand. He said "*Opfer.*" The bewildered Englishman searched his brain for the translation, and searched in vain. For the life of him he could not remember what it meant. But the word, for all his inability to translate it, touched his soul with ice. It was worse, far worse, than anything he had imagined. He felt like a lost, helpless creature, and all power to fight sank out of him from that moment.

"It is magnificent to be such a willing—" added Schliemann, sidling up to him with a dreadful leer on his face. He made use of the same word—"*Opfer.*"

"God! What could it all mean?" "Offer himself!" "True spirit of devotion!" "Willing," "unselfish," "magnificent!" *Opfer, Opfer, Opfer!* What in the name of heaven did it mean, that strange, mysterious word that struck such terror into his heart?

He made a valiant effort to keep his presence of mind and hold his nerves steady. Turning, he saw that Kalkmann's face was a dead white. Kalkmann! He understood that well enough. *Kalkmann* meant "Man of Chalk": he knew that. But what did "*Opfer*" mean? That was the real key to the situation. Words poured through his disordered mind in an endless stream— unusual, rare words he had perhaps heard but once in his life— while "*Opfer*," a word in common use, entirely escaped him. What an extraordinary mockery it all was!

Then Kalkmann, pale as death, but his face hard as iron, spoke a few low words that he did not catch, and the Brothers standing by the walls at once turned the lamps down so that the room became dim. In the half light he could only just discern their faces and movements.

"It is time," he heard Kalkmann's remorseless voice continue just behind him. "The hour of midnight is at hand. Let us prepare. He comes! He comes; Bruder Asmodelius comes!" His voice rose to a chant.

And the sound of that name, for some extraordinary reason, was terrible—utterly terrible; so that Harris shook from head to foot as he heard it. Its utterance filled the air like soft thunder, and a hush came over the whole room. Forces rose all about him, transforming the normal into the horrible, and the spirit of craven fear ran through all his being, bringing him to the verge of collapse.

Asmodelius! Asmodelius! The name was appalling. For he understood at last to whom it referred and the meaning that lay between its great syllables. At the same instant, too, he suddenly understood the meaning of that unremembered word. The import of the word "*Opfer*" flashed upon his soul like a message of death.

He thought of making a wild effort to reach the door, but the weakness of his trembling knees, and the row of black figures that stood between, dissuaded him at once. He would have screamed for help, but remembering the emptiness of the vast building, and the loneliness of the situation, he understood that no help could come that way, and he kept his lips closed. He stood still and did nothing. But he knew now what was coming.

Two of the Brothers approached and took him gently by the arm.

"Bruder Asmodelius accepts you," they whispered; "are you ready?"

Then he found his tongue and tried to speak. "But what have I to do with this Bruder Asm—Asmo—?" he stammered, a desperate rush of words crowding vainly behind the halting tongue.

The name refused to pass his lips. He could not pronounce it as they did. He could not pronounce it at all. His sense of helplessness then entered the acute stage, for this inability to speak the name produced a fresh sense of quite horrible confusion in his mind, and he became extraordinarily agitated.

"I came here for a friendly visit," he tried to say with a great effort, but, to his intense dismay, he heard his voice saying something quite different, and actually making use of that very word they had all used: "I came here as a willing *Opfer*," he heard his own voice say, "and *I am quite ready*."

He was lost beyond all recall now! Not alone his mind, but the very muscles of his body had passed out of control. He felt that he was hovering on the confines of a phantom or demon-world,—a world in which the name they had spoken constituted the Master-name, the word of ultimate power.

What followed he heard and saw as in a nightmare.

"In the half light that veils all truth, let us prepare to worship and adore," chanted Schliemann, who had preceded him to the end of the room.

"In the mists that protect our faces before the Black Throne, let us make ready the willing victim," echoed Kalkmann in his great bass.

They raised their faces, listening expectantly, as a roaring sound, like the passing of mighty projectiles, filled the air, far, far away, very wonderful, very forbidding. The walls of the room trembled.

"He comes! He comes! He comes!" chanted the Brothers in chorus.

The sound of roaring died away, and an atmosphere of still and utter cold established itself over all. Then Kalkmann, dark and unutterably stern, turned in the dim light and faced the rest.

"Asmodelius, our *Hauptbruder*, is about us," he cried in a voice that even while it shook was yet a voice of iron; "Asmodelius is about us. Make ready."

There followed a pause in which no one stirred or spoke. A tall Brother approached the Englishman; but Kalkmann held up his hand.

"Let the eyes remain uncovered," he said, "in honour of so freely giving himself." And to his horror Harris then realised for the first time that his hands were already fastened to his sides.

The Brother retreated again silently, and in the pause that followed all the figures about him dropped to their knees, leaving him standing alone, and as they dropped, in voices hushed with mingled reverence and awe, they cried, softly, odiously, appallingly, the name of the Being whom they momentarily expected to appear.

Then, at the end of the room, where the windows seemed to have disappeared so that he saw the stars, there rose into view far up against the night sky, grand and terrible, the outline of a man. A kind of grey glory enveloped it so that it resembled a steel-cased statue, immense, imposing, horrific in its distant splendour; while, at the same time, the face was so spiritually mighty, yet so proudly, so austerely sad, that Harris felt as he stared, that the sight was more than his eyes could meet, and that in another moment the power of vision would fail him altogether, and he must sink into utter nothingness.

So remote and inaccessible hung this figure that it was impossible to gauge anything as to its size, yet at the same time so strangely close, that when the grey radiance from its mightily broken visage, august and mournful, beat down upon his soul, pulsing like some dark star with the powers of spiritual evil, he felt almost as though he were looking into a face no farther removed from him in space than the face of any one of the Brothers who stood by his side.

And then the room filled and trembled with sounds that Harris understood full well were the failing voices of others who had preceded him in a long series down the years. There came first a plain, sharp cry, as of a man in the last anguish, choking for his breath, and yet, with the very final expiration of it, breathing the name of the Worship—of the dark Being who rejoiced to hear it. The cries of the strangled; the short, running gasp of the suffocated; and the smothered gurgling of the tightened throat, all these, and more, echoed back and forth between the walls, the very walls in which he now stood a prisoner, a sacrificial victim. The cries, too, not alone of the broken bodies, but—far worse—of beaten, broken souls. And as the ghastly chorus rose and fell, there came also the faces of the lost and unhappy creatures to whom they belonged, and, against that curtain of pale grey light, he saw float past him in the air, an array of white and piteous human countenances that seemed to beckon and gibber at him as though he were already one of themselves.

Slowly, too, as the voices rose, and the pallid crew sailed past, that giant form of grey descended from the sky and approached the room that contained the worshippers and their prisoner. Hands rose and sank about him in the darkness, and he felt that he was being draped in other garments than his own; a circlet of ice seemed to run about his head, while round the waist, enclosing the fastened arms, he felt a girdle tightly drawn. At last, about his very throat, there ran a soft and silken touch which, better than if there had been full light, and a mirror held to his face, he understood to be the cord of sacrifice—and of death.

At this moment the Brothers, still prostrate upon the floor, began again their mournful, yet impassioned chanting, and as they did so a strange thing happened. For, apparently without moving or altering its position, the huge Figure seemed, at once and suddenly, to be inside the room, almost beside him, and to fill the space around him to the exclusion of all else.

He was now beyond all ordinary sensations of fear, only a drab feeling as of death—the death of the soul—stirred in his heart. His thoughts no longer even beat vainly for escape. The end was near, and he knew it.

The dreadfully chanting voices rose about him in a wave: "We worship! We adore! We offer!" The sounds filled his ears and hammered, almost meaningless, upon his brain.

Then the majestic grey face turned slowly downwards upon him, and his very soul passed outwards and seemed to become absorbed in the sea of those anguished eyes. At the same moment a dozen hands forced him to his knees, and in the air before him he saw the arm of Kalkmann upraised, and felt the pressure about his throat grow strong.

It was in this awful moment, when he had given up all hope, and the help of gods or men seemed beyond question, that a strange thing happened. For before his fading and terrified vision there slid, as in a dream of light,—yet without apparent rhyme or reason—wholly unbidden and unexplained,—the face of that other man at the supper table of the railway inn. And the sight, even mentally, of that strong, wholesome, vigorous English face, inspired him suddenly with a new courage.

It was but a flash of fading vision before he sank into a dark and terrible death, yet, in some inexplicable way, the sight of that face stirred in him unconquerable hope and the certainty of deliverance. It was a face of power, a face, he now realised, of simple goodness such as might have been seen by men of old on the shores of Galilee; a face, by heaven, that could conquer even the devils of outer space.

And, in his despair and abandonment, he called upon it, and called with no uncertain accents. He found his voice in this overwhelming moment to some purpose; though the words he actually used, and whether they were in German or English, he could never remember. Their effect, nevertheless, was instantaneous. The Brothers understood, and that grey Figure of evil understood.

For a second the confusion was terrific. There came a great shattering sound. It seemed that the very earth trembled. But all Harris remembered afterwards was that voices rose about him in the clamour of terrified alarm—

"A man of power is among us! A man of God!"

The vast sound was repeated—the rushing through space as of huge projectiles—and he sank to the floor of the room, unconscious. The entire scene had vanished, vanished like smoke over the roof of a cottage when the wind blows.

And, by his side, sat down a slight un-German figure,—the figure of the stranger at the inn,—the man who had the "rather wonderful eyes."

* * * * *

When Harris came to himself he felt cold. He was lying under the open sky, and the cool air of field and forest was blowing upon his face. He sat up and looked about him. The memory of the late scene was still horribly in his mind, but no vestige of it remained. No walls or ceiling enclosed him; he was no longer in a room at all. There were no lamps turned low, no cigar smoke, no black forms of sinister worshippers, no tremendous grey Figure hovering beyond the windows.

Open space was about him, and he was lying on a pile of bricks and mortar, his clothes soaked with dew, and the kind stars shining brightly overhead. He was lying, bruised and shaken, among the heaped-up débris of a ruined building.

He stood up and stared about him. There, in the shadowy distance, lay the surrounding forest, and here, close at hand, stood the outline of the village buildings. But, underfoot, beyond question, lay nothing but the broken heaps of stones that betokened a building long since crumbled to dust. Then he saw that the stones were blackened, and that great wooden beams, half burnt, half rotten, made lines through the general débris. He stood, then, among the ruins of a burnt and shattered building, the weeds and nettles proving conclusively that it had lain thus for many years.

The moon had already set behind the encircling forest, but the stars that spangled the heavens threw enough light to enable him to make quite sure of what he saw. Harris, the silk merchant, stood among these broken and burnt stones and shivered.

Then he suddenly became aware that out of the gloom a figure had risen and stood beside him. Peering at him, he thought he recognised the face of the stranger at the railway inn.

"Are *you* real?" he asked in a voice he hardly recognised as his own.

"More than real—I'm friendly," replied the stranger; "I followed you up here from the inn."

Harris stood and stared for several minutes without adding anything. His teeth chattered. The least sound made him start; but the simple words in his own language, and the tone in which they were uttered, comforted him inconceivably.

"You're English too, thank God," he said inconsequently. "These German devils—" He broke off and put a hand to his eyes. "But what's become of them all—and the room—and— and—" The hand travelled down to his throat and moved nervously round his neck. He drew a long, long breath of relief. "Did I dream everything—everything?" he said distractedly.

He stared wildly about him, and the stranger moved forward

and took his arm. "Come," he said soothingly, yet with a trace of command in the voice, "we will move away from here. The high-road, or even the woods will be more to your taste, for we are standing now on one of the most haunted—and most terribly haunted—spots of the whole world."

He guided his companion's stumbling footsteps over the broken masonry until they reached the path, the nettles stinging their hands, and Harris feeling his way like a man in a dream. Passing through the twisted iron railing they reached the path, and thence made their way to the road, shining white in the night. Once safely out of the ruins, Harris collected himself and turned to look back.

"But, how is it possible?" he exclaimed, his voice still shaking. "How can it be possible? When I came in here I saw the building in the moonlight. They opened the door. I saw the figures and heard the voices and touched, yes touched their very hands, and saw their damned black faces, saw them far more plainly than I see you now." He was deeply bewildered. The glamour was still upon his eyes with a degree of reality stronger than the reality even of normal life. "Was I so utterly deluded?"

Then suddenly the words of the stranger, which he had only half heard or understood, returned to him.

"Haunted?" he asked, looking hard at him; "haunted, did you say?" He paused in the roadway and stared into the darkness where the building of the old school had first appeared to him. But the stranger hurried him forward.

"We shall talk more safely farther on," he said. "I followed you from the inn the moment I realised where you had gone. When I found you it was eleven o'clock—"

"Eleven o'clock," said Harris, remembering with a shudder.

"—I saw you drop. I watched over you till you recovered consciousness of your own accord, and now—now I am here to guide you safely back to the inn. I have broken the spell— the glamour—"

"I owe you a great deal, sir," interrupted Harris again,

beginning to understand something of the stranger's kindness, "but I don't understand it all. I feel dazed and shaken." His teeth still chattered, and spells of violent shivering passed over him from head to foot. He found that he was clinging to the other's arm. In this way they passed beyond the deserted and crumbling village and gained the high-road that led homewards through the forest.

"That school building has long been in ruins," said the man at his side presently; "it was burnt down by order of the Elders of the community at least ten years ago. The village has been uninhabited ever since. But the simulacra of certain ghastly events that took place under that roof in past days still continue. And the 'shells' of the chief participants still enact there the dreadful deeds that led to its final destruction, and to the desertion of the whole settlement. They were devil-worshippers!"

Harris listened with beads of perspiration on his forehead that did not come alone from their leisurely pace through the cool night. Although he had seen this man but once before in his life, and had never before exchanged so much as a word with him, he felt a degree of confidence and a subtle sense of safety and well-being in his presence that were the most healing influences he could possibly have wished after the experience he had been through. For all that, he still felt as if he were walking in a dream, and though he heard every word that fell from his companion's lips, it was only the next day that the full import of all he said became fully clear to him. The presence of this quiet stranger, the man with the wonderful eyes which he felt now, rather than saw, applied a soothing anodyne to his shattered spirit that healed him through and through. And this healing influence, distilled from the dark figure at his side, satisfied his first imperative need, so that he almost forgot to realise how strange and opportune it was that the man should be there at all.

It somehow never occurred to him to ask his name, or to

feel any undue wonder that one passing tourist should take so much trouble on behalf of another. He just walked by his side, listening to his quiet words, and allowing himself to enjoy the very wonderful experience after his recent ordeal, of being helped, strengthened, blessed. Only once, remembering vaguely something of his reading of years ago, he turned to the man beside him, after some more than usually remarkable words, and heard himself, almost involuntarily it seemed, putting the question: "Then are you a Rosicrucian, sir, perhaps?" But the stranger had ignored the words, or possibly not heard them, for he continued with his talk as though unconscious of any interruption, and Harris became aware that another somewhat unusual picture had taken possession of his mind, as they walked there side by side through the cool reaches of the forest, and that he had found his imagination suddenly charged with the childhood memory of Jacob wrestling with an angel,— wrestling all night with a being of superior quality whose strength eventually became his own.

"It was your abrupt conversation with the priest at supper that first put me upon the track of this remarkable occurrence," he heard the man's quiet voice beside him in the darkness, "and it was from him I learned after you left the story of the devil-worship that became secretly established in the heart of this simple and devout little community."

"Devil-worship! Here—!" Harris stammered, aghast.

"Yes—here;—conducted secretly for years by a group of Brothers before unexplained disappearances in the neighbourhood led to its discovery. For where could they have found a safer place in the whole wide world for their ghastly traffic and perverted powers than here, in the very precincts— under cover of the very shadow of saintliness and holy living?"

"Awful, awful!" whispered the silk merchant, "and when I tell you the words they used to me—"

"I know it all," the stranger said quietly. "I saw and heard everything. My plan first was to wait till the end and then to take steps for their destruction, but in the interest of your personal safety,"—he spoke with the utmost gravity and conviction,—"in the interest of the safety of your soul, I made my presence known when I did, and before the conclusion had been reached—"

"My safety! The danger, then, was real. They were alive and—" Words failed him. He stopped in the road and turned towards his companion, the shining of whose eyes he could just make out in the gloom.

"It was a concourse of the shells of violent men, spiritually developed but evil men, seeking after death—the death of the body—to prolong their vile and unnatural existence. And had they accomplished their object you, in turn, at the death of your body, would have passed into their power and helped to swell their dreadful purposes."

Harris made no reply. He was trying hard to concentrate his mind upon the sweet and common things of life. He even thought of silk and St. Paul's Churchyard and the faces of his partners in business.

"For you came all prepared to be caught," he heard the other's voice like some one talking to him from a distance; "your deeply introspective mood had already reconstructed the past so vividly, so intensely, that you were *en rapport* at once with any forces of those days that chanced still to be lingering. And they swept you up all unresistingly."

Harris tightened his hold upon the stranger's arm as he heard. At the moment he had room for one emotion only. It did not seem to him odd that this stranger should have such intimate knowledge of his mind.

"It is, alas, chiefly the evil emotions that are able to leave their photographs upon surrounding scenes and objects," the other added, "and who ever heard of a place haunted by a noble deed, or of beautiful and lovely ghosts revisiting the glimpses of the moon? It is unfortunate. But the wicked passions of men's hearts alone seem strong enough to leave pictures that persist;

the good are ever too lukewarm."

The stranger sighed as he spoke. But Harris, exhausted and shaken as he was to the very core, paced by his side, only half listening. He moved as in a dream still. It was very wonderful to him, this walk home under the stars in the early hours of the October morning, the peaceful forest all about them, mist rising here and there over the small clearings, and the sound of water from a hundred little invisible streams filling in the pauses of the talk. In after life he always looked back to it as something magical and impossible, something that had seemed too beautiful, too curiously beautiful, to have been quite true. And, though at the time he heard and understood but a quarter of what the stranger said, it came back to him afterwards, staying with him till the end of his days, and always with a curious, haunting sense of unreality, as though he had enjoyed a wonderful dream of which he could recall only faint and exquisite portions.

But the horror of the earlier experience was effectually dispelled; and when they reached the railway inn, somewhere about three o'clock in the morning, Harris shook the stranger's hand gratefully, effusively, meeting the look of those rather wonderful eyes with a full heart, and went up to his room, thinking in a hazy, dream-like way of the words with which the stranger had brought their conversation to an end as they left the confines of the forest—

"And if thought and emotion can persist in this way so long after the brain that sent them forth has crumbled into dust, how vitally important it must be to control their very birth in the heart, and guard them with the keenest possible restraint."

But Harris, the silk merchant, slept better than might have been expected, and with a soundness that carried him half-way through the day. And when he came downstairs and learned that the stranger had already taken his departure, he realised with keen regret that he had never once thought of asking his name.

"Yes, he signed the visitors' book," said the girl in reply to his question.

And he turned over the blotted pages and found there, the last entry, in a very delicate and individual handwriting—

"*John Silence*, London."

Case IV, *John Silence: Physician Extraordinary*, 1908

THE ATTIC

The forest-girdled village upon the Jura slopes slept soundly, although it was not yet many minutes after ten o'clock. The clang of the *couvre-feu* had indeed just ceased, its notes swept far into the woods by a wind that shook the mountains. This wind now rushed down the deserted street. It howled about the old rambling building called La Citadelle, whose roof towered gaunt and humped above the smaller houses—Château left unfinished long ago by Lord Wemyss, the exiled Jacobite. The families who occupied the various apartments listened to the storm and felt the building tremble. 'It's the mountain wind. It will bring the snow,' the mother said, without looking up from her knitting. 'And how sad it sounds.'

But it was not the wind that brought sadness as we sat round the open fire of peat. It was the wind of memories. The lamplight slanted along the narrow room towards the table where breakfast things lay ready for the morning. The double windows were fastened. At the far end stood a door ajar, and on the other side of it the two elder children lay asleep in the big bed. But beside the window was a smaller unused bed, that had been empty now a year. And tonight was the anniversary . . .

And so the wind brought sadness and long thoughts. The little chap that used to lie there was already twelve months gone, far, far beyond the Hole where the Winds came from, as he called it; yet it seemed only yesterday that I went to tell him a tuck-up story, to stroke Riquette, the old motherly cat that cuddled against his back and laid a paw beside his pillow like a human being, and to hear his funny little earnest whisper say, '*Oncle, tu sais, j'ai prié pour Petavel.*' For La Citadelle had its unhappy ghost—of Petavel, the usurer, who had hanged himself in the attic a century gone by, and was known to walk its dreary corridors in search of peace—and this wise Irish mother, calming the boys' fears with wisdom, had told him, 'If you pray for Petavel, you'll save his soul and make him happy, and he'll only love you.' And, thereafter, this little imaginative boy had done so every night. With a passionate seriousness he did it. He had wonderful, delicate ways like that. In all our hearts he made his fairy nests of wonder. In my own, I know, he lay closer than any joy imaginable, with his big blue eyes, his queer soft questionings, and his splendid child's unselfishness—a sun-kissed flower of innocence that, had he lived, might have sweetened half a world.

'Let's put more peat on,' the mother said, as a handful of rain like stones came flinging against the windows; 'that must be hail.' And she went on tiptoe to the inner room. 'They're sleeping like two puddings,' she whispered, coming presently back. But it struck me she had taken longer than to notice merely that; and her face wore an odd expression that made me uncomfortable. I thought she was somehow just about to laugh or cry. By the table a second she hesitated. I caught the flash of indecision as it passed. 'Pan,' she said suddenly—it was a nickname, stolen from my tuck-up stories, *he* had given me—'I wonder how Riquette got in.' She looked hard at me. 'It wasn't you, was it?' For we never let her come at night since he had gone. It was too poignant. The beastie always went cuddling and nestling into that empty bed. But this time it was not my doing, and I offered plausible explanations. 'But—she's on the bed. Pan, *would* you be so kind—' She left the sentence unfinished, but I easily understood, for a lump had somehow risen in my own throat too, and I remembered now that she had come out from the inner room so quickly—with a kind of hurried rush almost. I put 'mère Riquette' out into the corridor. A lamp stood on the chair outside the door of another occupant further down, and I urged her gently towards it. She turned and looked at me—straight up into my face; but, instead of going down as I suggested, she went slowly in the opposite direction. She stepped softly towards a door in the wall that led up broken stairs into the attics. There she sat down and waited. And so I left her, and came back hastily to the peat fire and companionship. The wind rushed in behind me and slammed the door.

And we talked then somewhat busily of cheerful things; of the children's future, the excellence of the cheap Swiss schools, of Christmas presents, skiing, snow, tobogganing. I led the talk away from mournfulness; and when these subjects were exhausted I told stories of my own adventures in distant parts of the world. But 'mother' listened the whole time—not to me. Her thoughts were all elsewhere. And her air of intently, secretly listening, bordered, I felt, upon the uncanny. For she often stopped her knitting and sat with her eyes fixed upon the air before her; she stared blankly at the wall, her head slightly on one side, her figure tense, attention strained—elsewhere. Or, when my talk positively demanded it, her nod was oddly mechanical and her eyes looked through and past me. The wind continued very loud and roaring; but the fire glowed, the room was warm and cosy. Yet she shivered, and when I drew attention to it, her reply, 'I do feel cold, but I didn't know I shivered,' was given as though she spoke across the air to someone else. But what impressed me even more uncomfortably were her repeated questions about Riquette. When a pause in my tales permitted, she would look up with 'I wonder where Riquette went?' or, thinking of the inclement night, 'I hope mère Riquette's not out of doors. Perhaps Madame Favre has taken her in?' I offered to go and see. Indeed I was already halfway across the room when there came the heavy bang at the door that rooted me to the ground where I stood. It was not wind. It was something alive that made it rattle. There was a second blow. A thud on the corridor boards followed, and then a high, odd voice that at first was as human as the cry of a child.

It is undeniable that we both started, and for myself I can answer truthfully that a chill ran down my spine; but what frightened me more than the sudden noise and the eerie cry was the way 'mother' supplied the immediate explanation. For behind the words 'It's only Riquette; she sometimes springs at the door like that; perhaps we'd better let her in,' was a certain touch of uncanny quiet that made me feel she had known the cat would come, and knew also why she came. One cannot explain such impressions further. They leave their vital touch, then go their way. Into the little room, however, in that moment there came between us this uncomfortable sense that the night held other purposes than our own—and that my companion was aware of them. There was something going on far, far removed from the routine of life as we were accustomed to it. Moreover, our usual routine was the eddy, while this was the main stream. It felt big, I mean.

And so it was that the entrance of the familiar, friendly creature brought this thing both itself and 'mother' knew, but whereof I as yet was ignorant. I held the door wide. The draught rushed through behind her, and sent a shower of sparks about the fireplace. The lamp flickered and gave a little gulp. And Riquette marched slowly past, with all the impressive dignity of her kind, towards the other door that stood ajar. Turning the corner like a shadow, she disappeared into the room where the two children slept. We heard the soft thud with which she leaped upon the bed. Then, in a lull of the wind, she came back again and sat on the oilcloth, staring into mother's' face. She mewed and put a paw out, drawing the black dress softly with half-opened claws. And it was all so horribly suggestive and pathetic, it revived such poignant memories, that I got up impulsively—I think I had actually said the words, 'We'd better put her out, mother, after all'—when my companion rose to her feet and forestalled me. She said another thing instead. It took my breath away to hear it. 'She wants us to go with her. Pan, will you come too?' The surprise on my face must have asked the question, for I do not remember saying anything. 'To the attic,' she said quietly.

She stood there by the table, a tall, grave figure dressed in black, and her face above the lampshade caught the full glare of light. Its expression positively stiffened me. She seemed so secure in her singular purpose. And her familiar appearance had so oddly given place to something wholly strange to me. She looked like another person—almost with the unwelcome transformation of the sleepwalker about her. Cold came over me as I watched her, for I remembered suddenly her Irish second-sight, her story years ago of meeting a figure on the attic stairs, the figure of Petavel. And the idea of this motherly, sedate, and wholesome woman, absorbed day and night in prosaic domestic duties, and yet 'seeing' things, touched the incongruous almost to the point of alarm. It was so distressingly convincing.

Yet she knew quite well that I would come. Indeed, following the excited animal, she was already by the door, and a moment later, still without answering or protesting, I was with them in the draughty corridor. There was something inevitable in her manner that made it impossible to refuse. She took the lamp from its nail on the wall, and following our four-footed guide, who ran with obvious pleasure just in front, she opened the door into the courtyard. The wind nearly put the lamp out, but a minute later we were safe inside the passage that led up flights of creaky wooden stairs towards the world of tenantless attics overhead.

And I shall never forget the way the excited Riquette first stood up and put her paws upon the various doors, trotted ahead, turned back to watch us coming, and then finally sat down and waited on the threshold of the empty, raftered space that occupied the entire length of the building underneath the roof. For her manner was more that of an intelligent dog than of a cat, and sometimes more like that of a human mind than either.

We had come up without a single word. The howling of the wind as we rose higher was like the roar of artillery. There were many broken stairs, and the narrow way was full of twists and turnings. It was a dreadful journey. I felt eyes watching us from all the yawning spaces of the darkness, and the noise of the storm smothered footsteps everywhere. Troops of shadows kept us company. But it was on the threshold of this big, chief attic, when 'mother' stopped abruptly to put down the lamp, that real fear took hold of me. For Riquette marched steadily forward into the middle of the dusty flooring, picking her way among the fallen tiles and mortar, as though she went towards—someone. She purred loudly and uttered little cries of excited pleasure. Her tail went up into the air, and she lowered her head with the unmistakable intention of being stroked. Her lips opened and shut. Her green eyes smiled. She was being stroked.

It was an unforgettable performance. I would rather have witnessed an execution or a murder than watch that mysterious creature twist and turn about in the way she did. Her magnified shadow was as large as a pony on the floor and rafters. I wanted to hide the whole thing by extinguishing the lamp. For, even before the mysterious action began, I experienced the sudden rush of conviction that others besides ourselves were in this attic—and standing very close to us indeed. And, although there was ice in my blood, there was also a strange swelling of the heart that only love and tenderness could bring.

But, whatever it was, my human companion, still silent, knew and understood. She *saw*. And her soft whisper that ran with the wind among the rafters, 'Il a prié pour Petavel et le bon Dieu l'a entendu,' did not amaze me one quarter as much as the expression I then caught upon her radiant face. Tears ran down the cheeks, but they were tears of happiness. Her whole figure seemed lit up. She opened her arms—picture of great Motherhood, proud, blessed, and tender beyond words. I thought she was going to fall, for she took quick steps forward; but when I moved to catch her, she drew me aside instead with a sudden gesture that brought fear back in the place of wonder.

'Let them pass,' she whispered grandly. 'Pan, don't you see . . . He's leading him into peace and safety . . . by the hand!' And her joy seemed to kill the shadows and fill the entire attic with white light. Then, almost simultaneously with her words, she swayed. I was in time to catch her, but as I did so, across the very spot where we had just been standing—two figures, I swear, went past us like a flood of light.

There was a moment next of such confusion that I did not see what happened to Riquette, for the sight of my companion kneeling on the dusty boards and praying with a curious sort of passionate happiness, while tears pressed between her covering fingers—the strange wonder of this made me utterly oblivious to minor details. . .

We were sitting round the peat fire again, and 'mother' was saying to me in the gentlest, tenderest whisper I ever heard from human lips—'Pan, I think perhaps that's why God took him . . .'

And when a little later we went in to make Riquette cosy in the empty bed, ever since kept sacred to her use, the mournfulness had lifted; and in the place of resignation was proud peace and joy that knew no longer sad or selfish questionings.

Bôle

Pan's Garden, 1912

THE TRANSFER

The child began to cry in the early afternoon—about three o'clock, to be exact. I remember the hour, because I had been listening with secret relief to the sound of the departing carriage. Those wheels fading into the distance down the gravel drive with Mrs. Frene, and her daughter Gladys to whom I was governess, meant for me some hours' welcome rest, and the June day was oppressively hot. Moreover, there was this excitement in the little country household that had told upon us all, but especially upon myself. This excitement, running delicately behind all the events of the morning, was due to some mystery, and the mystery was of course kept concealed from the governess. I had exhausted myself with guessing and keeping on the watch. For some deep and unexplained anxiety possessed me, so that I kept thinking of my sister's dictum that I was really much too sensitive to make a good governess, and that I should have done far better as a professional clairvoyante.

Mr. Frene, senior, 'Uncle Frank,' was expected for an unusual visit from town about teatime. That I knew. I also knew that his visit was concerned somehow with the future welfare of little Jamie, Gladys' seven-year-old brother. More than this, indeed, I never knew, and this missing link makes my story in a fashion incoherent—an important bit of the strange puzzle left out. I only gathered that the visit of Uncle Frank was of a condescending nature, that Jamie was told he must be upon his very best behaviour to make a good impression, and that Jamie, who had never seen his uncle, dreaded him horribly already in advance. Then, trailing thinly through the dying crunch of the carriage wheels this sultry afternoon, I heard the curious little wail of the child's crying, with the effect, wholly unaccountable, that every nerve in my body shot its bolt electrically, bringing me to my feet with a tingling of unequivocal alarm. Positively, the water ran into my eyes. I recalled his white distress that morning when told that Uncle Frank was motoring down for tea and that he was to be 'very nice indeed' to him. It had gone into me like a knife. All through the day, indeed, had run this nightmare quality of terror and vision.

'The man with the 'normous face?' he had asked in a little voice of awe, and then gone speechless from the room in tears that no amount of soothing management could calm. That was all I saw; and what he meant by 'the 'normous face' gave me only a sense of vague presentiment. But it came as anticlimax somehow—a sudden revelation of the mystery and excitement that pulsed beneath the quiet of the stifling summer day. I feared for him. For of all that commonplace household I loved Jamie best, though professionally I had nothing to do with him. He was a high-strung, ultra-sensitive child, and it seemed to me that no one understood him, least of all his honest, tender-hearted parents; so that his little wailing voice brought me from my bed to the window in a moment like a call for help.

The haze of June lay over that big garden like a blanket; the wonderful flowers, which were Mr. Frene's delight, hung motionless; the lawns, so soft and thick, cushioned all other sounds; only the limes and huge clumps of guelder roses hummed with bees. Through this muted atmosphere of heat and haze the sound of the child's crying floated faintly to my ears—from a distance. Indeed, I wonder now that I heard it at all, for the next moment I saw him down beyond the garden, standing in his white sailor suit alone, two hundred yards away. He was down by the ugly patch where nothing grew—the Forbidden Corner. A faintness then came over me at once, a faintness as of death, when I saw him *there* of all places-where he never was allowed to go, and where, moreover, he was usually too terrified to go. To see him standing solitary in that singular spot, above all to hear him crying there, bereft me momentarily of the power to act. Then, before I could recover my composure sufficiently to call him in, Mr. Frene came round the corner from the Lower Farm with the dogs, and, seeing his son, performed that office for me. In his loud, good-natured, hearty voice he called him, and Jamie turned and ran as though some spell had broken just in time—ran into the open arms of his fond but uncomprehending father, who carried him indoors on his shoulder, while asking 'what all this hubbub was about?' And, at their heels, the tailless sheepdogs followed, barking loudly, and performing what Jamie called their 'Gravel Dance,' because they ploughed up the moist, rolled gravel with their feet.

I stepped back swiftly from the window lest I should be seen. Had I witnessed the saving of the child from fire or drowning the relief could hardly have been greater. Only Mr. Frene, I felt sure, would not say and do the right thing quite. He would protect the boy from his own vain imaginings, yet not with the explanation that could really heal. They disappeared behind the rose trees, making for the house. I saw no more till later, when Mr. Frene, senior, arrived.

* * * * *

To describe the ugly patch as 'singular' is hard to justify, perhaps, yet some such word is what the entire family sought, though never—oh, never!—used. To Jamie and myself, though equally we never mentioned it, that treeless, flowerless spot was more than singular. It stood at the far end of the magnificent rose garden, a bald, sore place, where the black earth showed uglily in winter, almost like a piece of dangerous bog, and in summer baked and cracked with fissures where green lizards shot their fire in passing. In contrast to the rich luxuriance of death amid life, a centre of disease that cried for healing lest it spread. But it never did spread. Behind it stood the thick wood of silver birches and, glimmering beyond, the orchard meadow, where the lambs played.

The gardeners had a very simple explanation of its barrenness—that the water all drained off it owing to the lie of the slopes immediately about it, holding no remnant to keep the soil alive. I cannot say. It was Jamie—Jamie who felt its spell and haunted it, who spent whole hours there, even while afraid, and for whom it was finally labelled 'strictly out of bounds' because it stimulated his already big imagination, not wisely but too darkly—it was Jamie who buried ogres there and heard it crying in an earthy voice, swore that it shook its surface sometimes while he watched it, and secretly gave it food in the form of birds or mice or rabbits he found dead upon his wanderings. And it was Jamie who put so extraordinarily into words the *feeling* that the horrid spot had given me from the moment I first saw it.

'It's bad, Miss Gould,' he told me.

'But, Jamie, nothing in Nature is bad—exactly; only different from the rest sometimes.'

'Miss Gould, if you please, then it's empty. It's not fed. It's dying because it can't get the food it wants.' And when I stared into the little pale face where the eyes shone so dark and wonderful, seeking within myself for the right thing to say to him, he added, with an emphasis and conviction that made me suddenly turn cold: 'Miss Gould'—he always used my name like this in all his sentences—'it's hungry, don't you see? But I know what would make it feel all right.'

Only the conviction of an earnest child, perhaps, could have made so outrageous a suggestion worth listening to for an instant; but for me, who felt that things an imaginative child believed were important, it came with a vast disquieting shock of reality. Jamie, in this exaggerated way, had caught at the edge of a shocking fact—a hint of dark, undiscovered truth had leaped into that sensitive imagination. Why there lay horror in the words I cannot say, but I think some power of darkness trooped across the suggestion of that sentence at the end, 'I know what would make it feel all right.' I remember that I shrank from asking explanation. Small groups of other words, veiled fortunately by his silence, gave life to an unspeakable possibility that hitherto had lain at the back of my own consciousness. The way it sprang to life proves, I think, that my mind already contained it. The blood rushed from my heart as I listened. I remember that my knees shook. Jamie's idea was—had been all along—my own as well.

And now, as I lay down on my bed and thought about it all, I understood why the coming of his uncle involved somehow an experience that wrapped terror at its heart. With a sense of nightmare certainty that left me too weak to resist the preposterous idea, too shocked, indeed, to argue or reason it away, this certainty came with its full, black blast of conviction; and the only way I can put it into words, since nightmare horror really is not properly tellable at all, seems this: that there was something missing in that dying patch of garden; something lacking that it ever searched for; something, once found and taken, that would turn it rich and living as the rest; more—that there *was* some living person who could do this for it. Mr. Frene, senior, in a word, 'Uncle Frank,' was this person who out of his abundant life could supply the lack—unwittingly.

For this connection between the dying, empty patch and the person of this vigorous, wealthy, and successful man had already lodged itself in my subconsciousness before I was aware of it. Clearly it must have lain there all along, though hidden. Jamie's words, his sudden pallor, his vibrating emotion of fearful anticipation had developed the plate, but it was his weeping alone there in the Forbidden Corner that had printed it. The photograph shone framed before me in the air. I hid my eyes. But for the redness—the charm of my face goes to pieces unless my eyes are clear—I could have cried. Jamie's words that morning about the "normous face' came back upon me like a battering-ram.

Mr. Frene, senior, had been so frequently the subject of conversation in the family since I came, I had so often heard him discussed, and had then read so much about him in the papers—

his energy, his philanthropy, his success with everything he laid his hand to—that a picture of the man had grown complete within me. I knew him as he was—within; or, as my sister would have said—clairvoyantly. And the only time I saw him (when I took Gladys to a meeting where he was chairman, and later *felt* his atmosphere and presence while for a moment he patronisingly spoke with her) had justified the portrait I had drawn. The rest, you may say, was a woman's wild imagining; but I think rather it was that kind of divining intuition which women share with children. If souls could be made visible, I would stake my life upon the truth and accuracy of my portrait.

For this Mr. Frene was a man who drooped alone, but grew vital in a crowd—because he used their vitality. He was a supreme, unconscious artist in the science of taking the fruits of others' work and living—for his own advantage. He vampired, unknowingly no doubt, everyone with whom he came in contact; left them exhausted, tired, listless. Others fed him, so that while in a full room he shone, alone by himself and with no life to draw upon he languished and declined. In the man's immediate neighbourhood you felt his presence draining you; he took your ideas, your strength, your very words, and later used them for his own benefit and aggrandisement. Not evilly, of course; the man was good enough; but you felt that he was dangerous owing to the facile way he absorbed into himself all loose vitality that was to be had. His eyes and voice and presence devitalised you. Life, it seemed, not highly organised enough to resist, must shrink from his too near approach and hide away for fear of being appropriated, for fear, that is, of—death.

Jamie, unknowingly, put in the finishing touch to my unconscious portrait. The man carried about with him some silent, compelling trick of drawing out all your reserves—then swiftly pocketing them. At first you would be conscious of taut resistance; this would slowly shade off into weariness; the will would become flaccid; then you either moved away or yielded— agreed to all he said with a sense of weakness pressing ever closer upon the edges of collapse. With a male antagonist it might be different, but even then the effort of resistance would generate force that *he* absorbed and not the other. He never gave out. Some instinct taught him how to protect himself from that. To human beings, I mean, he never gave out. This time it was a very different matter. He had no more chance than a fly before the wheels of a huge—what Jamie used to call—'attraction' engine.

So this was how I saw him—a great human sponge, crammed and soaked with the life, or proceeds of life, absorbed from others—stolen. My idea of a human vampire was satisfied. He went about carrying these accumulations of the life of others. In this sense his 'life' was not really his own. For the same reason, I think, it was not so fully under his control as he imagined.

* * * * *

And in another hour this man would be here. I went to the window. My eye wandered to the empty patch, dull black there amid the rich luxuriance of the garden flowers. It struck me as a hideous bit of emptiness yawning to be filled and nourished. The idea of Jamie playing round its bare edge was loathsome. I watched the big summer clouds above, the stillness of the afternoon, the haze. The silence of the overheated garden was oppressive. I had never felt a day so stifling, motionless. It lay there waiting. The household, too, was waiting—waiting for the coming of Mr. Frene from London in his big motorcar.

And I shall never forget the sensation of icy shrinking and distress with which I heard the rumble of the car. He had arrived. Tea was all ready on the lawn beneath the lime trees, and Mrs. Frene and Gladys, back from their drive, were sitting in wicker chairs. Mr. Frene, junior, was in the hall to meet his brother, but Jamie, as I learned afterwards, had shown such hysterical alarm, offered such bold resistance, that it had been deemed wiser to keep him in his room. Perhaps, after all, his presence might not be necessary. The visit clearly had to do with something on the uglier side of life—money, settlements, or whatnot; I never knew exactly; only that his parents were anxious, and that Uncle Frank had to be propitiated. It does not matter. That has nothing to do with the affair. What has to do with it—or I should not be telling the story—is that Mrs. Frene sent for me to come down 'in my nice white dress, if I didn't mind,' and that I was terrified, yet pleased, because it meant that a pretty face would be considered a welcome addition to the visitor's landscape. Also, most odd it was, I felt my presence was somehow inevitable, that in some way it was intended that I should witness what I did witness. And the instant I came upon the lawn—I hesitate to set it down, it sounds so foolish, disconnected—I could have sworn, as my eyes met his, that a kind of sudden darkness came, taking the summer brilliance out of everything, and that it was caused by troops of small black horses that raced about us from his person—to attack.

After a first momentary approving glance he took no further notice of me. The tea and talk went smoothly; I helped to pass the plates and cups, filling in pauses with little under-talk to Gladys. Jamie was never mentioned. Outwardly all seemed well, but inwardly everything was awful—skirting the edge of things unspeakable, and so charged with danger that I could not keep my voice from trembling when I spoke.

I watched his hard, bleak face; I noticed how thin he was, and the curious, oily brightness of his steady eyes. They did not glitter, but they drew you with a sort of soft, creamy shine like Eastern eyes. And everything he said or did announced what I may dare to call the *suction* of his presence. His nature achieved this result automatically. He dominated us all, yet so gently that until it was accomplished no one noticed it.

Before five minutes had passed, however, I was aware of one thing only. My mind focused exclusively upon it, and so vividly that I marvelled the others did not scream, or run, or do something violent to prevent it. And it was this; that, separated merely by some dozen yards or so, this man, vibrating with the acquired vitality of others, stood within easy reach of that spot of yawning emptiness, waiting and eager to be filled. Earth scented her prey.

These two active 'centres' were within fighting distance; he so thin, so hard, so keen, yet really spreading large with the loose 'surround' of others' life he had appropriated, so practised and triumphant; that other so patient, deep, with so mighty a draw of the whole earth behind it, and—ugh!—so obviously aware that its opportunity at last had come.

I saw it all as plainly as though I watched two great animals prepare for battle, both unconsciously; yet in some inexplicable way I saw it, of course, within me, and not externally. The conflict would be hideously unequal. Each side had already sent out emissaries, how long before I could not tell, for the first evidence *he* gave that something was going wrong with him was when his voice grew suddenly confused, he missed his words, and his lips trembled a moment and turned flabby. The next second his face betrayed that singular and horrid change, growing somehow loose about the bones of the cheek, and larger, so that I remembered Jamie's miserable phrase. The emissaries of the two kingdoms, the human and the vegetable, had met, I make it out, in that very second. For the first time in his long career of battening on others, Mr. Frene found himself pitted against a vaster kingdom than he knew and, so finding, shook inwardly in that little part that was his definite actual self. He felt the huge disaster coming.

'Yes, John,' he was saying, in his drawling, self-congratulating voice, 'Sir George gave me that car—gave it to me as a present. Wasn't it char—?' and then broke off abruptly, stammered, drew breath, stood up, and looked uneasily about him. For a second there was a gaping pause. It was like the click which starts some huge machinery moving—that instant's pause before it actually starts. The whole thing, indeed, then went with the rapidity of machinery running down and beyond control. I thought of a giant dynamo working silently and invisible.

'What's that?' he cried, in a soft voice charged with alarm. 'What's that horrid place? And someone's crying there—who is it?'

He pointed to the empty patch. Then, before anyone could answer, he started across the lawn towards it, going every minute faster. Before anyone could move he stood upon the edge. He leaned over—peering down into it.

It seemed a few hours passed, but really they were seconds, for time is measured by the quality and not the quantity of sensations it contains. I saw it all with merciless, photographic detail, sharply etched amid the general confusion. Each side was intensely active, but only one side, the human, exerted *all* its force—in resistance. The other merely stretched out a feeler, as it were, from its vast, potential strength; no more was necessary. It was such a soft and easy victory. Oh, it was rather pitiful! There was no bluster or great effort, on one side at least. Close by his side I witnessed it, for I, it seemed, alone had moved and followed him. No one else stirred, though Mrs. Frene clattered noisily with the cups, making some sudden impulsive gesture with her hands, and Gladys, I remember, gave a cry—it was like a little scream—'Oh, mother, it's the heat, isn't it?' Mr. Frene, her father, was speechless, pale as ashes.

But the instant I reached his side, it became clear what had drawn me there thus instinctively. Upon the other side, among the silver birches, stood little Jamie. He was watching. I experienced—for him—one of those moments that shake the heart; a liquid fear ran all over me, the more effective because unintelligible really. Yet I felt that if I could know all, and what lay actually behind, my fear would be more than justified; that the thing was awful, full of awe.

And then it happened—a truly wicked sight—like watching a universe in action, yet all contained within a small square foot of space. I think he understood vaguely that if someone could only take his place he might be saved, and that was why, discerning instinctively the easiest substitute within reach, he saw the child and called aloud to him across the empty patch, 'James, my boy, come here!'

His voice was like a thin report, but somehow flat and lifeless, as when a rifle misses fire, sharp, yet weak; it had no 'crack' in it. It was really supplication. And, with amazement, I heard my own ring out imperious and strong, though I was not conscious of saying it, 'Jamie, don't move. Stay where you are!' But Jamie, the little child, obeyed neither of us. Moving up nearer to the edge, he stood there—laughing! I heard that laughter, but could have sworn it did not come from him. The empty, yawning patch gave out that sound.

Mr. Frene turned sideways, throwing up his arms. I saw his hard, bleak face grow somehow wider, spread through the air, and downwards. A similar thing, I saw, was happening at the same time to his entire person, for it drew out into the atmosphere in a stream of movement. The face for a second made me think of those toys of green india-rubber that children pull. It grew enormous. But this was an external impression only. What actually happened, I clearly understood, was that all this vitality and life he had transferred from others to himself for years was now in turn being taken from him and transferred—elsewhere.

One moment on the edge he wobbled horribly, then with that queer sideways motion, rapid yet ungainly, he stepped forward into the middle of the patch and fell heavily upon his face. His eyes, as he dropped, faded shockingly, and across the countenance was written plainly what I can only call an expression of destruction. He looked utterly destroyed. I caught a sound—from Jamie?—but this time not of laughter. It was like a gulp; it was deep and muffled and it dipped away into the earth. Again I thought of a troop of small black horses galloping away down a subterranean passage beneath my feet—plunging into the depths—their tramping growing fainter and fainter into buried distance. In my nostrils was a pungent smell of earth.

* * * * *

And then—all passed. I came back into myself. Mr. Frene, junior, was lifting his brother's head from the lawn where he had fallen from the heat, close beside the tea-table. He had never really moved from there. And Jamie, I learned afterwards, had been the whole time asleep upon his bed upstairs, worn out with his crying and unreasoning alarm. Gladys came running out with cold water, sponge and towel, brandy too—all kinds of things. 'Mother, it *was* the heat, wasn't it?' I heard her whisper, but I did not catch Mrs. Frene's reply. From her face it struck me that she was bordering on collapse herself. Then the butler followed, and they just picked him up and carried him into the house. He recovered even before the doctor came.

But the queer thing to me is that I was convinced the others all had seen what I saw, only that no one said a word about it; and to this day no one *has* said a word. And that was, perhaps, the most horrid part of all.

From that day to this I have scarcely heard a mention of Mr. Frene, senior. It seemed as if he dropped suddenly out of life. The papers never mentioned him. His activities ceased, as it were. His afterlife, at any rate, became singularly ineffective. Certainly he achieved nothing worth public mention. But it may be only that, having left the employ of Mrs. Frene, there was no particular occasion for me to hear anything.

The afterlife of that empty patch of garden, however, was quite otherwise. Nothing, so far as I know, was done to it by gardeners, or in the way of draining it or bringing in new earth, but even before I left in the following summer it had changed. It lay untouched, full of great, luscious, driving weeds and creepers, very strong, full—fed, and bursting thick with life.

Sandhills.

Pan's Garden, 1912

THE EMPTY SLEEVE

I

The Gilmer brothers were a couple of fussy and pernickety old bachelors of a rather retiring, not to say timid, disposition. There was grey in the pointed beard of John, the elder, and if any hair had remained to William it would also certainly have been of the same shade. They had private means. Their main interest in life was the collection of violins, for which they had the instinctive flair of true connoisseurs. Neither John nor William, however, could play a single note. They could only pluck the open strings. The production of tone, so necessary before purchase, was done vicariously for them by another.

The only objection they had to the big building in which they occupied the roomy top floor was that Morgan, liftman and caretaker, insisted on wearing a billycock with his uniform after six o'clock in the evening, with a result disastrous to the beauty of the universe. For "Mr. Morgan," as they called him between themselves, had a round and pasty face on the top of a round and conical body. In view, however, of the man's other rare qualities—including his devotion to themselves—this objection was not serious.

He had another peculiarity that amused them. On being found fault with, he explained nothing, but merely repeated the words of the complaint.

"Water in the bath wasn't really hot this morning, Morgan!"

"Water in the bath not reely 'ot, wasn't it, sir?"

Or, from William, who was something of a faddist:

"My jar of sour milk came up late yesterday, Morgan."

"Your jar sour milk come up late, sir, yesterday?"

Since, however, the statement of a complaint invariably resulted in its remedy, the brothers had learned to look for no further explanation. Next morning the bath *was* hot, the sour milk *was* "brortup" punctually. The uniform and billycock hat, though, remained an eyesore and source of oppression.

On this particular night John Gilmer, the elder, returning from a Masonic rehearsal, stepped into the lift and found Mr. Morgan with his hand ready on the iron rope.

"Fog's very thick outside," said Mr. John pleasantly; and the lift was a third of the way up before Morgan had completed his customary repetition: "Fog very thick outside, yes, sir." And Gilmer then asked casually if his brother were alone, and received the reply that Mr. Hyman had called and had not yet gone away.

Now this Mr. Hyman was a Hebrew, and, like themselves, a connoisseur in violins, but, unlike themselves, who only kept their specimens to look at, he was a skilful and exquisite player. He was the only person they ever permitted to handle their pedigree instruments, to take them from the glass cases where they reposed in silent splendour, and to draw the sound out of their wondrous painted hearts of golden varnish. The brothers loathed to see his fingers touch them, yet loved to hear their singing voices in the room, for the latter confirmed their sound judgment as collectors, and made them certain their money had been well spent. Hyman, however, made no attempt to conceal his contempt and hatred for the mere collector. The atmosphere of the room fairly pulsed with these opposing forces of silent emotion when Hyman played and the Gilmers, alternately writhing and admiring, listened. The occasions, however, were not frequent. The Hebrew only came by invitation, and both brothers made a point of being in. It was a very formal proceeding—something of a sacred rite almost.

John Gilmer, therefore, was considerably surprised by the information Morgan had supplied. For one thing, Hyman, he had understood, was away on the Continent.

"Still in there, you say?" he repeated, after a moment's reflection.

"Still in there, Mr. John, sir." Then, concealing his surprise from the liftman, he fell back upon his usual mild habit of complaining about the billycock hat and the uniform.

"You really should try and remember, Morgan," he said, though kindly. "That hat does *not* go well with that uniform!"

Morgan's pasty countenance betrayed no vestige of expression. "'At don't go well with the yewniform, sir," he repeated, hanging up the disreputable bowler and replacing it with a gold-braided cap from the peg. "No, sir, it don't, do it?" he added cryptically, smiling at the transformation thus effected.

And the lift then halted with an abrupt jerk at the top floor. By somebody's carelessness the landing was in darkness, and, to make things worse, Morgan, clumsily pulling the iron rope, happened to knock the billycock from its peg so that his sleeve, as he stooped to catch it, struck the switch and plunged the scene in a moment's complete obscurity.

And it was then, in the act of stepping out before the light was turned on again, that John Gilmer stumbled against something that shot along the landing past the open door. First he thought it must be a child, then a man, then—an animal. Its movement was rapid yet stealthy. Starting backwards instinctively to allow it room to pass, Gilmer collided in the darkness with Morgan, and Morgan incontinently screamed. There was a moment of stupid confusion. The heavy framework of the lift shook a little, as though something had stepped into it and then as quickly jumped out again. A rushing sound followed that resembled footsteps, yet at the same time was more like gliding—someone in soft slippers or stockinged feet, greatly hurrying. Then came silence again. Morgan sprang to the landing and turned up the electric light. Mr. Gilmer, at the same moment, did likewise to the switch in the lift. Light flooded the scene. Nothing was visible.

"Dog or cat, or something, I suppose, wasn't it?" exclaimed Gilmer, following the man out and looking round with bewildered amazement upon a deserted landing. He knew quite well, even while he spoke, that the words were foolish.

"Dog or cat, yes, sir, or—something," echoed Morgan, his eyes narrowed to pinpoints, then growing large, but his face stolid.

"The light should have been on." Mr. Gilmer spoke with a touch of severity. The little occurrence had curiously disturbed his equanimity. He felt annoyed, upset, uneasy.

For a perceptible pause the liftman made no reply, and his employer, looking up, saw that, besides being flustered, he was white about the jaws. His voice, when he spoke, was without its normal assurance. This time he did not merely repeat. He explained.

"The light *was* on, sir, when last *I* come up!" he said, with emphasis, obviously speaking the truth. "Only a moment ago," he added.

Mr. Gilmer, for some reason, felt disinclined to press for explanations. He decided to ignore the matter.

Then the lift plunged down again into the depths like a diving-bell into water; and John Gilmer, pausing a moment first to reflect, let himself in softly with his latchkey, and, after hanging up hat and coat in the hall, entered the big sitting-room he and his brother shared in common.

The December fog that covered London like a dirty blanket had penetrated, he saw, into the room. The objects in it were half shrouded in the familiar yellowish haze.

II

In dressing-gown and slippers, William Gilmer, almost invisible in his armchair by the gas-stove across the room, spoke at once. Through the thick atmosphere his face gleamed, showing an extinguished pipe hanging from his lips. His tone of voice conveyed emotion, an emotion he sought to suppress, of a quality, however, not easy to define.

"Hyman's been here," he announced abruptly. "You must have met him. He's this very instant gone out."

It was quite easy to see that something had happened, for "scenes" leave disturbance behind them in the atmosphere. But John made no immediate reference to this. He replied that he had seen no one—which was strictly true—and his brother thereupon, sitting bolt upright in the chair, turned quickly and faced him. His skin, in the foggy air, seemed paler than before.

"That's odd," he said nervously.

"What's odd?" asked John.

"That you didn't see—anything. You ought to have run into one another on the doorstep." His eyes went peering about the room. He was distinctly ill at ease. "You're positive you saw no one? Did Morgan take him down before you came? Did Morgan see him?" He asked several questions at once.

"On the contrary, Morgan told me he was still here with you. Hyman probably walked down, and didn't take the lift at all," he replied. "That accounts for neither of us seeing him." He decided to say nothing about the occurrence in the lift, for his brother's nerves, he saw plainly, were on edge.

William then stood up out of his chair, and the skin of his face changed its hue, for whereas a moment ago it was merely pale, it had now altered to a tint that lay somewhere between white and a livid grey. The man was fighting internal terror. For a moment these two brothers of middle age looked each other straight in the eye. Then John spoke:

"What's wrong, Billy?" he asked quietly. "Something's upset you. What brought Hyman in this way—unexpectedly? I thought he was still in Germany."

The brothers, affectionate and sympathetic, understood one another perfectly. They had no secrets. Yet for several minutes the younger one made no reply. It seemed difficult to choose his words apparently.

"Hyman played, I suppose—on the fiddles?" John helped him, wondering uneasily what was coming. He did not care much for the individual in question, though his talent was of such great use to them.

The other nodded in the affirmative, then plunged into rapid speech, talking under his breath as though he feared someone might overhear. Glancing over his shoulder down the foggy room, he drew his brother close.

"Hyman came," he began, "unexpectedly. He hadn't written, and I hadn't asked him. You hadn't either, I suppose?"

John shook his head.

"When I came in from the dining-room I found him in the passage. The servant was taking away the dishes, and he had let himself in while the front door was ajar. Pretty cool, wasn't it?"

"He's an original," said John, shrugging his shoulders. "And you welcomed him?" he asked.

"I asked him in, of course. He explained he had something glorious for me to hear. Silenski had played it in the afternoon, and he had bought the music since. But Silenski's 'Strad' hadn't the power—it's thin on the upper strings, you remember, unequal, patchy—and he said no instrument in the world could do it justice but our 'Joseph'—the small Guarnerius, you know, which he swears is the most perfect in the world."

"And what was it? Did he play it?" asked John, growing more uneasy as he grew more interested. With relief he glanced round and saw the matchless little instrument lying there safe and sound in its glass case near the door.

"He played it—divinely: a Zigeuner Lullaby, a fine, passionate, rushing bit of inspiration, oddly misnamed 'lullaby.' And, fancy, the fellow had memorized it already! He walked about the room on tiptoe while he played it, complaining of the light—"

"Complaining of the light?"

"Said the thing was crepuscular, and needed dusk for its full effect. I turned the lights out one by one, till finally there was only the glow of the gas logs. He insisted. You know that way he has with him? And then he got over me in another matter: insisted on using some special strings he had brought with him, and put them on, too, himself—thicker than the A and E *we* use."

For though neither Gilmer could produce a note, it was their pride that they kept their precious instruments in perfect condition for playing, choosing the exact thickness and quality of strings that suited the temperament of each violin; and the little Guarnerius in question always "sang" best, they held, with thin strings.

"Infernal insolence," exclaimed the listening brother, wondering what was coming next. "Played it well, though, didn't he, this Lullaby thing?" he added, seeing that William hesitated. As he spoke he went nearer, sitting down close beside him in a leather chair.

"Magnificent! Pure fire of genius!" was the reply with enthusiasm, the voice at the same time dropping lower. "Staccato like a silver hammer; harmonics like flutes, clear, soft, ringing; and the tone—well, the G string was a baritone, and the upper registers creamy and mellow as a boy's voice. John," he added, "that Guarnerius is the very pick of the period and"—again he hesitated—"Hyman loves it. He'd give his soul to have it."

The more John heard, the more uncomfortable it made him. He had always disliked this gifted Hebrew, for in his secret heart he knew that he had always feared and distrusted him. Sometimes he had felt half afraid of him; the man's very forcible personality was too insistent to be pleasant. His type was of the dark and sinister kind, and he possessed a violent will that rarely failed of accomplishing its desire.

"Wish I'd heard the fellow play," he said at length, ignoring his brother's last remark, and going on to speak of the most matter-of-fact details he could think of. "Did he use the Dodd bow, or the Tourte? That Dodd I picked up last month, you know, is the most perfectly balanced I have ever—"

He stopped abruptly, for William had suddenly got upon his feet and was standing there, searching the room with his eyes. A chill ran down John's spine as he watched him.

"What is it, Billy?" he asked sharply. "Hear anything?"

William continued to peer about him through the thick air.

"Oh, nothing, probably," he said, an odd catch in his voice; "only—I keep feeling as if there was somebody listening. Do you think, perhaps"—he glanced over his shoulder—"there is someone at the door? I wish—I wish you'd have a look, John."

John obeyed, though without great eagerness. Crossing the room slowly, he opened the door, then switched on the light. The passage leading past the bathroom towards the bedrooms beyond was empty. The coats hung motionless from their pegs.

"No one, of course," he said, as he closed the door and came back to the stove. He left the light burning in the passage. It was curious the way both brothers had this impression that they were not alone, though only one of them spoke of it.

"Used the Dodd or the Tourte, Billy—which?" continued John in the most natural voice he could assume.

But at that very same instant the water started to his eyes. His brother, he saw, was close upon the thing he really had to tell. But he had stuck fast.

III

By a great effort John Gilmer composed himself and remained in his chair. With detailed elaboration he lit a cigarette, staring hard at his brother over the flaring match while he did so. There he sat in his dressing-gown and slippers by the fireplace, eyes downcast, fingers playing idly with the red tassel. The electric light cast heavy shadows across the face. In a flash then, since emotion may sometimes express itself in attitude even better than in speech, the elder brother understood that Billy was about to tell him an unutterable thing.

By instinct he moved over to his side so that the same view of the room confronted him.

"Out with it, old man," he said, with an effort to be natural. "Tell me what you saw."

Billy shuffled slowly round and the two sat side by side, facing the fog-draped chamber.

"It was like this," he began softly, "only I was standing instead of sitting, looking over to that door as you and I do now. Hyman moved to and fro in the faint glow of the gas logs against the far wall, playing that 'crepuscular' thing in his most inspired sort of way, so that the music seemed to issue from himself rather than from the shining bit of wood under his chin, when—I noticed something coming over me that was"—he hesitated, searching for words—"that wasn't *all* due to the music," he finished abruptly.

"His personality put a bit of hypnotism on you, eh?"

William shrugged his shoulders.

"The air was thickish with fog and the light was dim, cast upwards upon him from the stove," he continued. "I admit all that. But there wasn't light enough to throw shadows, you see, and—"

"Hyman looked queer?" the other helped him quickly.

Billy nodded his head without turning.

"Changed there before my very eyes"—he whispered it—"turned animal—"

"Animal?" John felt his hair rising.

"That's the only way I can put it. His face and hands and body turned otherwise than usual. I lost the sound of his feet. When the bow-hand or the fingers on the strings passed into the light, they were"—he uttered a soft, shuddering little laugh—"furry, oddly divided, the fingers massed together. And he paced stealthily. I thought every instant the fiddle would drop with a crash and he would spring at me across the room."

"My dear chap—"

"He moved with those big, lithe, striding steps one sees"—John held his breath in the little pause, listening keenly—"one sees those big brutes make in the cages when their desire is aflame for food or escape, or—or fierce, passionate desire for anything they want with their whole nature—"

"The big felines!" John whistled softly.

"And every minute getting nearer and nearer to the door, as though he meant to make a sudden rush for it and get out."

"With the violin! Of course you stopped him?"

"In the end. But for a long time, I swear to you, I found it difficult to know what to do, even to move. I couldn't get my voice for words of any kind; it was like a spell."

"It *was* a spell," suggested John firmly.

"Then, as he moved, still playing," continued the other, "he seemed to grow smaller; to shrink down below the line of the gas. I thought I should lose sight of him altogether. I turned the light up suddenly. There he was over by the door—crouching."

"Playing on his knees, you mean?"

William closed his eyes in an effort to visualize it again.

"Crouching," he repeated, at length, "close to the floor. At least, I think so. It all happened so quickly, and I felt so bewildered, it was hard to see straight. But at first I could have sworn he was half his natural size. I called to him, I think I swore at him—I forget exactly, but I know he straightened up at once and stood before me down there in the light"—he pointed across the room to the door—"eyes gleaming, face white as chalk, perspiring like midsummer, and gradually filling out, straightening up, whatever you like to call it, to his natural size and appearance again. It was the most horrid thing I've ever seen."

"As an—animal, you saw him still?"

"No; human again. Only much smaller."

"What did he say?"

Billy reflected a moment.

"Nothing that I can remember," he replied. "You see, it was all over in a few seconds. In the full light, I felt so foolish, and nonplussed at first. To see him normal again baffled me. And, before I could collect myself, he had let himself out into the passage, and I heard the front door slam. A minute later—the same second almost, it seemed—you came in. I only remember grabbing the violin and getting it back safely under the glass case. The strings were still vibrating."

The account was over. John asked no further questions. Nor did he say a single word about the lift, Morgan, or the extinguished light on the landing. There fell a longish silence between the two men; and then, while they helped themselves to a generous supply of whisky-and-soda before going to bed, John looked up and spoke:

"If you agree, Billy," he said quietly, "I think I might write and suggest to Hyman that we shall no longer have need for his services."

And Billy, acquiescing, added a sentence that expressed something of the singular dread lying but half concealed in the atmosphere of the room, if not in their minds as well:

"Putting it, however, in a way that need not offend him."

"Of course. There's no need to be rude, is there?"

Accordingly, next morning the letter was written; and John, saying nothing to his brother, took it round himself by hand to the Hebrew's rooms near Euston. The answer he dreaded was forthcoming:

"Mr. Hyman's still away abroad," he was told. "But we're forwarding letters; yes. Or I can give you 'is address if you'll prefer it." The letter went, therefore, to the number in Königstrasse, Munich, thus obtained.

Then, on his way back from the insurance company where he went to increase the sum that protected the small Guarnerius from loss by fire, accident, or theft, John Gilmer called at the offices of certain musical agents and ascertained that Silenski, the violinist, was performing at the time in Munich. It was only some days later, though, by diligent inquiry, he made certain that at a concert on a certain date the famous virtuoso had played a Zigeuner Lullaby of his own composition—the very date, it turned out, on which he himself had been to the Masonic rehearsal at Mark Masons' Hall.

John, however, said nothing of these discoveries to his brother William.

IV

It was about a week later when a reply to the letter came from Munich—a letter couched in somewhat offensive terms, though it contained neither words nor phrases that could actually be found fault with. Isidore Hyman was hurt and angry. On his return to London a month or so later, he proposed to call and talk the matter over. The offensive part of the letter lay, perhaps, in his definite assumption that he could persuade the brothers to resume the old relations. John, however, wrote a brief reply to the effect that they had decided to buy no new fiddles; their collection being complete, there would be no occasion for them to invite his services as a performer. This was final. No answer came, and the matter seemed to drop. Never for one moment, though, did it leave the consciousness of John Gilmer. Hyman had said that he would come, and come assuredly he would. He secretly gave Morgan instructions that he and his brother for the future were always "out" when the Hebrew presented himself.

"He must have gone back to Germany, you see, almost at once after his visit here that night," observed William—John, however, making no reply.

One night towards the middle of January the two brothers came home together from a concert in Queen's Hall, and sat up later than usual in their sitting-room discussing over their whisky and tobacco the merits of the pieces and performers. It must have been past one o'clock when they turned out the lights in the passage and retired to bed. The air was still and frosty; moonlight over the roofs—one of those sharp and dry winter nights that now seem to visit London rarely.

"Like the old-fashioned days when we were boys," remarked William, pausing a moment by the passage window and looking out across the miles of silvery, sparkling roofs.

"Yes," added John; "the ponds freezing hard in the fields, rime on the nursery windows, and the sound of a horse's hoofs coming down the road in the distance, eh?" They smiled at the memory, then said good night, and separated. Their rooms were at opposite ends of the corridor; in between were the bathroom, dining-room, and sitting-room. It was a long, straggling flat. Half an hour later both brothers were sound asleep, the flat silent, only a dull murmur rising from the great city outside, and the moon sinking slowly to the level of the chimneys.

Perhaps two hours passed, perhaps three, when John Gilmer, sitting up in bed with a start, wide-awake and frightened, knew that someone was moving about in one of the three rooms that lay between him and his brother. He had absolutely no idea why he should have been frightened, for there was no dream or nightmare-memory that he brought over from unconsciousness, and yet he realized plainly that the fear he felt was by no means a foolish and unreasoning fear. It had a cause and a reason. Also— which made it worse—it was fully warranted. Something in his sleep, forgotten in the instant of waking, had happened that set every nerve in his body on the watch. He was positive only of two things—first, that it was the entrance of this person, moving so quietly there in the flat, that sent the chills down his spine; and, secondly, that this person was *not* his brother William.

John Gilmer was a timid man. The sight of a burglar, his eyes black-masked, suddenly confronting him in the passage, would most likely have deprived him of all power of decision—until the burglar had either shot him or escaped. But on this occasion some instinct told him that it was no burglar, and that the acute distress he experienced was not due to any message of ordinary physical fear. The thing that had gained access to his flat while he slept had first come—he felt sure of it—into his room, and had passed very close to his own bed, before going on. It had then doubtless gone to his brother's room, visiting them both stealthily to make sure they slept. And its mere passage through his room had been enough to wake him and set these drops of cold perspiration upon his skin. For it was—he felt it in every fibre of his body—something hostile.

The thought that it might at that very moment be in the room of his brother, however, brought him to his feet on the cold floor, and set him moving with all the determination he could summon towards the door. He looked cautiously down an utterly dark passage; then crept on tiptoe along it. On the wall were old-fashioned weapons that had belonged to his father; and feeling a curved, sheathless sword that had come from some Turkish campaign of years gone by, his fingers closed tightly round it, and lifted it silently from the three hooks whereon it lay. He passed the doors of the bathroom and dining-room, making instinctively for the big sitting-room where the violins were kept in their glass cases. The cold nipped him. His eyes smarted with the effort to see in the darkness. Outside the closed door he hesitated.

Putting his ear to the crack, he listened. From within came a faint sound of someone moving. The same instant there rose the sharp, delicate "ping" of a violin-string being plucked; and John Gilmer, with nerves that shook like the vibrations of that very string, opened the door wide with a fling and turned on the light at the same moment. The plucked string still echoed faintly in the air.

The sensation that met him on the threshold was the well-known one that things had been going on in the room which his unexpected arrival had that instant put a stop to. A second earlier and he would have discovered it all in the act. The atmosphere still held the feeling of rushing, silent movement with which the things had raced back to their normal, motionless positions. The immobility of the furniture was a mere attitude hurriedly assumed, and the moment his back was turned the whole business, whatever it might be, would begin again. With this presentment of the room, however—a purely imaginative one— came another, swiftly on its heels.

For one of the objects, less swift than the rest, had not quite regained its "attitude" of repose. It still moved. Below the window curtains on the right, not far from the shelf that bore the violins in their glass cases, he made it out, slowly gliding along the floor. Then, even as his eye caught it, it came to rest.

And, while the cold perspiration broke out all over him afresh, he knew that this still moving item was the cause both of his waking and of his terror. This was the disturbance whose presence he had divined in the flat without actual hearing, and whose passage through his room, while he yet slept, had touched every nerve in his body as with ice. Clutching his Turkish sword tightly, he drew back with the utmost caution against the wall and watched, for the singular impression came to him that the movement was not that of a human being crouching, but rather of something that pertained to the animal world. He remembered, flash-like, the movements of reptiles, the stealth of the larger felines, the undulating glide of great snakes. For the moment, however, it did not move, and they faced one another.

The other side of the room was but dimly lighted, and the noise he made clicking up another electric lamp brought the thing flying forward again—towards himself. At such a moment it seemed absurd to think of so small a detail, but he remembered his bare feet, and, genuinely frightened, he leaped upon a chair and swished with his sword through the air about him. From this better point of view, with the increased light to aid him, he then saw two things—first, that the glass case usually covering the Guarnerius violin had been shifted; and, secondly, that the moving object was slowly elongating itself into an upright position. Semi-erect, yet most oddly, too, like a creature on its hind legs, it was coming swiftly towards him. It was making for the door—and escape.

The confusion of ghostly fear was somehow upon him so that he was too bewildered to see clearly, but he had sufficient self-control, it seemed, to recover a certain power of action; for the moment the advancing figure was near enough for him to strike, that curved scimitar flashed and whirred about him, with such misdirected violence, however, that he not only failed to strike it even once, but at the same time lost his balance and fell forward from the chair whereon he perched—straight into it.

And then came the most curious thing of all, for as he dropped, the figure also dropped, stooped low down, crouched, dwindled amazingly in size, and rushed past him close to the ground like an animal on all fours. John Gilmer screamed, for he could no longer contain himself. Stumbling over the chair as he turned to follow, cutting and slashing wildly with his sword, he saw halfway down the darkened corridor beyond the scuttling outline of, apparently, an enormous—cat!

The door into the outer landing was somehow ajar, and the next second the beast was out, but not before the steel had fallen with a crashing blow upon the front disappearing leg, almost severing it from the body.

It was dreadful. Turning up the lights as he went, he ran after it to the outer landing. But the thing he followed was already well away, and he heard, on the floor below him, the same oddly gliding, slithering, stealthy sound, yet hurrying, that he had heard weeks before when something had passed him in the lift and Morgan, in his terror, had likewise cried aloud.

For a time he stood there on that dark landing, listening, thinking, trembling; then turned into the flat and shut the door. In the sitting-room he carefully replaced the glass case over the treasured violin, puzzled to the point of foolishness, and strangely routed in his mind. For the violin itself, he saw, had been dragged several inches from its cushioned bed of plush.

Next morning, however, he made no allusion to the occurrence of the night. His brother apparently had not been disturbed.

V

The only thing that called for explanation—an explanation not fully forthcoming—was the curious aspect of Mr. Morgan's countenance. The fact that this individual gave notice to the owners of the building, and at the end of the month left for a new post, was, of course, known to both brothers; whereas the story he told in explanation of his face was known only to the one who questioned him about it—John. And John, for reasons best known to himself, did not pass it on to the other. Also, for reasons best known to himself, he did not cross-question the liftman about those singular marks, or report the matter to the police.

Mr. Morgan's pasty visage was badly scratched, and there were red lines running from the cheek into the neck that had the appearance of having been produced by sharp points viciously applied—claws. He had been disturbed by a noise in the hall, he said, about three in the morning, a scuffle had ensued in the darkness, but the intruder had got clear away . . .

"A cat or something of the kind, no doubt," suggested John Gilmer at the end of the brief recital. And Morgan replied in his usual way: "A cat, or something of the kind, Mr. John, no doubt."

All the same, he had not cared to risk a second encounter, but had departed to wear his billycock and uniform in a building less haunted.

Hyman, meanwhile, made no attempt to call and talk over his dismissal. The reason for this was only apparent, however, several months later when, quite by chance, coming along Piccadilly in an omnibus, the brothers found themselves seated opposite to a man with a thick black beard and blue glasses. William Gilmer hastily rang the bell and got out, saying something half intelligible about feeling faint. John followed him.

"Did you see who it was?" he whispered to his brother the moment they were safely on the pavement.

John nodded.

"Hyman, in spectacles. He's grown a beard, too."

"Yes, but did you also notice—"

"What?"

"He had an empty sleeve."

"An empty sleeve?"

"Yes," said William; "he's lost an arm."

There was a long pause before John spoke. At the door of their club the elder brother added:

"Poor devil! He'll never again play on"—then, suddenly changing the preposition—"*with* a pedigree violin!"

And that night in the flat, after William had gone to bed, he looked up a curious old volume he had once picked up on a secondhand bookstall, and read therein quaint descriptions of how the "desire-body of a violent man" may assume animal shape, operate on concrete matter even at a distance; and, further, how a wound inflicted thereon can reproduce itself upon its physical counterpart by means of the mysterious so-called phenomenon of "repercussion."

Tales of the Uncanny and Supernatural, 1914

THE TERROR
OF THE TWINS

That the man's hopes had built upon a son to inherit his name and estates—a single son, that is—was to be expected; but no one could have foreseen the depth and bitterness of his disappointment, the cold, implacable fury, when there arrived instead—twins. For, though the elder legally must inherit, that other ran him so deadly close. A daughter would have been a more reasonable defeat. But twins—! To miss his dream by so feeble a device—!

* * * * *

The complete frustration of a hope deeply cherished for years may easily result in strange fevers of the soul, but the violence of the father's hatred, existing as it did side by side with a love he could not deny, was something to set psychologists thinking. More than unnatural, it was positively uncanny. Being a man of rigid self-control, however, it operated inwardly, and doubtless along some morbid line of weakness little suspected even by those nearest to him, preying upon his thought to such dreadful extent that finally the mind gave way. The suppressed rage and bitterness deprived him, so the family decided, of his reason, and he spent the last years of his life under restraint. He was possessed naturally of immense forces—of will, feeling, desire; his dynamic value truly tremendous, driving through life like a great engine; and the intensity of this concentrated and buried hatred was guessed by few. The twins themselves, however, knew it. They divined it, at least, for it operated ceaselessly against them side by side with the genuine soft love that occasionally sweetened it, to their great perplexity. They spoke of it only to each other, though.

"At twenty-one," Edward, the elder, would remark sometimes, unhappily, "we shall know more." "Too much," Ernest would reply, with a rush of unreasoning terror the thought never failed to evoke—*in him*. "Things father said always happened—in life." And they paled perceptibly. For the hatred, thus compressed into a veritable bomb of psychic energy, had found at the last a singular expression in the cry of the father's distraught mind. On the occasion of their final visit to the asylum, preceding his death by a few hours only, very calmly, but with an intensity that drove the words into their hearts like points of burning metal, he had spoken. In the presence of the attendant, at the door of the dreadful padded cell, he said it: "You are not two, but one. I still regard you as one. And at the coming of age, by h—, you shall find it out!"

The lads perhaps had never fully divined that icy hatred which lay so well concealed against them, but that this final sentence was a curse, backed by all the man's terrific force, they quite well realised; and accordingly, almost unknown to each other, they had come to dread the day inexpressibly. On the morning of that twenty-first birthday—their father gone these five years into the Unknown, yet still sometimes so strangely close to them—they shared the same biting, inner terror, just as they shared all other emotions of their life—intimately, without speech. During the daytime they managed to keep it at a distance; but when the dusk fell about the old house they knew the stealthy approach of a kind of panic sense. Their self-respect weakened swiftly . . . and they persuaded their old friend, and once tutor, the vicar, to sit up with them till midnight . . . He had humoured them to that extent, willing to forgo his sleep, and at the same time more than a little interested in their singular belief—that before the day was out, before midnight struck, that is, the curse of that terrible man would somehow come into operation against them.

Festivities over and the guests departed, they sat up in the library, the room usually occupied by their father, and little used since. Mr. Curtice, a robust man of fifty-five, and a firm believer in spiritual principalities and powers, dark as well as good, affected (for their own good) to regard the youths' obsession with a kindly cynicism. "I do not think it likely for one moment," he said gravely, "that such a thing would be permitted. All spirits are in the hands of God, and the violent ones more especially." To which Edward made the extraordinary reply: "Even if father does not come himself he will—*send!*" And Ernest agreed: "All this time he's been making preparations for this very day. We've both known it for a long time—by odd things that have happened, by our dreams, by nasty little dark hints of various kinds, and by these persistent attacks of terror that come from nowhere, especially of late. Haven't we, Edward?" Edward assenting with a shudder. "Father has been at us of late with renewed violence. Tonight it will be a regular assault upon our lives, or minds, or souls!"

"Strong personalities *may* possibly leave behind them forces that continue to act," observed Mr. Curtice with caution, while the brothers replied almost in the same breath: "That's exactly what we feel so curiously. Though—nothing has actually happened yet, you know, and it's a good many years now since—"

This was the way the twins spoke of it all. And it was their profound conviction that had touched their old friend's sense of duty. The experiment should justify itself—and cure them. Meanwhile none of the family knew. Everything was planned secretly.

The library was the quietest room in the house. It had shuttered bow-windows, thick carpets, heavy doors. Books lined the walls, and there was a capacious open fireplace of brick in which the wood logs blazed and roared, for the autumn night was chilly. Round this the three of them were grouped, the clergyman reading aloud from the Book of Job in low tones; Edward and Ernest, in dinner-jackets, occupying deep leather armchairs, listening. They looked exactly what they were—Cambridge "undergrads," their faces pale against their dark hair, and alike as two peas. A shaded lamp behind the clergyman threw the rest of the room into shadow. The reading voice was steady, even monotonous, but something in it betrayed an underlying anxiety, and although the eyes rarely left the printed page, they took in every movement of the young men opposite, and noted every change upon their faces. It was his aim to produce an unexciting atmosphere, yet to miss nothing; if anything did occur to see it from the very beginning. Not to be taken by surprise was his main idea . . . And thus, upon this falsely peaceful scene, the minutes passed the hour of eleven and slipped rapidly along towards midnight.

The novel element in his account of this distressing and dreadful occurrence seems to be that what happened— happened without the slightest warning or preparation. There was no gradual presentiment of any horror; no strange blast of cold air; no dwindling of heat or light; no shaking of windows or mysterious tapping upon furniture. Without preliminaries it fell with its black trappings of terror upon the scene.

The clergyman had been reading aloud for some considerable time, one or other of the twins—Ernest usually—making occasional remarks, which proved that his sense of dread was disappearing. As the time grew short and nothing happened they grew more at their ease. Edward, indeed, actually nodded, dozed, and finally fell asleep. It was a few minutes before midnight. Ernest, slightly yawning, was stretching himself in the big chair. "Nothing's going to happen," he said aloud, in a pause. "Your good influence has prevented it." He even laughed now. "What superstitious asses we've been, sir; haven't we—?"

Curtice, then, dropping his Bible, looked hard at him under the lamp. For in that second, even while the words sounded, there had come about a most abrupt and dreadful change; and so swiftly that the clergyman, in spite of himself, was taken utterly by surprise and had no time to think. There had swooped down upon the quiet library—so he puts it—an immense hushing silence, so profound that the peace already reigning there seemed clamour by comparison; and out of this enveloping stillness there rose through the space about them a living and abominable Invasion—soft, motionless, terrific. It was as though vast engines, working at full speed and pressure, yet too swift and delicate to be appreciable to any definite sense, had suddenly dropped down upon them—from nowhere. "It made me think," the vicar used to say afterwards, "of the Mauretania machinery compressed into a nutshell, yet losing none of its awful power."

" . . . haven't we?" repeated Ernest, still laughing. And Curtice, making no audible reply, heard the true answer in his heart: "Because everything has *already happened*—even as you feared."

Yet, to the vicar's supreme astonishment, Ernest still noticed—nothing!

"Look," the boy added, "Eddy's sound asleep—sleeping like a pig. Doesn't say much for your reading, you know, sir!" And he laughed again—lightly, even foolishly. But that laughter jarred, for the clergyman understood now that the sleep of the elder twin was either feigned—or *unnatural*.

And while the easy words fell so lightly from his lips, the monstrous engines worked and pulsed against him and against his sleeping brother, all their huge energy concentrated down into points fine as Suggestion, delicate as Thought. The Invasion affected everything. The very objects in the room altered incredibly, revealing suddenly behind their normal exteriors horrid little hearts of darkness. It was truly amazing, this vile metamorphosis. Books, chairs, pictures, all yielded up their pleasant aspect, and betrayed, as with silent mocking laughter, their inner soul of blackness—their *decay*. This is how Curtice tries to body forth in words what he actually witnessed . . . And Ernest, yawning, talking lightly, half foolishly—still noticed nothing!

For all this, as described, came about in something like ten seconds; and with it swept into the clergyman's mind, like a blow, the memory of that sinister phrase used more than once by Edward: "If father doesn't come, he will certainly—send." And Curtice understood that he had done both—both sent and come himself... That violent mind, released from its spell of madness in the body, yet still retaining the old implacable hatred, was now directing the terrible, unseen assault. This silent room, so hushed and still, was charged to the brim. The horror of it, as he said later, "seemed to peel the very skin from my back." ... And, while Ernest noticed nothing, Edward slept! ... The soul of the clergyman, strong with the desire to help or save, yet realising that he was alone against a Legion, poured out in wordless prayer to his Deity. The clock just then, whirring before it struck, made itself audible.

"By Jove! It's all right, you see!" exclaimed Ernest, his voice oddly fainter and lower than before. "There's midnight—and nothing's happened. Bally nonsense, all of it!" His voice had dwindled curiously in volume. "I'll get the whisky and soda from the hall." His relief was great and his manner showed it. But in him somewhere was a singular change. His voice, manner, gestures, his very tread as he moved over the thick carpet toward the door, all showed it. He seemed less real, less alive, reduced somehow to littleness, the voice without timbre or quality, the appearance of him diminished in some fashion quite ghastly. His presence, if not actually shrivelled, was at least impaired. Ernest had suffered a singular and horrible *decrease*...

The clock was still whirring before the strike. One heard the chain running up softly. Then the hammer fell upon the first stroke of midnight.

"I'm off," he laughed faintly from the door; "it's all been pure funk—on my part, at least. . . !" He passed out of sight into the hall. *The Power that throbbed so mightily about the room followed him out.* Almost at the same moment Edward woke up. But he woke with a tearing and indescribable cry of pain and anguish on his lips: "Oh, oh, oh! But it hurts! It hurts! I can't hold you;

leave me. It's breaking me asunder—"

The clergyman had sprung to his feet, but in the same instant everything had become normal once more—the room as it was before, the horror gone. There was nothing he could do or say, for there was no longer anything to put right, to defend, or to attack. Edward was speaking; his voice, deep and full as it never had been before: "By Jove, how that sleep has refreshed me! I feel twice the chap I was before—twice the chap. I feel quite splendid. Your voice, sir, must have hypnotised me to sleep . . ." He crossed the room with great vigour. "Where's—er—where's—Ernie, by the bye?" he asked casually, hesitating—almost searching— for the name. And a shadow as of a vanished memory crossed his face and was gone. The tone conveyed the most complete indifference where once the least word or movement of his twin had wakened solicitude, love. "Gone away, I suppose—gone to bed, I mean, of course."

Curtice has never been able to describe the dreadful conviction that overwhelmed him as he stood there staring, his heart in his mouth—the conviction, the positive certainty, that Edward had changed interiorly, had suffered an incredible accession to his existing personality. But he knew it as he watched. His mind, spirit, soul had most wonderfully increased. Something that hitherto the lad had known from the outside only, or by the magic of loving sympathy, had now passed, to be incorporated with his own being. And, being himself, it required no expression. Yet this visible increase was somehow terrible. Curtice shrank back from him. The instinct—he has never grasped the profound psychology of *that*, nor why it turned his soul dizzy with a kind of nausea—the instinct to strike him where he stood, passed, and a plaintive sound from the hall, stealing softly into the room between them, sent all that was left to him of self-possession into his feet. He turned and ran. Edward followed him—very leisurely.

They found Ernest, or what had been Ernest, crouching behind the table in the hail, weeping foolishly to himself. On his face lay blackness. The mouth was open, the jaw dropped; he dribbled hopelessly; and from the face had passed all signs of intelligence—of spirit.

For a few weeks he lingered on, regaining no sign of spiritual or mental life before the poor body, hopelessly disorganised, released what was left of him, from pure inertia—from complete and utter loss of vitality.

And the horrible thing—so the distressed family thought, at least—was that all those weeks Edward showed an indifference that was singularly brutal and complete. He rarely even went to visit him. I believe, too, it is true that he only once spoke of him by name; and that was when he said—

"Ernie? Oh, but Ernie is much better and happier where he is—!"

Tales of the Uncanny and Supernatural, 1914

THE WOLVES OF GOD

I

As the little steamer entered the bay of Kettletoft in the Orkneys the beach at Sanday appeared so low that the houses almost seemed to be standing in the water; and to the big, dark man leaning over the rail of the upper deck the sight of them came with a pang of mingled pain and pleasure. The scene, to his eyes, had not changed. The houses, the low shore, the flat treeless country beyond, the vast open sky, all looked exactly the same as when he left the island thirty years ago to work for the Hudson Bay Company in distant N. W. Canada. A lad of eighteen then, he was now a man of forty-eight, old for his years, and this was the homecoming he had so often dreamed about in the lonely wilderness of trees where he had spent his life. Yet his grim face wore an anxious rather than a tender expression. The return was perhaps not quite as he had pictured it.

Jim Peace had not done too badly, however, in the Company's service. For an islander, he would be a rich man now; he had not married, he had saved the greater part of his salary, and even in the faraway Post where he had spent so many years there had been occasional opportunities of the kind common to new, wild countries where life and law are in the making. He had not hesitated to take them. None of the big Company Posts, it was true, had come his way, nor had he risen very high in the service; in another two years his turn would have come, yet he had left of his own accord before those two years were up. His decision, judging by the strength in the features, was not due to impulse; the move had been deliberately weighed and calculated; he had renounced his opportunity after full reflection. A man with those steady eyes, with that square jaw and determined mouth, certainly did not act without good reason.

A curious expression now flickered over his weather-hardened face as he saw again his childhood's home, and the return, so often dreamed about, actually took place at last. An uneasy light flashed for a moment in the deep-set grey eyes, but was quickly gone again, and the tanned visage recovered its accustomed look of stern composure. His keen sight took in a dark knot of figures on the landing-pier—his brother, he knew, among them. A wave of homesickness swept over him. He longed to see his brother again, the old farm, the sweep of open country, the sand-dunes, and the breaking seas. The smell of long-forgotten days came to his nostrils with its sweet, painful pang of youthful memories.

How fine, he thought, to be back there in the old familiar fields of childhood, with sea and sand about him instead of the smother of endless woods that ran a thousand miles without a break. He was glad in particular that no trees were visible, and that rabbits scampering among the dunes were the only wild animals he need ever meet . . .

Those thirty years in the woods, it seemed, oppressed his mind; the forests, the countless multitudes of trees, had wearied him. His nerves, perhaps, had suffered finally. Snow, frost and sun, stars, and the wind had been his companions during the long days and endless nights in his lonely Post, but chiefly— trees. Trees, trees, trees! On the whole, he had preferred them in stormy weather, though, in another way, their rigid hosts, 'mid the deep silence of still days, had been equally oppressive. In the clear sunlight of a windless day they assumed a waiting, listening, watching aspect that had something spectral in it, but when in motion—well, he preferred a moving animal to one that stood stock-still and stared. Wind, moreover, in a million trees, even the lightest breeze, drowned all other sounds—the howling of the wolves, for instance, in winter, or the ceaseless harsh barking of the husky dogs he so disliked.

Even on this warm September afternoon a slight shiver ran over him as the background of dead years loomed up behind the present scene. He thrust the picture back, deep down inside himself. The self-control, the strong, even violent will that the face betrayed, came into operation instantly. The background was background; it belonged to what was past, and the past was over and done with. It was dead. Jim meant it to stay dead.

The figure waving to him from the pier was his brother. He knew Tom instantly; the years had dealt easily with him in this quiet island; there was no startling, no unkindly change, and a deep emotion, though unexpressed, rose in his heart. It was good to be home again, he realized, as he sat presently in the cart, Tom holding the reins, driving slowly back to the farm at the north end of the island. Everything he found familiar, yet at the same time strange. They passed the school where he used to go as a little barelegged boy; other boys were now learning their lessons exactly as he used to do. Through the open window he could hear the droning voice of the schoolmaster, who, though invisible, wore the face of Mr. Lovibond, his own teacher.

"Lovibond?" said Tom, in reply to his question. "Oh, he's been dead these twenty years. He went south, you know—Glasgow, I think it was, or Edinburgh. He got typhoid."

Stands of golden plover were to be seen as of old in the fields, or flashing overhead in swift flight with a whir of wings, wheeling and turning together like one huge bird. Down on the empty shore a curlew cried. Its piercing note rose clear above the noisy clamour of the gulls. The sun played softly on the quiet sea, the air was keen but pleasant, the tang of salt mixed sweetly with the clean smells of open country that he knew so well. Nothing of essentials had changed, even the low clouds beyond the heaving uplands were the clouds of childhood.

They came presently to the sand-dunes, where rabbits sat at their burrow-mouths, or ran helter-skelter across the road in front of the slow cart.

"They're safe till the colder weather comes and trapping

begins," he mentioned. It all came back to him in detail.

"And they know it, too—the canny little beggars," replied Tom. "Any rabbits out where you've been?" he asked casually.

"Not to hurt you," returned his brother shortly.

Nothing seemed changed, although everything seemed different. He looked upon the old, familiar things, but with other eyes. There were, of course, changes, alterations, yet so slight, in a way so odd and curious, that they evaded him; not being of the physical order, they reported to his soul, not to his mind. But his soul, being troubled, sought to deny the changes; to admit them meant to admit a change in himself he had determined to conceal even if he could not entirely deny it.

"Same old place, Tom," came one of his rare remarks. "The years ain't done much to it." He looked into his brother's face a moment squarely. "Nor to you, either, Tom," he added, affection and tenderness just touching his voice and breaking through a natural reserve that was almost taciturnity.

His brother returned the look; and something in that instant passed between the two men, something of understanding that no words had hinted at, much less expressed. The tie was real, they loved each other, they were loyal, true, steadfast fellows. In youth they had known no secrets. The shadow that now passed and vanished left a vague trouble in both hearts.

"The forests," said Tom slowly, "have made a silent man of you, Jim. You'll miss them here, I'm thinking."

"Maybe," was the curt reply, "but I guess not."

His lips snapped to as though they were of steel and could never open again, while the tone he used made Tom realize that the subject was not one his brother cared to talk about particularly. He was surprised, therefore, when, after a pause, Jim returned to it of his own accord. He was sitting a little sideways as he spoke, taking in the scene with hungry eyes. "It's a queer thing," he observed, "to look round and see nothing but clean empty land, and not a single tree in sight. You see, it don't look natural quite."

Again his brother was struck by the tone of voice, but this time by something else as well he could not name. Jim was excusing himself, explaining. The manner, too, arrested him. And thirty years disappeared as though they had not been, for it was thus Jim acted as a boy when there was something unpleasant he had to say and wished to get it over. The tone, the gesture, the manner, all were there. He was edging up to something he wished to say, yet dared not utter.

"You've had enough of trees then?" Tom said sympathetically, trying to help, "and things?"

The instant the last two words were out he realized that they had been drawn from him instinctively, and that it was the anxiety of deep affection which had prompted them. He had guessed without knowing he had guessed, or rather, without intention or attempt to guess. Jim had a secret. Love's clairvoyance had discovered it, though not yet its hidden terms.

"I have—" began the other, then paused, evidently to choose his words with care. "I've had enough of trees." He was about to speak of something that his brother had unwittingly touched upon in his chance phrase, but instead of finding the words he sought, he gave a sudden start, his breath caught sharply. "What's that?" he exclaimed, jerking his body round so abruptly that Tom automatically pulled the reins. "What is it?"

"A dog barking," Tom answered, much surprised. "A farm dog barking. Why? What did you think it was?" he asked, as he flicked the horse to go on again. "You made me jump," he added, with a laugh. "You're used to huskies, ain't you?"

"It sounded so—not like a dog, I mean," came the slow explanation. "It's long since I heard a sheepdog bark, I suppose it startled me."

"Oh, it's a dog all right," Tom assured him comfortingly, for his heart told him infallibly the kind of tone to use. And presently, too, he changed the subject in his blunt, honest fashion, knowing that, also, was the right and kindly thing to do. He pointed out the old farms as they drove along, his brother silent again, sitting stiff and rigid at his side. "And it's good to have you back, Jim, from those outlandish places. There are not too many of the family left now—just you and I, as a matter of fact."

"Just you and I," the other repeated gruffly, but in a sweetened tone that proved he appreciated the ready sympathy and tact. "We'll stick together, Tom, eh? Blood's thicker than water, ain't it? I've learnt that much, anyhow."

The voice had something gentle and appealing in it, something his brother heard now for the first time. An elbow nudged into his side, and Tom knew the gesture was not solely a sign of affection, but grew partly also from the comfort born of physical contact when the heart is anxious. The touch, like the last words, conveyed an appeal for help. Tom was so surprised he couldn't believe it quite.

Scared! Jim scared! The thought puzzled and afflicted him who knew his brother's character inside out, his courage, his presence of mind in danger, his resolution. Jim frightened seemed an impossibility, a contradiction in terms; he was the kind of man who did not know the meaning of fear, who shrank from nothing, whose spirits rose highest when things appeared most hopeless. It must, indeed, be an uncommon, even a terrible danger that could shake such nerves; yet Tom saw the signs and read them clearly. Explain them he could not, nor did he try. All he knew with certainty was that his brother, sitting now beside him in the cart, hid a secret terror in his heart. Sooner or later, in his own good time, he would share it with him.

He ascribed it, this simple Orkney farmer, to those thirty years of loneliness and exile in wild desolate places, without companionship, without the society of women, with only Indians, husky dogs, a few trappers or fur-dealers like himself, but none of the wholesome, natural influences that sweeten life within reach. Thirty years was a long, long time. He began planning schemes to help. Jim must see people as much as possible, and his mind ran quickly over the men and women available. In women the neighbourhood was not rich, but there were several men of the right sort who might be useful, good fellows all. There was John Rossiter, another old Hudson Bay man, who had been factor at Cartwright, Labrador, for many years, and had returned long ago to spend his last days in civilization. There was Sandy McKay, also back from a long spell of rubber-planting in Malay . . . Tom was still busy making plans when they reached the old farm and presently sat down to their first meal together since that early breakfast thirty years ago before Jim caught the steamer that bore him off to exile—an exile that now returned him with nerves unstrung and a secret terror hidden in his heart.

"I'll ask no questions," he decided. "Jim will tell me in his own good time. And meanwhile, I'll get him to see as many folks as possible." He meant it too; yet not only for his brother's sake. Jim's terror was so vivid it had touched his own heart too.

"Ah, a man can open his lungs here and breathe!" exclaimed Jim, as the two came out after supper and stood before the house, gazing across the open country. He drew a deep breath as though to prove his assertion, exhaling with slow satisfaction again. "It's good to see a clear horizon and to know there's all that water between—between me and where I've been." He turned his face to watch the plover in the sky, then looked towards the distant shoreline where the sea was just visible in the long evening light. "There can't be too much water for me," he added, half to himself. "I guess they can't cross water—not that much water at any rate."

Tom stared, wondering uneasily what to make of it.

"At the trees again, Jim?" he said laughingly. He had overheard the last words, though spoken low, and thought it best not to ignore them altogether. To be natural was the right way, he believed, natural and cheery. To make a joke of anything unpleasant, he felt, was to make it less serious. "I've never seen a tree come across the Atlantic yet, except as a mast—dead," he added.

"I wasn't thinking of the trees just then," was the blunt reply, "but of—something else. The damned trees are nothing, though I hate the sight of 'em. Not of much account, anyway"— as though he compared them mentally with another thing. He puffed at his pipe, a moment.

"They certainly can't move," put in his brother, "nor swim either."

"Nor another thing," said Jim, his voice thick suddenly, but not with smoke, and his speech confused, though the idea in his mind was certainly clear as daylight. "Things can't hide behind 'em—can they?"

"Not much cover hereabouts, I admit," laughed Tom, though the look in his brother's eyes made his laughter as short as it sounded unnatural.

"That's so," agreed the other. "But what I meant was"—he threw out his chest, looked about him with an air of intense relief, drew in another deep breath, and again exhaled with satisfaction—"if there are no trees, there's no hiding."

It was the expression on the rugged, weathered face that sent the blood in a sudden gulping rush from his brother's heart. He had seen men frightened, seen men afraid before they were actually frightened; he had also seen men stiff with terror in the face both of natural and so-called supernatural things; but never in his life before had he seen the look of unearthly dread that now turned his brother's face as white as chalk and yet put the glow of fire in two haunted burning eyes.

Across the darkening landscape the sound of distant barking had floated to them on the evening wind.

"It's only a farm-dog barking." Yet it was Jim's deep, quiet voice that said it, one hand upon his brother's arm.

"That's all," replied Tom, ashamed that he had betrayed himself, and realizing with a shock of surprise that it was Jim who now played the role of comforter—a startling change in their relations. "Why, what did you think it was?"

He tried hard to speak naturally and easily, but his voice shook. So deep was the brothers' love and intimacy that they could not help but share.

Jim lowered his great head. "I thought," he whispered, his grey beard touching the other's cheek, "maybe it was the wolves"—an agony of terror made both voice and body tremble—"the Wolves of God!"

II

The interval of thirty years had been bridged easily enough; it was the secret that left the open gap neither of them cared or dared to cross. Jim's reason for hesitation lay within reach of guesswork, but Tom's silence was more complicated.

With strong, simple men, strangers to affectation or pretence, reserve is a real, almost a sacred thing. Jim offered nothing more; Tom asked no single question. In the latter's mind lay, for one thing, a singular intuitive certainty: that if he knew the truth he would lose his brother. How, why, wherefore, he had no notion; whether by death, or because, having told an awful thing, Jim would hide—physically or mentally—he knew not, nor even asked himself. No subtlety lay in Tom, the Orkney farmer. He merely felt that a knowledge of the truth involved separation which was death.

Day and night, however, that extraordinary phrase which, at its first hearing, had frozen his blood, ran on beating in his mind. With it came always the original, nameless horror that had held him motionless where he stood, his brother's bearded lips against his ear: *The Wolves of God*. In some dim way, he sometimes felt—tried to persuade himself, rather—the horror did not belong to the phrase alone, but was a sympathetic echo of what Jim felt himself. It had entered his own mind and heart. They had always shared in this same strange, intimate way. The deep brotherly tie accounted for it. Of the possible transference of thought and emotion he knew nothing, but this was what he meant perhaps.

At the same time he fought and strove to keep it out, not because it brought uneasy and distressing feelings to him, but because he did not wish to pry, to ascertain, to discover his brother's secret as by some kind of subterfuge that seemed too near to eavesdropping almost. Also, he wished most earnestly to protect him. Meanwhile, in spite of himself, or perhaps because of himself, he watched his brother as a wild animal watches its young. Jim was the only tie he had on earth. He loved him with a brother's love, and Jim, similarly, he knew, loved him. His job was difficult. Love alone could guide him.

He gave openings, but he never questioned:

"Your letter did surprise me, Jim. I was never so delighted in my life. You had still two years to run."

"I'd had enough," was the short reply. "God, man, it was good to get home again!"

This, and the blunt talk that followed their first meeting, was all Tom had to go upon, while those eyes that refused to shut watched ceaselessly always. There was improvement, unless, which never occurred to Tom, it was self-control; there was no more talk of trees and water, the barking of the dogs passed unnoticed, no reference to the loneliness of the backwoods life passed his lips; he spent his days fishing, shooting, helping with the work of the farm, his evenings smoking over a glass—he was more than temperate—and talking over the days of long ago.

The signs of uneasiness still were there, but they were negative, far more suggestive, therefore, than if open and direct. He desired no company, for instance—an unnatural thing, thought Tom, after so many years of loneliness.

It was this and the awkward fact that he had given up two years before his time was finished, renouncing, therefore, a comfortable pension—it was these two big details that stuck with such unkind persistence in his brother's thoughts. Behind both, moreover, ran ever the strange whispered phrase. What the words meant, or whence they were derived, Tom had no possible inkling. Like the wicked refrain of some forbidden song, they haunted him day and night, even his sleep not free from them entirely. All of which, to the simple Orkney farmer, was so new an experience that he knew not how to deal with it at all. Too strong to be flustered, he was at any rate bewildered. And it was for Jim, his brother, he suffered most.

What perplexed him chiefly, however, was the attitude his brother showed towards old John Rossiter. He could almost have imagined that the two men had met and known each other out in Canada, though Rossiter showed him how impossible that was, both in point of time and of geography as well. He had brought them together within the first few days, and Jim, silent, gloomy, morose, even surly, had eyed him like an enemy. Old Rossiter, the milk of human kindness as thick in his veins as cream, had taken no offence. Grizzled veteran of the wilds, he had served his full term with the Company and now enjoyed his well-earned pension. He was full of stories, reminiscences, adventures of every sort and kind; he knew men and values, had seen strange things that only the true wilderness delivers, and he loved nothing better than to tell them over a glass. He talked with Jim so genially and affably that little response was called for luckily, for Jim was glum and unresponsive almost to rudeness. Old Rossiter noticed nothing. What Tom noticed was, chiefly perhaps, his brother's acute uneasiness. Between his desire to help, his attachment to Rossiter, and his keen personal distress, he knew not what to do or say. The situation was becoming too much for him.

The two families, besides—Peace and Rossiter—had been neighbours for generations, had intermarried freely, and were related in various degrees. He was too fond of his brother to feel ashamed, but he was glad when the visit was over and they were out of their host's house. Jim had even declined to drink with him.

"They're good fellows on the island," said Tom on their way

home, "but not specially entertaining, perhaps. We all stick together though. You can trust 'em mostly."

"I never was a talker, Tom," came the gruff reply. "You know that." And Tom, understanding more than he understood, accepted the apology and made generous allowances.

"John likes to talk," he helped him. "He appreciates a good listener."

"It's the kind of talk I'm finished with," was the rejoinder. "The Company and their goings-on don't interest me any more. I've had enough."

Tom noticed other things as well with those affectionate eyes of his that did not want to see yet would not close. As the days drew in, for instance, Jim seemed reluctant to leave the house towards evening. Once the full light of day had passed, he kept indoors. He was eager and ready enough to shoot in the early morning, no matter at what hour he had to get up, but he refused point blank to go with his brother to the lake for an evening flight. No excuse was offered; he simply declined to go.

The gap between them thus widened and deepened, while yet in another sense it grew less formidable.

Both knew, that is, that a secret lay between them for the first time in their lives, yet both knew also that at the right and proper moment it would be revealed. Jim only waited till the proper moment came. And Tom understood. His deep, simple love was equal to all emergencies. He respected his brother's reserve. The obvious desire of John Rossiter to talk and ask questions, for instance, he resisted staunchly as far as he was able. Only when he could help and protect his brother did he yield a little. The talk was brief, even monosyllabic; neither the old Hudson Bay fellow nor the Orkney farmer ran to many words:

"He ain't right with himself," offered John, taking his pipe out of his mouth and leaning forward. "That's what I don't like to see." He put a skinny hand on Tom's knee, and looked earnestly into his face as he said it.

"Jim!" replied the other. "Jim ill, you mean!" It sounded ridiculous.

"His mind is sick."

"I don't understand," Tom said, though the truth bit like rough-edged steel into the brother's heart.

"His soul, then, if you like that better."

Tom fought with himself a moment, then asked him to be more explicit.

"More'n I can say," rejoined the laconic old backwoodsman. "I don't know myself. The woods heal some men and make others sick."

"Maybe, John, maybe." Tom fought back his resentment. "You've lived, like him, in lonely places. You ought to know." His mouth shut with a snap, as though he had said too much. Loyalty to his suffering brother caught him strongly. Already his heart ached for Jim. He felt angry with Rossiter for his divination, but perceived, too, that the old fellow meant well and was trying to help him. If he lost Jim, he lost the world—his all.

A considerable pause followed, during which both men puffed their pipes with reckless energy. Both, that is, were a bit excited. Yet both had their code, a code they would not exceed for worlds.

"Jim," added Tom presently, making an effort to meet the sympathy halfway, "ain't quite up to the mark, I'll admit that."

There was another long pause, while Rossiter kept his eyes on his companion steadily, though without a trace of expression in them—a habit that the woods had taught him.

"Jim," he said at length, with an obvious effort, "is skeered. And it's the soul in him that's skeered."

Tom wavered dreadfully then. He saw that old Rossiter, experienced backwoodsman and taught by the Company as he was, knew where the secret lay, if he did not yet know its exact terms. It was easy enough to put the question, yet he hesitated, because loyalty forbade.

"It's a dirty outfit somewheres," the old man

mumbled to himself.

Tom sprang to his feet, "If you talk that way," he exclaimed angrily, "you're no friend of mine—or his." His anger gained upon him as he said it. "Say that again," he cried, "and I'll knock your teeth—"

He sat back, stunned a moment.

"Forgive me, John," he faltered, shamed yet still angry. "It's pain to me, it's pain. Jim," he went on, after a long breath and a pull at his glass, "Jim *is* scared, I know it." He waited a moment, hunting for the words that he could use without disloyalty. "But it's nothing he's done himself," he said, "nothing to his discredit. I know *that*."

Old Rossiter looked up, a strange light in his eyes.

"No offence," he said quietly.

"Tell me what you know," cried Tom suddenly, standing up again.

The old factor met his eye squarely, steadfastly. He laid his pipe aside.

"D'ye really want to hear?" he asked in a lowered voice. "Because, if you don't—why, say so right now. I'm all for justice," he added, "and always was."

"Tell me," said Tom, his heart in his mouth. "Maybe, if I knew—I might help him." The old man's words woke fear in him. He well knew his passionate, remorseless sense of justice.

"Help him," repeated the other. "For a man skeered in his soul there ain't no help. But—if you want to hear—I'll tell you."

"Tell me," cried Tom. "I *will* help him," while rising anger fought back rising fear.

John took another pull at his glass.

"Jest between you and me like."

"Between you and me," said Tom. "Get on with it."

There was a deep silence in the little room. Only the sound of the sea came in, the wind behind it.

"The Wolves," whispered old Rossiter. "The Wolves of God."

Tom sat still in his chair, as though struck in the face. He shivered. He kept silent and the silence seemed to him long and curious. His heart was throbbing, the blood in his veins played strange tricks. All he remembered was that old Rossiter had gone on talking. The voice, however, sounded far away and distant. It was all unreal, he felt, as he went homewards across the bleak, windswept upland, the sound of the sea forever in his ears . . .

Yes, old John Rossiter, damned be his soul, had gone on talking. He had said wild, incredible things. Damned be his soul! His teeth should be smashed for that. It was outrageous, it was cowardly, it was not true.

"Jim," he thought, "my brother, Jim!" as he ploughed his way wearily against the wind. "I'll teach him. I'll teach him to spread such wicked tales!" He referred to Rossiter. "God blast these fellows! They come home from their outlandish places and think they can say anything! I'll knock his yellow dog's teeth . . . !"

While, inside, his heart went quailing, crying for help, afraid.

He tried hard to remember exactly what old John had said. Round Garden Lake—that's where Jim was located in his lonely Post—there was a tribe of Redskins. They were of unusual type. Malefactors among them—thieves, criminals, murderers—were not punished. They were merely turned out by the Tribe to die.

But how?

The Wolves of God took care of them. What were the Wolves of God?

A pack of wolves the Redskins held in awe, a sacred pack, a spirit pack—God curse the man! Absurd, outlandish nonsense! Superstitious humbug! A pack of wolves that punished malefactors, killing but never eating them. "Torn but not eaten," the words came back to him, "white men as well as red. They could even cross the sea . . . "

"He ought to be strung up for telling such wild yarns. By God—I'll teach him!"

"Jim! My brother, Jim! It's monstrous."

But the old man, in his passionate cold justice, had said a yet more terrible thing, a thing that Tom would never forget, as he never could forgive it: "You mustn't keep him here; you must send him away. We cannot have him on the island." And for that, though he could scarcely believe his ears, wondering afterwards whether he heard aright, for that, the proper answer to which was a blow in the mouth, Tom knew that his old friendship and affection had turned to bitter hatred.

"If I don't kill him, for that cursed lie, may God—and Jim—forgive me!"

III

It was a few days later that the storm caught the islands, making them tremble in their sea-born bed. The wind tearing over the treeless expanse was terrible, the lightning lit the skies. No such rain had ever been known. The building shook and trembled. It almost seemed the sea had burst her limits, and the waves poured in. Its fury and the noises that the wind made affected both the brothers, but Jim disliked the uproar most. It made him gloomy, silent, morose. It made him—Tom perceived it at once—uneasy. "Scared in his soul"—the ugly phrase came back to him.

"God save anyone who's out tonight," said Jim anxiously, as the old farm rattled about his head. Whereupon the door opened as of itself. There was no knock. It flew wide, as if the wind had burst it. Two drenched and beaten figures showed in the gap against the lurid sky—old John Rossiter and Sandy. They laid their fowling pieces down and took off their capes; they had been up at the lake for the evening flight and six birds were in the game bag. So suddenly had the storm come up that they had been caught before they could get home.

And, while Tom welcomed them, looked after their creature wants, and made them feel at home as in duty bound, no visit, he felt at the same time, could have been less opportune. Sandy did not matter—Sandy never did matter anywhere, his personality being negligible—but John Rossiter was the last man Tom wished to see just then. He hated the man; hated that sense of implacable justice that he knew was in him; with the slightest excuse he would have turned him out and sent him on to his own home, storm or no storm. But Rossiter provided no excuse; he was all gratitude and easy politeness, more pleasant and friendly to Jim even than to his brother. Tom set out the whisky and sugar, sliced the lemon, put the kettle on, and furnished dry coats while the soaked garments hung up before the roaring fire that Orkney makes customary even when days are warm.

"It might be the equinoctials," observed Sandy, "if it wasn't late October." He shivered, for the tropics had thinned his blood.

"This ain't no ordinary storm," put in Rossiter, drying his drenched boots. "It reminds me a bit"—he jerked his head to the window that gave seawards, the rush of rain against the panes half drowning his voice—"reminds me a bit of yonder." He looked up, as though to find someone to agree with him, only one such person being in the room.

"Sure, it ain't," agreed Jim at once, but speaking slowly, "no ordinary storm." His voice was quiet as a child's. Tom, stooping over the kettle, felt something cold go trickling down his back. "It's from acrost the Atlantic too."

"All our big storms come from the sea," offered Sandy, saying just what Sandy was expected to say. His lank red hair lay matted on his forehead, making him look like an unhappy collie dog.

"There's no hospitality," Rossiter changed the talk, "like an islander's," as Tom mixed and filled the glasses. "He don't even ask 'Say when?'" He chuckled in his beard and turned to Sandy, well pleased with the compliment to his host. "Now, in Malay," he added dryly, "it's probably different, I guess." And the two men, one from Labrador, the other from the tropics, fell to bantering one another with heavy humour, while Tom made things comfortable and Jim stood silent with his back to the fire. At each blow of the wind that shook the building, a suitable remark was made, generally by Sandy: "Did you hear that now?"

"Ninety miles an hour at least." "Good thing you build solid in this country!" while Rossiter occasionally repeated that it was an "uncommon storm" and that "it reminded" him of the northern tempests he had known "out yonder."

Tom said little, one thought and one thought only in his heart—the wish that the storm would abate and his guests depart. He felt uneasy about Jim. He hated Rossiter. In the kitchen he had steadied himself already with a good stiff drink, and was now halfway through a second; the feeling was in him that he would need their help before the evening was out. Jim, he noticed, had left his glass untouched. His attention, clearly, went to the wind and the outer night; he added little to the conversation.

"Hark!" cried Sandy's shrill voice. "Did you hear that? That wasn't wind, I'll swear." He sat up, looking for all the world like a dog pricking its ears to something no one else could hear.

"The sea coming over the dunes," said Rossiter. "There'll be an awful tide tonight and a terrible sea off the Swarf. Moon at the full, too." He cocked his head sideways to listen. The roaring was tremendous, waves and wind combining with a result that almost shook the ground. Rain hit the glass with incessant volleys like duck shot.

It was then that Jim spoke, having said no word for a long time.

"It's good there's no trees," he mentioned quietly. "I'm glad of that."

"There'd be fearful damage, wouldn't there?" remarked Sandy. "They might fall on the house too."

But it was the tone Jim used that made Rossiter turn stiffly in his chair, looking first at the speaker, then at his brother. Tom caught both glances and saw the hard keen glitter in the eyes. This kind of talk, he decided, had got to stop, yet how to stop it he hardly knew, for his were not subtle methods, and rudeness to his guests ran too strong against the island customs. He refilled the glasses, thinking in his blunt fashion how best to achieve his object, when Sandy helped the situation without knowing it.

"That's my first," he observed, and all burst out laughing. For Sandy's tenth glass was equally his "first," and he absorbed his liquor like a sponge, yet showed no effects of it until the moment when he would suddenly collapse and sink helpless to the ground. The glass in question, however, was only his third, the final moment still far away.

"Three in one and one in three," said Rossiter, amid the general laughter, while Sandy, grave as a judge, half emptied it at a single gulp. Good-natured, obtuse as a carthorse, the tropics, it seemed, had first worn out his nerves, then removed them entirely from his body. "That's Malay theology, I guess," finished Rossiter. And the laugh broke out again. Whereupon, setting his glass down, Sandy offered his usual explanation that the hot lands had thinned his blood, that he felt the cold in these "arctic islands," and that alcohol was a necessity of life with him. Tom, grateful for the unexpected help, encouraged him to talk, and Sandy, accustomed to neglect as a rule, responded readily. Having saved the situation, however, he now unwittingly led it back into the danger zone.

"A night for tales, eh?" he remarked, as the wind came howling with a burst of strangest noises against the house. "Down there in the States," he went on, "they'd say the evil spirits were out. They're a superstitious crowd, the natives. I remember once—" And he told a tale, half foolish, half interesting, of a mysterious track he had seen when following buffalo in the jungle. It ran close to the spoor of a wounded buffalo for miles, a track unlike that of any known animal, and the natives, though unable to name it, regarded it with awe. It was a good sign, a kill was certain. They said it was a spirit track.

"You got your buffalo?" asked Tom.

"Found him two miles away, lying dead. The mysterious spoor came to an end close beside the carcass. It didn't continue."

"And that reminds me—" began old Rossiter, ignoring Tom's attempt to introduce another subject. He told them of the haunted island at Eagle River, and a tale of the man who would not stay buried on another island off the coast. From that he went on to describe the strange man-beast that hides in the deep forests of Labrador, manifesting but rarely, and dangerous to men who stray too far from camp, men with a passion for wild life over-strong in their blood—the great mythical Wendigo. And while he talked, Tom noticed that Sandy used each pause as a good moment for a drink, but that Jim's glass still remained untouched.

The atmosphere of incredible things, thus, grew in the little room, much as it gathers among the shadows round a forest campfire when men who have seen strange places of the world give tongue about them, knowing they will not be laughed at— an atmosphere, once established, it is vain to fight against. The ingrained superstition that hides in every mother's son comes up at such times to breathe. It came up now. Sandy, closer by several glasses to the moment, Tom saw, when he would be suddenly drunk, gave birth again, a tale this time of a Scottish planter who had brutally dismissed a native servant for no other reason than that he disliked him. The man disappeared completely, but the villagers hinted that he would—soon indeed that he had— come back, though "not quite as he went." The planter armed, knowing that vengeance might be violent. A black panther, meanwhile, was seen prowling about the bungalow. One night a noise outside his door on the veranda roused him. Just in time to see the black brute leaping over the railings into the compound, he fired, and the beast fell with a savage growl of pain. Help arrived and more shots were fired into the animal, as it lay, mortally wounded already, lashing its tail upon the grass. The lanterns, however, showed that instead of a panther, it was the servant they had shot to shreds.

Sandy told the story well, a certain odd conviction in his tone and manner, neither of them at all to the liking of his host. Uneasiness and annoyance had been growing in Tom for some time already, his inability to control the situation adding to his anger. Emotion was accumulating in him dangerously; it was directed chiefly against Rossiter, who, though saying nothing definite, somehow deliberately encouraged both talk and atmosphere. Given the conditions, it was natural enough the talk should take the turn it did take, but what made Tom more and more angry was that, if Rossiter had not been present, he could have stopped it easily enough. It was the presence of the old Hudson Bay man that prevented his taking decided action. He was afraid of Rossiter, afraid of putting his back up. That was the truth. His recognition of it made him furious.

"Tell us another, Sandy McKay," said the veteran. "There's a lot in such tales. They're found the world over—men turning into animals and the like."

And Sandy, yet nearer to his moment of collapse, but still showing no effects, obeyed willingly. He noticed nothing; the whisky was good, his tales were appreciated, and that sufficed him. He thanked Tom, who just then refilled his glass, and went on with his tale. But Tom, hatred and fury in his heart, had reached the point where he could no longer contain himself, and Rossiter's last words inflamed him. He went over, under cover of a tremendous clap of wind, to fill the old man's glass. The latter refused, covering the tumbler with his big, lean hand. Tom stood over him a moment, lowering his face. "You keep still," he whispered ferociously, but so that no one else heard it. He glared into his eyes with an intensity that held danger, and Rossiter, without answering, flung back that glare with equal, but with a calmer, anger.

The wind, meanwhile, had a trick of veering, and each time it shifted, Jim shifted his seat too. Apparently, he preferred to face the sound, rather than have his back to it.

"Your turn now for a tale," said Rossiter with purpose, when Sandy finished. He looked across at him, just as Jim, hearing the burst of wind at the walls behind him, was in the act of moving his chair again. The same moment the attack rattled the door and windows facing him. Jim, without answering, stood for a moment still as death, not knowing which way to turn.

"It's beatin' up from all sides," remarked Rossiter, "like it was goin' round the building."

There was a moment's pause, the four men listening with awe to the roar and power of the terrific wind. Tom listened too, but at the same time watched, wondering vaguely why he didn't cross the room and crash his fist into the old man's chattering mouth. Jim put out his hand and took his glass, but did not raise it to his lips. And a lull came abruptly in the storm, the wind sinking into a moment's dreadful silence. Tom and Rossiter turned their heads in the same instant and stared into each other's eyes. For Tom the instant seemed enormously prolonged. He realized the challenge in the other and that his rudeness had roused it into action. It had become a contest of wills—Justice battling against Love.

Jim's glass had now reached his lips, and the chattering of his teeth against its rim was audible.

But the lull passed quickly and the wind began again, though so gently at first, it had the sound of innumerable swift footsteps treading lightly, of countless hands fingering the doors and windows, but then suddenly with a mighty shout as it swept against the walls, rushed across the roof and descended like a battering-ram against the farther side.

"God, did you hear that?" cried Sandy. "It's trying to get in!" and having said it, he sank in a heap beside his chair, all of a sudden completely drunk. "It's wolves or panthersh," he mumbled in his stupor on the floor, "but whatsh's happened to Malay?" It was the last thing he said before unconsciousness took him, and apparently he was insensible to the kick on the head from a heavy farmer's boot. For Jim's glass had fallen with a crash and the second kick was stopped midway. Tom stood spellbound, unable to move or speak, as he watched his brother suddenly cross the room and open a window into the very teeth of the gale.

"Let be! Let be!" came the voice of Rossiter, an authority in it, a curious gentleness too, both of them new. He had risen, his lips were still moving, but the words that issued from them were inaudible, as the wind and rain leaped with a galloping violence into the room, smashing the glass to atoms and dashing a dozen loose objects helter-skelter on to the floor.

"I saw it!" cried Jim, in a voice that rose above the din and clamour of the elements. He turned and faced the others, but it was at Rossiter he looked. "I saw the leader." He shouted to make himself heard, although the tone was quiet. "A splash of white on his great chest. I saw them all!"

At the words, and at the expression in Jim's eyes, old Rossiter, white to the lips, dropped back into his chair as if a blow had struck him. Tom, petrified, felt his own heart stop. For through the broken window, above yet within the wind, came the sound of a wolf-pack running, howling in deep, full-throated chorus, mad for blood. It passed like a whirlwind and was gone. And, of the three men so close together, one sitting and two standing, Jim alone was in that terrible moment wholly master of himself.

Before the others could move or speak, he turned and looked full into the eyes of each in succession. His speech went back to his wilderness days:

"I done it," he said calmly. "I killed him—and I got ter go."

With a look of mystical horror on his face, he took one stride, flung the door wide, and vanished into the darkness.

So quick were both words and action, that Tom's paralysis passed only as the draught from the broken window banged the door behind him. He seemed to leap across the room, old Rossiter, tears on his cheeks and his lips mumbling foolish words, so close upon his heels that the backward blow of fury Tom aimed at his face caught him only in the neck and sent him reeling sideways to the floor instead of flat upon his back.

"Murderer! My brother's death upon you!" he shouted as he tore the door open again and plunged out into the night.

And the odd thing that happened then, the thing that touched old John Rossiter's reason, leaving him from that moment till his death a foolish man of uncertain mind and memory, happened when he and the unconscious, drink-sodden Sandy lay alone together on the stone floor of that farmhouse room.

Rossiter, dazed by the blow and his fall, but in full possession of his senses, and the anger gone out of him owing to what he had brought about, this same John Rossiter sat up and saw Sandy also sitting up and staring at him hard. And Sandy was sober as a judge, his eyes and speech both clear, even his face unflushed.

"John Rossiter," he said, "it was not God who appointed you executioner. It was the devil." And his eyes, thought Rossiter, were like the eyes of an angel.

"Sandy McKay," he stammered, his teeth chattering and breath failing him. "Sandy McKay!" It was all the words that he could find. But Sandy, already sunk back into his stupor again, was stretched drunk and incapable upon the farmhouse floor, and remained in that condition till the dawn.

Jim's body lay hidden among the dunes for many months and in spite of the most careful and prolonged searching. It was another storm that laid it bare. The sand had covered it. The clothes were gone, and the flesh, torn but not eaten, was naked to the December sun and wind.

The Wolves of God and Other Fey Stories, 1921

THE TARN
OF SACRIFICE

John Holt, a vague excitement in him, stood at the door of the little inn, listening to the landlord's directions as to the best way of reaching Scarsdale. He was on a walking tour through the Lake District, exploring the smaller dales that lie away from the beaten track and are accessible only on foot.

The landlord, a hard-featured north countryman, half innkeeper, half sheep farmer, pointed up the valley. His deep voice had a friendly burr in it.

"You go straight on till you reach the head," he said, "then take to the fell. Follow the 'sheep-trod' past the Crag. Directly you're over the top you'll strike the road."

"A road up there!" exclaimed his customer incredulously.

"Aye," was the steady reply. "The old Roman road. The same road," he added, "the savages came down when they burst through the Wall and burnt everything right up to Lancaster—"

"They were held—weren't they—at Lancaster?" asked the other, yet not knowing quite why he asked it.

"I don't rightly know," came the answer slowly. "Some say they were. But the old town has been that built over since, it's hard to tell." He paused a moment. "At Ambleside," he went on presently, "you can still see the marks of the burning, and at the little fort on the way to Ravenglass."

Holt strained his eyes into the sunlit distance, for he would soon have to walk that road and he was anxious to be off. But the landlord was communicative and interesting. "You can't miss it," he told him. "It runs straight as a spear along the fell top till it meets the Wall. You must hold to it for about eight miles. Then you'll come to the Standing Stone on the left of the track—"

"The Standing Stone, yes?" broke in the other a little eagerly.

"You'll see the Stone right enough. It was where the Romans came. Then bear to the left down another 'trod' that comes into the road there. They say it was the war-trail of the folk that set up the Stone."

"And what did they use the Stone for?" Holt inquired, more as though he asked it of himself than of his companion.

The old man paused to reflect. He spoke at length.

"I mind an old fellow who seemed to know about such things called it a Sighting Stone. He reckoned the sun shone over it at dawn on the longest day right on to the little holm in Blood Tarn. He said they held sacrifices in a stone circle there." He stopped a moment to puff at his black pipe. "Maybe he was right. I have seen stones lying about that may well be that."

The man was pleased and willing to talk to so good a listener. Either he had not noticed the curious gesture the other made, or he read it as a sign of eagerness to start. The sun was warm, but a sharp wind from the bare hills went between them with a sighing sound. Holt buttoned his coat about him. "An odd name for a mountain lake—Blood Tarn," he remarked, watching the landlord's face expectantly.

"Aye, but a good one," was the measured reply. "When I was a boy the old folk had a tale that the savages flung three Roman captives from that crag into the water. There's a book been written about it; they say it was a sacrifice, but most likely they were tired of dragging them along, *I* say. Anyway, that's what the writer said. One, I mind, now you ask me, was a priest of some heathen temple that stood near the Wall, and the other two were his daughter and her lover." He guffawed. At least he made a strange noise in his throat. Evidently, thought Holt, he was sceptical yet superstitious. "It's just an old tale handed down, whatever the learned folk may say," the old man added.

"A lonely place," began Holt, aware that a fleeting touch of awe was added suddenly to his interest.

"Aye," said the other, "and a bad spot too. Every year the Crag takes its toll of sheep, and sometimes a man goes over in the mist. It's right beside the track and very slippery. Ninety foot of a drop before you hit the water. Best keep round the tarn and leave the Crag alone if there's any mist about. Fishing? Yes, there's some quite fair trout in the tarn, but it's not much fished. Happen one of the shepherd lads from Tyson's farm may give it a turn with an 'otter,'" he went on, "once in a while, but he won't stay for the evening. He'll clear out before sunset."

"Ah! Superstitious, I suppose?"

"It's a gloomy, chancy spot—and with the dusk falling," agreed the innkeeper eventually. "None of our folk care to be caught up there with night coming on. Most handy for a shepherd, too— but Tyson can't get a man to bide there." He paused again, then added significantly: "Strangers don't seem to mind it though. It's only our own folk—"

"Strangers!" repeated the other sharply, as though he had been waiting all along for this special bit of information. "You don't mean to say there are people living up there?" A curious thrill ran over him.

"Aye," replied the landlord, "but they're daft folk—a man and his daughter. They come every spring. It's early in the year yet, but I mind Jim Backhouse, one of Tyson's men, talking about them last week." He stopped to think. "So they've come back," he went on decidedly. "They get milk from the farm."

"And what on earth are they doing up there?" Holt asked.

He asked many other questions as well, but the answers were poor, the information not forthcoming. The landlord would talk for hours about the Crag, the tarn, the legends and the Romans, but concerning the two strangers he was uncommunicative. Either he knew little, or he did not want to discuss them; Holt felt it was probably the former. They were educated town-folk, he gathered with difficulty, rich apparently, and they spent their time wandering about the fell, or fishing. The man was often seen upon the Crag, his girl beside him, barelegged, dressed as a peasant. "Happen they come for their health, happen the father is a learned man studying the Wall"—exact information was not forthcoming.

The landlord "minded his own business," and inhabitants were too few and far between for gossip. All Holt could extract amounted to this: the couple had been in a motor accident some years before, and as a result they came every spring to spend a month or two in absolute solitude, away from cities and the excitement of modern life. They troubled no one and no one troubled them.

"Perhaps I may see them as I go by the tarn," remarked the walker finally, making ready to go. He gave up questioning in despair. The morning hours were passing.

"Happen you may," was the reply, "for your track goes past their door and leads straight down to Scarsdale. The other way over the Crag saves half a mile, but it's rough going along the scree." He stopped dead. Then he added, in reply to Holt's goodbye: "In my opinion it's not worth it," yet what he meant exactly by "it" was not quite clear.

* * * * *

The walker shouldered his knapsack. Instinctively he gave the little hitch to settle it on his shoulders—much as he used to give to his pack in France. The pain that shot through him as he did so was another reminder of France. The bullet he had stopped on the Somme still made its presence felt at times . . . Yet he knew, as he walked off briskly, that he was one of the lucky ones. How many of his old pals would never walk again, condemned to hobble on crutches for the rest of their lives! How many, again, would never even hobble! More terrible still, he remembered, were the blind. . . The dead, it seemed to him, had been more fortunate . . .

He swung up the narrowing valley at a good pace and was soon climbing the fell. It proved far steeper than it had appeared from the door of the inn, and he was glad enough to reach the top and fling himself down on the coarse springy turf to admire the view below.

The spring day was delicious. It stirred his blood. The world beneath looked young and stainless. Emotion rose through him in a wave of optimistic happiness. The bare hills were half hidden by a soft blue haze that made them look bigger, vaster, less earthly than they really were. He saw silver streaks in the valleys that he knew were distant streams and lakes. Birds soared between. The dazzling air seemed painted with exhilarating light and colour. The very clouds were floating gossamer that he could touch. There were bees and dragonflies and fluttering thistledown. Heat vibrated. His body, his physical sensations, so-called, retired into almost nothing. He felt himself, like his surroundings, made of air and sunlight. A delicious sense of resignation poured upon him. He, too, like his surroundings, was composed of air and sunshine, of insect wings, of soft, fluttering vibrations that the gorgeous spring day produced . . . It seemed that he renounced the heavy dues of bodily life, and enjoyed the delights, momentarily at any rate, of a more ethereal consciousness.

Near at hand, the hills were covered with the faded gold of last year's bracken, which ran down in a brimming flood till it was lost in the fresh green of the familiar woods below. Far in the hazy distance swam the sea of ash and hazel. The silver birch sprinkled that lower world with fairy light.

Yes, it was all natural enough. He could see the road quite clearly now, only a hundred yards away from where he lay. How straight it ran along the top of the hill! The landlord's expression recurred to him: "Straight as a spear." Somehow, the phrase seemed to describe exactly the Romans and all their works . . . The Romans, yes, and all their works. . .

He became aware of a sudden sympathy with these long dead conquerors of the world. With them, he felt sure, there had been no useless, foolish talk. They had known no empty words, no bandying of foolish phrases. "War to end war," and "Regeneration of the race"—no hypocritical nonsense of that sort had troubled their minds and purposes. They had not attempted to cover up the horrible in words. With them had been no childish, vain pretence. They had gone straight to their ends.

Other thoughts, too, stole over him, as he sat gazing down upon the track of that ancient road; strange thoughts, not wholly welcome. New, yet old, emotions rose in a tide upon him. He began to wonder . . . Had he, after all, become brutalized by the War? He knew quite well that the little "Christianity" he inherited had soon fallen from him like a garment in France. In his attitude to Life and Death he had become, frankly, pagan. He now realized, abruptly, another thing as well: in reality he had never been a "Christian" at any time. Given to him with his mother's milk, he had never accepted, felt at home with Christian dogmas. To him they had always been an alien creed. Christianity met none of his requirements . . .

But what were his "requirements"? He found it difficult to answer.

Something, at any rate, different and more primitive, he thought . . .

Even up here, alone on the mountain-top, it was hard to be absolutely frank with himself. With a kind of savage, honest determination, he bent himself to the task. It became suddenly important for him. He must know exactly where he stood. It seemed he had reached a turning point in his life. The War, in the objective world, had been one such turning point; now he had reached another, in the subjective life, and it was more important than the first.

As he lay there in the pleasant sunshine, his thoughts went back to the fighting. A friend, he recalled, had divided people into those who enjoyed the War and those who didn't. He was obliged to admit that he had been one of the former—he had thoroughly enjoyed it. Brought up from a youth as an engineer, he had taken to a soldier's life as a duck takes to water. There had been plenty of misery, discomfort, wretchedness; but there had been compensations that, for him, outweighed them. The fierce excitement, the primitive, naked passions, the wild fury, the reckless indifference to pain and death, with the loss of the normal, cautious, pettifogging little daily self all these involved, had satisfied him. Even the actual killing . . .

He started. A slight shudder ran down his back as the cool wind from the open moorlands came sighing across the soft spring sunshine. Sitting up straight, he looked behind him a moment, as with an effort to turn away from something he disliked and dreaded because it was, he knew, too strong for him. But the same instant he turned round again. He faced the vile and dreadful thing in himself he had hitherto sought to deny, evade. Pretence fell away. He could not disguise from himself, that he had thoroughly enjoyed the killing; or, at any rate, had not been shocked by it as by an unnatural and ghastly duty. The shooting and bombing he performed with an effort always, but the rarer moments when he had been able to use the bayonet . . . the joy of feeling the steel go home . . .

He started again, hiding his face a moment in his hands, but he did not try to evade the hideous memories that surged. At times, he knew, he had gone quite mad with the lust of slaughter; he had gone on long after he should have stopped. Once an officer had pulled him up sharply for it, but the next instant had been killed by a bullet. He thought he had gone on killing, but he did not know. It was all a red mist before his eyes and he could only remember the sticky feeling of the blood on his hands when he gripped his rifle . . .

And now, at this moment of painful honesty with himself, he realized that his creed, whatever it was, must cover all that; it must provide some sort of a philosophy for it; must neither apologize nor ignore it. The heaven that it promised must be a man's heaven. The Christian heaven made no appeal to him, he could not believe in it. The ritual must be simple and direct. He felt that in some dim way he understood why those old people had thrown their captives from the Crag. The sacrifice of an animal victim that could be eaten afterwards with due ceremonial did not shock him. Such methods seemed simple, natural, effective. Yet would it not have been better—the horrid thought rose unbidden in his inmost mind—better to have cut their throats with a flint knife . . . slowly?

Horror-stricken, he sprang to his feet. These terrible thoughts he could not recognize as his own. Had he slept a moment in the sunlight, dreaming them? Was it some hideous nightmare flash that touched him as he dozed a second? Something of fear and awe stole over him. He stared round for some minutes into the emptiness of the desolate landscape, then hurriedly ran down to the road, hoping to exorcize the strange sudden horror by vigorous movement. Yet when he reached the track he knew that he had not succeeded. The awful pictures were gone perhaps, but the mood remained. It was as though some new attitude began to take definite form and harden within him.

He walked on, trying to pretend to himself that he was some forgotten legionary marching up with his fellows to defend the Wall. Half unconsciously he fell into the steady tramping pace of his old regiment: the words of the ribald songs they had sung going to the front came pouring into his mind. Steadily and almost mechanically he swung along till he saw the Stone as a black speck on the left of the track, and the instant he saw it there rose in him the feeling that he stood upon the edge of an adventure that he feared yet longed for. He approached the great granite monolith with a curious thrill of anticipatory excitement, born he knew not whence.

But, of course, there was nothing. Common sense, still operating strongly, had warned him there would be, could be, nothing. In the waste the great Stone stood upright, solitary, forbidding, as it had stood for thousands of years. It dominated the landscape somewhat ominously. The sheep and cattle had used it as a rubbing-stone, and bits of hair and wool clung to its rough, weather-eaten edges; the feet of generations had worn a cup-shaped hollow at its base. The wind sighed round it plaintively. Its bulk glistened as it took the sun.

A short mile away the Blood Tarn was now plainly visible; he could see the little holm lying in a direct line with the Stone, while, overhanging the water as a dark shadow on one side, rose the cliff-like rock they called "the Crag." Of the house the landlord had mentioned, however, he could see no trace, as he relieved his shoulders of the knapsack and sat down to enjoy his lunch. The tarn, he reflected, was certainly a gloomy place; he could understand that the simple superstitious shepherds did not dare to live there, for even on this bright spring day it wore a dismal and forbidding look. With failing light, when the Crag sprawled its big lengthening shadow across the water, he could well imagine they would give it the widest possible berth. He strolled down to the shore after lunch, smoking his pipe lazily— then suddenly stood still. At the far end, hidden hitherto by a fold in the ground, he saw the little house, a faint column of blue smoke rising from the chimney, and at the same moment a woman came out of the low door and began to walk towards the tarn. She had seen him, she was moving evidently in his direction; a few minutes later she stopped and stood waiting on the path—waiting, he well knew, for him.

And his earlier mood, the mood he dreaded yet had forced himself to recognize, came back upon him with sudden redoubled power. As in some vivid dream that dominates and paralyses the will, or as in the first stages of an imposed hypnotic spell, all question, hesitation, refusal sank away. He felt a pleasurable resignation steal upon him with soft, numbing effect. Denial and criticism ceased to operate, and common sense died with them. He yielded his being automatically to the deeps of an adventure he did not understand. He began to walk towards the woman.

It was, he saw as he drew nearer, the figure of a young girl, nineteen or twenty years of age, who stood there motionless with her eyes fixed steadily on his own. She looked as wild and picturesque as the scene that framed her. Thick black hair hung loose over her back and shoulders; about her head was bound a green ribbon; her clothes consisted of a jersey and a very short skirt which showed her bare legs browned by exposure to the sun and wind. A pair of rough sandals covered her feet. Whether the face was beautiful or not he could not tell; he only knew that it attracted him immensely and with a strength of appeal that he at once felt curiously irresistible. She remained motionless against the boulder, staring fixedly at him till he was close before her. Then she spoke:

"I am glad that you have come at last," she said in a clear, strong voice that yet was soft and even tender. "We have been expecting you."

"You have been expecting me!" he repeated, astonished beyond words, yet finding the language natural, right and true. A stream of sweet feeling invaded him, his heart beat faster, he felt happy and at home in some extraordinary way he could not understand yet did not question.

"Of course," she answered, looking straight into his eyes with welcome unashamed. Her next words thrilled him to the core of his being. "I have made the room ready for you."

Quick upon her own, however, flashed back the landlord's words, while common sense made a last faint effort in his thought. He was the victim of some absurd mistake evidently. The lonely life, the forbidding surroundings, the associations of the desolate hills had affected her mind. He remembered the accident.

"I am afraid," he offered, lamely enough, "there is some mistake. I am not the friend you were expecting. I—" He stopped. A thin slight sound as of distant laughter seemed to echo behind the unconvincing words.

"There is no mistake," the girl answered firmly, with a quiet smile, moving a step nearer to him, so that he caught the subtle perfume of her vigorous youth. "I saw you clearly in the Mystery Stone. I recognized you at once."

"The Mystery Stone," he heard himself saying, bewilderment increasing, a sense of wild happiness growing with it.

Laughing, she took his hand in hers. "Come," she said, drawing him along with her, "come home with me. My father will be waiting for us; he will tell you everything, and better far than I can."

He went with her, feeling that he was made of sunlight and that he walked on air, for at her touch his own hand responded as with a sudden fierceness of pleasure that he failed utterly to understand, yet did not question for an instant. Wildly, absurdly, madly it flashed across his mind: "This is the woman I shall marry—*my* woman. I am her man."

They walked in silence for a little, for no words of any sort offered themselves to his mind, nor did the girl attempt to speak. The total absence of embarrassment between them occurred to him once or twice as curious, though the very idea of embarrassment then disappeared entirely. It all seemed natural and unforced, the sudden intercourse as familiar and effortless as though they had known one another always.

"The Mystery Stone," he heard himself saying presently, as the idea rose again to the surface of his mind. "I should like to know more about it. Tell me, dear."

"I bought it with the other things," she replied softly.

"What other things?"

She turned and looked up into his face with a slight expression of surprise; their shoulders touched as they swung along; her hair blew in the wind across his coat. "The bronze collar," she answered in the low voice that pleased him so, "and this ornament that I wear in my hair."

He glanced down to examine it. Instead of a ribbon, as he had first supposed, he saw that it was a circlet of bronze, covered with a beautiful green patina and evidently very old. In front, above the forehead, was a small disk bearing an inscription he could not decipher at the moment. He bent down and kissed her hair, the girl smiling with happy contentment, but offering no sign of resistance or annoyance.

"And," she added suddenly, "the dagger."

Holt started visibly. This time there was a thrill in her voice that seemed to pierce down straight into his heart. He said nothing, however. The unexpectedness of the word she used, together with the note in her voice that moved him so strangely, had a disconcerting effect that kept him silent for a time. He did not ask about the dagger. Something prevented his curiosity finding expression in speech, though the word, with the marked accent she placed upon it, had struck into him like the shock of sudden steel itself, causing him an indecipherable emotion of both joy and pain. He asked instead, presently, another question, and a very commonplace one: he asked where she and her father had lived before they came to these lonely hills. And the form of his question—his voice shook a little as he said it— was, again, an effort of his normal self to maintain its already precarious balance.

The effect of his simple query, the girl's reply above all, increased in him the mingled sensations of sweetness and menace, of joy and dread, that half alarmed, half satisfied him. For a moment she wore a puzzled expression, as though making an effort to remember.

"Down by the sea," she answered slowly, thoughtfully, her voice very low. "Somewhere by a big harbour with great ships coming in and out. It was there we had the break—the shock— an accident that broke us, shattering the dream we share Today." Her face cleared a little. "We were in a chariot," she went on more easily and rapidly, "and father—my father was injured, so that I went with him to a palace beyond the Wall till he grew well."

"You were in a chariot?" Holt repeated. "Surely not."

"Did I say chariot?" the girl replied. "How foolish of me!" She shook her hair back as though the gesture helped to clear her mind and memory. "That belongs, of course, to the other dream. No, not a chariot; it was a car. But it had wheels like a chariot— the old war-chariots. You know."

"Disk-wheels," thought Holt to himself. He did not ask about the palace. He asked instead where she had bought the Mystery Stone, as she called it, and the other things. Her reply bemused and enticed him farther, for he could not unravel it. His whole inner attitude was shifting with uncanny rapidity and completeness. They walked together, he now realized, with linked arms, moving slowly in step, their bodies touching. He felt the blood run hot and almost savage in his veins. He was aware how amazingly precious she was to him, how deeply, absolutely necessary to his life and happiness. Her words went past him in the mountain wind like flying birds.

"My father was fishing," she went on, "and I was on my way to join him, when the old woman called me into her dwelling and showed me the things. She wished to give them to me, but I refused the present and paid for them in gold. I put the fillet on my head to see if it would fit, and took the Mystery Stone in my hand. Then, as I looked deep into the stone, this present dream died all away. It faded out. I saw the older dreams again— *our* dreams."

"The older dreams!" interrupted Holt. "Ours!" But instead of saying the words aloud, they issued from his lips in a quiet whisper, as though control of his voice had passed a little from him. The sweetness in him became more wonderful, unmanageable; his astonishment had vanished; he walked and talked with his old familiar happy Love, the woman he had sought so long and waited for, the woman who was his mate, as he was hers, she who alone could satisfy his inmost soul.

"The old dream," she replied, "the very old—the oldest of all perhaps—when we committed the terrible sacrilege. I saw the High Priest lying dead—whom my father slew—and the other whom *you* destroyed. I saw you prise out the jewel from the image of the god—with your short bloody spear. I saw, too, our flight to the galley through the hot, awful night beneath the stars—and our escape . . . "

Her voice died away and she fell silent.

"Tell me more," he whispered, drawing her closer against his side. "What had *you* done?" His heart was racing now. Some fighting blood surged uppermost. He felt that he could kill, and the joy of violence and slaughter rose in him.

"Have you forgotten so completely?" she asked very low, as he pressed her more tightly still against his heart. And almost beneath her breath she whispered into his ear, which he bent to catch the little sound: "I had broken my vows with you."

"What else, my lovely one—my best beloved—what more did you see?" he whispered in return, yet wondering why the fierce pain and anger that he felt behind still lay hidden from betrayal.

"Dream after dream, and always we were punished. But the last time was the clearest, for it was here—here where we now walk together in the sunlight and the wind—it was here the savages hurled us from the rock."

A shiver ran through him, making him tremble with an unaccountable touch of cold that communicated itself to her as well. Her arm went instantly about his shoulder, as he stooped and kissed her passionately. "Fasten your coat about you," she said tenderly, but with troubled breath, when he released her, "for this wind is chill although the sun shines brightly. We were glad, you remember, when they stopped to kill us, for we were tired and our feet were cut to pieces by the long, rough journey from the Wall." Then suddenly her voice grew louder again and the smile of happy confidence came back into her eyes. There was the deep earnestness of love in it, of love that cannot end or die. She looked up into his face. "But soon now," she said, "we shall be free. For you have come, and it is nearly finished—this weary little present dream."

"How," he asked, "shall we get free?" A red mist swam momentarily before his eyes.

"My father," she replied at once, "will tell you all. It is quite easy."

"Your father, too, remembers?"

"The moment the collar touches him," she said, "he is a priest again. See! Here he comes forth already to meet us, and to bid you welcome."

Holt looked up, startled. He had hardly noticed, so absorbed had he been in the words that half intoxicated him, the distance they had covered. The cottage was now close at hand, and a tall, powerfully built man, wearing a shepherd's rough clothing, stood a few feet in front of him. His stature, breadth of shoulder and thick black beard made up a striking figure. The dark eyes, with fire in them, gazed straight into his own, and a kindly smile played round the stern and vigorous mouth.

"Greeting, my son," said a deep, booming voice, "for I shall call you my son as I did of old. The bond of the spirit is stronger than that of the flesh, and with us three the tie is indeed of triple strength. You come, too, at an auspicious hour, for the omens are favourable and the time of our liberation is at hand." He took the other's hand in a grip that might have killed an ox and yet was warm with gentle kindliness, while Holt, now caught wholly into the spirit of some deep reality he could not master yet accepted, saw that the wrist was small, the fingers shapely, the gesture itself one of dignity and refinement.

"Greeting, my father," he replied, as naturally as though he said more modern words.

"Come in with me, I pray," pursued the other, leading the way, "and let me show you the poor accommodation we have provided, yet the best that we can offer."

He stooped to pass the threshold, and as Holt stooped likewise the girl took his hand and he knew that his bewitchment was complete. Entering the low doorway, he passed through a kitchen, where only the roughest, scantiest furniture was visible, into another room that was completely bare. A heap of dried bracken had been spread on the floor in one corner to form a bed. Beside it lay two cheap, coloured blankets. There was nothing else.

"Our place is poor," said the man, smiling courteously, but with that dignity and air of welcome which made the hovel seem a palace. "Yet it may serve, perhaps, for the short time that you will need it. Our little dream here is well-nigh over, now that you have come. The long weary pilgrimage at last draws to a close." The girl had left them alone a moment, and the man stepped closer to his guest. His face grew solemn, his voice deeper and more earnest suddenly, the light in his eyes seemed actually to flame with the enthusiasm of a great belief. "Why have you tarried thus so long, and where?" he asked in a lowered tone that vibrated in the little space. "We have sought you with prayer and fasting, and she has spent her nights for you in tears. You lost the way, it must be. The lesser dreams entangled your feet, I see." A touch of sadness entered the voice, the eyes held pity in them. "It is, alas, too easy, I well know," he murmured. "It is too easy."

"I lost the way," the other replied. It seemed suddenly that his heart was filled with fire. "But now," he cried aloud, "now that I have found her, I will never, never let her go again. My feet are steady and my way is sure."

"Forever and ever, my son," boomed the happy, yet almost solemn answer, "she is yours. Our freedom is at hand."

He turned and crossed the little kitchen again, making a sign that his guest should follow him. They stood together by the door, looking out across the tarn in silence. The afternoon sunshine fell in a golden blaze across the bare hills that seemed to smoke with the glory of the fiery light. But the Crag loomed dark in shadow overhead, and the little lake lay deep and black beneath it.

"Acella, Acella!" called the man, the name breaking upon his companion as with a shock of sweet delicious fire that filled his entire being, as the girl came the same instant from behind the cottage. "The Gods call me," said her father. "I go now to the hill. Protect our guest and comfort him in my absence."

Without another word, he strode away up the hillside and presently was visible standing on the summit of the Crag, his arms stretched out above his head to heaven, his great head thrown back, his bearded face turned upwards. An impressive, even a majestic figure he looked, as his bulk and stature rose in dark silhouette against the brilliant evening sky. Holt stood motionless, watching him for several minutes, his heart swelling in his breast, his pulses thumping before some great nameless pressure that rose from the depths of his being. That inner attitude which seemed a new and yet more satisfying attitude to life than he had known hitherto, had crystallized. Define it he could not, he only knew that he accepted it as natural. It satisfied him. The sight of that dignified, gaunt figure worshipping upon the hilltop enflamed him . . .

"I have brought the stone," a voice interrupted his reflections, and turning, he saw the girl beside him. She held out for his inspection a dark square object that looked to him at first like a black stone lying against the brown skin of her hand. "The Mystery Stone," the girl added, as their faces bent down together to examine it. "It is there I see the dreams I told you of."

He took it from her and found that it was heavy, composed apparently of something like black quartz, with a brilliant polished surface that revealed clear depths within. Once, evidently, it had been set in a stand or frame, for the marks where it had been attached still showed, and it was obviously of great age. He felt confused, the mind in him troubled yet excited, as he gazed. The effect upon him was as though a wind rose suddenly and passed across his inmost subjective life, setting its entire contents in rushing motion.

"And here," the girl said, "is the dagger."

He took from her the short bronze weapon, feeling at once instinctively its ragged edge, its keen point, sharp and effective still. The handle had long since rotted away, but the bronze tongue, and the holes where the rivets had been, remained, and, as he touched it, the confusion and trouble in his mind increased to a kind of turmoil, in which violence, linked to something tameless, wild and almost savage, was the dominating emotion. He turned to seize the girl and crush her to him in a passionate embrace, but she held away, throwing back her lovely head, her eyes shining, her lips parted, yet one hand stretched out to stop him.

"First look into it with me," she said quietly. "Let us see together."

She sat down on the turf beside the cottage door, and Holt, obeying, took his place beside her. She remained very still for some minutes, covering the stone with both hands as though to warm it. Her lips moved. She seemed to be repeating some kind of invocation beneath her breath, though no actual words were audible. Presently her hands parted. They sat together gazing at the polished surface. They looked within.

"There comes a white mist in the heart of the stone," the girl whispered. "It will soon open. The pictures will then grow. Look!" she exclaimed after a brief pause, "they are forming now."

"I see only mist," her companion murmured, gazing intently. "Only mist I see."

She took his hand and instantly the mist parted. He found himself peering into another landscape which opened before his eyes as though it were a photograph. Hills covered with heather stretched away on every side.

"Hills, I see," he whispered. "The ancient hills—"

"Watch closely," she replied, holding his hand firmly.

At first the landscape was devoid of any sign of life; then suddenly it surged and swarmed with moving figures. Torrents of men poured over the hill-crests and down their heathery sides in columns. He could see them clearly—great hairy men, clad in skins, with thick shields on their left arms or slung over their backs, and short stabbing spears in their hands. Thousands upon thousands poured over in an endless stream. In the distance he could see other columns sweeping in a turning movement. A few of the men rode rough ponies and seemed to be directing the march, and these, he knew, were the chiefs . . .

The scene grew dimmer, faded, died away completely. Another took its place:

By the faint light he knew that it was dawn. The undulating

country, less hilly than before, was still wild and uncultivated. A great wall, with towers at intervals, stretched away till it was lost in shadowy distance. On the nearest of these towers he saw a sentinel clad in armour, gazing out across the rolling country. The armour gleamed faintly in the pale glimmering light, as the man suddenly snatched up a bugle and blew upon it. From a brazier burning beside him he next seized a brand and fired a great heap of brushwood. The smoke rose in a dense column into the air almost immediately, and from all directions, with incredible rapidity, figures came pouring up to man the wall. Hurriedly they strung their bows, and laid spare arrows close beside them on the coping. The light grew brighter. The whole country was alive with savages; like the waves of the sea they came rolling in enormous numbers. For several minutes the wall held. Then, in an impetuous, fearful torrent, they poured over . . .

It faded, died away, was gone again, and a moment later yet another took its place:

But this time the landscape was familiar, and he recognized the tarn. He saw the savages upon the ledge that flanked the dominating Crag; they had three captives with them. He saw two men. The other was a woman. But the woman had fallen exhausted to the ground, and a chief on a rough pony rode back to see what had delayed the march. Glancing at the captives, he made a fierce gesture with his arm towards the water far below. Instantly the woman was jerked cruelly to her feet and forced onwards till the summit of the Crag was reached. A man snatched something from her hand. A second later she was hurled over the brink.

The two men were next dragged on to the dizzy spot where she had stood. Dead with fatigue, bleeding from numerous wounds, yet at this awful moment they straightened themselves, casting contemptuous glances at the fierce savages surrounding them. They were Romans and would die like Romans. Holt saw their faces clearly for the first time.

He sprang up with a cry of anguished fury.

"The second man!" he exclaimed. "You saw the second man!"

The girl, releasing his hand, turned her eyes slowly up to his, so that he met the flame of her ancient and undying love shining like stars upon him out of the night of time.

"Ever since that moment," she said in a low voice that trembled, "I have been looking, waiting for you—"

He took her in his arms and smothered her words with kisses, holding her fiercely to him as though he would never let her go. "I, too," he said, his whole being burning with his love, "I have been looking, waiting for you. Now I have found you. We have found each other . . . !"

The dusk fell slowly, imperceptibly. As twilight slowly draped the gaunt hills, blotting out familiar details, so the strong dream, veil upon veil, drew closer over the soul of the wanderer, obliterating finally the last reminder of Today. The little wind had dropped and the desolate moors lay silent, but for the hum of distant water falling to its valley bed. His life, too, and the life of the girl, he knew, were similarly falling, falling into some deep shadowed bed where rest would come at last. No details troubled him, he asked himself no questions. A profound sense of happy peace numbed every nerve and stilled his beating heart.

He felt no fear, no anxiety, no hint of alarm or uneasiness vexed his singular contentment. He realized one thing only— that the girl lay in his arms, he held her fast, her breath mingled with his own. They had found each other. What else mattered?

From time to time, as the daylight faded and the sun went down behind the moors, she spoke. She uttered words he vaguely heard, listening, though with a certain curious effort, before he closed the thing she said with kisses. Even the fierceness of his blood was gone. The world lay still, life almost ceased to flow. Lapped in the deeps of his great love, he was redeemed, perhaps, of violence and savagery . . .

"Three dark birds," she whispered, "pass across the sky . . . they fall beyond the ridge. The omens are favourable. A hawk now follows them, cleaving the sky with pointed wings."

"A hawk," he murmured. "The badge of my old Legion."

"My father will perform the sacrifice," he heard again, though it seemed a long interval had passed, and the man's figure was now invisible on the Crag amid the gathering darkness. "Already he prepares the fire. Look, the sacred island is alight. He has the black cock ready for the knife."

Holt roused himself with difficulty, lifting his face from the garden of her hair. A faint light, he saw, gleamed fitfully on the holm within the tarn. Her father, then, had descended from the Crag, and had lit the sacrificial fire upon the stones. But what did the doings of the father matter now to him?

"The dark bird," he repeated dully, "the black victim the Gods of the Underworld alone accept. It is good, Acella, it is good!" He was about to sink back again, taking her against his breast as before, when she resisted and sat up suddenly.

"It is time," she said aloud. "The hour has come. My father climbs, and we must join him on the summit. Come!"

She took his hand and raised him to his feet, and together they began the rough ascent towards the Crag. As they passed along the shore of the Tarn of Blood, he saw the fire reflected in the ink-black waters; he made out, too, though dimly, a rough circle of big stones, with a larger flagstone lying in the centre. Three small fires of bracken and wood, placed in a triangle with its apex towards the Standing Stone on the distant hill, burned briskly, the crackling material sending out sparks that pierced the columns of thick smoke. And in this smoke, peering, shifting, appearing and disappearing, it seemed he saw great faces moving. The flickering light and twirling smoke made clear sight difficult. His bliss, his lethargy were very deep. They left the tarn below them and hand in hand began to climb the final slope.

Whether the physical effort of climbing disturbed the deep pressure of the mood that numbed his senses, or whether the cold draught of wind they met upon the ridge restored some vital detail of Today, Holt does not know. Something, at any rate, in him wavered suddenly, as though a centre of gravity had shifted slightly. There was a perceptible alteration in the balance of thought and feeling that had held invariable now for many hours. It seemed to him that something heavy lifted, or rather, began to lift—a weight, a shadow, something oppressive that obstructed light. A ray of light, as it were, struggled through the thick darkness that enveloped him. To him, as he paused on the ridge to recover his breath, came this vague suggestion of faint light breaking across the blackness. It was objective.

"See," said the girl in a low voice, "the moon is rising. It lights the sacred island. The blood-red waters turn to silver."

He saw, indeed, that a huge three-quarter moon now drove with almost visible movement above the distant line of hills; the little tarn gleamed as with silvery armour; the glow of the sacrificial fires showed red across it. He looked down with a shudder into the sheer depth that opened at his feet, then turned to look at his companion. He started and shrank back. Her face, lit by the moon and by the fire, shone pale as death; her black hair framed it with a terrible suggestiveness; the eyes, though brilliant as ever, had a film upon them. She stood in an attitude of both ecstasy and resignation, and one outstretched arm pointed towards the summit where her father stood.

Her lips parted, a marvellous smile broke over her features, her voice was suddenly unfamiliar: "He wears the collar," she uttered. "Come. Our time is here at last, and we are ready. See, he waits for us!"

There rose for the first time struggle and opposition in him; he resisted the pressure of her hand that had seized his own and drew him forcibly along. Whence came the resistance and the opposition he could not tell, but though he followed her, he was aware that the refusal in him strengthened. The weight of darkness that oppressed him shifted a little more, an inner light increased; The same moment they reached the summit and stood beside—the priest. There was a curious sound of fluttering. The figure, he saw, was naked, save for a rough blanket tied loosely about the waist.

"The hour has come at last," cried his deep booming voice that woke echoes from the dark hills about them. "We are alone now with our Gods." And he broke then into a monotonous rhythmic chanting that rose and fell upon the wind, yet in a tongue that sounded strange; his erect figure swayed slightly with its cadences; his black beard swept his naked chest; and his face, turned skywards, shone in the mingled light of moon above and fire below, yet with an added light as well that burned within him rather than without. He was a weird, magnificent figure, a priest of ancient rites invoking his deathless deities upon the unchanging hills.

But upon Holt, too, as he stared in awed amazement, an inner light had broken suddenly. It came as with a dazzling blaze that at first paralysed thought and action. His mind cleared, but too abruptly for movement, either of tongue or hand, to be possible. Then, abruptly, the inner darkness rolled away completely. The light in the wild eyes of the great chanting, swaying figure, he now knew was the light of mania.

The faint fluttering sound increased, and the voice of the girl was oddly mingled with it. The priest had ceased his invocation. Holt, aware that he stood alone, saw the girl go past him carrying a big black bird that struggled with vainly beating wings.

"Behold the sacrifice," she said, as she knelt before her father and held up the victim. "May the Gods accept it as presently They shall accept us too!"

The great figure stooped and took the offering, and with one blow of the knife he held, its head was severed from its body. The blood spattered on the white face of the kneeling girl. Holt was aware for the first time that she, too, was now unclothed; but for a loose blanket, her white body gleamed against the dark heather in the moonlight. At the same moment she rose to her feet, stood upright, turned towards him so that he saw the dark hair streaming across her naked shoulders, and, with a face of ecstasy, yet ever that strange film upon her eyes, her voice came to him on the wind:

"Farewell, yet not farewell! We shall meet, all three, in the underworld. The Gods accept us!"

Turning her face away, she stepped towards the ominous figure behind, and bared her ivory neck and breast to the knife. The eyes of the maniac were upon her own; she was as helpless and obedient as a lamb before his spell.

Then Holt's horrible paralysis, if only just in time, was lifted. The priest had raised his arm, the bronze knife with its ragged edge gleamed in the air, with the other hand he had already gathered up the thick dark hair, so that the neck lay bare and open to the final blow. But it was two other details, Holt thinks, that set his muscles suddenly free, enabling him to act with the swift judgment which, being wholly unexpected, disconcerted both maniac and victim and frustrated the awful culmination. The dark spots of blood upon the face he loved, and the sudden final fluttering of the dead bird's wings upon the ground—these two things, life actually touching death, released the held-back springs.

He leaped forward. He received the blow upon his left arm and hand. It was his right fist that sent the High Priest to earth with a blow that, luckily, felled him in the direction away from the dreadful brink, and it was his right arm and hand, he became aware some time afterwards only, that were chiefly of use in carrying the fainting girl and her unconscious father back to the shelter of the cottage, and to the best help and comfort he could provide . . .

It was several years afterwards, in a very different setting, that he found himself spelling out slowly to a little boy the lettering cut into a circlet of bronze the child found on his study table. To the child he told a fairy tale, then dismissed him to play with his mother in the garden. But, when alone, he rubbed away the verdigris with great care, for the circlet was thin and frail with age, as he examined again the little picture of a tripod from which smoke issued, incised neatly in the metal. Below it, almost as sharp as when the Roman craftsman cut it first, was the name Acella. He touched the letters tenderly with his left hand, from which two fingers were missing, then placed it in a drawer of his desk and turned the key.

"That curious name," said a low voice behind his chair. His wife had come in and was looking over his shoulder. "You love it, and I dread it." She sat on the desk beside him, her eyes troubled. "It was the name father used to call me in his illness."

Her husband looked at her with passionate tenderness, but said no word.

"And this," she went on, taking the broken hand in both her own, "is the price you paid to me for his life. I often wonder what strange good deity brought you upon the lonely moor that night, and just in the very nick of time. You remember . . . ?"

"The deity who helps true lovers, of course," he said with a smile, evading the question. The deeper memory, he knew, had closed absolutely in her since the moment of the attempted double crime. He kissed her, murmuring to himself as he did so, but too low for her to hear, "Acella! *My* Acella . . . !"

The Wolves of God and Other Fey Stories, 1921

"VENGEANCE IS MINE"

I

An active, vigorous man in Holy Orders, yet compelled by heart trouble to resign a living in Kent before full middle age, he had found suitable work with the Red Cross in France; and it rather pleased a strain of innocent vanity in him that Rouen, whence he derived his Norman blood, should be the scene of his activities.

He was a gentle-minded soul, a man deeply read and thoughtful, but goodness perhaps his outstanding quality, believing no evil of others. He had been slow, for instance, at first to credit the German atrocities, until the evidence had compelled him to face the appalling facts. With acceptance, then, he had experienced a revulsion which other gentle minds have probably also experienced—a burning desire, namely, that the perpetrators should be fitly punished.

This primitive instinct of revenge—he called it a lust—he sternly repressed; it involved a descent to lower levels of conduct irreconcilable with the progress of the race he so passionately believed in. Revenge pertained to savage days. But, though he hid away the instinct in his heart, afraid of its clamour and persistency, it revived from time to time, as fresh horrors made it bleed anew. It remained alive, unsatisfied; while, with its analysis, his mind strove unconsciously. That an intellectual nation should deliberately include frightfulness as a chief item in its creed perplexed him horribly; it seemed to him conscious spiritual evil openly affirmed. Some genuine worship of Odin, Wotan, Moloch lay still embedded in the German outlook, and beneath the veneer of their pretentious culture. He often wondered, too, what effect the recognition of these horrors must have upon gentle minds in other men, and especially upon imaginative minds. How did they deal with the fact that this appalling thing existed in human nature in the twentieth century? Its survival, indeed, caused his belief in civilization as a whole to waver. Was progress, his pet ideal and cherished faith, after all a mockery? Had human nature not advanced . . . ?

His work in the great hospitals and convalescent camps beyond the town was tiring; he found little time for recreation, much less for rest; a light dinner and bed by ten o'clock was the usual way of spending his evenings. He had no social intercourse, for everyone else was as busy as himself. The enforced solitude, not quite wholesome, was unavoidable. He found no outlet for his thoughts. Firsthand acquaintance with suffering, physical and mental, was no new thing to him, but this close familiarity, day by day, with maimed and broken humanity preyed considerably on his mind, while the fortitude and cheerfulness shown by the victims deepened the impression of respectful, yearning wonder made upon him. They were so young, so fine and careless, these lads whom the German lust for power had robbed of limbs, and eyes, of mind, of life itself. The sense of horror grew in him with cumulative but unrelieved effect.

With the lengthening of the days in February, and especially when March saw the welcome change to summer time, the natural desire for open air asserted itself. Instead of retiring early to his dingy bedroom, he would stroll out after dinner through the ancient streets. When the air was not too chilly, he would prolong these outings, starting at sunset and coming home beneath the bright mysterious stars. He knew at length every turn and winding of the old-world alleys, every gable, every tower and spire, from the *Vieux Marché*, where Joan of Arc was burnt, to the busy quays, thronged now with soldiers from half a dozen countries. He wandered on past grey gateways of crumbling stone that marked the former banks of the old tidal river. An English army, five centuries ago, had camped here among reeds and swamps, besieging the Norman capital, where now they brought in supplies of men and material upon modern docks, a mighty invasion of a very different kind. Imaginative reflection was his constant mood.

But it was the haunted streets that touched him most, stirring some chord his ancestry had planted in him. The forest of spires thronged the air with strange stone flowers, silvered by moonlight as though white fire streamed from branch and petal; the old church towers soared; the cathedral touched the stars. After dark the modern note, paramount in the daylight, seemed hushed; with sunset it underwent a definite night-change. Although the darkened streets kept alive in him the menace of fire and death, the crowding soldiers, dipped to the face in shadow, seemed somehow negligible; the leaning roofs and gables hid them in a purple sea of mist that blurred their modern garb, steel weapons, and the like. Shadows themselves, they entered the being of the town; their feet moved silently; there was a hush and murmur; the brooding buildings absorbed them easily.

Ancient and modern, that is, unable successfully to mingle, let fall grotesque, incongruous shadows on his thoughts. The spirit of medieval days stole over him, exercising its inevitable sway upon a temperament already predisposed to welcome it. Witchcraft and wonder, pagan superstition and speculation, combined with an ancestral tendency to weave a spell, half of acceptance, half of shrinking, about his imaginative soul in which poetry and logic seemed otherwise fairly balanced. Too weary for critical judgment to discern clear outlines, his mind, during these magical twilight walks, became the playground of opposing forces, some power of dreaming, it seems, too easily in the ascendant. The soul of ancient Rouen, stealing beside his footsteps in the dusk, put forth a shadowy hand and touched him.

This shadowy spell he denied as far as in him lay, though

the resistance offered by reason to instinct lacked true driving power. The dice were loaded otherwise in such a soul. His own blood harked back unconsciously to the days when men were tortured, broken on the wheel, walled up alive, and burnt for small offences. This shadowy hand stirred faint ancestral memories in him, part instinct, part desire. The next step, by which he saw a similar attitude flowering full blown in the German frightfulness, was too easily made to be rejected. The German horrors made him believe that this ignorant cruelty of olden days threatened the world now in a modern, organized shape that proved its survival in the human heart. Shuddering, he fought against the natural desire for adequate punishment, but forgot that repressed emotions sooner or later must assert themselves. Essentially irrepressible, they may force an outlet in distorted fashion. He hardly recognized, perhaps, their actual claim, yet it was audible occasionally. For, owing to his loneliness, the natural outlet, in talk and intercourse, was denied.

Then, with the softer winds, he yearned for country air. The sweet spring days had come; morning and evening were divine; above the town the orchards were in bloom. Birds blew their tiny bugles on the hills. The midday sun began to burn.

It was the time of the final violence, when the German hordes flung like driven cattle against the Western line where free men fought for liberty. Fate hovered dreadfully in the balance that spring of 1918; Amiens was threatened, and if Amiens fell, Rouen must be evacuated. The town, already full, became now overfull. On his way home one evening he passed the station, crowded with homeless new arrivals. "Got the wind up, it seems, in Amiens!" cried a cheery voice, as an officer he knew went by him hurriedly. And as he heard it the mood of the spring became of a sudden uppermost. He reached a decision. The German horror came abruptly closer. This further overcrowding of the narrow streets was more than he could face.

It was a small, personal decision merely, but he *must* get out among woods and fields, among flowers and wholesome, growing things, taste simple, innocent life again. The following evening he would pack his haversack with food and tramp the four miles to the great *Forêt Verte*—delicious name!—and spend the night with trees and stars, breathing his full of sweetness, calm and peace. He was too accustomed to the thunder of the guns to be disturbed by it. The song of a thrush, the whistle of a blackbird, would easily drown that. He made his plan accordingly.

The next two nights, however, a warm soft rain was falling; only on the third evening could he put his little plan into execution. Anticipatory enjoyment, meanwhile, lightened his heart; he did his daily work more competently, the spell of the ancient city weakened somewhat. The shadowy hand withdrew.

II

Meanwhile, a curious adventure intervened.

His good and simple heart, disciplined these many years in the way a man should walk, received upon its imaginative side, a stimulus that, in his case, amounted to a shock. That a strange and comely woman should make eyes at him disturbed his equilibrium considerably; that he should enjoy the attack, though without at first responding openly—even without full comprehension of its meaning—disturbed it even more. It was, moreover, no ordinary attack.

He saw her first the night after his decision when, in a mood of disappointment due to the rain, he came down to his lonely dinner. The room, he saw, was crowded with new arrivals, from Amiens, doubtless, where they had "the wind up." The wealthier civilians had fled for safety to Rouen. These interested and, in a measure, stimulated him. He looked at them sympathetically, wondering what dear home-life they had so hurriedly relinquished at the near thunder of the enemy guns, and, in so doing, he noticed, sitting alone at a small table just in front of his own—yet with her back to him—a woman.

She drew his attention instantly. The first glance told him that she was young and well-to-do; the second, that she was unusual. What precisely made her unusual he could not say, although he at once began to study her intently. Dignity, atmosphere, personality, he perceived beyond all question. She sat there with an air. The becoming little hat with its challenging feather slightly tilted, the set of the shoulders, the neat waist and slender outline; possibly, too, the hair about the neck, and the faint perfume that was wafted towards him as the serving girl swept past, combined in the persuasion. Yet he felt it as more than a persuasion. She attracted him with a subtle vehemence he had never felt before. The instant he set eyes upon her his blood ran faster. The thought rose passionately in him, almost the words that phrased it: "I wish I knew her."

This sudden flash of response his whole being certainly gave—to the back of an unknown woman. It was both vehement and instinctive. He lay stress upon its instinctive character; he was aware of it before reason told him why. That it was "in response" he also noted, for although he had not seen her face and she assuredly had made no sign, he felt that attraction which involves also invitation. So vehement, moreover, was this response in him that he felt shy and ashamed the same instant, for it almost seemed he had expressed his thought in audible words. He flushed, and the flush ran through his body; he was conscious of heated blood as in a youth of twenty-five, and when a man past forty knows this touch of fever he may also know, though he may not recognize it, that the danger signal which means possible abandon has been lit. Moreover, as though to prove his instinct justified, it was at this very instant that the woman turned and stared at him deliberately. She looked into his eyes, and he looked into hers. He knew a moment's keen distress, a sharpest possible discomfort, that after all he *had* expressed his desire audibly. Yet, though he blushed, he did not lower his eyes. The embarrassment passed instantly, replaced by a thrill of strangest pleasure and satisfaction. He knew a tinge of inexplicable dismay as well. He felt for a second helpless before what seemed a challenge in her eyes. The eyes were too compelling. They mastered him.

In order to meet his gaze she had to make a full turn in her chair, for her table was placed directly in front of his own. She did so without concealment. It was no mere attempt to see what lay behind by making a half-turn and pretending to look elsewhere; no corner of the eye business; but a full, straight, direct, significant stare. She looked into his soul as though she called him, he looked into hers as though he answered. Sitting there like a statue, motionless, without a bow, without a smile, he returned her intense regard unflinchingly and yet unwillingly. He made no sign. He shivered again . . . It was perhaps ten seconds before she turned away with an air as if she had delivered her message and received his answer, but in those ten seconds a series of singular ideas crowded his mind, leaving an impression that ten years could never efface. The face and eyes produced a kind of intoxication in him. There was almost recognition, as though she said: "Ah, there you are! I was waiting; you'll have to come, of course. You must!" And just before she turned away she smiled.

He felt confused and helpless.

The face he described as unusual; familiar, too, as with the atmosphere of some long forgotten dream, and if beauty perhaps was absent, character and individuality were supreme. Implacable resolution was stamped upon the features, which yet were sweet and womanly, stirring an emotion in him that he could not name and certainly did not recognize. The eyes, slanting a little upwards, were full of fire, the mouth voluptuous but very firm, the chin and jaw most delicately modelled, yet with a masculine strength that told of inflexible resolve. The resolution, as a whole, was the most relentless he had ever seen upon a human countenance. It dominated him. "How vain to resist the will," he thought, "that lies behind!" He was conscious of enslavement; she conveyed a message that he must obey, admitting compliance with her unknown purpose.

That some extraordinary wordless exchange was registered thus between them seemed very clear; and it was just at this moment, as if to signify her satisfaction, that she smiled. At his feeling of willing compliance with some purpose in her mind, the smile appeared. It was faint, so faint indeed that the eyes betrayed it rather than the mouth and lips; but it was there; he saw it and he thrilled again to this added touch of wonder and enchantment. Yet, strangest of all, he maintains that with the smile there fluttered over the resolute face a sudden arresting tenderness, as though some wild flower lit a granite surface with its melting loveliness. He was aware in the clear strong eyes of unshed tears, of sympathy, of self-sacrifice he called maternal, of clinging love. It was this tenderness, as of a soft and gracious mother, and this implacable resolution, as of a stern, relentless man, that left upon his receptive soul the strange impression of sweetness yet of domination.

The brief ten seconds were over. She turned away as deliberately as she had turned to look. He found himself trembling with confused emotions he could not disentangle, could not even name; for, with the subtle intoxication of compliance in his soul lay also a vigorous protest that included refusal, even a violent refusal given with horror. This unknown woman, without actual speech or definite gesture, had lit a flame in him that linked on far away and out of sight with the magic of the ancient city's medieval spell. Both, he decided, were undesirable, both to be resisted.

He was quite decided about this. She pertained to forgotten yet unburied things, her modern aspect a mere disguise, a disguise that some deep unsatisfied instinct in him pierced with ease.

He found himself equally decided, too, upon another thing which, in spite of his momentary confusion, stood out clearly: the magic of the city, the enchantment of the woman, both attacked a constitutional weakness in his blood, a line of least resistance. It wore no physical aspect, breathed no hint of ordinary romance; the mere male and female, moral or immoral touch was wholly absent; yet passion lurked there, tumultuous if hidden, and a tract of consciousness, long untravelled, was lit by sudden ominous flares. His character, his temperament, his calling in life as a former clergyman and now a Red Cross worker, being what they were, he stood on the brink of an adventure not dangerous alone but containing a challenge of fundamental kind that involved his very soul.

No further thrill, however, awaited him immediately. He left his table before she did, having intercepted no slightest hint of desired acquaintanceship or intercourse. He, naturally, made no advances; she, equally, made no smallest sign. Her face remained hidden, he caught no flash of eyes, no gesture, no hint of possible invitation. He went upstairs to his dingy room, and in due course fell asleep. The next day he saw her not, her place in the dining-room was empty; but in the late evening of the following day, as the soft spring sunshine found him prepared for his postponed expedition, he met her suddenly on the stairs. He was going down with haversack and in walking kit to an early dinner, when he saw her coming up; she was perhaps a dozen steps below him; they must meet. A wave of confused, embarrassed pleasure swept him. He realized that this was no chance meeting. She meant to speak to him.

Violent attraction and an equally violent repulsion seized him. There was no escape, nor, had escape been possible, would he have attempted it. He went down four steps, she mounted four towards him; then he took one and she took one. They met. For a moment they stood level, while he shrank against the wall to let her pass. He had the feeling that but for the support of that wall he must have lost his balance and fallen into her, for the sunlight from the landing window caught her face and lit it, and she was younger, he saw, than he had thought, and far more comely. Her atmosphere enveloped him, the sense of attraction and repulsion became intense. She moved past him with the slightest possible bow of recognition; then, having passed, she turned.

She stood a little higher than himself, a step at most, and she thus looked down at him. Her eyes blazed into his. She smiled, and he was aware again of the domination and the sweetness. The perfume of her near presence drowned him; his head swam. "We count upon you," she said in a low firm voice, as though giving a command; "I know . . . we may. We do." And, before he knew what he was saying, trembling a little between deep pleasure and a contrary impulse that sought to choke the utterance, he heard his own voice answering. "You can count upon me. . . " And she was already halfway up the next flight of stairs ere he could move a muscle, or attempt to thread a meaning into the singular exchange.

Yet meaning, he well knew, there was.

She was gone; her footsteps overhead had died away. He stood there trembling like a boy of twenty, yet also like a man of forty in whom fires, long dreaded, now blazed sullenly. She had opened the furnace door, the draught rushed through. He felt again the old unwelcome spell; he saw the twisted streets 'mid leaning gables and shadowy towers of a day forgotten; he heard the ominous murmurs of a crowd that thirsted for wheel and scaffold and fire; and, aware of vengeance, sweet and terrible, aware, too, that he welcomed it, his heart was troubled and afraid.

In a brief second the impression came and went; following it swiftly, the sweetness of the woman swept him: he forgot his shrinking in a rush of wild delicious pleasure. The intoxication in him deepened. She had recognized him! She had bowed and even smiled; she had spoken, assuming familiarity, intimacy, including him in her secret purposes! It was this sweet intimacy cleverly injected, that overcame the repulsion he acknowledged, winning complete obedience to the unknown meaning of her words. This meaning, for the moment, lay in darkness; yet it was a portion of his own self, he felt, that concealed it of set purpose. He kept it hid, he looked deliberately another way; for, if he faced it with full recognition, he knew that he must resist it to the death. He allowed himself to ask vague questions—then let her dominating spell confuse the answers so that he did not hear them. The challenge to his soul, that is, he evaded.

What is commonly called sex lay only slightly in his troubled emotions; her purpose had nothing that kept step with chance acquaintanceship. There lay meaning, indeed, in her smile and voice, but these were no handmaids to a vulgar intrigue in a foreign hotel. Her will breathed cleaner air; her purpose aimed at some graver, mightier climax than the mere subjection of an elderly victim like himself. That will, that purpose, he felt certain, were implacable as death, the resolve in those bold eyes was not a common one. For, in some strange way, he divined the strong maternity in her; the maternal instinct was deeply, even predominantly, involved; he felt positive that a divine tenderness, deeply outraged, was a chief ingredient too. In some way, then, she needed him, yet not she alone, for the pronoun "we" was used, and there were others with her; in some way, equally, a part of him was already her and their accomplice, an unresisting slave, a willing co-conspirator.

He knew one other thing, and it was this that he kept concealed so carefully from himself. His recognition of it was subconscious possibly, but for that very reason true: her purpose was consistent with the satisfaction at last of a deep instinct in him that clamoured to know gratification. It was for these odd, mingled reasons that he stood trembling when she left him on the stairs, and finally went down to his hurried meal with a heart that knew wonder, anticipation, and delight, but also dread.

III

The table in front of him remained unoccupied; his dinner finished, he went out hastily.

As he passed through the crowded streets, his chief desire was to be quickly free of the old muffled buildings and airless alleys with their clinging atmosphere of other days. He longed for the sweet taste of the heights, the smells of the forest whither he was bound. This *Forêt Verte*, he knew, rolled for leagues towards the north, empty of houses as of human beings; it was the home of deer and birds and rabbits, of wild boar too. There would be spring flowers among the brushwood, anemones, celandine, oxslip, daffodils. The vapours of the town oppressed him, the warm and heavy moisture stifled; he wanted space and the sight of clean simple things that would stimulate his mind with lighter thoughts.

He soon passed the Rampe, skirted the ugly villas of modern Bihorel and, rising now with every step, entered the *Route Neuve*. He went unduly fast; he was already above the Cathedral spire; below him the Seine meandered round the chalky hills, laden with war-barges, and across a dip, still pink in the afterglow, rose the blunt Down of Bonsecours with its antiaircraft batteries. Poetry and violent fact crashed everywhere; he longed to top the hill and leave these unhappy reminders of death behind him. In front the sweet woods already beckoned through the twilight. He hastened. Yet while he deliberately fixed his imagination on promised peace and beauty, an undercurrent ran sullenly in his mind, busy with quite other thoughts. The unknown woman and her singular words, the following mystery of the ancient city, the soft beating wonder of the two together, these worked their incalculable magic persistently about him. Repression merely added to their power. His mind was a prey to some shadowy, remote anxiety that, intangible, invisible, yet knocked with ghostly fingers upon some door of ancient memory . . . He watched the moon rise above the eastern ridge, in the west the afterglow of sunset still hung red. But these did not hold his attention as they normally must have done. Attention seemed elsewhere. The undercurrent bore him down a siding, into a backwater, as it were, that clamoured for discharge.

He thought suddenly, then, of weather, what he called "German weather"—that combination of natural conditions which so oddly favoured the enemy always. It had often occurred to him as strange; on sea and land, mist, rain and wind, the fog and drying sun worked ever on *their* side. The coincidence was odd, to say the least. And now this glimpse of rising moon and sunset sky reminded him unpleasantly of the subject. Legends of pagan weather-gods passed through his mind like hurrying shadows. These shadows multiplied, changed form, vanished and returned. They came and went with incoherence, a straggling stream, rushing from one point to another, manoeuvring for position, but all unled, unguided by his will. The physical exercise filled his brain with blood, and thought danced undirected, picture upon picture driving by, so that soon he slipped from German weather and pagan gods to the witchcraft of past centuries, of its alleged association with the natural powers of the elements, and thus, eventually, to his cherished beliefs that humanity had advanced.

Such remnants of primitive days were grotesque superstition, of course. But had humanity advanced? Had the individual progressed after all? Civilization, was it not the merest artificial growth? And the old perplexity rushed through his mind again—the German barbarity and blood-lust, the savagery, the undoubted sadic impulses, the frightfulness taught with cool calculation by their highest minds, approved by their professors, endorsed by their clergy, applauded by their women even— all the unwelcome, undesired thoughts came flocking back upon him, escorted by the trooping shadows. They lay, these questions, still unsolved within him; it was the undercurrent, flowing more swiftly now, that bore them to the surface. It had acquired momentum; it was leading somewhere.

They were a thoughtful, intellectual race, these Germans; their music, literature, philosophy, their science—how reconcile the opposing qualities? He had read that their herd-instinct was unusually developed, though betraying the characteristics of a low wild savage type—the lupine. It might be true. Fear and danger wakened this collective instinct into terrific activity, making them blind and humourless; they fought best, like wolves, in contact; they howled and whined and boasted loudly all together to inspire terror; their *Hymn of Hate* was but an elaboration of the wolf's fierce bark, giving them herd-courage; and a savage discipline was necessary to their lupine type.

These reflections thronged his mind as the blood coursed in his veins with the rapid climbing; yet one and all, the beauty of the evening, the magic of the hidden town, the thoughts of German horror, German weather, German gods, all these, even the odd detail that they revived a pagan practice by hammering nails into effigies and idols—all led finally to one blazing centre that nothing could dislodge nor anything conceal; a woman's voice and eyes. To these he knew quite well, was due the undesired intensification of the very mood, the very emotions, the very thoughts he had come out on purpose to escape.

"It is the night of the vernal equinox," occurred to him suddenly, sharp as a whispered voice beside him. He had no notion whence the idea was born. It had no particular meaning, so far as he remembered.

"It had *then* . . . " said the voice imperiously, rising, it seemed, directly out of the undercurrent in his soul.

It startled him. He increased his pace. He walked very quickly, whistling softly as he went.

The dusk had fallen when at length he topped the long, slow hill, and left the last of the atrocious straggling villas well behind him. The ancient city lay far below in murky haze and smoke, but tinged now with the silver of the growing moon.

IV

He stood now on the open plateau. He was on the heights at last.

The night air met him freshly in the face, so that he forgot the fatigue of the long climb uphill, taken too fast somewhat for his years. He drew a deep draught into his lungs and stepped out briskly.

Far in the upper sky light flaky clouds raced through the reddened air, but the wind kept to these higher strata, and the world about him lay very still. Few lights showed in the farms and cottages, for this was the direct route of the Gothas, and nothing that could help the German hawks to find the river was visible.

His mind cleared pleasantly; this keen sweet air held no mystery; he put his best foot foremost, whistling still, but a little more loudly than before. Among the orchards he saw the daisies glimmer. Also, he heard the guns, a thudding concussion in the direction of the coveted Amiens, where, some sixty miles as the crow flies, they roared their terror into the calm evening skies. He cursed the sound, in the town below it was not audible. Thought jumped then to the men who fired them, and so to the prisoners who worked on the roads outside the hospitals and camps he visited daily. He passed them every morning and night, and the N.C.O. invariably saluted his Red Cross uniform, a salute he returned, when he could not avoid it, with embarrassment.

One man in particular stood out clearly in this memory; he had exchanged glances with him, noted the expression of his face, the number of his gang printed on coat and trousers—"82." The fellow had somehow managed to establish a relationship; he would look up and smile or frown; if the news, from his point of view, was good, he smiled; if it was bad, he scowled; once, insolently enough—when the Germans had taken Albert, Péronne, Bapaume—he grinned.

Something about the sullen, close-cropped face, typically Prussian, made the other shudder. It was the visage of an animal, neither evil nor malignant, even good-natured sometimes when it smiled, yet of an animal that could be fierce with the lust of happiness, ferocious with delight. The sullen savagery of a human wolf lay in it somewhere. He pictured its owner impervious to shame, to normal human instinct as civilized people know these. Doubtless he read his own feelings into it. He could imagine the man doing anything and everything, regarding chivalry and sporting instinct as proof of fear or weakness. He could picture this member of the wolf-pack killing a woman or a child, mutilating, cutting off little hands even, with the conscientious conviction that it was right and sensible to destroy *any* individual of an enemy tribe. It was, to him, an atrocious and inhuman face.

It now cropped up with unpleasant vividness, as he listened to the distant guns and thought of Amiens with its back against the wall, its inhabitants flying—

Ah! Amiens . . . ! He again saw the woman staring into his obedient eyes across the narrow space between the tables. He smelt the delicious perfume of her dress and person on the stairs. He heard her commanding voice, her very words: "We count on you . . . I know we can . . . we do." And her background was of twisted streets, dark alleyways and leaning gables . . .

He hurried, whistling loudly an air that he invented suddenly, using his stick like a golf club at every loose stone his feet encountered, making as much noise as possible. He told himself he was a parson and a Red Cross worker. He looked up and saw that the stars were out. The pace made him warm, and he shifted his haversack to the other shoulder. The moon, he observed, now cast his shadow for a long distance on the sandy road.

After another mile, while the air grew sharper and twilight surrendered finally to the moon, the road began to curve and dip, the cottages lay farther out in the dim fields, the farms and barns occurred at longer intervals. A dog barked now and again; he saw cows lying down for the night beneath shadowy fruit-trees. And then the scent in the air changed slightly, and a darkening of the near horizon warned him that the forest had come close.

This was an event. Its influence breathed already a new perfume; the shadows from its myriad trees stole out and touched him. Ten minutes later he reached its actual frontier cutting across the plateau like a line of sentries at attention. He slowed down a little. Here, within sight and touch of his long-desired objective, he hesitated. It stretched, he knew from the map, for many leagues to the north, uninhabited, lonely, the home of peace and silence; there were flowers there, and cool sweet spaces where the moonlight fell. Yet here, within scent and touch of it, he slowed down a moment to draw breath. A forest on the map is one thing; visible before the eyes when night has fallen, it is another. It is real.

The wind, not noticeable hitherto, now murmured towards him from the serried trees that seemed to manufacture darkness out of nothing. This murmur hummed about him. It enveloped him. Piercing it, another sound that was not the guns just reached him, but so distant that he hardly noticed it. He looked back. Dusk suddenly merged in night. He stopped.

"How practical the French are," he said to himself—aloud— as he looked at the road running straight as a ruled line into the heart of the trees. "They waste no energy, no space, no time. Admirable!"

It pierced the forest like a lance, tapering to a faint point in the misty distance. The trees ate its undeviating straightness as though they would smother it from sight, as though its rigid outline marred their mystery. He admired the practical makers of the road, yet sided, too, with the poetry of the trees. He stood there staring, waiting, dawdling . . . About him, save for this murmur of the wind, was silence. Nothing living stirred. The world lay extraordinarily still. That other distant sound had died away.

He lit his pipe, glad that the match blew out and the damp tobacco needed several matches before the pipe drew properly. His puttees hurt him a little, he stooped to loosen them. His haversack swung round in front as he straightened up again, he shifted it laboriously to the other shoulder. A tiny stone in his right boot caused irritation. Its removal took a considerable time, for he had to sit down, and a log was not at once forthcoming. Moreover, the laces gave him trouble, and his fingers had grown thick with heat and the knots were difficult to tie . . .

"There!" He said it aloud, standing up again. "Now at last, I'm ready!" Then added a mild imprecation, for his pipe had gone out while he stooped over the recalcitrant boot, and it had to be lighted once again. "Ah!" he gasped finally with a sigh as, facing the forest for the third time, he shuffled his tunic straight, altered his haversack once more, changed his stick from the right hand to the left—and faced the foolish truth without further pretence.

He mopped his forehead carefully, as though at the same time trying to mop away from his mind a faint anxiety, a very faint uneasiness, that gathered there. Was someone standing near him? Had somebody come close? He listened intently. It was the blood singing in his ears, of course, that curious distant noise. For, truth to tell, the loneliness bit just below the surface of what he found enjoyable. It seemed to him that somebody was coming, someone he could not see, so that he looked back over his shoulder once again, glanced quickly right and left, then peered down the long opening cut through the woods in front— when there came suddenly a roar and a blaze of dazzling light from behind, so instantaneously that he barely had time to obey the instinct of self-preservation and step aside. He actually leapt. Pressed against the hedge, he saw a motorcar rush past him like a whirlwind, flooding the sandy road with fire; a second followed it; and, to his complete amazement, then, a third.

They were powerful, private cars, so-called. This struck him instantly. Two other things he noticed, as they dived down the throat of the long white road—they showed no taillights. This made him wonder. And, secondly, the drivers, clearly seen, were women. They were not even in uniform—which made him wonder even more. The occupants, too, were women. He caught the outline of toque and feather—or was it flowers?—against the closed windows in the moonlight as the procession rushed past him.

He felt bewildered and astonished. Private motors were rare, and military regulations exceedingly strict; the danger of spies dressed in French uniform was constant; cars armed with machine guns, he knew, patrolled the countryside in all directions. Shaken and alarmed, he thought of favoured persons fleeing stealthily by night, of treachery, disguise and swift surprise; he thought of various things as he stood peering down the road for ten minutes after all sight and sound of the cars had died away. But no solution of the mystery occurred to him. Down the white throat the motors vanished. His pipe had gone out; he lit it, and puffed furiously.

His thoughts, at any rate, took temporarily a new direction now. The road was not as lonely as he had imagined. A natural reaction set in at once, and this proof of practical, modern life banished the shadows from his mind effectually. He started off once more, oblivious of his former hesitation. He even felt a trifle shamed and foolish, pretending that the vanished mood had not existed. The tobacco had been damp. His boot had really hurt him.

Yet bewilderment and surprise stayed with him. The swiftness of the incident was disconcerting; the cars arrived and vanished with such extraordinary rapidity; their noisy irruption into this peaceful spot seemed incongruous; they roared, blazed, rushed and disappeared; silence resumed its former sway.

But the silence persisted, whereas the noise was gone.

This touch of the incongruous remained with him as he now went ever deeper into the heart of the quiet forest. This odd incongruity of dreams remained.

V

The keen air stole from the woods, cooling his body and his mind; anemones gleamed faintly among the brushwood, lit by the pallid moonlight. There were beauty, calm and silence, the slow breathing of the earth beneath the comforting sweet stars. War, in this haunt of ancient peace, seemed an incredible anachronism. His thoughts turned to gentle happy hopes of a day when the lion and the lamb would yet lie down together, and a little child would lead them without fear. His soul dwelt with peaceful longings and calm desires.

He walked on steadily, until the inflexible straightness of the endless road began to afflict him, and he longed for a turning to the right or left. He looked eagerly about him for a woodland path. Time mattered little; he could wait for the sunrise and walk home "beneath the young grey dawn"; he had food and matches, he could light a fire, and sleep—No!—after all, he would not light a fire, perhaps; he might be accused of signalling to hostile aircraft, or a *garde forestière* might catch him. He would not bother with a fire. The night was warm, he could enjoy himself and pass the time quite happily without artificial heat; probably he would need no sleep at all . . . And just then he noticed an opening on his right, where a seductive pathway led in among the trees. The moon, now higher in the sky, lit this woodland trail enticingly; it seemed the very opening he had looked for, and with a thrill of pleasure he at once turned down it, leaving the ugly road behind him with relief.

The sound of his footsteps hushed instantly on the leaves and moss; the silence became noticeable; an unusual stillness followed; it seemed that something in his mind was also hushed. His feet moved stealthily, as though anxious to conceal his presence from surprise. His steps dragged purposely; their rustling through the thick dead leaves, perhaps, was pleasant to him. He was not sure.

The path opened presently into a clearing where the

moonlight made a pool of silver, the surrounding brushwood fell away; and in the centre a gigantic outline rose. It was, he saw, a beech tree that dwarfed the surrounding forest by its grandeur. Its bulk loomed very splendid against the sky, a faint rustle just audible in its myriad tiny leaves. Dipped in the moonlight, it had such majesty of proportion, such symmetry, that he stopped in admiration. It was, he saw, a multiple tree, five stems springing with attempted spirals out of an enormous trunk; it was immense; it had a presence, the space framed it to perfection. The clearing, evidently, was a favourite resting place for summer picknickers, a playground, probably, for city children on holiday afternoons; woodcutters, too, had been here recently, for he noticed piled brushwood ready to be carted. It indicated admirably, he felt, the limits of his night expedition. Here he would rest awhile, eat his late supper, sleep perhaps round a small—No! again—a fire he need *not* make; a spark might easily set the woods ablaze, it was against both forest and military regulations. This idea of a fire, otherwise so natural, was distasteful, even repugnant, to him. He wondered a little why it recurred. He noticed this time, moreover, something unpleasant connected with the suggestion of a fire, something that made him shrink; almost a ghostly dread lay hidden in it.

This startled him. A dozen excellent reasons, supplied by his brain, warned him that a fire was unwise; but the true reason, supplied by another part of him, concealed itself with care, as though afraid that reason might detect its nature and fix the label on. Disliking this reminder of his earlier mood, he moved forward into the clearing, swinging his stick aggressively and whistling. He approached the tree, where a dozen thick roots dipped into the earth. Admiring, looking up and down, he paced slowly round its prodigious girth, then stood absolutely still. His heart stopped abruptly, his blood became congealed. He saw something that filled him with a sudden emptiness of terror. On this western side the shadow lay very black; it was between the thick limbs, half stem, half root, where the dark hollows gave easy hiding-places, that he was positive he detected movement. A portion of the trunk had moved.

He stood stock still and stared—not three feet from the trunk—when there came a second movement. Concealed in the shadows there crouched a living form. The movement defined itself immediately. Half reclining, half standing, a living being pressed itself close against the tree, yet fitting so neatly into the wide scooped hollows, that it was scarcely distinguishable from its ebony background. But for the chance movement he must have passed it undetected. Equally, his outstretched fingers might have touched it. The blood rushed from his heart, as he saw this second movement.

Detaching itself from the obscure background, the figure rose and stood before him. It swayed a little, then stepped out into the patch of moonlight on his left. Three feet lay between them. The figure then bent over. A pallid face with burning eyes thrust forward and peered straight into his own.

The human being was a woman. The same instant he recognized the eyes that had stared him out of countenance in the dining-room two nights ago. He was petrified. She stared him out of countenance now.

And, as she did so, the undercurrent he had tried to ignore so long swept to the surface in a tumultuous flood, obliterating his normal self. Something elaborately built up in his soul by years of artificial training collapsed like a house of cards, and he knew himself undone.

"They've got me . . . !" flashed dreadfully through his mind. It was, again, like a message delivered in a dream where the significance of acts performed and language uttered, concealed at the moment, is revealed much later only.

"After all—they've got me . . . !"

VI

The dialogue that followed seemed strange to him only when looking back upon it. The element of surprise again was negligible if not wholly absent, but the incongruity of dreams, almost of nightmare, became more marked. Though the affair was unlikely, it was far from incredible. So completely were this man and woman involved in some purpose common to them both that their talk, their meeting, their instinctive sympathy at the time seemed natural. The same stream bore them irresistibly towards the same far sea. Only, as yet, this common purpose remained concealed. Nor could he define the violent emotions that troubled him. Their exact description was in him, but so deep that he could not draw it up. Moonlight lay upon his thought, merging clear outlines.

Divided against himself, the cleavage left no authoritative self in control; his desire to take an immediate decision resulted in a confused struggle, where shame and pleasure, attraction and revulsion mingled painfully. Incongruous details tumbled helter-skelter about his mind: for no obvious reason, he remembered again his Red Cross uniform, his former holy calling, his nationality too; he was a servant of mercy, a teacher of the love of God; he was an English gentleman. Against which rose other details, as in opposition, holding just beyond the reach of words, yet rising, he recognized well enough, from the bedrock of the human animal, whereon a few centuries have imposed the thin crust of refinement men call civilization. He was aware of joy and loathing.

In the first few seconds he knew the clash of a dreadful fundamental struggle, while the spell of this woman's strange enchantment poured over him, seeking the reconciliation he himself could not achieve. Yet the reconciliation *she* sought meant victory or defeat; no compromise lay in it. Something imperious emanating from her already dominated the warring elements towards a coherent whole. He stood before her, quivering with emotions he dared not name. Her great womanhood he recognized, acknowledging obedience to her undisclosed intentions. And this idea of coming surrender terrified him. Whence came, too, that queenly touch about her that made him feel he should have sunk upon his knees?

The conflict resulted in a curious compromise. He raised his hand; he saluted; he found very ordinary words.

"You passed me only a short time ago," he stammered, "in the motors. There were others with you—"

"Knowing that you would find us and come after. We count on your presence and your willing help." Her voice was firm as with unalterable conviction. It was persuasive too. He nodded, as though acquiescence seemed the only course.

"We need your sympathy; we must have your power too."

He bowed again. "My power!" Something exulted in him. But he murmured only. It was natural, he felt; he gave consent without a question.

Strange words he both understood and did not understand. Her voice, low and silvery, was that of a gentle, cultured woman, but command rang through it with a clang of metal, terrible behind the sweetness. She moved a little closer, standing erect before him in the moonlight, her figure borrowing something of the great tree's majesty behind her. It was incongruous, this gentle and yet sinister air she wore. Whence came, in this calm peaceful spot, the suggestion of a wild and savage background to her? Why were there tumult and oppression in his heart, pain, horror, tenderness and mercy, mixed beyond disentanglement? Why did he think already, but helplessly, of escape, yet at the same time burn to stay? Whence came again, too, a certain queenly touch he felt in her?

"The gods have brought you," broke across his turmoil in a half whisper whose breath almost touched his face. "You belong to us."

The deeps rose in him. Seduced by the sweetness and the power, the warring divisions in his being drew together. His under-self more and more obtained the mastery she willed. Then something in the French she used flickered across his mind with a faint reminder of normal things again.

"Belgian—" he began, and then stopped short, as her instant rejoinder broke in upon his halting speech and petrified him. In her voice sang that triumphant tenderness that only the feminine powers of the Universe may compass: it seemed the sky sang with her, the mating birds, wild flowers, the south wind and the running streams. All these, even the silver birches, lent their fluid, feminine undertones to the two pregnant words with which she interrupted him and completed his own unfinished sentence:

"—and mother."

With the dreadful calm of an absolute assurance, she stood and watched him.

His understanding already showed signs of clearing. She stretched her hands out with a passionate appeal, a yearning gesture, the eloquence of which should explain all that remained unspoken. He saw their grace and symmetry, exquisite in the moonlight, then watched them fold together in an attitude of prayer. Beautiful mother hands they were; hands made to smooth the pillows of the world, to comfort, bless, caress, hands that little children everywhere must lean upon and love-perfect symbol of protective, self-forgetful motherhood.

This tenderness he noted; he noted next—the strength. In the folded hands he divined the expression of another great world-power, fulfilling the implacable resolution of the mouth and eyes. He was aware of relentless purpose, more—of merciless revenge, as by a protective motherhood outraged beyond endurance. Moreover, the gesture held appeal; these hands, so close that their actual perfume reached him, sought his own in help. The power in himself as man, as male, as father—this was required of him in the fulfillment of the unknown purpose to which this woman summoned him. His understanding cleared still more.

The couple faced one another, staring fixedly beneath the giant beech that overarched them. In the dark of his eyes, he knew, lay growing terror. He shivered, and the shiver passed down his spine, making his whole body tremble. There stirred in him an excitement he loathed, yet welcomed, as the primitive male in him, answering the summons, reared up with instinctive, dreadful glee to shatter the bars that civilization had so confidently set upon its freedom. A primal emotion of his under-being, ancient lust that had too long gone hungry and unfed, leaped towards some possible satisfaction. It was incredible; it was, of course, a dream. But judgment wavered; increasing terror ate his will away. Violence and sweetness, relief and degradation, fought in his soul, as he trembled before a power that now slowly mastered him. This glee and loathing formed their ghastly partnership. He could have strangled the woman where she stood. Equally, he could have knelt and kissed her feet.

The vehemence of the conflict paralysed him.

"A mother's hands . . . " he murmured at length, the words escaping like bubbles that rose to the surface of a seething cauldron and then burst.

And the woman smiled as though she read his mind and saw his little trembling. The smile crept down from the eyes towards the mouth; he saw her lips part slightly; he saw her teeth.

But her reply once more transfixed him. Two syllables she uttered in a voice of iron:

"Louvain."

* * * * *

The sound acted upon him like a Word of Power in some Eastern fairy tale. It knit the present to a past that he now recognized could never die. Humanity had *not* advanced. The hidden source of his secret joy began to glow. For this woman focused in him passions that life had hitherto denied, pretending they were atrophied, and the primitive male, the naked savage rose up, with glee in its lustful eyes and blood upon its lips. Acquired civilization, a pitiful mockery, split through its thin veneer and fled.

"Belgian . . . Louvain . . . Mother . . . " he whispered, yet astonished at the volume of sound that now left his mouth. His voice had a sudden fullness. It seemed a caveman roared the words.

She touched his hand, and he knew a sudden intensification of life within him; immense energy poured through his veins; a medieval spirit used his eyes; great pagan instincts strained and urged against his heart, against his very muscles. He longed for action.

And he cried aloud: "I am with you, with you to the end!"

Her spell had vivified beyond all possible resistance that primitive consciousness which is ever the bedrock of the human animal.

A racial memory, inset against the forest scenery, flashed suddenly through the depths laid bare. Below a sinking moon dark figures flew in streaming lines and groups; tormented cries went down the wind; he saw torn, blasted trees that swayed and rocked; there was a leaping fire, a gleaming knife, an altar. He saw a sacrifice.

It flashed away and vanished. In its place the woman stood, with shining eyes fixed on his face, one arm outstretched, one hand upon his flesh. She shifted slightly, and her cloak swung open. He saw clinging skins wound closely about her figure; leaves, flowers and trailing green hung from her shoulders, fluttering down the lines of her triumphant physical beauty. There was a perfume of wild roses, incense, ivy bloom, whose subtle intoxication drowned his senses. He saw a sparkling girdle round the waist, a knife thrust through it tight against the hip. And his secret joy, the glee, the pleasure of some unlawful and unholy lust leaped through his blood towards the abandonment of satisfaction.

The moon revealed a glimpse, no more. An instant he saw her thus, half savage and half sweet, symbol of primitive justice entering the present through the door of vanished centuries.

The cloak swung back again, the outstretched hand withdrew, but from a world he knew had altered.

Today sank out of sight. The moon shone pale with terror and delight on Yesterday.

VII

Across this altered world a faint new sound now reached his ears, as though a human wail of anguished terror trembled and changed into the cry of some captured helpless animal. He thought of a wolf apart from the comfort of its pack, savage yet abject. The despair of a last appeal was in the sound. It floated past, it died away. The woman moved closer suddenly.

"All is prepared," she said, in the same low, silvery voice; "we must not tarry. The equinox is come, the tide of power flows. The sacrifice is here; we hold him fast. We only awaited you." Her shining eyes were raised to his. "Your soul is with us now?" she whispered.

"My soul is with you."

"And midnight," she continued, "is at hand. We use, of course, their methods. Henceforth the gods—their old-world gods—shall work on our side. They demand a sacrifice, and justice has provided one."

His understanding cleared still more then; the last veil of confusion was drawing from his mind. The old, old names went thundering through his consciousness—Odin, Wotan, Moloch—accessible ever to invocation and worship of the rightful kind. It seemed as natural as though he read in his pulpit the prayer for rain, or gave out the hymn for those at sea. That was merely an empty form, whereas this was real. Sea, storm and earthquake, all natural activities, lay under the direction of those elemental powers called the gods. Names changed, the principle remained.

"Their weather shall be ours," he cried, with sudden passion, as a memory of unhallowed usages he had thought erased from life burned in him; while, stranger still, resentment stirred— revolt—against the system, against the very deity he had worshipped hitherto. For these had never once interfered to help the cause of right; their feebleness was now laid bare before his eyes. And a twofold lust rose in him. "Vengeance is ours!" he cried in a louder voice, through which this sudden loathing of the cross poured hatred. "Vengeance and justice! Now bind the victim! Bring on the sacrifice!"

"He is already bound." And as the woman moved a little, the curious erection behind her caught his eye—the piled brushwood he had imagined was the work of woodmen, picnickers, or playing children. He realized its true meaning.

It now delighted and appalled him. Awe deepened in him, a wind of ice passed over him. Civilization made one more fluttering effort. He gasped, he shivered; he tried to speak. But no words came. A thin cry, as of a frightened child, escaped him.

"It is the only way," the woman whispered softly. "We steal from them the power of their own deities." Her head flung back with a marvellous gesture of grace and power; she stood before him a figure of perfect womanhood, gentle and tender, yet at the same time alive and cruel with the passions of an ignorant and savage past. Her folded hands were clasped, her face turned heavenwards. "I am a mother," she added, with amazing passion, her eyes glistening in the moonlight with unshed tears. "We all"—she glanced towards the forest, her voice rising to a wild and poignant cry—"all, all of us are mothers!"

It was then the final clearing of his understanding happened, and he realized his own part in what would follow. Yet before the realization he felt himself not merely ineffective, but powerless. The struggling forces in him were so evenly matched that paralysis of the will resulted. His dry lips contrived merely a few words of confused and feeble protest.

"Me!" he faltered. "My help—?"

"Justice," she answered; and though softly uttered, it was as though the medieval towers clanged their bells. That secret, ghastly joy again rose in him; admiration, wonder, desire followed instantly. A fugitive memory of Joan of Arc flashed by, as with armoured wings, upon the moonlight. Some power similarly heroic, some purpose similarly inflexible, emanated from this woman, the savour of whose physical enchantment, whose very breath, rose to his brain like incense. Again he shuddered. The spasm of secret pleasure shocked him. He sighed. He felt alert, yet stunned.

Her words went down the wind between them:

"You are so weak, you English," he heard her terrible whisper, "so nobly forgiving, so fine, yet so forgetful. You refuse the weapon *they* place within your hands." Her face thrust closer, the great eyes blazed upon him. "If we would save the children"—the voice rose and fell like wind—"we must worship where they worship, we must sacrifice to their savage deities..."

The stream of her words flowed over him with this nightmare magic that seemed natural, without surprise. He listened, he trembled, and again he sighed. Yet in his blood there was sudden roaring.

"... Louvain ... the hands of little children ... we have the proof," he heard, oddly intermingled with another set of words that clamoured vainly in his brain for utterance; "the diary in his own handwriting, his gloating pleasure ... the little, innocent hands..."

"Justice is mine!" rang through some fading region of his now fainting soul, but found no audible utterance.

"... Mist, rain and wind ... the gods of German Weather ... We all ... are mothers..."

"I will repay," came forth in actual words, yet so low he hardly heard the sound. But the woman heard.

"*We!*" she cried fiercely, "*we* will repay!"...

"God!" The voice seemed torn from his throat. "Oh God—*my* God!"

"*Our* gods," she said steadily in that tone of iron, "are near. The sacrifice is ready. And *you*—servant of mercy, priest of a younger deity, and English—you bring the power that makes it effectual. The circuit is complete."

It was perhaps the tears in her appealing eyes, perhaps it was her words, her voice, the wonder of her presence; all combined possibly in the spell that finally then struck down his will as with a single blow that paralysed his last resistance. The monstrous, half-legendary spirit of a primitive day recaptured him completely; he yielded to the spell of this tender, cruel woman, mother and avenging angel, whom horror and suffering had flung back upon the practices of uncivilized centuries. A common desire, a common lust and purpose, degraded both of them. They understood one another. Dropping back into a gulf of savage worship that set up idols in the place of God, they prayed to Odin and his awful crew . . .

It was again the touch of her hand that galvanized him. She raised him; he had been kneeling in slavish wonder and admiration at her feet. He leaped to do the bidding, however terrible, of this woman who was priestess, queen indeed, of a long-forgotten orgy.

"Vengeance at last!" he cried, in an exultant voice that no longer frightened him. "Now light the fire! Bring on the sacrifice!"

There was a rustling among the nearer branches, the forest stirred; the leaves of last year brushed against advancing feet. Yet before he could turn to see, before even the last words had wholly left his lips, the woman, whose hand still touched his fingers, suddenly tossed her cloak aside, and flinging her bare arms about his neck, drew him with impetuous passion towards her face and kissed him, as with delighted fury of exultant passion, full upon the mouth. Her body, in its clinging skins, pressed close against his own; her heat poured into him. She held him fiercely, savagely, and her burning kiss consumed his modern soul away with the fire of a primal day.

"The gods have given you to us," she cried, releasing him. "Your soul is ours!"

She turned—they turned together—to look for one upon whose last hour the moon now shed her horrid silver.

VIII

This silvery moonlight fell upon the scene.

Incongruously he remembered the flowers that soon would know the cuckoo's call; the soft mysterious stars shone down; the woods lay silent underneath the sky.

An amazing fantasy of dream shot here and there. "I am a man, an Englishman, a padre!" ran twisting through his mind, as though *she* whispered them to emphasize the ghastly contrast of reality. A memory of his own Kentish village with its Sunday school fled past, his dream of the Lion and the Lamb close after it. He saw children playing on the green . . . He saw their happy little hands . . .

Justice, punishment, revenge—he could not disentangle them. No longer did he wish to. The tide of violence was at his lips, quenching an ancient thirst. He drank. It seemed he could drink forever. These tender pictures only sweetened horror. That kiss had burned his modern soul away.

The woman waved her hand; there swept from the underbrush a score of figures dressed like herself in skins, with leaves and flowers entwined among their flying hair. He was surrounded in a moment. Upon each face he noted the same tenderness and terrible resolve that their commander wore. They pressed about him, dancing with enchanting grace, yet with full-blooded abandon, across the chequered light and shadow. It was the brimming energy of their movements that swept him off his feet, waking the desire for fierce rhythmical expression. His own muscles leaped and ached; for this energy, it seemed, poured into him from the tossing arms and legs, the shimmering bodies whence hair and skins flung loose, setting the very air awhirl. It flowed over into inanimate objects even, so that the trees waved their branches although no wind stirred—hair, skins and hands, rushing leaves and flying fingers touched his face, his neck, his arms and shoulders, catching him away into this orgy of an ancient, sacrificial ritual. Faces with shining eyes peered into his, then sped away; grew in a cloud upon the moonlight; sank back in shadow; reappeared, touched him, whispered, vanished. Silvery limbs gleamed everywhere. Chanting rose in a wave, to fall away again into forest rustlings; there were smiles that flashed, then fainted into moonlight, red lips and gleaming teeth that shone, then faded out. The secret glade, picked from the heart of the forest by the moon, became a torrent of tumultuous life, a whirlpool of passionate emotions Time had not killed.

But it was the eyes that mastered him, for in their yearning, mating so incongruously with the savage grace—in the eyes shone ever tears. He was aware of gentle women, of womanhood, of accumulated feminine power that nothing could withstand, but of feminine power in majesty, its essential protective tenderness roused, as by tribal instinct, into a collective fury of implacable revenge. He was, above all, aware of motherhood—of mothers. And the man, the male, the father in him rose like a storm to meet it.

From the torrent of voices certain sentences emerged; sometimes chanted, sometimes driven into his whirling mind as though big whispers thrust them down his ears. "You are with us to the end," he caught. "We have the proof. And punishment is ours!"

It merged in wind, others took its place:

"We hold him fast. The old gods wait and listen."

The body of rushing whispers flowed like a storm-wind past.

A lovely face, fluttering close against his own, paused an instant, and starry eyes gazed into his with a passion of gratitude, dimming a moment their stern fury with a mother's tenderness: "For the little ones . . . it is necessary, it is the only way . . . Our own children . . . " The face went out in a gust of blackness, as the chorus rose with a new note of awe and reverence, and a score of throats uttered in unison a single cry: "The raven! The White Horses! His signs! Great Odin hears!"

He saw the great dark bird flap slowly across the clearing, and melt against the shadow of the giant beech; he heard its hoarse, croaking note; the crowds of heads bowed low before its passage. The White Horses he did not see; only a sound as of considerable masses of air regularly displaced was audible far overhead. But the veiled light, as though great thunderclouds had risen, he saw distinctly. The sky above the clearing where he stood, panting and dishevelled, was blocked by a mass that owned unusual outline. These clouds now topped the forest, hiding the moon and stars. The flowers went out like nightlights blown. The wind rose slowly, then with sudden violence. There was a roaring in the treetops. The branches tossed and shook.

"The White Horses!" cried the voices, in a frenzy of adoration. "He is here!"

It came swiftly, this collective mass; it was both apt and terrible. There was an immense footstep. It was there.

Then panic seized him, he felt an answering tumult in himself, the Past surged through him like a sea at flood. Some inner sight, peering across the wreckage of Today, perceived an outline that in its size dwarfed mountains, a pair of monstrous shoulders, a face that rolled through a full quarter of the heavens. Above the ruin of civilization, now fulfilled in the microcosm of his own being, the menacing shadow of a forgotten deity peered down upon the earth, yet upon one detail of it chiefly—the human group that had been wildly dancing, but that now chanted in solemn conclave about a forest altar.

For some minutes a dead silence reigned; the pouring winds left emptiness in which no leaf stirred; there was a hush, a stillness that could be felt. The kneeling figures stretched forth a level sea of arms towards the altar; from the lowered heads the hair hung down in torrents, against which the naked flesh shone white; the skins upon the rows of backs gleamed yellow. The obscurity deepened overhead. It was the time of adoration. He knelt as well, arms similarly outstretched, while the lust of vengeance burned within him.

Then came, across the stillness, the stirring of big wings, a rustling as the great bird settled in the higher branches of the beech. The ominous note broke through the silence; and with one accord the shining backs were straightened. The company rose, swayed, parting into groups and lines. Two score voices resumed the solemn chant. The throng of pallid faces passed to and fro like great fireflies that shone and vanished. He, too, heard his own voice in unison, while his feet, as with instinctive knowledge, trod the same measure that the others trod.

Out of this tumult and clearly audible above the chorus and the rustling feet rang out suddenly, in a sweetly fluting tone, the leader's voice:

"The Fire! But first the hands!"

A rush of figures set instantly towards a thicket where the underbrush stood densest. Skins, trailing flowers, bare waving arms and tossing hair swept past on a burst of perfume. It was as though the trees themselves sped by. And the torrent of voices shook the very air in answer:

"The Fire! But first—the hands!"

Across this roaring volume pierced then, once again, that wailing sound which seemed both human and nonhuman—the anguished cry as of some lonely wolf in metamorphosis, apart from the collective safety of the pack, abjectly terrified, feeling the teeth of the final trap, and knowing the helpless feet within the steel. There was a crash of rending boughs and tearing branches. There was a tumult in the thicket, though of brief duration—then silence.

He stood watching, listening, overmastered by a diabolical sensation of expectancy he knew to be atrocious. Turning in the direction of the cry, his straining eyes seemed filled with blood; in his temples the pulses throbbed and hammered audibly. The next second he stiffened into a stone-like rigidity, as a figure, struggling violently yet half collapsed, was borne hurriedly past by a score of eager arms that swept it towards the beech tree, and then proceeded to fasten it in an upright position against the trunk. It was a man bound tight with thongs, adorned with leaves and flowers and trailing green. The face was hidden, for the head sagged forward on the breast, but he saw the arms forced flat against the giant trunk, held helpless beyond all possible escape; he saw the knife, poised and aimed by slender, graceful fingers above the victim's wrists laid bare; he saw the—hands.

"An eye for an eye," he heard, "a tooth for a tooth!" It rose in awful chorus. Yet this time, although the words roared close about him, they seemed farther away, as if wind brought them through the crowding trees from far off.

"Light the fire! Prepare the sacrifice!" came on a following wind; and, while strange distance held the voices as before, a new faint sound now audible was very close. There was a crackling. Some ten feet beyond the tree a column of thick smoke rose in the air; he was aware of heat not meant for modern purposes; of yellow light that was not the light of stars.

The figure writhed, and the face swung suddenly sideways. Glaring with panic hopelessness past the judge and past the hanging knife, the eyes found his own. There was a pause of perhaps five seconds, but in these five seconds centuries rolled by. The priest of Today looked down into the well of time. For five hundred years he gazed into those twin eyeballs, glazed with the abject terror of a last appeal. They recognized one another.

The centuries dragged appallingly. The drama of civilization, in a sluggish stream, went slowly by, halting, meandering, losing itself, then reappearing. Sharpest pains, as of a thousand knives, accompanied its dreadful, endless lethargy. Its million hesitations made him suffer a million deaths of agony. Terror, despair and anger, all futile and without effect upon its progress, destroyed a thousand times his soul, which yet some hope—a towering, indestructible hope—a thousand times renewed. This despair and hope alternately broke his being, ever to fashion it anew. His torture seemed not of this world. Yet hope survived. The sluggish stream moved onward, forward . . .

There came an instant of sharpest, dislocating torture. The yellow light grew slightly brighter. He saw the eyelids flicker.

It was at this moment he realized abruptly that he stood alone, apart from the others, unnoticed apparently, perhaps forgotten; his feet held steady; his voice no longer sang. And at this discovery a quivering shock ran through his being, as though the will were suddenly loosened into a new activity, yet an activity that halted between two terrifying alternatives.

It was as though the flicker of those eyelids loosed a spring.

Two instincts, clashing in his being, fought furiously for the mastery. One, ancient as this sacrifice, savage as the legendary figure brooding in the heavens above him, battled fiercely with another, acquired more recently in human evolution, that had not yet crystallized into permanence. He saw a child, playing in a Kentish orchard with toys and flowers the little innocent hands made living . . . he saw a lowly manger, figures kneeling round it, and one star shining overhead in piercing and prophetic beauty.

Thought was impossible; he saw these symbols only, as the two contrary instincts, alternately hidden and revealed, fought for permanent possession of his soul. Each strove to dominate him; it seemed that violent blows were struck that wounded physically; he was bruised, he ached, he gasped for breath; his body swayed, held upright only, it seemed, by the awful appeal in the fixed and staring eyes.

The challenge had come at last to final action; the conqueror, he well knew, would remain an integral portion of his character, his soul.

It was the old, old battle, waged eternally in every human heart, in every tribe, in every race, in every period, the essential principle indeed, behind the great world-war. In the stress and confusion of the fight, as the eyes of the victim, savage in victory, abject in defeat—the appealing eyes of that animal face against the tree stared with their awful blaze into his own, this flashed clearly over him. It was the battle between might and right, between love and hate, forgiveness and vengeance, Christ and the Devil. He heard the menacing thunder of "an eye for an eye, a tooth for a tooth," then above its angry volume rose suddenly another small silvery voice that pierced with sweetness:— "Vengeance is mine, I will repay . . . " sang through him as with unimaginable hope.

Something became incandescent in him then. He realized a singular merging of powers in absolute opposition to each other. It was as though they harmonized. Yet it was through this small, silvery voice the apparent magic came. The words, of course, were his own in memory, but they rose from his modern soul, now reawakening . . . He started painfully. He noted again that he stood apart, alone, perhaps forgotten of the others. The woman, leading a dancing throng about the blazing brushwood, was far from him. Her mind, too sure of his compliance, had momentarily left him. The chain was weakened. The circuit knew a break.

But this sudden realization was not of spontaneous origin. His heart had not produced it of its own accord. The unholy tumult of the orgy held him too slavishly in its awful sway for the tiny point of his modern soul to have pierced it thus unaided. The light flashed to him from an outside, natural source of simple loveliness—the singing of a bird. From the distance, faint and exquisite, there had reached him the silvery notes of a happy thrush, awake in the night, and telling its joy over and over again to itself. The innocent beauty of its song came through the forest and fell into his soul . . .

The eyes, he became aware, had shifted, focusing now upon an object nearer to them. The knife was moving. There was a convulsive wriggle of the body, the head dropped loosely forward, no cry was audible. But, at the same moment, the inner battle ceased and an unexpected climax came. Did the soul of the bully faint with fear? Did the spirit leave him at the actual touch of earthly vengeance? The watcher never knew. In that appalling moment when the knife was about to begin the mission that the fire would complete, the roar of inner battle ended abruptly, and that small silvery voice drew the words of invincible power from his reawakening soul. "Ye do it also unto me . . . " pealed o'er the forest.

He reeled. He acted instantaneously. Yet before he had dashed the knife from the hand of the executioner, scattered the pile of blazing wood, plunged through the astonished worshippers with a violence of strength that amazed even himself; before he had torn the thongs apart and loosened the fainting victim from the tree; before he had uttered a single word or cry, though it seemed to him he roared with a voice of thousands—he witnessed a sight that came surely from the Heaven of his earliest childhood days, from that Heaven whose God is love and whose forgiveness was taught him at his mother's knee.

With superhuman rapidity it passed before him and was gone. Yet it was no earthly figure that emerged from the forest, ran with this incredible swiftness past the startled throng, and reached the tree. He saw the shape; the same instant it was there; wrapped in light, as though a flame from the sacrificial fire flashed past him over the ground. It was of an incandescent brightness, yet brightest of all were the little outstretched hands. These were of purest gold, of a brilliance incredibly shining.

It was no earthly child that stretched forth these arms of generous forgiveness and took the bewildered prisoner by the hand just as the knife descended and touched the helpless wrists. The thongs were already loosened, and the victim, fallen to his knees, looked wildly this way and that for a way of possible escape, when the shining hands were laid upon his own. The murderer rose. Another instant and the throng must have been upon him, tearing him limb from limb. But the radiant little face looked down into his own; she raised him to his feet;

with superhuman swiftness she led him through the infuriated concourse as though he had become invisible, guiding him safely past the furies into the cover of the trees. Close before his eyes, this happened; he saw the waft of golden brilliance, he heard the final gulp of it, as wind took the dazzling of its fiery appearance into space. They were gone . . .

IX

He stood watching the disappearing motorcars, wondering uneasily who the occupants were and what their business, whither and why did they hurry so swiftly through the night? He was still trying to light his pipe, but the damp tobacco would not burn.

The air stole out of the forest, cooling his body and his mind; he saw the anemones gleam; there was only peace and calm about him, the earth lay waiting for the sweet, mysterious stars. The moon was higher; he looked up; a late bird sang. Three strips of cloud, spaced far apart, were the footsteps of the South Wind, as she flew to bring more birds from Africa. His thoughts turned to gentle, happy hopes of a day when the lion and the lamb should lie down together, and a little child should lead them. War, in this haunt of ancient peace, seemed an incredible anachronism.

He did not go farther; he did not enter the forest; he turned back along the quiet road he had come, ate his food on a farmer's gate, and over a pipe sat dreaming of his sure belief that humanity had advanced. He went home to his hotel soon after midnight. He slept well, and next day walked back the four miles from the hospitals, instead of using the car. Another hospital searcher walked with him. They discussed the news.

"The weather's better anyhow," said his companion. "In our favour at last!"

"That's something," he agreed, as they passed a gang of

prisoners and crossed the road to avoid saluting.

"Been another escape, I hear," the other mentioned. "He won't get far. How on earth do they manage it? The M.O. had a yarn that he was helped by a motorcar. I wonder what they'll do to him."

"Oh, nothing much. Bread and water and extra work, I suppose?"

The other laughed. "I'm not so sure," he said lightly. "Humanity hasn't advanced very much in that kind of thing."

A fugitive memory flashed for an instant through the other's brain as he listened. He had an odd feeling for a second that he had heard this conversation before somewhere. A ghostly sense of familiarity brushed his mind, then vanished. At dinner that night the table in front of him was unoccupied. He did not, however, notice that it was unoccupied.

The Wolves of God and Other Fey Stories, 1921

KING'S EVIDENCE

When Flanagan left his nursing home that November afternoon the last rays of the red sunset lay over Regent's Park. It was very still. The air was raw, but the sky was clear, if with a hint of possible fog to come.

Flanagan was on his way to South Kensington by the Underground. He was in high spirits. His fear of open spaces—agoraphobia so-called—at last was really cured. He no longer dreaded to cross a square, a lawn, a field. This terrible affliction, inherited from shell-shock, was a thing of the past, thank heaven. For months he had been unable even to cross the open garden of the home. Gradually, the specialists had weaned him from that awful terror. Already he had made small journeys alone. Now he was fit for a longer effort.

'It'll do you good,' said the Matron, seeing him off. 'Go and have tea with your pal. An open space won't bother you a bit, and anyhow there are no open spaces on the Underground. Be back for dinner at 7.0.'

And Tim Flanagan, young Canadian soldier, who knew nothing of London beyond the precincts of his nursing home, started off full of confidence. Exact directions—first right, second left, etc., lay in his pocket. To a man of the backwoods it was child's play. He took the Underground at Regent's Park and reached South Kensington easily, of course. Then, leaving the train twenty minutes later and coming up to street level, he entered a world of blackness he had never known before, though he had read about it—a genuine London pea-soup fog.

'Gosh!' he said to himself. 'This is the real thing!'

The station hall itself was darkened with all its lights. He faced a wall of opaque, raw, stifling gloom that stung his eyes and bit into his throat. The change was so sudden, it amazed him. But the novelty at first stimulated him, accustomed as he was to the clear Canadian air. It seemed unbelievable, but it was true. He watched the people grope their way out into the street—and vanish. He hesitated. A slight shiver ran over him.

'Come on now, Tim Flanagan!' he said. 'You know the directions by heart,'—and he plunged down into the filthy blackness of the open street. First to the right, second to the left—and within five minutes he was completely lost.

He stood still, aware suddenly that he must keep himself in hand. He repeated calmly the directions he knew so well. But got them mixed. How many turns had he made so far? He wasn't sure. Memory was already out of gear a little. Too dark to read the paper in his pocket. Nothing to help him—no stars, wind, scent, sound of running water, moss on the north side of the trees.

Groping figures emerged, vanished, reappeared, dissolved. He heard shuffling feet, sticks tapping. Saw an occasional taxi crawling by the kerb, the passenger walking. They loomed, faded, were gone. A swirl in the fog showed a faint light, and he staggered towards it and recognized an island. Thank heaven for that refuge! A figure or two arrived and left as he stood there, clutching the lamp-post. They asked the way, choking, he asked the way, coughing. They lurched off and the murk covered them. Like blind fish, he thought, on the ocean bed. But his confusion and bewilderment became serious, with unpleasant symptoms he thought done with for ever. There were no carts, no taxis now, no figures either. He was alone, an empty space about him— the two things he dreaded most. He waved his stick. It struck nothing solid. In spite of the cold, he was sweating. And panic slowly raised its ugly head.

'I must get across to the pavement. I must cross that open space. I *must* . . . !'

It took him fifteen minutes, most of the way on his hands and knees, but the moment of collapse was close as he crawled along pluckily by the pavement railings—then saw a slight thickening of the fog beneath the next lamp, grotesquely magnified. Was it real? It moved. It moved towards him. It was a human being. If it was a human being he could speak to—be with—he would be saved. It came close up against his face. It was a woman.

He gasped out at it, pulling himself up by the railing.

'Lost your way like me, Ma'am? D'you know where you are? Morley Place I'm looking for. For heaven's sake . . .'

His voice stopped dead. The woman was peering down at him. He saw her face quite clearly—the brilliant, frightened eyes, the skin white like linen. She was young, wrapped in a dark fur coat. She had beauty—beauty of a sort. He didn't care who or what she was. To him she meant—safety only.

There was no answer to his questions. She whispered—as though speech was difficult: 'Where am I? I came out so suddenly. I can't find my way back . . .' and was gone from his side into the swirling fog.

And Flanagan, without an instant's hesitation, went after her. He *must* be with a human being. She moved swiftly, seemed sure of her way, she never faltered. Terrified he might lose sight of her, he kept breathlessly at her heels. She uttered no sound, no cry, not once did she turn her head. But her unfaltering speed helped to restore his own confidence. She knew her way now beyond all question. But two things struck him as odd—first that she made no sound—he heard no footsteps—second that she left a curious faint perfume in the air, a perfume that made him uneasy—connecting it somehow with misery and pain.

Abruptly then she swerved, so abruptly that he almost touched her, and passed through an iron gate—across a tiny garden to a house.

She did not turn her head, but he heard her queer whispering voice again: 'I've found it. Now I can get back.'

'May I come in too?' he cried, exhausted. 'Don't leave me! If I'm left alone I shall go mad!'

There was no answer. She passed like a feather up the stone

steps and vanished into the house. The front door, he noticed, was ajar already. Nor did she close it behind her. He followed her—into a pitchblack hall, then collapsed in a heap on the stone floor. But he was safe. The open spaces of the street were behind him. He heard a door open and close upstairs. Complete silence followed.

A couple of minutes later he struggled to his feet, switched on his electric torch, and realized at once that the house was untenanted. Dust-sheets covered the hall furniture. Through a door, half open, he saw pictures screened on the walls, brackets draped. But companionship—human companionship was what he wanted—and *must* have—or his mind would go. He was shaking like a leaf. So he crept upstairs on tiptoe and reached the landing. Then stood still. His knees felt like blotting-paper.

He saw a long corridor with closed doors. And he cautiously tried three in succession—empty rooms, furniture under dust-sheets, blinds down, mattresses rolled up. At the fourth door he knew he was right, for the strange, unpleasant odour caught his nostrils. And this time he knew instantly why it brought pain and misery—anaesthetic, ether or chloroform.

His next glance showed him the young woman lying in her fur coat on the bed. The body lay at full length. Motionless. He had seen death too often to be mistaken, much less afraid. He stole up, felt her cheek, still warm. An hour or so ago she was alive. He gently raised a closed eyelid, but hurriedly let it fall again, and in the presence of death instinctively he took off his hat, laying it on the bed. His hand then, moving towards the heart, encountered a hard knob—the head of a long steel hat-pin driven up to its hilt. But his own private terror was now lost in something greater. He drew the pin out slowly and placed it on her breast. And in doing so he noticed a blood stain on his finger. At which instant there was a loud clanging noise downstairs—the front-door being closed. A frenzied realization of his position blazed into his mind—a dead woman, alone together in an empty house, blood on my hand, fingerprints on the door-handle and pin, body still warm, police!

The sinister combination cleared his brain. Heart racing madly, he switched out his light, and darted across the landing to the room opposite—seeing as he ran the flicker of an electric torch on banisters and ceiling, as the man holding it rapidly climbed the stairs. He managed it just in time. Through the crack of his own door he saw the outline of the man slip into the room where the dead—the murdered—woman lay and close the door carefully behind him. Only his outline had been visible, blurred in the deep shadows behind the torch he carried.

The one thing Flanagan knew was that he must get away instantly. He crept out, stole along the landing on tiptoe, and began the perilous descent with the utmost caution. Each time a board creaked, his heart missed a beat. He tested each step. Half-way down, to his horror, his foot tripped in a rod— with an uproar like a handgrenade in his forgotten trenches. Concealment was now impossible. He took the last flight in a leap, shot across the hall, tore open the front door, just as his pursuer, with torch in hand, had reached the top of the stairs. The light flashed down on to him for a second? He wasn't sure. He banged the door, and plunged headlong into the welcome all-obscuring fog outside.

He ran wildly, fast as he could, across the little garden out into the street. The fog held no terrors for him now. His one object was to put distance between him and that house of death. Sense of direction he had none. There was no sound of steps behind him. For ten, fifteen minutes, he raced along. He must have gone a long way—a mile at least—when his legs failed him, his mind went black, his strength was gone, and the terror of open spaces rose over him like ice. He dropped in his tracks clinging to the cold, wet area railing—one thought only hideously clear in his brain before it stopped functioning—he had left his hat beside the body on the bed.

Unconsciousness followed. He had no recollection exactly— till a voice sounded, a man's voice, kindly.

'Can I be of any assistance? Come, let me help you. Take my arm. I'm a physician. Luckily, too, you're just outside my house . . .'

And Flanagan felt himself half dragged, half pushed into a warm, well-lit hall, the stranger having opened the door with a latchkey. A few minutes later, he was sipping whiskey before a blazing fire, trying to stammer his thanks and gratitude.

'Got lost,' he managed to say, 'agor—agoraphobia, sir, you know . . . shell-shock . . . you've saved me . . .'

And some fifteen minutes later, whiskey, warmth and experienced human sympathy had worked wonders. The doctor's handling of the terrified youth was masterly. Flanagan found fuller control come back. He even smoked a cigarette with pleasure.

'You know,' the doctor was saying in his pleasant, gentle voice, 'I rather guessed it might be shell-shock. I've seen so many cases . . .' as Flanagan now began to take him in more fully; elderly, with a very determined, implacable look sometimes behind what was a good, almost a benevolent face. A man not to be trifled with, he felt. 'And I'm encouraged', the doctor went on smilingly, 'to hazard a second guess—that you've had another violent shock too—quite recently.' He looked hard into Flanagan's eyes. 'Am I not right—eh? Yes, I felt sure of it.' There came a little pause. 'Now, why not tell me about it,' came the suggestion, soothingly, yet with more authority in the tone. 'It will help you—relieve your mind. Suppression is bad, remember. And we're complete strangers to one another. I don't know your name. You don't know mine. Tell me about it. Confession,' he laughed, 'is good for the soul, they say . . .'

Flanagan hesitated. 'It's too incredible,' he mumbled, though burning to get it out of him. 'You just couldn't believe it, sir.'

In the end he told it, all of it, faithfully.

'Pretty tall story, isn't it, sir?'

'Tall, yes,' came the quiet reply, 'but not incredible—as I know from many a strange experience.' He paused and sipped his drink. 'In fact, as one confidence deserves another,' he went on, '*I* might now tell *you* of an oddly similar case that came my way. It may make you feel more comfortable,' he added with skilful tact, 'to hear *my* story. I won't give names, of course. It's about an officer at the front—great friend of mine—middle-aged, rich, just married to a young girl—a cheap, pleasure-loving sort, utterly worthless, I'm afraid. While he was fighting for his country, she took a lover. Planned to run away. Only somehow the husband got wind of it out in France. He got leave, too, just in the nick of time . . .'

'Well rid of her,' Flanagan put in.

'Perhaps,' said the doctor. 'Only he determined to make that riddance final.'

Flanagan gasped, but not audibly. And that implacable look on the other's face had hardened him a little. He listened more closely, he watched more closely, too. He was thinking hard. Reflecting. A touch of uneasiness stirred in him.

'Go on, please,' he said.

The doctor went on; in a lowered tone. 'They met, he found out, this guilty pair, in an empty house, a house belonging to the husband. And the woman, using her latchkey, slipped in. She left the door ajar for the lover. She found death waiting for her. It was a *painless* death. Her lover, for some reason, was late. The fog possibly. It must have been a night rather like this, I gather . . .'

'The lover,' Flanagan whispered, for his voice failed him somehow, 'the lover didn't come, you mean?'

'A man *did* come in,' was the doctor's quiet answer, 'but he hardly tallied with the description the husband had. A stranger, apparently. Saw the door ajar and came in for shelter perhaps— just as you might have done.'

Flanagan felt a shiver run down his spine. 'And the husband,' he asked under his breath, 'where was *he* all this time?'

'Oh,' came the answer at once, 'waiting outside—concealed in the fog. Watching. He saw the man go in, of course. Five minutes later he went in after him.'

Flanagan stood up with a sudden jerk. 'I'll be going,' he said abruptly, and added some words of mumbled thanks. The doctor said nothing. He too rose to his feet. They passed into the hall.

'But you can't go out in the fog like that,' said the doctor, quietly enough. 'Why, you've got no hat. Here, I'll lend you one.' And he casually took a hat from a row on the rack and Flanagan mechanically put it on his head. He didn't shake the offered hand. Perhaps he hadn't seen it. He went out.

The fog had lifted a bit. He found his station easily. Open spaces did not bother him.

In the bright light of the train he took off the borrowed hat and looked it over. It was his own hat.

1936

THE MAGIC MIRROR

IT was the last night on board the *Borotania*, as she was due in New York next morning. Most of the passengers were busy packing up in their cabins, so that when I strolled into the smoking-room I found it nearly empty, with only a straggler or two lined up at the bar. Fatty, however, was sitting in his usual corner with his two inseparables, Jimmy and Baldy, whose real names I never discovered.

When I came in Baldy was talking about systems at roulette.

"There are no systems worth a curse," he was saying. "It's all boloney to say there are. And most of the wheels are crooked, anyhow."

"I guess you're right," Fatty agreed, "though I did once come across a system that was infallible. The trouble was I couldn't work it long enough to make a real killing."

"And how was that? " Jimmy enquired.

"Just that the inventor faded away before we could clean up," explained Fatty. "Hard luck, you call it! Hard luck isn't the right word. It was a catastrophe. That's what it was, Baldy—a catastrophe!

"Well, let's have the whole lie. Fatty," said Jimmy and Baldy together, "and we'll tell you what we think."

"It's gospel truth," came the rejoinder, "and no lie at all, though I can't blame you if you don't believe it. It was about the strangest thing I ever ran up against—which is saying a lot. To this day I don't know what to make of it. It worked. I will say that for it. But it's got me beat just the same.

"It is some years ago now," Fatty resumed, delighted to have even what he considered a dud audience of two, "that I stayed on rather late at Monte. The season was over, and the Sporting

Club, together with a whole lot of the better hotels, closed down. I had my quarters in a small pub on the Rue des Moulins, I remember, as my own joint was closed, too. The grub wasn't too good, and I used to drop in now and again at Quinto's to get myself a good lunch.

"One day, after lunch, I turned into the public gardens to smoke a cigar and look at the flowers before creeping home for a nap and I remember that the cigar, given to me up at the golf course by a millionaire friend of mine, was particularly good. I was enjoying it, smoking away and feeling at peace with all the world, when I noticed a curious-looking figure moving along the path towards me. He was an oldish fellow with a straggly white beard, and he was wearing a funny sort of hat on his head. I had never seen a hat quite like it before, but I found out afterwards that it was called a "terai", or some sort of name like that, and that it was worn a lot in India.

"There were plenty of empty seats all round me and I prayed to God the old fellow wouldn't come and sit down within talking distance of me and my cigar. Yet that was exactly what he did. The old bozo comes tottering along till he gets to my bench, and then he parks himself bang down quite close to me. Yes, he parked himself just next door, so that I expected the next minute he would turn and ask me for a match.

"But he had his match all right—his stinking cheroot, too— and he lights up and puffs away without a spot of trouble. Now, as you boys know, if there is one thing I cannot stand, it's the smoke from one of those greenhouse bug-killers, so as soon as he got going I was for going, too. I sort of shifted my legs before getting up, and it was just then he turns and looks at me. Did I say "looks at me"? I can only tell you duds that there was something in his eyes that made me think of lightning. He spoke at the same time. And his first remark somehow took my breath away. I mean by that I hadn't expected it.

' "Could you tell me something about the gambling here? " he asks.

' "Sure, " I says, getting my breath back a bit, "sure I can. What 's troubling you, stranger? "

'His eyes flashed that queer way again, but all he gives me back was innocent enough. "I understand they play a game called roulette," he says, "but I don't know anything about it. I'd like to."

' "The less you know, the cheaper for you," I tells him, knowing the answer pat. For he didn't look to me like a man to play the tables, what with his "Oxford voice" and his strange face that was half a monk and half, I guess, a scholar. "Keep your money, " I adds, "if you 've got any."

' "But I want to make some money," he explains straight off the reel and quite honest-sounding. "I've got a plan that's certain."

'And this time I looks him straight in the eye, lightning or no lightning—though I admit there was something in his eye that made me sort of wonder.

' "Now, listen, pal," I tell him, with a fatherly touch that I knew didn't quite come off. "Listen to me, will you? Every train that pulls into this burg has some sucker on it that thinks he's going to make good dough, but only one in ten thousand ever gets away with it. You take my advice and beat it back to Timbuctoo, or wherever you hail from, and just forget it." And I takes a good puff at my cigar for having given good advice for once, feeling easy in my conscience, if you know what I mean.

' "I come from Tibet, not Timbuctoo," he corrects me slap, flashing those googly eyes my way, "and I've got with me a magic mirror. I can't lose. It's a magic mirror from Tibet, you see." And his stinking cheroot puffed across into my face and made me cough.

'Well, of course, I knew then that the old boy was nuts. That Tibet-and-magic business proved it. And yet there was something about him that had me guessing. I had the feeling that he knew a thing or two I didn't know. I can't express it quite. I knew I was on the wrong tack, anyway. He had something I'd never met before. I was under-rating. him. He was child-like crazy, if you like, but he was something else as well. I only know I let my cigar that—millionaire cigar—go out. That shows you, maybe!

' "What's the great idea?" I says, more easily than I felt. "Are you going to flash light from the mirror into the croupier's eye and then grab some dough? If so, I can tell you right now that those methods won't work here. Maybe they're all right back in the sticks in your Tibet, but they won't cut any ice here in Monte!"

'He gave me a sort of patient, half-contemptuous look as though I was a kid.

' "The mirror," he says quietly, "shows me what to play— numbers and colors, or whatever the foolishness is." And he pulls down that awful hat over his lightning blinkers, puffs out a poisonous cloud, and looks out over the flowers in the garden. In other words, he showed me plain enough that he thought I wasn't yet born.

'Well, this had me fair flummoxed. I just don't know what to say next. I lit up my cigar again, then threw it away as it no longer tasted good. After a bit I got going again. I asked him how he got his mirror, thinking it a fair question. And he gives me a long spiel about how he had been interpreter with a British expedition into Tibet, and how some lama gave him the mirror. Good stuff, too, right enough. He did the lama some service or other.

' "They call them devil-mirrors," he told me.

' "For why?" I asks, wondering what he'll throw me next.

' "Because they bring death and riches," is the answer.

' "Meself," I tells him, "I don't fancy mirrors like that."

' "You've never seen one," he says, knowing all the answers.

' "True," I tells him. "Maybe I don't want to."

'He said nothing for a bit then. I had the feeling he thought I was a nitwit from Kalamazoo. And that's just what I felt, without knowing why—as though he was giving me the works and I was just dumb.

'Then he gets going again.

"I am an old man now," he says. "I'm over a hundred, if you care to know, and I wish to try this mirror before I die. I promised the lama I would. I must. Only, I need a helper. I cannot do it all alone."

'Well, this flummoxed me right down to the bone. Either he was nuts or I was! Over a hundred, indeed! Why, those eyes belonged to a young man! I thought it over for a bit. "Where was I?" I asked myself. "In Monte or in some weird Tibetan monastery?"

' "Of course," I says at length, "if that's the way you look at it, I've got nothing to say. Have you got the mirror with you? I'd sure like to have a look at it."

' "Certainly," he agrees, and pulls out of his pocket a little chamois-leather bag and produces from it a small bronze mirror. I handled it cautiously, giving it the once-over. It had some curious figures twined round the polished surface—naked men and women, and their faces were awful. I'm pretty hard-boiled myself, but, believe me, those faces made me shudder so I could hardly bear to look at them. The old boy's mug, too, had something in common with them, it strikes me.

' "Now," he says, watching me hard, "do you notice anything peculiar about it?"

'I looked carefully and turned the mirror round in various directions so as to get the reflection of the gardens and the trees. "No," I tells him at last, "I can't say that I do."

' "Have you seen your own face in it?" he asked at length, with a smile I didn't care much about. His question gave me quite a shock.

' "No," I tell him "I have not."

' "Just as well," he says, "for if you did you would die."

'With that I hands him back his mirror as quick as I could, but he only laughs quietly to himself and slips it back into its bag. And then I began thinking things over to myself a bit. After all, I thought, you don't get handed devils' mirrors in Tibet for nothing. I guess the old boy had to do his stuff before the lama gave it to him—something pretty tough, too, or one of the local gorillas could have handled it. And so I came to the conclusion it was better not to ask any more questions. The only thing that really mattered was whether the mirror would work or not.

‘ "Go in and try it," I says to him straight. "Why not?"

'But he has the answer to that, too. "I must have someone with me," he explains again. "When I see the numbers in the glass I can't attend to putting the money on as well. I need a helper, someone I can trust. And I trust you."

I had got this far when a wave of suspicion came over me. The old boy was a "con" man, and he was sure trying to play me for a sucker. I expected every moment his confederate would come rolling up with some plausible yarn, and that they would start stringing me along to put up some dough. I kept my eyes wide open, but I saw no one. And to fill in time I asked him about Tibet. He told me plenty about the country and certainly seemed to know his stuff all right, but as I couldn't check up on it, this didn't get us very far. It sounded genuine, all the same. He said he had been born at a mission station right on the frontier and that his nurse had been a Tibetan woman. When his parents died he had got a job with the Indian Government, and had now retired with a pension and was on his way to England. He told me a lot, too, about having promised the lama something about the mirror, but I just couldn't make head or tail of that. He wanted, anyway, to use it for getting money, and here in Monte he saw a chance. So I let it go at that.

‘ "Sure you've never seen a roulette wheel?" I asks him.

‘ "Never," says he.

‘ "Well, I'll take you right along and show you one," I says, and I bring the old bird down the street till we get to a shop that has them in the window. Half the shops in Monte stock them, as you know, so that we hadn't far to go. I watches the old fox careful to see if he's going to do an act, but he seems genuinely interested, and he soon got wise to the numbers and dozens and all that, and how it worked. Then I asks him how the mirror's going to show him what to back.

' "I shall see the numbers or the colour in the glass," says he.

' "Well, if you've got any dough," I suggests, "let's go to the rooms and give the thing a whirl."

' "I have a thousand francs," he says, "if you think that will be enough."

' "Plenty," I tell him, "if the mirror's any good. But let's start gently with a hundred-franc stake, just to see how she goes. If we win, we go on; if we lose, we don't. How's that strike you?"

' "We shall win," he says, calm as you like, "and half the winnings will be yours. You are entitled to them for your kindness to a stranger."

'Well, this little spiel goes down very well with me, so I just says "Thank you," and takes his hand on it. Talk of a grip! That old hundred-per-center had a fist like iron. Anyway, we wanders over to the Casino and I gets him a ticket for the *salle privee* and in we goes. And, let me tell you, the old bozo was on the up-and-up all right, for when we gets to the rooms he hands over his *mille* and asks me to do the staking while he consults his little mirror.

'Now, as chance would have it, the rooms weren't crowded, and we got a coupla good seats right at the end of one of the tables. I had changed the note into *plaques*, and we were all set. The old guy trots out his mirror and starts staring into it. I watches him close. After a minute or two his face kind of changes. His skin went whiter and his features became sort of fixed and hard. I thought at first he'd dropped off to sleep maybe with his eyes wide open, only I caught a flash of what I call the lightning in them and knew he was just too concentrated to blink. You might have thought he was a flapper going to put the lip-stick on with that mirror in front of him. It was sure a queer sight. I notice the croupier nearest to us seems kind of inquisitive and keeps looking at him, but he doesn't say anything.

'They were paying out just when we sat down, but now they spin the wheel and it is time to stake. I glance at the old crank and he mutters "Fifteen," hardly moving his lips. It was fifteen the time before, but all the same, my *plaque* goes on, and sure enough, up she comes—fifteen! Now that, of course, might be just luck, but it gave me confidence, all right, so when next time the old bird mumbles "Twenty-one," I shoves on two *plaques* to see if I can't give the bank a jolt.

'And would you believe it, boys? Up she comes as pretty as a picture, while I rakes in the dough, trying not to grin like a Cheshire cat as I does it. And so it goes on, just as smooth and easy as I'm telling you, and we sure gave the bank a ride that afternoon. But I thinks it wise to stop at last, as the old fellow is beginning to look kind of petered out, it strikes me; so I take him away to the bar and give him a good slug of brandy, and we split the dough as he said, and then I take him back in a *fiacre* to his joint.'

"How much did you win?" asks Baldy.

"Sixty *mille* between us up to date, and giving him back his *mille* as agreed."

"Next morning," Fatty continued, "I went round bright and early to see how he was making out, and I found him in rather poor shape. So I tried to persuade him to give the rooms a miss that day. Nothing doing!

' "Lead me to the tables," he says, firm as a rock. "It was your brandy that upset me a little, for, you see, I never touch alcohol," and by his voice you mighta thought he was some Professor at Oxford starting up his lecture.

' "Anyway," I suggests, "let 's have a good feed first," and I makes in the direction of Quinto's, for there was a bit of time to fill before the rooms opened. But will he eat? Not a damned swallow, I tell you! Not a single bite!

' "I shall see better, " he whispers to me, "if I have no food. But please do not let me stop you. I will wait till you have had a meal."

So that's what happened. "A crank," I says to myself, "must turn his own handle the way he wants," and I left him to it while I enjoyed the best blow-out ever with plenty of good liquor to wash it down, and the old boy doesn't hurry me one little bit, sitting there quiet and silent as an Indian idol. And when I'd lit my cigar we roll away in a *fiacre* back to the Casino.

'We go to the same table again and I notice the croupier recognises the old guy, and exchanges a quick look with another croupier, and the pair of them watch that mirror pretty close, though there's nothing they can say or do about it, for any guy can look in his pocket-mirror if he wants to and see if his hair's straight. And, believe me, that mirror does its stuff again fit to beat the band. Or, I should say, beat the bank. For it just couldn't miss. Every time my pal mutters his number, up it comes, though sometimes I don't quite catch what he mumbles and so hold back and don't put a *plaque* on. And when that happens he gives me one of those sort of lightning looks that puts the blame on *me* all right. After that I watches his lips. I make no further mistakes, but start playing the dough real heavy, till we'd won so much I swear I couldn't count it, and I could see that the croupiers don't like it one little bit, they don't.

'And so it goes on and on, boys, with me watching those mumbling lips like a cat watches a mouse, and making no more miss-hits, till sudden I notice that those lips of his seem kind of white. No blood in them, I mean. I give his face the once-over, and that don't look right to me, either. Made me think of a bladder with the air running out on it. Something was wrong, it seems to me, and I decided we'd had enough for one day and I'd better get him out.

' "Come on," I whispers to him. "Let's go. Give it a rest till tomorrow, pal."

' "One more turn," he whispers back, but the flash from those gig-lamps not quite so bright. "I'm seeing better than ever before."

'So I agrees to that. One turn more can't do us any harm, and he sure was seeing perfect.

"Thirteen," he mutters. And on go my *plaques*.

'Now it so happens that he can reach the number easier than

me, so I hand him the dough while I shove a maximum myself on *impair*, just to give the bank a final trimming before we blow.

'The wheel is spinning lovely when I hear a kind of gasp and a sigh from the old boy, but when I turns quick to look at him he seems okay. A moment later the ball settles nice and comfortable in thirteen, and they pay me on *impair* right enough. Then a strange thing happens. The croupier is in the act of shoving the money over to pay the old guy on his number when he stops, then pulls it back again as though the bank had won. I catches my breath and stares a moment. And everybody stares with me. The room had filled to the brim and everybody had been watching our play. There came sudden an awful silence.

'I got my breath back. "What's the matter?" cries out. "Pay the old man his winnings!"

'And the croupier turned to me without a smile.

' "*On ne paye pas les morts*," he said quietly, raking the money in.

'The old boy was dead—dead as a door-nail. He had croaked while the wheel was spinning. Can you beat it for bad luck? I looks round quick to see that no one had pinched the mirror, but I'm damned if it isn't broken into a thousand pieces.

'Isn't life just plain hell?'

The Bystander, March 16, 1938